THE ASH REMAINS

-THE LAW OF TEETH: BOOK 1-

C. WILLIAM PHILLIPS

The Ash Remains

Published by AMCLER Publishing

This is a work of fiction. Names, characters, places, organizations, and events are either products of the author's imagination or used fictitiously. Any resemblance to actual persons, living or dead, events, or locales is entirely coincidental.

Artificial Intelligence was not used in the drafting or editing of this book or any images found therein or related to the book.

First Edition

Cover art by Jason Dement

Cover design by Joshua Adams

Map illustration by Enkrotian

Edited by Dr. Jenna Niece

ISBN: 979-8-9993559-4-2

Printed in the USA

For Mom.

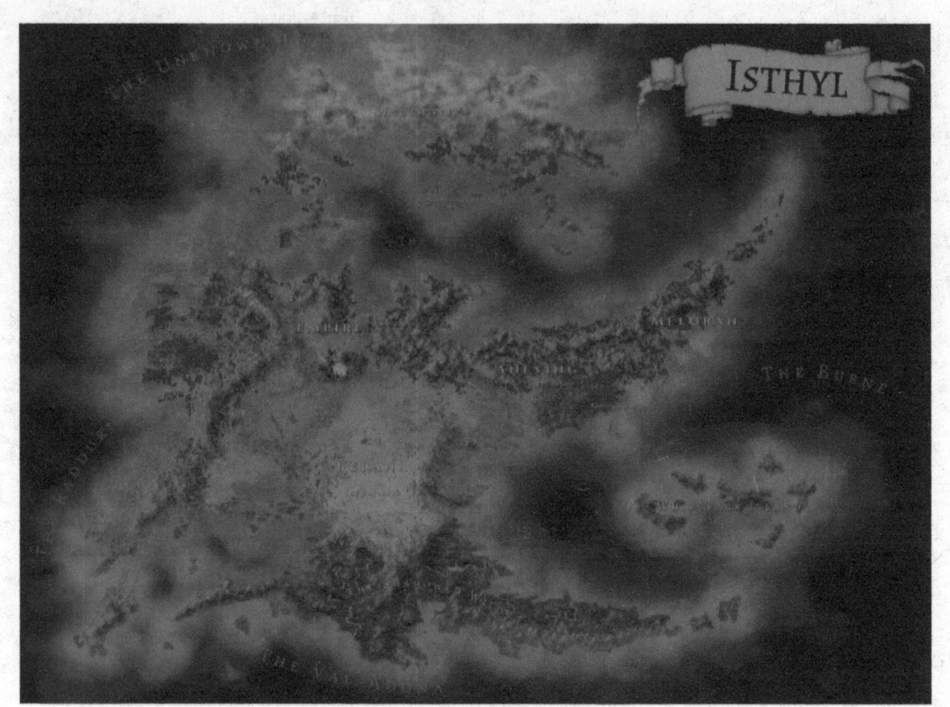
ISTHYL

Prologue

The Wall

"TO ARMS!"

The calls came rolling down the hall, one after another. Nak awoke to pounding on his barracks door.

"TO ARMS! ENEMY AT THE GATES!"

A driving rain slammed against the window by Nak's head as the world came into focus.

"ENEMY AT THE GATES! TO ARMS!"

Nak threw off his sheets and put his bare feet on the cold stone floor as realization buzzed to the front of his foggy mind. *Enemy at the gates?* A thousand questions followed the first. How had there been no warning? Where were the envoys? Why was there no attempt to treat before the attack? How large is the force? *How many of my friends will die tonight?*

He paused as he fastened the clasps on his dinged iron breastplate. *Will I die tonight?*

Pushing the thought away, Nak cinched on his padded leather bracers, retrieved a helmet from under his bunk, and grabbed a longsword and shield that hung from a hook on the wall by the door. All around him, his fellow soldiers bustled about, dressing and arming themselves. Outside the heavy wooden door hung on black wrought-iron hinges, the cries were still coming.

"ENEMY AT THE GATES! TO ARMS!"

Nak breathed deep and heaved open the door. Soldiers were running by, fully armed and armored as commanders called out orders above the din. Nak pulled the old banged up iron helmet over his head and made sure it was tight, slapping it twice with a gloved hand before running out to join his fellow soldiers in their jog to the battlements, sheathed longsword in hand. As he went, he strapped his wooden shield, emblazoned with the sigil of Aneving province: a red tree on a green field.

Nak's feet carried him through turn after turn of gray stone hallways, sending him down the corridors of the old keep. With every step, he drew closer to the battlements overlooking the town that sat at the foot of the castle. He realized as he turned yet another corner that his mouth had gone dry. He licked his lips as he tried to block out the fear that clawed at his chest, but he only chapped them further.

Then all at once, the huge ornate doors that led out onto the landing loomed ahead of him, like the gateway to a dream. Every step that brought him closer to that huge wooden door seemed to carry Nak further and further from peace. His heart felt as though it were caught in a blacksmith's hot irons. Each beat brought new fire, and every pang of heat made Nak wonder if he might simply die of the pressure in his chest and save the attackers the trouble of killing him.

Finally, after what seemed to be both an eternity and a moment, Nak passed through the doors and was outside. The pounding rain had picked up in intensity, and a howling wind swept across the battlements. Nak took his place with his unit, as he had rehearsed a thousand times. He stood on the most outset wall of the keep.

Push the ladders back, he thought. *Don't get cute, just kick down those ladders.* The words of his drill sergeant echoed through his head. *Don't get cute. Don't be a hero. Just be a good soldier and come out the other side if you can.*

Nak drew his sword and discarded the scabbard behind him somewhere. He gave it a couple swings, slicing through drops of rain just to get a feel for it. His heart was pounding in his ears, but even that wasn't loud enough to drown out the war drums being beaten below.

Nak finally allowed himself to glimpse the opposing army, and it nearly caused him to faint. Ten thousand men at least stretched out beneath him, torches as far as he could see. A million glimmering points of flame and steel, so many that Nak wasn't sure if he was looking at a battlefield or the night sky.

What happened to the army? Nak thought, his mind reeling. Not a week before, the Duke had sent the vast majority of their forces to meet the enemy in force, drive them back. *Three-thousand head of Aneving Cavalry. Another two-thousand footmen,* Nak thought, taking a mental tally of the force. *Were they routed that thoroughly?*

A glance at his fellow soldiers on either side of him told Nak he wasn't the only one doing the math. The remaining garrison was barely a thousand men. They were outnumbered ten-to-one at least. He tightened his grip on the longsword and closed his eyes.

Just knock down the ladders. The walls will hold.

Breathing slowly, he listened. Down below, there were cries of war, marching songs, whinnying horses, and of course the ever-present pounding drums. Up on the battlements, there were sergeants and commanders yelling at their men through the howling wind and driving rain. Other than that, there was not a sound. No soldiers spoke. No songs were being sung. Deeper in the castle, he knew the Duke and his family were being secured, along with the other noble families in residence. If they failed to hold the wall, the nobility would be ushered out of the castle via some secret escape route. Men would die to give them time to flee.

Nak swallowed and opened his eyes. There was nothing to do but wait now. Wait for the enemy to begin the attack.

Just knock down the ladders. Just knock down the damn ladders.

The march stretched on for what seemed like hours to Nak. Then without warning, it stopped. The drums stopped, the singing stopped, all noise ceased in an instant. The men on the walls didn't speak either. They all knew what was about to happen, Nak assumed. He figured most of them had never seen so much as a tavern brawl, much less an actual siege. They'd never fought someone who wanted to kill them. Never thought they'd have to.

Nak's memory flashed with images of men who'd wanted him dead. Even patrols could turn deadly in some neighborhoods. And it's doubly likely when you're shaking down shop-owners for protection on the side. Nak groaned, gripped his sword tighter. It felt good in his hand, nicely balanced, fresh from the castle forges not a month past. Shouts from the soldiers around him snapped him back to reality. He opened his eyes and saw them, just beginning to crest on their way up.

Ladders.

The ladders started their descent toward the walls, and the noise resumed. A massive *boom* echoed from a hundred feet below, from what Nak could only assume was a battering ram hitting the huge oak doors to the main keep. With no vanguard force to stop them, the enemy had marched right to the gate of Aneving and started breaking it down.

The ladders fell in slow motion toward him and the other men on the wall. Nak jumped as a *twang* of bowstrings sounded behind him, and a volley of arrows went to meet them. Some found their marks, but most fell to the ground, toward some poor soul who might as well have been miles from the actual fighting.

Atop each ladder was a screaming raider, clad in mismatched armor, certainly scavenged from previous kills. The one falling toward Nak was a slight man, wearing a breastplate taken from a Rovignon guard, dented and beaten, but his arms were bare, save his chainmail gauntlets. His legs were covered in a rusted chainmail skirt, with padded breeches, soiled from days of marching underneath. Scraggly, unkempt patches of hair covered his knotted and scarred pate, one eye glaring at Nak with wild, untethered rage, the other socket empty and lidless.

He fell with a shriek, rolling off the ladder as it slammed into the wall of the keep, massive metal hinges biting ruts into the smooth grey stone. As the attacker popped out of his roll and onto his feet, Nak caught the crazed look in his one remaining eye. In an instant, his short iron sword was coming for Nak's neck. He barely managed to get his shield up, warding off the blow and returning the favor with a sideways swing of his own. The smaller man twisted away from the attack and went for the back of Nak's head. The blow made impact, skewing his helmet to the side and obscuring his vision. Nak's ears rang loudly. So loudly, he barely managed to fall to one knee and avoid a would-be killing blow to his neck. From there, Nak stabbed upward over his shoulder, hoping to find something. Castle steel beat scavenged plate and Nak felt his sword find flesh, crunching through the stolen armor and sliding across bone before bursting out the man's back.

The slight man's weight slumped against the hilt of Nak's sword as his own iron blade clattered to the stones. Nak shrugged him off, laying him down and pulling his sword free. He adjusted his helmet, then watched the man's eye fade, his blood running with the pouring rain through the canyons between stones.

Nak shook his head and tried to free himself from the cold pit in his stomach as he turned back to the battle. His brothers in arms had set to work on the great metal hinges of the ladder but were getting nowhere. Nak rushed over to help them, for all the good it did.

On all sides, the song of steel rang out as swords clashed and shields splintered. Men screamed as they died and screamed as they killed, and ever-present was the *boom* of the battering ram and the deep, pounding beating of the war drum.

Nak could hear more men coming up the ladder. He checked his shield. It was barely scarred by the blow it had taken. Merely another scar added to its pockmarked face. The man who crested the ladder this time was shirtless, covered in filth with a mane of matted hair reaching down his back. He wielded two small battleaxes. Nak tightened his grip on his sword.

Just push down the ladders.

As he reached the top of the ladder, the shirtless man jumped off toward Nak. A quick sidestep meant he landed hard and bounced on the slick castle wall. One axe skittered off into the chaos. Nak seized the opportunity and rushed him. As the man got to one knee, Nak caught him full-bore with the front of his shield, sending him to his back and causing him to lose his one remaining axe. Nak wasted no time in sliding his sword between the man's unguarded ribs. A quick twist of the blade put an end to any protest from the attacker.

As Nak stood and freed his sword from the man's abdomen, he turned just in time to see two more besiegers climbing off the ladder and onto the wall. These two were better-armored, clad in full plate, dinged from battles untold. Their heads were covered by full helms with slits for visors, and they both hefted huge, black-bladed greatswords that they wielded with two hands. As the first one reached the top of the ladder and grabbed the wall, one of Nak's fellow soldiers swung at him hard with his sword. The knight caught the blow on one forearm, shrugging it off like nothing more than a child's toy. It might as well have leapt from its owner's hands as it careened off into the darkness below. The soldier fled, apparently not wanting to fight two fully armored men with no weapon.

Nak groaned. *Damn.*

The rain surrounded the two attackers like a curtain, veiling them from sight. The dark iron armor seemed to hide them in the night. For a moment, Nak struggled to see them at all. Then, all at once, a massive black blade came screaming through the air, slicing raindrops in two. He sidled to the right and the strike clanged off the stones. Before the soldier could lift his blade, Nak took a step toward him, but was stopped by an incoming cross-body swing coming for his head. He ducked under it, then stood and swung to his right, his sword clanging off the soldier's armor.

The first attacker was standing now, and advancing on Nak. He raised his shield and deflected a thrust, then swung down hard with his own blade, catching his opponent on an armored shoulder. A mailed fist knocked his sword away, then caught Nak on the side of the head, knocking his helmet off and sending him sprawling to his back in the water.

He barely managed to raise his shield in time to stop a downward stab. As fast as he could think to, Nak hooked his booted foot behind the knee of the man standing over him and pulled hard. He came crashing down in a mess of dark armor and a grunt. Rain was blinding Nak, soaking his hair. The metallic taste of blood filled his mouth from his busted lip. A flick of his tongue told him one of his front teeth had been broken in half by the punch.

Nak heard the crunching of plate armor as the other soldier advanced from somewhere behind him. He rolled to his stomach, then rose to one knee and swung his shield up and to the left as hard as he could. Luck was on his side and he'd swung true, deflecting an overhand strike and causing the armored man to stumble slightly. Nak saw an opportunity as the opposing soldier teetered. He ran at him, shield-first. The collision was hard, and Nak felt as though he'd run smack into a wall. The wall gave way, though, and the soldier tumbled over the side of the keep, screaming to a bloody and broken end somewhere below.

Nak wiped the water from his eyes as best he could with his free hand gloved. A quick glance back told him the other soldier was getting up, albeit slowly. He shook his head, tried to right himself in the driving rain. His footing was becoming untrustworthy, the water and blood sloshing around his boots and making him slip when he tried to set his feet. His breath came in ragged gasps, and his entire body ached. On all sides of him, the battle was raging. The attackers were still bashing against the gate down below. Nak assumed someone must be putting up a fight down there, but the ladder crews were beginning to gain a foothold on the walls.

He heard the coming attack just in time to dive to the left, splashing into the water just as a hard downward swing bit into the stone in a shower of sparks. The enemy soldier recovered quickly and swung down at Nak as he backpedaled. Nak caught the blow with his shield, but the soldier swung again, and again, relentlessly. He went at his work like a woodsman cutting down a tree. After three blows, the shield began to splinter. Two more blows and the left side cracked. As he hacked away, Nak felt his arm begin to go numb.

Just before the shield broke completely, a spear burst through the soldier's chest as he raised his sword over his head. He stopped, dropping the sword as blood dripped from the spear. It clanged to the ground, bouncing wildly. The large armored man dropped to his knees, then fell to the side. Where he'd stood was one of Nak's fellow soldiers. He didn't know the man's name, but he'd seen him on the grounds. He helped him up, then gave a nod and ran off. Nak unfastened the ruins of his shield and discarded it, then retrieved his sword from the standing water where he'd dropped it and shook it off.

Knock down the ladders.

Nak threw his weight against the enormous ladder. Nothing. He redoubled his efforts, dropping his sword and seizing the ladder with both hands, pushing and straining like an ox yoked to a cart in the mud. His muscles burned as if he were shoving against the castle wall itself. At some point–he didn't remember seeing it happen–one of his fellow soldiers joined in. Together, they heaved. It budged, so they did it again. More soldiers appeared, as if from the ether, and together they hefted it again. Finally, with a rending squeal, the hinges gave way, and the ladder crashed to the ground below, the men still climbing it left to scream as they plummeted back to their fellows.

Nak breathed as the battle raged around him. The *boom* beneath him continued to drone on as the battering ram kept its steady beat, pounding into the gates. Screams echoed all around him, along with the singing sound of steel on steel. Volleys of flaming arrows flew over his head, seeking victims on the battlefield below.

All at once, a guttural scream split the air. It was so loud, Nak felt it was coming from inside his own head. Long and low it carried on, shaking the very stones under his feet. Silence fell on the battlefield, on both sides. Nak looked up, but between the blinding rain and pitch-black sky, nothing revealed itself.

A crack of lightning illuminated the beast, painting it against a canvas of purple clouds. Long and lean, it writhed through the sky, the beats of its wings sending gusts of air to the ground. The call came almost instantly.

"DRAGON!"

A plume of orange flame unfurled from the beast's open maw, sizzling the air and boiling the rain. It came crashing down on the upper battlements behind Nak. Even from two hundred yards, he could feel the heat.

Of course, he'd heard the stories of dragonfire as a boy, but no one had seen dragons in battle for decades. He'd always thought of it as fantasy, but as he watched a drill sergeant explode in a gory mess of boiling blood and bits of flesh, it all became viscerally real.

The beast swung low, and as it sped by, Nak glimpsed the shimmering, silver-clad warrior on its back. His cloak, a massive shock of red fabric flowed whipping in the breeze past the tip of the dragon's tail and off into the night. On his back, an enormous sword hung sheathed, at least eight feet long and a foot wide, with a hilt that added another foot, at least. Though, as Nak watched, he realized the sword wasn't scabbarded at all, but rather hovered just behind its wielder, floating completely on its own.

A Rider! Thoughts swirled in Nak's head. *Where did he come from?*

He hefted his sword and, as the dragon looped up into the sky to ready for another attack, ran like mad for the door to the keep. He ran past troops of both sides, some fleeing and some fighting, and over the charred bones of his comrades. The beast shrieked again and shook the world, but Nak's eyes were set on the door, even as his heart pounded into his throat.

Two-hundred yards.

One-hundred.

Fifty.

A gust of wind knocked Nak onto his back. The dragon landed hard on the roof of the keep, coiled over the door, its tail flicking at the darkness. The Rider sat elegantly on its back, staring at him from behind silver plate with eyes unseen. The beast's head hung low, directly in Nak's path. As he looked up to meet the Rider's implacable gaze, he noticed thin wisps of purple smoke coiling from the eye slits in his helmet. He shivered involuntarily at the sight and cast a quick glance behind, which told him he was surrounded. At least ten men boxed him in, with the dragon and its master in front.

Nak lifted himself to his feet. Silence engulfed him. Silence, save the screams. The battle was nearly done already. All that remained was finishing off any remaining soldiers who wouldn't kneel and killing the nobility, if they hadn't escaped. Nak's thoughts drifted to the newborn Prince Alric. He banished the thoughts and gripped his sword.

The rain had stopped. A moonless evening breeze swept across Nak's face, carrying the scent of hot blood and roasted flesh to his nose as thunder rumbled and lightning danced in lace along the clouds.

Nak's breaths came in heaves as he weighed his options. There was no way he could fight his way backwards, and what was the point? The only thing awaiting him there were more enemy soldiers.

No, he decided. *The dragon is the only way. Maybe I can move fast enough and reach the Rider...*

His thoughts tapered off as he realized the fantasy of it all. As far as he knew, he was the last opposition left. There would be no miracle, he knew. No song to be sung of his slaying a great dragon and its Rider.

The dragon's eyes never moved from Nak as he watched it, baring its mouth full of greatswords. A low rumble emanated from its belly, and orange sparks danced along its shimmering silver and red scales.

Nak's heart pounded louder than any of the war drums from the battle, louder than the battering ram, louder even than the dragon's cry. It pounded right in his ears, up against his brain. He spun his sword in his hand, then screamed as he charged.

A spout of red-orange flame unfurled from the dragon's mouth and rocketed toward him. He didn't even have time to feel the heat before it engulfed him.

Part One
Seclusion

Chapter One

The Monastery

Mun-Alin. Our home. What a toil it must've been to build. But by the Six, there is no view like the one it affords.

-Log of Dragonmaster Rykas, 874th Lord of Mun-Alin

Wind whipped across Wik's face, bringing tears to the corners of her eyes. She closed them tight against the frigid mountain air and breathed out slowly. The sounds around her seemed to brighten: the chirping of birds, the whistling of the wind through an empty mountain cave, the breathing of the old man standing a few feet away, observing her with annoyed stoicism. She held her breath, bathing in the warmth of all those little moments. Then she reached for the well of power within her.

With her eyes closed, she could almost see it: a great,

undulating pool of pure, untouched power. *The very life of the world,* Meristofales had told her. Resting within all people, but accessible to very few. She tried to pull on it, take just a little. No more than a thimbleful, is how the old man had told her to think of it. Apparently, visualizing it as an actual pool of liquid was supposed to help her harness it.

The power flowed to her. Just a touch, just like she told it. It filled the thimble she held in her mind with a viscous liquid that glowed gold and white. And then it kept flowing. And on, and on, and on. Until the thimble overflowed and it began running over her feet and around her ankles. Surprised, she let loose a breath she'd been holding.

All at once, the delicate little thread she had pulled tight popped loose, and chaos reigned. The abandoned mountain cave was now a great yawning cavern cut into the mountain by the force of her power. The birds fled in terror. The old man watching nearby was nearly knocked off his feet by a blast of wind that might've dwarfed the beating of some dragons' wings.

For Wik's part, her body felt immediately alight with warmth that threatened to burn her from the inside. She gasped as her eyes shot open, cold air forcing her to blink painfully as she went to her hands and knees, crawling off the stone platform upon which she was situated. Her hands found the wet snow and she rubbed it on her arms, her face, her eyes, and in her mouth. The burning subsided, settling in as a tingling pain in her throat. Wik laid in the snow, gasping and trying to blink away the stubborn tears, but of course she couldn't. Not all of them were from the mountain air.

That's where she was when the old man approached.

Meristofales's boots gave away his approach, tapping across the ancient stones as he marched over to her. She looked up at him from where she lay flat on her back on the stones.

"Wik," he said through gritted teeth. "Do I need to go over it again?"

Wik sighed and rubbed her face before shaking her head, even though she knew he'd do it anyway.

"All people," he intoned, same as the hundred times before, "contain within themselves a reserve of incredible power. For most, they never access it unless they find themselves in a life-threatening situation and do it by accident. But for some" –he leveled his stare at her meaningfully– "accessing this power is as intuitive as breathing. They might not even realize they're doing it. But intuition will not take you to the heights of magic use. Only training can do that. So we will continue to do this, every day, until you *get. it. right.*"

Wik stood with some effort and shook off the snow, then looked at the old Rider. Meristofales's hard gray eyes gave way after a moment and he chuckled, a smile creasing the leathery corners of his ancient mouth.

"Girl," he said, clapping her on the shoulder and guiding her back to the meditation circle, "you will either be my greatest success, or the reason for my crossing over."

Wik looked at her feet. "Let's hope it's the former."

Meristofales laughed as he shook her goodnaturedly by the shoulder. "Let's go again."

Eoradon laid back against the warmth of Iaxal's belly and breathed deep. The rough scales of her hide flexed with every breath she took, her abdomen rising and falling in time with the puffs of wistful smoke that curled from her nostrils. Every breath also brought with it the slightest thrum, deep within her. She couldn't help it, he knew, and knowing something so simple was beyond her reach brought a sly smile to his lips.

You seem more at-ease than normal, her thoughts spoke directly into his mind. Decades ago, when he'd come to this place, the voices of the dragons had felt like an intrusion in his mind. Now, he was scarcely even cognizant of them. He and Iaxal had been speaking without talking for so long, it was more than just second nature. It was the only way he could imagine his life.

I am, he thought back. And why shouldn't he be? The sun was out, lighting up the mountains with that sort of angry red-orange fire only the brightest mornings could manage. There was a breeze, but not really enough he'd call it "windy." And he was with her, taking it all in.

Iaxal lifted her enormous green and yellow-scaled head and sniffed the frigid air, then thrummed a little deeper. *It's nice today. There's a faint odor of sparrow on the air. A flock of them should pass within a mile of the monastery later this afternoon.*

Eoradon chuckled. *So I guess I know what you'll be doing for dinner*. She thrummed happily at the thought.

An enormous explosion rocked the air as a physical blast of wind cut through the courtyard where they lazed. Eoradon huddled in the protection of Iaxal's wing, raised the instant she thought there might be danger. After a couple tense heartbeats, she lowered the wing and Eoradon spied Meristofales standing sternly over Wik.

Eoradon shook his head as he laid back against Iaxal. *That girl seems to get further and further from controlling that power every day*, he thought.

Iaxal snorted. *She has great potential. It's harder for you to sense it, because your human senses about magic are extremely dull. But for dragonkind, it is eminently apparent what power she possesses.*

Eoradon raised a brow as he turned to look at the dragon. *And what kind of power is that?*

Iaxal's great head turned slowly to regard him through her enormous golden eyes, flecked with green. *That girl*, she thought, *has the deepest reserve of anyone in this monastery.* She eyed him purposefully before continuing. *Including you.*

Eoradon chuckled, but Iaxal didn't seem to be joking. *Iaxal,* he began. *I have pure imperial blood. My family possesses the deepest reserves ever recorded.*

Iaxal turned away from him and curled her head over the stump of her right foreleg. *Aye, Rodo, you're right. And they refill. It's why your ancestors ruled Ir-Anan for...how many generations?*

He sighed. *A thousand, supposedly. But historians argue it couldn't be more than a few hundred.*

Right, she said in his mind. *But this girl—Wik—has a well of power to rival even my own. If she can ever learn to harness it...*

Eoradon suppressed a shiver that ran down his spine. If she was that strong, he wondered if Meristofales even ought to be training her. He banished the thought immediately, but still—he'd seen what that kind of power could do, and had no desire to see it again.

His father laid by the throne, struggling to stand, sputtering blood...

He shook himself. Nothing to be gained by looking back.

Something on your mind? Iaxal thrummed as her thoughts

wound through his.

He grunted and did his best to hide what he'd seen. *Nothing.*

She thrummed deeper. *You were a child, Rodo. There was nothing you–*

It was decades ago, he cut her off. *A different life. A different world. Certainly a different person.*

She didn't speak again, but he could feel her presence in his mind. Sad and pitiful, she waited there for whenever he would be ready. Eoradon sighed, then reached his hand out and rubbed her warm belly. She thrummed, vibrating his hand.

Rialin shielded his eyes and laid low against his mount as the mountains streamed past on either side. He felt stinging tears gathering at the corners of his eyes as they banked around another craggy spire and sped through the valley of stone on the other side.

His mount, a young dragon with scales colored red with highlights of light blue, brought his wings close to his body and dove toward the floor of the valley, some thousand feet below. Rialin's stomach leapt into his throat as they executed the maneuver, even after so many years of riding dragons. About a hundred feet from the stony, bramble-covered valley floor, the dragon snapped out his wings and glided for a distance before flapping and beginning the climb back up.

Rialin was constantly amazed by the dragons' adeptness in the air. The beasts were certainly useful for that, if little else. He gave the monster a mental whiplash, or as close as he could manage. It grunted, smoke puffing from its nostrils as it increased its pace.

The wind whipped Rialin's hair away from his face as they

banked around a peak, so close he could've reached out and grazed the stone face of the mountain if he'd wanted. Another stone wall, looming to his left, cast them into a cold, lingering shadow as they flew. And then, all at once, they burst into the stark sunlight, and the monastery loomed before them.

Its enormity still took Rialin by surprise, all these decades later. Carved from the sheer side of Mun-Alin, the largest peak in the Crags, it took up most of the mountain with its structure. The secrets of its construction had been lost long before Rialin had come here, but the evidence of the ancient Riders' ingenuity still loomed over them. As evidence of that thought, he reached out and could feel his blade resting where it was strapped to his saddle. The enormous Rider blades were one of his order's primary weapons. Nearly eight feet long, the weapon was damned near impossible for a normal person to wield, but light as a feather in the hands of the Rider for whom it was forged. Rialin was no smith, but from his understanding, drops of blood from both dragon and rider were included in the smelting process of the blades, giving the Rider the ability to manipulate the weapon with their mind.

For all the good they do from behind the walls of the monastery, Rialin thought.

His beast came to a skidding landing on one of the dozens of platforms that jutted from the main structure of the monastery. The creature's claws left deep ruts in the stone, throwing bits of gravel and sediment up as he came to halt. Rialin unbuckled his saddle straps and hopped to the ground, as nimbly as possible with his knees popping and cracking the whole time. He groaned as he stretched his back. The magic of the Riders slowed his aging considerably, but it couldn't stop it completely. And at his age, even with magic's aid, his joints occasionally got stiff. Sharp steps reverberating off stone told Rialin that Ferao was striding toward him.

"Get him taken care of," Rialin said, gesturing over his shoulder to the dragon, now sniffing around the platform impatiently.

"Ah, stone and sky, Rialin," Ferao said, his northern accent thick in his rolling R's. "You cannae ride him like this. You'll put him in an early grave."

Rialin removed his flight mask and ran a gloved hand through his hair. "If he can't keep up, I'll just get another one."

Ferao rolled his eyes and patted the beast on the neck. "The dragons won't give you another one, even if the old man petitions them. You know they're angry with you."

Rialin grimaced. "Meristofales doesn't want me grounded, and the dragons have to keep making bonds or they gradually lose their intelligence, right? I can't imagine they'd risk losing a Rider, given how short we are on supply of new recruits." He gestured to the mostly empty courtyard. "Look at this place. It's a joke. And Meristofales knows it."

Ferao held his hands up. "Ain't my place to get involved in all that, Rialin." He patted the dragon again. "Just take care of the poor thing. He's done aught to draw your ire."

Rialin nodded. "True. But he's done aught to gain my respect, either. I will withdraw the one from him when he's earned the other." And with that, he turned and strode toward the courtyard.

Wik squeezed her eyes shut and tried to control her breathing. In. Out. In. Out. But every time she actively *tried* to breathe, she found it suddenly impossible to do. She shook her head and refocused. The old man was still watching. She needed to show him *something*, or he might never let her near a dragon.

The pool of magical essence appeared in her mind. Carefully, so slowly she felt she was hardly doing anything at all, she reached for it. Once again, the golden strands of viscous magical liquid flowed to her. She took it, careful not to let go of her held breath.

Just a small amount, she thought to herself. *Don't overdo it.* Meristofales wasn't speaking, but she swore she could *feel* his presence. Maybe she could? Was that...another pool? Iridescent white, shimmering light, far wider than hers but more shallow, wisps of glittery smoke wafting from its surface. Like shadows in the corner of her eye, it vanished when she focused on it. But she could've sworn she'd seen it.

She felt something slip ever so slightly out of her control. She turned her attention to it, reaching wildly with her mind for the bit of power, but she was too slow and it zipped away from her. And like a child trying to catch raindrops, she'd lost it.

The frustration caused her to sigh, and she immediately felt her mistake. The initial bit of magical energy was nothing more than a gust. But when she sighed, she severed her focus. The pool of energy disappeared and she slammed back into the physical world with what felt like the force of being dropped off the side of the mountain. The power inside her, now disconnected from its stabilizing force, had to be used. It was burning her from the inside. She could *feel* her insides cooking, roiling under the strain. Her eyes felt like they were going to burst from her skull from the pressure.

Distantly, she heard Meristofales scream, "Out there! Away! *OUT THERE!*" He sounded so far away, she could barely make out what he said over the blood thundering in her ears. She spun, unsure of where she was even looking, just hoping it was away from him and the rest of the monastery.

And then she screamed. When she did, the heat and power burst from her mouth like a river through a weak dam. Flames, glowing an incredible yellow and green, exploded from her mouth. When the geyser impacted a statue of some former Dragonmaster, it didn't simply burn the stone. The magical fire met the statue like a liquid. It *melted* the statue to a boiling orange puddle in a matter of seconds.

The power vanished from her as quickly as it had threatened to destroy her, leaving Wik utterly drained. She stared momentarily at the wreckage of the monastery's former leader, his likeness now lost forever. And then the pain. Blisters formed immediately on the inside of Wik's mouth and down her throat. Her head throbbed from the rapid heating and cooling. Her stomach revolted and if she'd had anything left in it, she would've vomited where she stood. As it was, she fell to her knees and gagged, spitting brown bile onto the stone.

All at once, her vision swam and she fell onto her side. She gasped, but barely got any breath. Subsequent gasps brought similar results. The panic set in. She couldn't breathe. She clawed at her chest and throat, eyes rolling, looking anywhere, everywhere for help.

Then Meristofales was there. He slid up beside her in a crouch. He ripped off a glove and his leathered hand went to her side. He pulled her shirt up, slid his hand underneath to rest on her bare abdomen.

"You burst your lung," he said. She barely heard him. Her vision was going dark. Just before she passed out she heard him say again, a faint glow emanating from his hand, "Stone and sky, the damned fool's burst her lung."

Chapter Two

Princely Heritage

The boy shows promise. I hope he will prove worth the trouble of housing him here.

-Log of Dragonmaster Rykas, 874th Lord of Mun-Alin

The meeting hall bustled with activity as all the active Riders crowded in amongst each other. Though, as Eoradon thought about it, perhaps "bustled" was the wrong word. The hall was enormous, meant to accommodate hundreds of Riders, with viewing perches available from the massive open roof for their dragons, as well. However, their numbers were so dramatically thinned after their years in exile that only thirty-six Riders remained, many of them aged beyond usefulness. Some, it had to be noted, were older even than Meristofales, and he'd seen over two hundred winters now.

Not many sharp swords in this lot, Eoradon thought, then winced as Iaxal sent her reproach through their bond.

The dragons that cared to attend these meetings perched higher up in the chamber. From what Eoradon could tell, only Iaxal, Uanari, and a couple of the other, older dragons bothered to come anymore. For their part, his and Meristofales's partners lounged on the roof, massive scaled heads hanging down through the viewing hole. Iaxal, a brilliant green and yellow, and Uanari, deep purple and black, three times her size at least.

Eoradon suppressed a shiver. Uanari was Meristofales's partnered dragon, and he was by far the most powerful dragon Eoradon had ever seen. Mindnumbingly huge, his thrum could shake the entire monastery when he really got into it. He'd never heard him roar, but from the stories, he could shear mountaintops. "The King of Dragons," as he was sometimes called around the monastery, was unfailingly loyal to Meristofales, though. Good for the rest of them, as far Eoradon was concerned. He certainly never wanted to be on the beast's bad side.

The crowd, if it could be called that, quieted as Meristofales stepped up on the dais at the center of the hall and raised his hand. As the din retreated and most people found seats, their leader, Lord Dragonmaster Meristofales, cleared his throat.

"Before we begin," he said, his gravelly voice carrying that distinctive Lowland accent effortlessly to the entire chamber. "I want to let you know, Wik is recovering well from the...mishap we all saw yesterday."

This was met with a chorus of chuckles, with a few groans mixed in for good measure. Eoradon stayed silent. He knew well enough the girl had few friends among those gathered here. Meristofales was surely aware of it, too, but he was desperate for her to find her footing. He didn't want to be the Dragonmaster that oversaw the end of the Order, he'd told Eoradon that bit himself. Eoradon only hoped his fear didn't outlast his willingness to preserve their way of life.

"Unfortunately," Meristofales continued in that slow, intentional cadence of his, "Dragonmaster Lokend's likeness was unrecoverable." Laughter rippled through the assembly. Eoradon chuckled, too. He thought Meristofales even allowed himself a slight smile.

Of course, as always, there was one among them who refused to let himself show any mirth. Eoradon glared at Rialin. The other Rider noticed, probably because he was already glaring back. Eoradon felt Iaxal's anger rise in his mind. She was thinking about her foot. His own anger rose to meet hers before he tamped it back down.

Not now, he told her in his mind. *The day will come.*

He thought he could feel her thrum even down here. *It had better,* was her response. Her anger was still white-hot when Rialin bothered to show his face. Which, to be fair, didn't happen much anymore. He was always off scouting or whatever he damned-well pleased. Eoradon looked away and the moment passed, even if his anger was only abated.

Meristofales was still talking down below. "Rialin tells me the ashfall from the Emergance has calmed to the east."

The older man indicated Rialin with a nod, which he returned with a much smaller, almost imperceptible one of his own. Meristofales opened his mouth to speak again, almost certainly dismissing the meeting because—well, what more was there to discuss? The only Rider who did any actual riding these days was Rialin, and he was under instruction to fly high enough he wouldn't be seen. But before the old man could get a word out, Rialin spoke up.

"Dragonmaster," he said, his voice silky smooth, just like it always had been. Eoradon turned sharply and looked at him. Up above, he heard Iaxal thrum. Thankfully, Uanari didn't follow suit. Rialin was standing, facing Meristofales. "When will we be allowed to take on new recruits? Other than your pet project, no foundlings have come to us in nearly twenty years. The older of our number know this—we are wasting away."

There was a moment of silence as his words settled over the gathered Riders. A spike of shock from Iaxal cut through Eoradon's mind. Meristofales spoke first.

"Rialin, you know we are under a binding order to remain in seclusion." His voice was sympathetic, but his face was set.

"How long?" Rialin asked, taking a step toward the elderly Dragonmaster. "You haven't seen the state of the world. I have. The empire is shattered, turned to fiefdoms and city-states, ruled by cruel men at best and warlords at worst. They need us, Meristofales." Another moment of silence, then he spoke again, pointing up to the lounging dragons. "As do they. You know they need the bond as much as we do. More. The last thing we need is feral dragons roaming the skies again."

A hushed murmur spread through the assembly as Meristofales cleared his throat. Eoradon leaned forward to listen.

"Rialin, I cannot lift the seclusion order."

"Then what *can* you do?" he asked, a little too loudly, a little too imploring.

Eoradon stood and took the steps two at a time down to the floor, where Rialin stood. Both he and Meristofales turned to regard him as he made his entrance.

Rialin rolled his eyes. "Ah, the little prince has graced us with his presence."

Eoradon gritted his teeth. "Your jibes don't sting half as hard as you might think, Rialin."

The other Rider barked a humorless laugh. "Oh no, I daresay my sword stings more." He looked up to where Iaxal was lounging. "Isn't that right, little bird?"

Anger flashed through Eoradon's mind and he fought to tamp it down. For just a moment, he felt the arcing pain through her leg as her foot had been cut away, hot blood spraying over the cool windblown grass of the valley. She climbed to her feet, glaring down and thrumming loud.

Peace, Iaxal, Eoradon said to her through their connection. *Peace.*

Out loud, Eoradon fought for control the same anger, clawing up at him now. Without realizing, he'd taken a step toward Rialin. The other Riders were paying attention now, if they weren't before. Standing, leaned forward on their knees, with arms crossed over their chests, they were watching.

When Eoradon spoke, he found he couldn't unclench his teeth, so it came out more of a hiss than real words.

"*Watch. Your. Mouth.*"

Rialin's eyes went a little wide at the level of vitriol, but the placid smile never wavered. "You should come with me, the next time I leave the monastery to scout. Go and survey your kingdom."

Before he knew it was happening, Eoradon had his fist clenched and pulled back. He hesitated for just a moment, suddenly acutely aware of how many eyes were watching them. One set of eyes stood out from the rest.

Meristofales's cool gray orbs, adorned by furrowed brows of much the same shade, hardened as Eoradon met them. He bellowed, with an intonation more thunderclap than human voice.

"*Stop this at once!*"

Eoradon froze. Rialin, too, hands halfway up to a defensive stance. They glowered at each other, but neither dared defy the Dragonmaster.

"You two will not make this assembly more of a mockery than it already is," he said. His words, like iron, bound Eoradon. He was helpless against this old man and his commands. "Both of you, out. *Now.*"

Rialin found his way, as he always did, to the gardens on the highest level of the monastery. The air was thin up here, even more so than on the grounds down below. The oppressive mountain fortress was beneath him, and nothing but the sky stretched out above, yawning and empty, save some wispy clouds and migratory birds heading south for the thaw.

Rialin breathed deep, held the cold air in his lungs, then huffed it out as he thought again of Eoradon's outburst in the assembly. Oh, how he'd love to catch the prince up here without Meristofales or the beast to protect him. They could settle the old scores then, finally put an end to the dance they'd kept up for most of the last twenty years.

Flames shooting miles high, nowhere to run, all alone at the end of the world.

Boots clicking on the stone behind roused Rialin from his reminiscing. He didn't need to turn to know who it would be, but he did anyway. Meristofales's aged face was turned skyward, lips upturned in a smile. The old man smiled a lot, to Rialin. He never could figure out where he got so much good humor.

"It's a beautiful day," the Dragonmaster said.

Rialin shrugged. "Most days are, up here."

Meristofales nodded in agreement, then let his face drop back into shadow before opening his eyes. "You're welcome," he said, fixing Rialin with that slate stare.

Rialin creased his brows. "For what, exactly?"

Meristofales settled slowly onto a bench and regarded him with one eye, the other squeezed shut against the sun. "For not letting Eoradon kick your ass."

Rialin sputtered a chuckle, caught off guard. "Ah, yes, that." He smiled a little, then crossed to where Meristofales sat and joined him on the bench. For a beat, they both simply sat and enjoyed the soft breeze, the quiet that comes with high places and thin air.

Meristofales was the first one to break the silence.

"You know I can't override the order of seclusion," he said, his voice low despite their being alone.

Rialin sighed. "The people who issued that order are decades in the dirt. There must be a way."

For a moment, Rialin thought Meristofales genuinely looked his age. He hunched, closed his eyes, and let his head hang, blowing air from his nose. It was over in a flash, but Rialin had seen him let his guard down for once.

"There are things you do not know, Rialin." Meristofales sighed. "And I cannot reopen the monastery until other things have come to pass."

Rialin screwed his brows up, confused. "Until what has come to pass?" he asked, incredulous.

Meristofales looked at him from under bushy gray brows. "There are things you do not know," he repeated. Before Rialin could speak again, the old man held up a spotted hand. "But here is what you *should* know. The Riders will not die with us, Rialin. And I will not be here forever. This monastery must have a Dragonmaster. And given your status and skill, I have to imagine the choice will be between you..." he let the moment hang in silence, "...or someone of Imperial descent."

"Ah." Rialin rocked back on the bench, looked up at the wisps of clouds making their way across the blue expanse. "So that's it, then? Me or him?"

"Probably," Meristofales said simply.

Rialin exhaled as he thought through how best to phrase the next bit. 'The craven prince will never consent to lead, and you know it."

Meristofales smiled slightly. "Oh, there's more to Eoradon than you assume. He'll do it if asked." He leveled a stare at Rialin. "But I think we both know his leadership is best served elsewhere."

Rialin scoffed at that. "Hasn't he spent thirty years saying he'll never go back to Ir-Anan?"

The aged Rider shrugged. "People say a lot of things."

Rialin sighed. "I will do what is needed."

"I'm glad to hear it." Meristofales grunted as he stood and stretched. "But a Dragonmaster should probably have a properly bonded dragon."

Rialin couldn't stop himself chuckling. "Then one should

prove itself worthy."

Meristofales nodded, and Rialin thought he caught the ghost of a smile on his lips for a moment. "You know the bond is stronger when you fully give in to it. You'd gain—"

"I'd gain one more thing that can kill me," Rialin snapped. "And another set of eyes and ears in my head. My sword works." He shrugged. "I'm fine with that. The dragons are welcome to stop sending hatchlings for me to bond." His eyes rolled up to meet the older man's. "But you know they won't."

Meristofales breathed out hard, but said nothing. He turned to leave, but stopped and looked back at Rialin. "Will you be here long?"

Rialin shook his head. "Just long enough to resupply. I'm hearing tell of some battle in Aneving. I plan to head that direction in short order and see what's happened."

Meristofales nodded and turned away. "Fair winds, Rider."

Rialin smiled to himself. "Fair winds."

Meristofales replaced his quill in the inkwell, closed the enormous volume of the *Dragonmaster's Account* with a *thump*, then leaned back and rubbed his sore eyes. He could feel Uanari's rumbling presence in his mind before the dragon spoke.

Meristofales, he said in a voice like crackling thunder, rattling the Dragonmaster's thoughts. *They want to speak*.

Meristofales shook himself to clarity. *Speak?* He tried and failed to stamp out the panic he suddenly felt rising in his chest. *About what?*

I do not know. But we must go.

And in a flash, he was gone, ripped away and spiraling through vast expanses of clouds imbued with every color imaginable. Great and horrible storms sprang to life all around him, thunder and lightning rocking him as he flew. Then, all at once, he came to a shuddering stop, floating in the middle of a great empty sky, lightning lacing the clouds around him and lighting the scene. In front of him, monstrous faces were lit momentarily by the arcing lightning, then submerged once more into purple and black shadows, their eyes glowing like diamonds in all different colors. He knew Uanari was here somewhere. His consciousness would've also made the trip, though it always seemed he had more control over this place and could remain out of sight.

No such luck for Meristofales. He was stuck, hovering in that great open sky, unable to move except to talk.

"Human..." One of the enormous creatures in the clouds spoke. He could never determine which one was speaking, or even if they were separate beings, or the many faces of one horrible god. "You have...been brought to us...to answer for your choices..." The creature spoke in a slow, droning cadence, as if forming words was a great strain. "The bond...grows...*weak*." When it spoke the last word, more lightning flashed, and Meristofales would've sworn the things were grimacing, as if in pain.

"I cannot take on new acolytes," Meristofales said, trying and failing to keep the tremble out of his voice. "Because of the order of sequester."

Thunder rumbled and the creature spoke again. "My... children...lose their wits. Become...as animals."

Meristofales hesitated, looking for the words before continuing. "I understand. But magic binds my hands. My predecessors were committed to the withdrawal of the Riders, and the monastery remaining separated from the affairs of the Kingdoms of Men." He swallowed. A little half-truth never hurt anyone.

Except possibly him, right now. A great strike of lightning smashed down past his face, the wind picked up into a gale, and a deep rumble of thunder threatened to shake the teeth from his head. But eventually, it subsided enough for the voice to boom again.

"You...must...change it." He began to protest, but the voice continued. "You have served...many years. Perhaps *too* many." Thunder rumbled as the voice stopped droning for a moment. "You would...do well to remember..." Lightning arced in all directions, illuminating the faces, all opened in a massive roar, seemingly coming to devour Meristofales. He reflexively put his hands in front of his face, but the faces stopped just short of him and spoke again in a growling whisper that shook the very air. "You rule...because *we allow it*. You can...be replaced."

And with that, he snapped back to the chair in his study, unsure as always whether the experience had been real or not.

Chapter Three

Escape

Many dangerous things lurk beneath the dark canopy of Aneving's Great Eastern Forest.

-Log of Dragonmaster Nirus, 740th Lord of Mun-Alin

Toddy threw the dice. They landed poorly, as was typical for his dice.

"For all the stupid things," he grumbled.

"Oh yes," squealed Pig. "I love when you give me your money. Pay up, please." And Pig extended his fat fingers and snatched the meager coins from Toddy's gloved hand.

"Damned cheat," Toddy mumbled.

"Ay, what the hell did you—" Pig's indignation was cut off as the men around them rose and looked to the road. Pig and Toddy looked that way, too. A lone man was approaching the barricade. Hunched, wrapped in a green cloak, pulled over his head against the rain and cold. He trudged along down the rutted trail they let pass for a road in these parts, stumbling slightly as his foot slipped, then righting himself. He was a big fellow, anyone could've seen that. But bent and worn. Old, Toddy decided. And he turned back to roll the dice again.

"Oi!" Hodge called out from the front of the little barricade, which, if Toddy was being honest, was little more than a sideways wagon and some crates. No one expected any traffic to come this way after the battle, but still, the Vicar wanted someone watching every road, so here they'd sat, listening to the chaos of the battle.

"Battle" was really quite a strong term for what had happened. It was a complete and utter rout. Hodge said the soldiers they'd turned when they came out to harry the army had all but handed them the city. The dragon had probably been overkill, in retrospect, but it brought people to heel very quickly, from what Toddy had picked up. But then, it wasn't his job to wonder why the Vicar and his generals did what they did.

It was his job to watch the road.

"Oi!" Hodge called again. "What's your business, old-timer?"

The man came to a stop and looked up at Hodge from beneath his brow.

"Just passing through. Coming from Aneving," he said in a gravelly cadence. He tried to step around Hodge, but the Commanding Officer stepped back into his path, blocking him again.

"Aneving's besieged," Hodge said, the suspicion in his voice pricking Toddy's ear. "No one in, or out."

"Right, right." The man looked around at the four of them. Hodge, up front, then Pig and the new man, Colt? Then Toddy in the back, no more than a knife for defense. But then, he wasn't supposed to be fighting. They'd told him to mind the others' equipment, keep it sharp and shiny and ready to fight. From the looks of their armor now, he reckoned, he'd failed on that point.

Hodge squinted at him. "Come on, soldier. You can't hide the look in those eyes. You've been a fighting man, haven't you?"

Toddy thought Hodge had gone mad until the old man gave a sly smile and a grunt, then stood to his full height. Toddy stopped himself from gasping, barely. The man was enormous, a full half-head taller than Hodge, who was the tallest of their company. Wide-set shoulders and a thick neck led to an aged face, still mostly hidden in shadow.

"Fair enough," the man said, and even that had grown deeper, more gravelly and grinding. "Not all men are made for lying."

Hodge chuckled. "So, honesty then?"

The man seemed to consider that, then nodded. "Honesty."

A beat passed.

"Honestly," he said, "if you don't stand aside and let me pass, I'll cut through the four of you before you can even draw a sword." He jerked his head to the treeline some fifty yards away. "And your man in the trees, the one aiming the arrow at me now? I'll kill him after. I don't run like I used to, but I think I've got a few chases through the woods left in me." He levelled a glare at their little group, going from man to man. "So, deal?" He turned back to Hodge, who looked flummoxed.

"We can't let you leave," he said, chuckling. "Besides, just cause you say you're some big man don't mean you are." And Hodge reached for his sword.

The next part happened so fast, Toddy barely registered it.

Before Hodge even gripped the hilt of his sword, the old man had flung a throwing knife from inside his cloak, caught the Commanding Officer in the neck. Pig and Colt stumbled back as he whipped a sword out, cutting Colt's neck with one motion. Then he rotated and twisted away as an arrow split the air where he'd been a moment before. And then, as if he were cutting a cake, he brought that sword down in an overhand swing and chopped deep into Pig's head, down through his nose and into his mouth. He yanked the blade free, and blood spurted in gouts from the open head. The stranger gritted his teeth, his gaze swinging all around. He was barely breathing hard.

He turned to face where the arrow had come from. "You!" he roared, all pretense gone from his voice as he hissed through gritted teeth and a bloody face. "You in the trees! This is your last chance to start fuckin' running!" A beat followed, then the sounds of someone crashing through the trees floated toward them.

Then the old man's hard blue eyes found Toddy, still dumbly holding dice out to throw them. He turned and looked at the terrifying swordsman, who was just now walking toward him, his booted feet biting deep into the mud.

"No, no, no, no..." Toddy was saying. It was pointless of course. Just a bad roll of the dice.

A look of pity crossed the man's bearded face as he brought the sword swinging down.

Sen wiped his sword on the back of the coat belonging to the young man he'd just killed, smearing even more blood on him. After a moment's inspection of the blade, he slid it back into the sheath at his waist, then turned to feeling the pockets of the four men he'd just slaughtered, looking for anything worth taking. The road ahead was long, and he knew they'd need coin for food and shelter.

After finding little, aside from some scattered gold coins on a crate by the wagon, he turned and trudged back down the road. Back to the child.

The little boy was huddled behind some rocks about a half-mile away from the barricade, wet and shivering and sniveling, much like he had been since that woman had thrust him into Sen's arms as he fought to escape the castle. The screams of the dragon and the screams of the people echoed in his mind still.

Sen shook himself. No time to dwell on that. Duke Visarch had given him a duty. That woman had given him a child. And both required him to head west, to Ir-Anan.

The boy's big, wet eyes snapped to Sen as he approached. "Are we safe?" he asked in that dithering, scared way he spoke.

Sen sighed. "No, boy, we're not safe." He slung his pack over his shoulder. He turned to leave, then begrudgingly turned back and offered the boy his hand. "Come on, now. Let's get down the road a ways before dark."

It was less than an hour into their walk when the boy complained of his legs hurting and asked Sen to carry him. He'd refused at first, but after another moment, the boy started to whimper and, well, he was a hard bastard, but he wasn't heartless. So it was, the boy sleeping in his arms, that Sen trudged on down the narrow little pigpath of a road.

Nightfall came, and Sen struck camp off the road, in the trees. He didn't risk a fire, but unrolled the one sleeping bundle he had and, grumbling as he did so, tucked the boy's small body into its warmth. He laid next to it and did not sleep, but rather laid awake, listening for danger, but hearing only the small child's soft snores. After a couple hours, sleep finally broke down his tired mind's defenses and claimed him.

He awoke to screaming. The boy was screaming. Sen ripped a dagger from his belt and looked at the boy, lying next to him. He was curled into a ball, screaming like nothing Sen had ever heard. Great, bubbling sobs wracked his little body as he looked about, his eyes wide and unseeing.

"Hey," Sen said, shaking him gently, then harder. "Hey, boy, are you alright?"

"Mommy!" the boy burbled. "Mommy! Daddy!"

Sen sighed, then put the knife away and patted the boy on the chest. "It's alright, now. Shh, son, it's alright." After a few more gurgled cries, he stilled, drifting back to sleep, his head against Sen's leg, tiny fist curled tight in his cloak.

Sen passed the next few hours to sunrise in fitful non-sleep, any stirring from the boy causing him to start. At first light, he gently rolled the boy away from him, strung the short bow he kept on the side of his pack, and stalked further into the woods. Hunting was light. The storm, then the bloody dragon, had forced most of the small game to flee.

As he rounded a crag of rock and looked into a clearing in the dead trees, though, Sen spotted the corpse of a large deer, bloated and beginning to decay. Nothing was edible about that. But perched on top of the corpse sat two fat buzzards, gorging themselves on the viscera. Sen sighed and sighted in with his bow.

By the time the boy stirred an hour later, Sen had set a steaming bowl of gamey, stringy meat by him.

"What is it?" he asked, never taking his eyes from the bowl.

"Vult—," Sen began, then thought better of it. "A bird. It's good." He took a bite of his own portion to show the boy it was safe. In truth, it was chewy, and he'd have killed for a piece of chicken or mutton, but he'd learned the hard way that sometimes you must use the tools you have.

The boy tentatively took a gristly piece of meat between his thumb and forefinger and placed it in his mouth. He spat it out almost immediately.

"Ugh!" the boy gagged. "That's bad!"

Sen sighed. He wanted to tell the boy he was wrong, snap at him for being rude, but in truth, he was right. Sen dumped the meat and returned the bowls to the pack, along with the rest of camp. After kicking some dirt over the meager flame he'd built to cook the carrion, they took off back toward the road.

"Where are we going?" the boy asked from behind as they pushed through the tall grass of a meadow.

"Ir-Anan," Sen responded over his shoulder. "You'll be safe there. They have places for children with..." he hesitated, then went on. "...with no family."

"Oh." The boy's voice was suddenly quiet and very small. "So my mommy and daddy are...they're dead?"

Sen winced, then stopped and turned to face the boy. "Most people from the castle are dead. So, I guess they probably are."

The boy looked at his feet, clearly about to cry. As he whimpered, Sen found himself kneeling—despite the pain he constantly fought in his knees—and turning the boy's chin up so they looked into each other's faces.

"But *we* aren't dead, are we?" The boy sniffled, then shook his head. Sen continued. "So, we've got to keep living, so there's someone to tell the stories about your ma and da. So other people can remember them. That's what we can do for the dead."

The boy still looked about to sob, but nodded his head and wiped his eyes.

"Okay," he said, his voice a little stronger. "I'll try."

Sen nodded. "That's a good lad. Come on, let's keep moving."

As they struck out again, they'd taken no more than a few steps when the boy called out again.

"Hey," he said in that curious way children do. "What's your name?"

"Sen," Sen said.

"Sen," the boy repeated, as if trying to commit it to memory. "My name's Erickanthous. But everyone called me Erick."

Sen nodded. "Erick. Good name."

A beat of silence, save their grassy footfalls.

The boy piped up again. "Sen, how old are you?"

Chapter Four

The Sword

The sacred blades of the Riders of Mun-Alin are greater than simple swords. They are an extension of the bond of Rider and dragon, forged from their own blood and tempered in dragonflame. I only wish we knew more of their construction, but those secrets are lost to the annals of this place's history. For now, we must make do with only greatswords. Perhaps in time, we will learn to forge finer weapons.

-Log of Dragonmaster Valene, 698th Lord of Mun-Alin

Wik groaned.Opening her eyes was a task. Breathing felt near impossible. Her mind reeled.

What happened?

In a horrifying moment, it came rushing back to her. The lava, the statue, Meristofales screaming at her, then...*the pain*. Her insides had nearly burned. In fact, she could feel now that some of her insides *had* indeed burned.

She felt at the bandages wrapped around her abdomen and her breath caught from the pain of the simple movement. So, she laid back on her cot and took in the room they'd stuck her in. It was in the monastery's rarely-used infirmary, set off in the corner of the vast space.

Feordan, the Rider in charge of medical care, pushed into the room through the curtains that served as walls for Wik's privacy. The woman was one of the older Riders, though Wik had to admit she'd never actually *seen* the dragon to which she was bonded. Supposedly, he was so brilliantly colored, he was near-blinding to look at in the sunlight.

"Oh!" Feordan exclaimed, ancient eyebrows going up. "You're awake?" It was more of a question than a statement, and when Wik tried to respond in the affirmative, she was taken by a coughing fit that rattled her bones and threaten to rip through the bandages.

"Don't speak," Feordan said, too late, as she bustled over to Wik's cot and set to checking her wounds. "Everything looks to be healing. I'm doing my best to heal you with magic from my reserve, but it's difficult and slow going. Soon enough, though, you should be able to get up and walk around. And talk, of course."

Wik tried to protest, tell her not to use her magic on her, but it was futile. She couldn't speak without immense pain, and Feordan outranked her in every conceivable way, both in practical knowledge and experience. And of course, she knew she needed the help anyway. If what she'd heard Meristofales say as she lost consciousness was right, she'd burst a lung, and so far as she knew, organs didn't grow back without magical intervention.

After checking a few more things in the small room, Feordan

bid her goodnight and extinguished all but one small candle at the bedside. Given the monastery was cut from a mountain, Wik didn't think candles posed much risk, but either way, she was grateful for the dimness to soothe her splitting skull.

Laying there in the cool darkness, Wik squeezed her eyes shut as she felt her chest constrict. Tears welled behind her eyelids, and she balled her hands into fists, fighting, fighting to keep her body under control.

Not again, she thought. *Not again, dammit.* Memories of other days, other failures floated unbidden to the front of her mind, accompanied by the faces of the other Riders, watching her struggle. Chief among them, the hardened visage of Meristofales. She wilted under the thought of that steely gaze.

I'm sorry, she thought as the tears squeezed from her eyes.

When sleep did eventually claim her, she found her mind wandering to the edge of that pool of effervescent white liquid. Here, in the calm of the otherwise empty infirmary, away from the howling wind outside, away from Meristofales's instruction, away from the silent stares of the Riders, she found she could focus on it more intently.

Wisps of glittering smoke curled from its mirrorlike surface, taunting—no, begging her to take it and use it. It beckoned to her, and in that moment she felt the power and what it offered. Those faces, standing in judgment, waiting for her failure dissipated in the face of the power. It seemed to ache for her, and she found herself desiring it. Slowly, almost without her noticing, Wik's hand had begun to stretch outward, reaching for that shimmering pool, that nameless strength. The strength to flatten mountains, to spew lava, to rain hell on her enemies—it all sat there, resting within her like a coiled snake, ready to strike.

With an effort, she stopped herself reaching for the pool. She knew its strength, she knew it was too much for her, and she knew she wasn't ready to wield it. Not fully, anyway. Even still, feeling it there, resting in the recesses of her mind, was a comfort.

Wik awoke some time later to Feordan moving through the little room, fussing with some medicinal knick-knack or the other.

"Don't worry," the elderly Rider said when she saw Wik was awake. "I'll be out of your way in just a moment. Breakfast is over there." She gestured with her chin to the cooling plate of food on the room's only table. After Feordan found something elsewhere to occupy herself with, Wik gingerly tried standing and found, to her surprise, her pain was diminishing. She ventured a try and found she could make words, albeit quietly and with much more rasp than was normal for her.

She ate slowly, taking her time and making sure not to overeat with the first actual meal she'd been given since her accident. They'd served her eggs, hard flour biscuits, with a jam of some sort, surely made from the mountaintop gardens. It was less than exciting, but Wik cleaned her plate. She knew healing magic left the patient famished, but she was surprised just how easily she was rid of the food. After breakfast, Wik wrapped herself in one of the plain homespun brown robes Feordan had left in her room, then returned to bed.

As she contemplated going back to sleep, she heard rustling outside her curtain walls, and after a moment, an aged hand pushed through the gap in the fabric.

"Wik? May I come in?" Meristofales's voice called from the other side.

Wik swallowed her surprise and responded "Yeah—I mean, yes, of course, Dragonmaster."

The old man stepped through the curtains and found her with those knowing gray eyes. Then he smiled, and any nerves or tension she'd felt at his visit melted away.

"You gave me quite a scare," he said, that thick accent cutting through his words and giving them an odd lyrical quality. "How're you feeling?"

Wik exhaled and let herself relax slowly on her bed. "A little better all the time," she croaked, then coughed. Her voice was certainly not back to normal. "Rider Feordan is taking good care of me."

Meristofales nodded and glanced toward the elderly woman, busying herself with something outside the curtains. "Aye, Feo's a good one." Wik almost thought she heard a tinge of something beyond the appreciation of a job well done. She mentally filed it away to tease him about later. He turned back to Wik. "Follow her advice and you'll be making new headaches for me in no time."

Wik nodded, then grimaced as she remembered her victim. "The statue?"

Meristofales laughed, a hearty, deep sound that surprised her with its suddenness. "Oh, I think he's well and truly finished now. You did him in for sure." Wik groaned before her mentor waved it away. "He died a thousand years before I was born, girl. Don't trouble yourself with his offense."

She nodded, still uneasy. Her throat was starting to hurt again, and her eyelids were feeling heavy, even with the Dragonmaster right in front of her. Meristofales must've sensed her fatigue, as he rubbed his aged hands together and stood with a little groan.

"I'll leave you to your sleep. You need your rest." He turned back to face her, as though he'd forgotten something. Wik shook herself to pay attention. "One more thing. Your training needs to continue. But I'd rather you not burn down anymore of my predecessors. So I've enlisted some help from a friend of mine."

Wik was about to ask what he meant when she felt it. A presence, pushing on the edges of her mind, as unstoppable to her as a lava flow to an ant. Slowly, with seemingly no effort at all, the visitor entered her mind and spoke.

Wik. The voice was all-encompassing, rattling her like an earthquake. She saw flashes of black scales and teeth, yellow eyes as large as horses, staring beyond the horizon—a sense of knowledge and scope of power like she'd never known. She fell over from the impact of it.

Meristofales never moved, just gave her another knowing smile. "Uanari doesn't need to spend much time training me anymore. And we thought he could help you hone your skills in a place you can't destroy." He turned to leave again, looking back over his shoulder as he went, and Wik thought she heard the beginnings of a laugh as he spoke. "Have fun!"

Eoradon could not see his sword, but he could feel it floating in the air nearby. Like an extension of himself, it spun around him in his seated position, gradually increasing in speed until the wind from it was rustling his hair and tugging at his clothes. Then, just as suddenly as it began moving, he brought it to a stop in front of him.

Nudging it this way and that with his mind, he set it to

slicing through the air around him, coming within inches of slicing him in half, but never touching him once. These were forms he'd practiced for decades now, beaten into him by trainers over the years. Most of all, of course, Meristofales.

Moving on to the next form, he stood and retrieved a standard metal side-sword, then set to doing a combination of side-sword forms and Rider blade forms, together. This was more standard combat, back in the Riders' glory days. A Rider couldn't maneuver the Rider blade's enormous length around a battlefield very easily, light as it may feel in their hand. The side-sword allowed them to fight in close quarters without fear of killing their allies. But of course, the ability to telepathically control their larger sword let them keep it active, even when they may be otherwise engaged.

Eoradon spun, stepped, slashed, thrust, jabbed, all in a whirling dance of steel. In one of his favorite moves this form allowed, he stabilized his larger sword in the air at waist-height, stepped up onto its flattened blade, then threw himself off the other side in a spinning downward slash. Here, his sword met only air. In a real fight, he'd have split some poor soldier clean in half.

Of course, the Riders don't go to battle anymore, he thought. *Now, we hide behind our tons of stone and wait to die.*

As much as Eoradon was loathe to admit it, he knew Rialin had a point. The monastery had grown stale and stagnant. Old and feeble, most Riders posed more of a threat to themselves than an enemy. Wik's melting of a statue not even a week ago confirmed it to him, as if he hadn't already known.

I will wither and die in these halls. As will we all. And when we're gone, Wik will roam them until she's driven mad by the loneliness. And in a thousand years, some enterprising treasure hunter will find us, take our swords and armor, and the great Dragon Riders of legend will be reduced to trinkets on a shelf and knick-knacks in a drawer.

Eoradon finished the form, the blades coming together in a ringing of steel at the end. Huffing breath, he returned the side-sword to its sheath and left the Rider blade to hover, point down, just behind him as he retrieved his things. He stopped to look out from the platform on which he stood after binding his hair back out of his eyes from where it had fallen during training. Mentally, he made a note to cut the golden locks back to a manageable length later tonight.

The mountains surrounding the monastery reflected the early-morning sun in brilliant hues, rainbows dancing off the melting snow at the peaks. The wind whipped at Eoradon's loose-fitting shirt, cooled the sweat accumulated on his brow, and brought the crisp, clean smells of the sunrise to his nostrils. He closed his eyes and breathed deep. The smells of the valley far below, the birds travelling on the wind, and the ovens just being lit in the monastery kitchens all found him in that moment. He let it take him back to a time before: before the monastery, before he'd ever seen a dragon, before his father—

Blood pooling on a marble floor, his father laying in a heap at the foot of the throne, warriors in strange armor, swords drawn.

He was snapped back to the moment by a scrabbling sound nearby. He turned to find the poor beast most recently bound to Rialin pulling hard on a lead, trying to get away from Ferao and

Theostalin. They were saddling it. Eoradon felt anger flare in his chest.

He's leaving again, he said to Iaxal in his mind. She was hunting a few peaks over, but he knew she'd hear.

He could've sworn she simply returned an audible growl, but after a moment she continued. *So soon.*

It's not a surprise. He never stays long.

The anger from Iaxal cooled slightly as she responded. *Part of you wants to go, too.*

Eoradon chuckled. *I wouldn't even know what to do.*

That's not a no, Iaxal pointed out.

It's a bad idea. I'm needed here.

This time Iaxal laughed. Which, coming from a dragon's telepathic link, was more of a deep chortle. *Rodo, you can lie to yourself and Meristofales, but please spare me. Unless you're sweeping a floor or cooking a meal, you're doing less than nothing by lurking around the monastery.* The words sank as deep as a knife might've, but Eoradon couldn't argue with the truth of her observation. *Besides,* she continued. *There was a time you would've never touched the ground, if you'd had the choice.*

Eoradon stared after Rialin as he mounted the functionally wild dragon and took to the sky. Then he looked at his feet and turned back to the monastery. *A long time ago.*

Iaxal didn't respond, but he could feel her there, a warmth in his mind. He knew she wouldn't force the issue, but there was some small part of him that hoped beyond hope someone would.

Chapter Five
First Flight

24 years ago

Eoradon rose from a night of fitful non-sleep to find the monastery already buzzing with activity. He'd barely swung his feet over the side of his straw-stuffed mattress when he felt his stomach roil as he remembered what awaited him today. Visions of open sky plagued him, the world spinning wildly around him as he fell unabated to the dirt miles below.

And so ends Eoradon, heir to the throne of Ir-Anan.

A shudder ran down his spine as he fought to keep his meager dinner from the night before in its place. *First flight,* he thought, mentally echoing the words of First Ranger Meristofales the previous day.

"It's a big day for you lot tomorrow," he'd said to the sweat-drenched trainees kneeling in the courtyard under the dying rays of the afternoon sun as it began forming the silhouette of the mountain that stood watch over them. "You'll all be airborne for the first time."

Eoradon found the First Ranger to be just as intimidating as most of the dragons that called the monastery home. Meristofales wasn't the tallest or most musclebound of the Riders, but he carried himself like a titan among men. His leathers were always oiled to perfection and his cloak never seemed to be dirty, despite his many trips off the mountain to scout. His close-cropped black beard and hair, combined with the slate gray of his eyes made him seem more mountain than man.

And of course, there was the living shadow he rode upon. Uanari the Black was spoken of only in hushed whispers by the trainees. The monster was easily the size of three normal dragons put together, but somehow it moved in near silence along the ground. Until the creature beat its enormous wings, it was entirely possible to not know it was anywhere near.

But when Uanari *did* take flight, it was like watching night descend upon the day. The sheer breadth of the beast's body was enough to cause a near-eclipse, and the wind from his passing could throw unprepared men to the ground.

Eoradon shivered again as he laced his leather boots. Still fighting nausea, he stepped from his room, made the short walk down to the mess hall, and looked around at the various designations of Riders readying themselves for the day, streaky purple and orange light of pre-dawn shining through the windows. He initially moved to retrieve a breakfast of pork sausage, eggs, and flour cakes with jam, but his stomach had other plans. In the end, he settled down at the table with his fellow trainees, holding a bright red apple.

As he sat down, a pair of eyes full of thinly-veiled disdain caught him from the other end of the table. Rialin didn't bother hiding how he felt about Eoradon. And why should he? He was lowborn, as were most of the Riders. Here, being Heir to the throne of Ir-Anan didn't make Eoradon special. It made him a target.

Today, Eoradon didn't have it in him to fight with the other boy, so he simply sighed and said, "Yes?"

Rialin coughed out a laugh around his mouthful of glazed ham. "Oh, have I been granted an audience with the prince?"

Eoradon felt a pang in his stomach. Was that the nerves? Or did Rialin's words find their mark more often than he let on? Either way, Eoradon had resolved a long time ago to not give the lowborn boy the satisfaction of seeing him hurt. He wanted to use his royal heritage against him, so Eoradon would make armor of it.

He put on his best princely smile before responding. "You're one of my citizens, Rialin. I'm never too busy for *you*." And then he took a flourishing bite of the apple. It was much more bitter than he'd expected, and he nearly coughed it up, but managed to chew and swallow.

Rialin rolled his eyes. "Just don't fall off the dragon, *your highness*," he said, sarcasm all but dripping from his mouth. "We'd hate to cause a succession crisis." Ferao, one of Rialin's hangers-on, laughed too loudly at that, signaling both of them to return to their meal, victorious.

Eoradon considered throwing his apple at the commoner's head, but thought better of it and tossed it back on the stone table instead. Try as he might, Eoradon couldn't find the humor in the jokes about succession Rialin seemed to find so funny. Of course, there was already a succession crisis, and everyone in the monastery knew it. Eoradon's father and brother were dead, and he was missing, far beyond the reach of the people who killed his family and shattered the oldest empire Isthyl had ever known.

Eoradon wondered sometimes if the people knew where he was, or if they thought him craven. He'd asked Meristofales not long ago when he would be strong enough to retake his family's throne, but the ranger had simply laughed and said, "One day, boy. Just be patient. It's going nowhere."

Of course, Meristofales had no way of knowing that. Or did he? Eoradon considered that. Meristofales left the monastery more than basically anyone. Of all the Riders there, he would have the best idea of what's happening with the succession.

Does he know something I don't? Eoradon wondered to himself. He didn't have time to finish the thought, however, because at that moment, their instructors for the day swaggered into the mess hall, bringing the scent of oiled leather, sweat, and the burnt-rock smell that accompanied the dragons.

There were four experienced Riders working with them today: Meristofales, not a hair out of place, as always. Nirial, a musclebound woman whose hair was pulled back in a long blonde braid down to her lower back. Feordan, a slight woman who normally manned the infirmary. Eoradon hadn't been expecting her. He'd never even seen her dragon. And then there was Liran. Tall, with sharp features and a shock of messy brown hair that he had to constantly fight to keep out of his face, Liran looked as if he'd been painted to life from legend. He wore the traditional riding leathers, stained to a dark brown and worn from use. The insignia of the monastery was burned into the front of his chestpiece, and his massive purple cloak was bundled up and thrown over his shoulder, so as to not drag the floor.

Eoradon suppressed a flash of jealousy as he looked at the Riders with their cloaks. The cloak was the final step in a Rider's training journey. Once they were awarded, a Rider was considered fully-vested, and no longer in training. His time would come, he knew, but it was still years away.

Liran caught Eoradon's eye and smiled, and Eoradon couldn't help but return the gesture. He'd been lucky to befriend the Rider a couple years prior, and had been able to get some extra help with sword work and magical training, which had helped immensely when he'd been made to duel or demonstrate an aptitude for controlled magic.

Of course, none of it had helped prepare him for today. The thought of being carried along in the sky by a dragon made Eoradon want to vomit the single bite of apple back onto the table, so he tried to think of literally anything else. Of course, trying not to think of something is a surefire way to think of nothing else, so he simply swallowed hard and closed his eyes.

Within an hour, Eoradon found himself outside in the main courtyard, standing in a line with the other trainees, and trying very hard not to look at any of the four instructors. Of course, Meristofales demanded attention when he spoke, and Eoradon found he didn't have the stomach to look away from the First Ranger.

"Trainees," he began in his booming cadence. "Today, you will cross the threshold from a ward of this monastery, to a contributing member of its ranks. You have trained with swords and magic. You have learned to make medicines and herbal remedies. You have been told of our world and its history, and our place in it. But today…" He paused, letting the moment sink in. An eerie silence overtook the courtyard. Other than the wind moving amongst the gathered onlookers, nothing moved. "…you take flight." And with his final words, the skies filled with a chorus of dragon calls.

Dozens of pairs of wings erupted from all around them and took to the sky. Some spouted fire, others corkscrewed and flipped, and still others roared and screamed and shook Eoradon's skull. He had to admit, even after spending years at the monastery and seeing dragons every day, there was something magnificent about them. The sun, glinting off scales and teeth, fire bursting from their mouths, the lithe and easy movements of the world's apex predator in flight. It all served to paint a surreal, incredible picture. And at its center, he found himself, no less terrified to climb on one of the creatures' backs.

Just as he was adjusting to the din, a great dark shadow fell across the courtyard. At first, he assumed a cloud had moved in front of the sun, but when he looked up, he saw only the great mass of Uanari the Black, blotting the sun. He did not roar or spout flame or flip like the others. Instead, he simply thrummed, a low vibration from his chest. Dragons often did this when they were contented or comfortable, but Uanari's thrum was no reassuring thing. Eoradon would've sworn he felt the ground shake beneath his boots, and he fought the urge to reach out and steady himself against something.

After a moment, Uanari stopped thrumming and banked off, letting the sun out again. When Eoradon looked to his fellow trainees, he saw the same trepidation he felt reflected in their faces, though it was tinged with more excitement than he could muster.

He was surprised, however, to see that same look on the faces of the other instructors. Meristofales looked triumphant, and Eoradon wondered briefly if there was some other game being played that he could not see.

Meristofales strode over to Rialin and clasped him on the shoulder. Rialin looked relieved at first, but when he glanced toward Uanari's massive form, still visible in the sky like a cloud of smoke that refuses to dissipate, a flash of unease crossed his brow. Eoradon smiled at that. A smack on the back snapped him back to reality, and he looked up to see Liran throwing an arm around his shoulder.

"Ready for your first flight?" Liran asked, a smile showing his perfect white teeth.

Eoradon groaned in response, causing Liran to laugh.

"Come on, your highness." Eoradon ignored the jibe at his heritage. Coming from Liran, it felt good natured, whereas Rialin managed to inject venom into every syllable.

Eoradon followed Liran down to the stables. He remembered when he first arrived at the monastery, and how wrong he'd been when he pictured the area. What he'd known to be stables back home in Ir-Anan were paltry little nothings compared to the great dragon stables of the monastery. The room was an enormous open cavern, carved out of the mountain itself. History lessons had taught Eoradon that this was once a natural cave, but the Riders who established the monastery had used their dragons' claws to hollow out the massive space it now was. A huge open hole at one end served as the entrance and exit for the dragons themselves, as they now streamed in from Meristofales's show above. Uanari was last, and even with the size of the hole through which he crawled, it was a bit of a squeeze. Eoradon wondered to himself whether they'd had to expand the entrance for him at some point.

Liran leading the way, Eoradon followed him to his own dragon. Xialan was waiting for them, and Eoradon was taken, as always, by her beauty. She was on the smaller side, for dragons, but still twice the size of the largest horse he'd ever seen. Her body was long and lithe, adorned by scales of gold and pink that made her a stunning sight when flying during a sunset. Two long whiskers trailed from her face, and her enormous eyes, almost too large for her angular face, seemed to take in every detail of her surroundings.

Eoradon watched as Liran patted her snout, and then they both looked at each other in complete silence for almost a full minute. Eoradon had to stop himself from rolling his eyes. *Riders and their telepathic conversations,* he thought as he coughed and drew their attention back to him. Liran chuckled sheepishly and offered mumbled apologies before setting to the task of teaching Eoradon to saddle a dragon.

The process took nearly an hour, with Liran demonstrating the more complex parts multiple times for Eoradon's benefit, ensuring he knew which clasps and buckles went where, how to cinch each piece tight without making it uncomfortable, and reassuring him that his own dragon partner would help him when the time came.

As the midmorning sun neared its apex, Liran smiled and patted the saddle, then said the most frightening words Eoradon could imagine.

"All done!" he beamed. "Ready to fly?"

Eoradon was *not* ready to fly, but he was given no choice in the matter. Liran put a hand on his shoulder and guided him to the saddle. His grip wasn't painful, but it was firm as he all but lifted Eoradon into the saddle and cinched him into the seat behind the Rider. Most saddles only accommodated one Rider, but these were specially-designed for trainees to take assisted flights, so Eoradon fit comfortably enough, aside from his roiling stomach and pounding heart.

"Hey," Liran's voice snapped him out of his cloud of terror for a moment. He looked down at his mentor. "It's going to be alright. Your fear is temporary. But once you're up there..." he trailed off as he looked out at the sky. When he spoke again, his voice was very small and far away. "...it all just falls away beneath you. Out there, that's the real world. All this—" he waved a hand to include everything around them "—this is the dream. Just wait. You'll see." He flashed a smile, then set to checking his own trappings.

Liran made sure his sidesword was secured to the saddle, but still easily reachable, double-checked the fastenings on his cloak and leathers, then handed one face shield to Eoradon before strapping one over his own face.

For his part, Eoradon's worry still gnawed at him. Liran's explanation of the beauty of flying was exciting and tempting, but it was a fantasy. He'd heard too much of the rigorous discipline required by Riders in flight to believe they could be so cavalier about how it feels to fly. Either way, he would soon see for himself.

Liran climbed into the saddle, and Xialan began to thrum slightly. The odd vibration under him made Eoradon jump, which prompted a laugh from Liran.

"She's eager!" he said over his shoulder. "They love it more than we do, even. Flying is *life* to a dragon. They'd rather be dead than grounded."

As if confirming this, Xialan turned toward the launching pad and cavern exit and began to lope. The dragon's run was less than comfortable, jostling Eoradon in the saddle and forcing him to take hold of the handles at his sides with a white-knuckled grip. As they drew closer to the sky with every bound, he was sure he was about to throw up. Just when he thought this couldn't be any *less* graceful, any *more* uncomfortable, Xialan leapt from the cavern, into the open sky.

And fell.

The wind tore at Eoradon and stole his scream as Xialin nosed down into a straight dive. They were picking up speed at a terrible rate, the mountain face rushing past and the ground coming to meet them. Eoradon felt like he was being torn from the saddle, his hands being forced loose from the handles he gripped so hard he thought he might break his fingers. Liran was leaned over, tight to Xialin's neck.

All thought left Eoradon as he screamed over and over and over again. His nightmares of falling from the back of a dragon replayed in his mind, all layered over top of one another, endlessly taunting him.

Here lies Eoradon, heir to the throne of Ir-Anan. The dumb shit fell off a dragon in a training exercise.

Then, as suddenly as it had begun, Xialan spread her wings and slowed their descent. She turned her nose up, whiskers trailing proudly in the late-morning sun as she sharply banked and pulled up out of the dive.

Eoradon vomited into the open sky, his stomach rebelling in

full now. When he stopped retching, he heard Liran cackling over the blood rushing in his ears. A deep, knee-slapping laugh that forced him to remove his eyeshield for a moment to wipe away tears.

"Sorry," he said between gasps as the laughter abated. "Sorry, Your Highness. The temptation was just too great."

Eoradon gulped air, trying to force his mind to calm. Even still, he briefly considered shoving Liran off the dragon. But right as he was planning how he could explain that away as an accident, he opened his eyes and looked out at the sky. And as he did so, he felt his entire world tip slightly, shift on its axis, and become something new.

A massive expanse rolled out beneath them, green and blue and gray and brown coming together in a canvas of bucolic perfection. From this height, it all appeared very far away, like children's toys for the gods. At the base of the mountains, verdant land spread out in all directions. A massive road wound through it, and along the way, it was dotted with farms and small towns. In the distance, Eoradon could see the road leading to what he thought was a city, situated against a slate cliffside, a river cutting through the ground across a large field.

"Ir-Anan," he whispered, breath caught in his throat as he looked at the capital city of the empire—*his* empire.

"Aye," Liran said, making Eoradon start. He was shocked the wind hadn't snatched the words away. "I wanted you to see it. How long's it been now, since you've been home?"

Eoradon swallowed. "Ten years. I was six when..." *Blood everywhere, screaming attendants, Meristofales scooped him up, held him tight as they soared through a moonless sky.*

"Right," Liran interjected, seeming to sense Eoradon's trepidation. "Have you ever seen your home like this?" He inclined his head toward the massive city, levels upon rotating levels, like rings stacked on a giant's fingers, ascending to the heavens. The slate black cliff face provided a canvas for the bright and colorful capital city to shine like a painter's brush strokes, and on a clear day like this one, it was evermore the beauty of man's achievement.

Eoradon shook his head numbly. "No. I barely remember seeing it at all."

Liran took that in for a moment before speaking again. "Well," he said, turning to flash that perfect smile at him again. "Let's go in for a closer look, shall we?"

Eoradon's heart leapt into his throat again, and this time not from fear of flying. He gave a mute nod and they were off. Xialan cut through the sky like a broadsword through freshly baked bread. She dipped from their lofty height to skim along the farmland, so close Eoradon was sure he could brush the golden strands of wheat with his fingers if he were braver. Then she banked, shot straight up, corkscrewed, dropped back down like a falling arrow, and they were snaking along the surface of the great Dominae River, the wake of their passing causing great curtains of water to spray tens of feet into the air before cascading back down in a shower of kaleidoscopic droplets. Then, she took back to the sky with great wingbeats, ascending up and up and up until they met the clouds again. They sped along inside the clouds for a while; just as Eoradon began to wonder if they were lost, the clouds gave way to brilliant sunshine as they burst forth into daylight, the great churning mass of Ir-Anan looming before them.

Eoradon's breath caught in his throat as he stared at the immensity of his birthright. Ir-Anan, capital city of the realm of men, occupied the entirety of the sky, casting its shadow across the acres of farmland surrounding the base of its lowest level. The city ascended in concentric circles, the largest being the original base level, the smallest being the topmost layer. In truth, as Eoradon had always heard it told, Ir-Anan was cities on top of cities, as the rich continually sought to escape the poor and be closer to the Six, the warriors who'd ascended to godhood after killing the vengeful old gods. It hadn't yet worked, apparently, as Eoradon could see construction beginning on the foundations of yet another, smaller level.

And it was still dwarfed by the bisected mountain against which it leaned. No one was still alive who knew the truth of Ir-Anan's founding, but whoever had done it apparently had the power to split mountains and discard the halves they no longer needed. In this instance, the other half of the mountain, creatively named "Otherhalf," sat miles away and barely visible, thousands of acres of lush farmland resting in the space between.

Eoradon didn't like to think about the creature, or more terrifyingly, the *person* who could've performed such an act. Maybe it really *was* the proof of the gods' existence, as the temple leaders liked to say. Either way, right now, the whole visage represented something totally different to Eoradon.

This was *home*. And yet, it felt so alien and far away now. Maybe the monastery was really where he belonged? It was certainly the place he felt most comfortable, and yet he still knew, innately, he was not *their* prince.

Xialan veered toward the city, following the shape of the

rings clockwise, giving Eoradon an unobstructed view. He spied smoke rising from countless chimneys, flowing up the levels and dissipating into the air. Roofs of buildings, drab and brown down low, multicolored and stained glass as the levels ascended. And at the core, the masterpiece of construction that was the imperial palace.

The palace ran vertically through the heart of the city, and it was the thing around which all the many levels of the city were built. Each level of the palace itself was an homage to the era of its construction, and so it grew more and more grand as it reached heavenward. The highest level, where Eoradon's father had sat when he ruled the world, was plated in gold, the enormous pillar entwined by twin dragons, diamond-coated flames erupting from their mouths over the entryway.

Eoradon remembered looking up at those dueling dragons as a young boy, watching his father, the emperor, walk between the flames like a hero from legend. He'd seemed so strong, so impervious then. Of course, "All Men Bleed," as the pamphlets calling for his assassination had read, and a knife kills a king as easily as a beggar.

"Feeling homesick?" Liran's words snapped Eoradon back to the moment.

"A little," Eoradon said. "I just...feel like someone out of time and out of place."

Liran nodded as he directed Xialan to head back to the monastery. "I understand. But you're learning how to lead, how to be a warrior and retake your throne, right?"

"I suppose," Eoradon hadn't voiced his fears, but Liran seemed to hear his thoughts.

"You don't think you can go back?"

"I don't think there's a point. I'm sure they have a new emperor." Eoradon sighed and gripped the handles on the saddle tightly as Xialan ascended.

"They actually don't," said Liran.

Eoradon started. "What? How?" His voice squeaked on the second word and he silently cursed.

Liran nodded. "They're ruled by a council now, from the senate. No emperor." Liran delivered this information with the verbal equivalent of a shrug.

"Why?" was all Eoradon could say. He was stunned the people would wait this long before either electing a new leader or finding a distant cousin to sit the throne.

Liran turned in the saddle and looked pointedly at him. "The people are waiting. For you."

They arrived back at the monastery a few moments later, Eoradon's mind still reeling.

The people are waiting for me? he thought. *How is that even possible? They really think I'm coming back?*

Xialan landed in the stables and Eoradon disembarked to find Meristofales striding over purposefully. He groaned and waited for Liran to intercept him. But of course, things never work out as they're supposed to, so Liran continued to get the saddle off of Xialan, paying no mind to the First Ranger's approach.

"Eoradon," said Meristofales, his deep voice rich and textured as he rubbed at his chin. He glanced to Xialin, and Eoradon followed his gaze. He saw the dragon give a slight, but definite nod. Then Meristofales spoke again. "Come with me."

Eoradon followed Meristofales into the bowels of the

monastery, past training rooms, weapons rooms, armor halls, and mess halls, until they finally reached a new milestone: the hatchery.

The hatchery was nestled deep in the mountain, where the residual lava flow could help warm the eggs. Eoradon had never seen it before, as there was virtually only one reason trainees would venture there.

The realization struck Eoradon and his heart began to flutter. The excitement was building until he was gestured through the door by Meristofales, who gave him a slight smile and wink as he went by.

Inside the sweltering room stood Dragonmaster Rykas, dressed in a simple robe, long gray hair and beard bound up and out of the way. He stood before a small nest, full of eggs of varying colors. Wordlessly, but with a smile, Rykas presented a green and gold egg to him. As Eoradon turned it over in his hand, he saw it had a slight scaliness to its exterior, and it was hot to the touch. He kept switching hands to avoid the heat.

"Eoradon," Rykss said evenly. "You have been selected to forge a bond. Are you ready?"

Eoradon nodded dumbly and hugged the dragon egg closer to his chest.

Rykas smiled. "Good. I thought so."

As if on cue, the egg split down the middle, and it fell open to reveal a small dragon, green and gold, barely larger than the lizards he used to see running across the streets in the Ir-Anan summer.

As the dragon slowly opened her eyes and looked into his, his world tilted again, rearranged into something new, as he felt a probing touch against the borders of his mind. He welcomed it, and the warmth of her presence made him shudder.

Iaxal, she said, and he knew with no other context that it was her name.

"Eoradon," he said, patting his chest.

"In your mind," Rykas said gently. "Build the bond."

Eoradon shook his head, silently chastising himself for making such a simple mistake, then mentally relayed his name to Iaxal. In response, the hatchling stretched in his hands, shaking slightly as she unfolded her wings, still wet with dew from the egg.

Rykas clasped a hand on Eoradon's shoulder and squeezed slightly. "You're one of us now, Prince." He said the words with what seemed like genuine kindness, but Eoradon couldn't help but wonder at the truth of them, regardless.

I don't know if I'm theirs, he thought to Iaxal, watching her eyes flick up to meet his. *But I know I'm yours. Always.*

Her reply came instantly and without hesitation.

Always.

Chapter Six

The Aging Oak

These damnable cultists will be the death of me.

-Log of Dragonmaster Wren, 500th Lord of Mun-Alin

Sen stretched his sore body and groaned. The nights of sleeping on the ground were catching up to him, a fact he accepted with bitter hatred. There was a day, not long ago in his memory, when he could've gone a year without sleeping in a bed, and never given it a second thought. Now, a couple days' camping had him cracking and popping like a tree in a storm.

Erick leapt up from the ground with nary a creak and set to gathering his sleeping roll into the pack Sen had fashioned for him a few days back. He wanted to help, he'd said. So Sen had obliged. To his credit, the boy had been a diligent little trooper, and Sen had met more than one grown man, fully committed to a career of soldiering, who complained with every footfall.

When camp was packed, they found themselves back on the

road, drudging ever westward toward Ir-Anan. Sen walked, his thick green travelling cloak pulled up over his head, which he found in desperate need of a shave. His thinning gray hair was well past the stubble phase now, sprouting over his pate like moss on an old oak. His beard had grown wild and unkempt, and he swore he could smell himself.

The boy looked better, all things considered. A little leaner, a little tougher than when they'd begun, but he appeared mostly well-fed and taken care of.

I made a promise to that woman, Sen thought, remembering the night Aneving Keep fell. *I'd like to keep one of those someday.*

His mind wandered back to that night. It was chaos. The army had arrived under the cover of darkness, using the storm to further mask their approach. He wasn't completely sure, but it seemed as though the vanguard the Duke had sent to harry the invaders had somehow been turned against them. With only a meager force defending the walls and gate, the Vicar's forces had no trouble cracking the Keep like an egg.

That was bad enough. But then they'd loosed that monster. Sen shuddered as he remembered the dragon's scream. He'd barely caught sight of it from a window, backdropped by the lightning, riding the storm like some demon in a story. Maybe it was. He thought on that, then silently chastised himself.

No, he thought. *Just a man. Just a man and a beast.*

Be that as it may, he'd never seen ruinous power and wanton destruction the likes of what that monster unleashed on Aneving. Its flames melted the very stones of the upper walls and catwalks. Men exploded into pulpy messes when they were caught in its wake.

They hadn't even needed the army. No weapon in the Keep could stand against it.

Then there was the rider. Sen had heard stories of the legendary Dragon Riders, obviously. His father had threatened to give him over to them more than once when he'd misbehaved as a child. But they'd quite famously not been seen in nearly twenty years; after his recent encounter, Sen was fine if they waited another twenty before making a reappearance.

The man had sat astride that creature as casually as a child riding a pony at a carnival. Clad in shining plate armor, Sen didn't readily see an opening to attack or force him to the ground, nevermind if he was able to draw that monstrous sword from his back. Of course, the dragon provided even fewer opportunities to fight back. It was covered in gray scales, looking as impenetrable as its Rider's plate.

Sen had caught that glimpse of the chaos out the window and taken off, looking for the Duke, determined to aid in his escape, whether they told him he was "retired" or not. But the Duke was determined to stay and try to parlay for his people.

"No, Sen," he'd said, standing in his crumbling throne room as a panicked crowd surged around them. "My place is here. But for you, I have another task. Go west, to Ir-Anan. Make sure they know. The Vicar will not stop at Aneving. He will demand the empire. Go and warn them." And with that, he'd shoved an official writ in Sen's hand, identifying him as an Envoy of Aneving. Then the damned fool had drawn his father's sword and taken off toward the bloody dragon. Sen had watched him toss the blade down at the dragon's feet and yell "Parlay!" right before he'd been turned to a red mist by a spout of flame.

Erick kicked a stone down the path and snapped Sen back to the moment. He walked a couple steps behind Sen, thumbs tucked into the straps of his pack. A small knife rested on his belt. Sen had given him that, too. One of his extras. The boy wanted to learn to throw it, and Sen felt no guilt in showing him how. Who knew what awaited them around the next curve in the road, or lurking behind a tree when they set up camp that night? He needed to have *some* defense, Sen figured. Just in case.

The thought of Erick in danger made Sen's throat tighten a little, and he admonished himself silently for it. He was too attached to this boy, and he knew it. His face made Sen think of times long gone, and other small children who fell asleep in his arms. It was foolish, he knew.

But what was a grandfather with no grandchildren supposed to do?

He still couldn't place Erick, or figure out who his parents were. The wash woman who'd thrust him into Sen's arms as he rushed down the stairwell and out of the Keep had seemed too old to be the boy's mother, and Erick had been tightlipped about the whole thing the couple of times Sen had asked.

Ultimately, he supposed it didn't matter. Whoever they were, they were certainly gone now. And with Aneving Keep gone the way of dust in the wind, whatever intrigue or politics had led to his residence there was also a moot point. Now, he and Sen were just an old man and a boy, walking west.

Though, of course that was only *partly* true, in the end. Nothing was so simple as that, when all was laid bare. And Sen knew that time would come eventually.

He dreaded it. The boy didn't look at him with fear or

trepidation, and Sen hated the idea of seeing his eyes go wide, fear gripping him. But he'd seen it before. He'd see it again, he knew. Retired, or not.

They camped that night in a clearing about a hundred yards into the woods. Sen risked a small fire, tired of sleeping on cold, hard ground, and needing something to warm his bones. Besides, they hadn't seen even a single fellow traveler since the pitiful blockade Sen had destroyed over a week ago.

They dined on a dinner of quail eggs Sen had foraged the day before, and each had an apple they'd picked from a tree along the side of the road. While they chewed, Erick pelted Sen with questions, as had become their nightly routine.

"Where are you from?"

"What were your parents like?"

"What's your favorite food?"

"How fast can you run?"

Sen tried to answer the boy to the best of his memory, though he wasn't sure how to explain to a small child, still wiry with energy many hours after waking, that old men don't run unless they're being chased. As they got to know each other better, Sen even found himself chuckling and recalling memories of his youth, things he'd not told anyone since his wife died.

He told Erick about growing up on a farm, how he'd been the youngest of five brothers and was always the weakest of the bunch, and how his older brothers had to do twice the chores every night, just catching him up so he wasn't stuck out in the dark. He'd told him how his mother had been meek and kind, never so much as spoken out of turn, and how his brothers were strong and brave, the type of men he'd wanted to be.

"What about your dad?" Erick queried him around a mouthful of berries one night.

Sen had sighed and responded, "Unfortunately, he's the type of man I *did* grow into."

During their quail-egg dinner, though, Erick finally worked up to the question Sen had been dreading.

"Sen," he said, chewing all the while.

"Chew first, then ask," Sen cut him off. They might be in the woods, but dammit, the boy could learn some manners.

Erick nodded impatiently, swallowed, and started again.

"Sen, how many people have you killed?"

Sen drew in a deep breath and held it a moment before blowing it out his nose. "I don't know," he said, not looking at Erick.

The boy nodded, then looked down for a moment. "A lot?"

Sen nodded gravely, still not meeting his eye. "A lot. Too many."

There was a beat of silence in which Sen chewed unenthusiastically on the last of his supper. Then the boy spoke again.

"They probably deserved it."

Sen barked a surprised laugh. "Some might've," he agreed, still smiling as he tossed his apple core into the fire. "Most probably didn't."

Erick shrugged. "If you did it, you probably thought they were bad guys." Then he yawned and stretched out on his sleeping roll.

Sen nodded. "Aye. I did." His smile faded. He rubbed his eyes, then stretched out on his own roll, his back to Erick. Invariably, he woke in the mornings with Erick having crawled over him and curled up in his dirty travelling cloak, but every night they fell asleep back to back. For protection, he had told the boy. In truth, if he let himself see Erick as any more than a ward, he was doomed to love the boy like his own.

Which he isn't, Sen thought. *He's not yours, and yours ain't coming back.*

He drifted off, not bothering to douse the fire.

He was punished for his carelessness with a boot to the gut. Sen wheezed, spit flying from his mouth, all his air stolen by the kick. Before he could reach for his knife, a pair of strong hands had him pinned to the ground by the shoulders, a set of snarling yellow teeth looming in front of his vision.

"Don't fuckin' move, old-timer." The teeth's owner was a spindly, dirty man, wiry strong and in the throes of bloodlust now. Black spittle adorned his cracked lips, and Sen could see rot spreading in his gums. He managed to draw in a wheezing breath, then immediately regretted it. The stench from the man's mouth was overpowering, and he was insisting on keeping his maw open.

"No...money," Sen coughed.

The man leered over at what was assuredly one of his compatriots. "This fuckin' fool thinks we want his fuckin' money," he cackled, and it sounded to Sen like two other voices joined in. He looked back at Sen and snarled a mean smile. "We want all you got, old man." His eyes travelled down to Sen's mouth and they took on a hungry quality. Sen had an idea what he meant, but had no intention of finding out.

"Take the food," he said, his voice coming back to him now. "Take our packs. They're yours."

The squalid little man laughed again, more of a crow's barking than a man's joviality. "Ain't none of it mine, friend." Those hungry yellow eyes squinted with glee as he leaned even closer and whispered reverently. "All things to the God of Teeth."

Damnable cultists, Sen thought with revulsion. As he took in what he could of the man now, he spotted the telltale white robes, red piping running down the sides and front. These were predictably soiled to the point of being little more than rags.

Sen concluded the conversation by stabbing him in the leg with the knife he'd worked free from his belt. The bastard howled and let go of Sen's shoulders. Now freed, Sen punched him across the jaw, and felt the feeble bone break under his force. The impact threw the attacker into the remnants of their fire, and he set to screaming as embers caught on his greasy clothes and growing flames licked his filthy body.

Sen rolled to his belly, then his knees, knife in hand, looking for the others. There were three more, rather than two as he'd thought. All were equally as repulsive as their leader. Sen sized them up quickly, his mind moving without thought.

One on the right, bow in loose grip, only one arrow visible, not drawn. No armor, wearing little more than rags. Two on the left, better armed. A rusty sword for one, twin daggers for the other. Still no armor, but older, stronger. One had an arm around a young boy's neck—

He was snapped back to the moment by the realization. They had Erick, of course they did. They would've never risked waking him until the boy was in hand. Sen's arm was already cocked to throw the knife at the one with the sword, but was stilled by the sight of Erick, a knife to his neck, tears streaming down his face as he tried to scream around the filthy hand covering his mouth.

"Stop right fuckin' there!" screeched the one holding Erick. It was a woman. That surprised Sen for just a moment, but it didn't matter. She'd die all the same. "I'll cut his fuckin' neck!"

Sen stood slowly. "No, you won't."

She looked at her compatriots, but they seemed to be losing their will to fight as Sen stood to his full height. The screams of their friend, burning alive on the ground, surely didn't give them any courage.

"Your god wants human flesh, isn't that right?" The girl tried and failed to cover a look of surprise. "It's easy to talk about killing for a god, when your victims are asleep or tied up." Sen took a step toward her and she shrank back, but her knife did not move. Behind him, he heard the one with the bow shuffling. "A whole different thing when they're standing in front of you, holding a knife." He let his voice drop, drifting back to a different time. A different man. "Come now. Let the boy go. Give yourself a chance to walk away."

She was shaking, but to her credit, she did not drop the knife. "How do I know you won't kill me anyway?"

The one with the sword turned to face her. "The god demands a sacrifice!"

Her eyes didn't leave Sen as she spoke. "We can't do anything for him if we're dead!"

Sen laughed. A practiced laugh, one he'd used many times. There was no mirth, only the lingering notes of dangerous intent. "I'm an old man. I've no use for killing you. But that boy—" He pointed at Erick with the tip of his knife. "—is not yours. And you'll not be hurting him."

She looked shakily at her comrades, then spat a curse and

shoved Erick back to him. Sen caught him, pulled him into a one-armed embrace. The one on the ground had stopped moving, but Erick wouldn't look away from him.

The wretches took off into the brush, leaving them alone with the burned body. Sen gently turned Erick away from the body and sat him down, then wrapped him in his sleeping roll. As he turned to leave camp, the boy spoke.

"Where are you going?" he asked, his voice small.

Sen retrieved the longsword and bow from his pack. When he spoke, his voice was grave. "I'm going to go kill them."

Sen crept through the underbrush, easily tracking the trio's mad dash away from his camp. He'd followed them for about a half-mile when he came upon a clearing, a rough little shack constructed in the middle. The stench of death was overwhelming.

He watched the shack from the treeline, hidden in the shadows until he determined they were still here. He saw them bustling about, trying to pack things to flee, evidently.

All those years, spent clearing out their encampments, Sen thought. *And they're still scuttling about in the wilderness*.

Though, Sen had to admit, this setup was a far cry from the other camps he'd seen from the Cult of Teeth. They'd been set up in sprawling cities of tents, huts, and cabins. For a long time, no one knew what they really did. They even had a representative in the Duke's court in Aneving for many years. Then, an escaped prisoner had found their way to a guard, and the secrets of the Cult of Teeth found their way to the surface.

Sen suppressed a shiver and focused on the acolytes moving busily around the ramshackle hut.

"Jarus," the female one snapped at the one who'd held the bow. "You shit, you could've shot him in the back and saved us all this trouble."

The one called Jarus huffed out a response. "Y'know it would've never worked, Serana! Probably couldn't've got it through his fuckin' back anyway."

"On that, we agree, you useless shit." And with that, Serana returned to the shack. As she entered, Sen thought he saw her moving down, as if descending stairs.

That left Jarus all alone to kick the dirt and curse the girl. Sen nocked an arrow, drew the bow back to his ear, and let it fly without hesitation. The arrow flew true, burying itself in the nape of Jarus's neck halfway up the shaft and assuredly poking out his face on the other side. His body dropped without a sound to the soft earth.

The lookout gone, Sen was moving again. He retrieved the arrow from Jarus's neck and returned it to his quiver. His first instinct was to kick in the door and cut them to ribbons. But he knew that was folly. He had no idea what protections this place had. For all he knew, there was an army of monsters down there.

More likely, some poor shits who couldn't fight back. But, we take no chances.

Sen worked his way around the back of the shack, where he found a dusty little square of ground that must've constituted a yard at one time. A twine dog collar lay in the dirt, attached to a rope, tied around a post. No dog, though.

Must've been dinner, Sen thought, then shuddered a little, and continued surveying the ground.

For the most part, the shack was all the construction he could find, though there was an old garden, long grown over with weeds, and a dry well. Satisfied he'd seen what the place had to offer, Sen moved toward the shack's door. As he was about to open it, it burst open from the other side. Sen managed to roll away and scramble around the corner.

"Jarus?" A male voice this time.

The other one, with the sword, Sen thought.

"Where are you? Serana's like to sacrifice *you* at this point." Sen risked a peek around the corner. The owner of the voice was a little bigger than the one he'd killed back at camp. Not as tall as Jarus had been, but thicker, his muscles more taut. He reminded Sen of a piece of wire, coiled too tight.

Sen could see the rusty old longsword dangling from the man's hip, scabbard long since lost. He barely looked like he knew how to swing it, anyway, but he'd never get the chance. Sen loosed a throwing knife, which lodged between his shoulder blades with a *thunk.* The wretch grunted, then dropped to his knees, scratching at his back, trying to reach the knife, to no avail. Sen was on him in an instant.

He impacted the smaller man with a spear tackle, rolled him on the ground, then came up with his legs wrapped around his abdomen, his hands affixed over his nose and mouth. Sen tensed his muscles, tightening his grip. The other man thrashed and fought for his breath, but Sen had him tight now. After a minute of fighting, the body went slack in Sen's grip. He ended it with a swift jerk of the wretch's neck and a chorus of *pops*.

With two of the cultists dead, Sen approached the door again, and pulled it open. Inside, he was greeted with, indeed, a staircase into a torch-lit hole. Hesitantly, he began down the steps.

Around twenty feet down, the stairs flattened into a tunnel, held up by wooden beams, torches inserted into the walls. Most of the torches seemed to be burned out, so Sen grabbed one from the staircase and carried it with him into the oppressive dark. As he walked, he noticed the tunnel became more and more haphazard as it went on. Where the stairs and initial tunnelway were clearly dug by someone with experience in excavation, the work got very sloppy as he went, until the supports all but disappeared, or were barely more than tree limbs. Sen had to stoop to avoid hitting his head. There was light up ahead, where the space seemingly opened up, and Sen caught occasional whiffs of *something* cooking.

When he reached the chamber at the end of the tunnel, he found it to be a dimly lit little alcove, still not tall enough for him to stand up in. Sen counted five dirty bed rolls scattered around the room. A large cauldron in the middle roiled over a fire, the smoke from which was vented above ground via a large metal pipe. It wasn't very effective. The room was nearly full of smog, making it difficult to see or maneuver.

Serana, the female cultist, was busy tossing something into the pot. As Sen watched, he realized, to his revulsion, it was pieces of a chopped up human body.

They're eating the sacrifices? That was extreme, even for the Cult. He knew there was only one way for this to end. He drew his sword. In the process of freeing the blade from its scabbard, he knocked his hand against one of the makeshift wooden supports holding the doorway to the room up.

Serana spun, saw him, and the color drained from her face. She screamed, an earsplitting sound, then hurled a human hand at him. Sen slipped to the side, letting the appendage careen into darkness, and tried to draw his sword again but once more found the confined space too cumbersome as he stumbled against a wall and smacked his head on the low ceiling.

And then she was on him. She was on her turf now, and her stooped, slouched posture aided her in the claustrophobic fight. She didn't seem to be armed with her knives from before, but she made for his eyes, scratching him with fingernails that were closer to talons. She bloodied his face and lip, but he managed to keep her from his eyes. She weighed next to nothing, and Sen flung her away with one arm once he'd regained control.

This time, he didn't bother standing or drawing a blade. From one knee, he launched himself at her, catching her full-tilt in the stomach and driving her into the ground. He felt ribs break as he slammed her into the dirt. Her breath was a ragged wheeze as he lifted himself from her. Only then did Sen draw his knife and put it to her grimy throat.

"I thought," she croaked through broken teeth and bloody spit. "You'd let us live."

Sen scowled down at her. "You were dead the moment you touched the boy." He drove the knife slowly into her windpipe. Her eyes went wide with terror as she realized what he'd done. He hadn't slashed her throat, which would've been a quick death. He'd simply taken her air. This would last for minutes as she gasped, sucked, and gulped for air that would never come. She tried to scream, but he'd stolen that, too.

Sen sat on her, pinning her spindly arms to the floor, and watched her die in the flickering light of that den of horrors. In the old days, he might have enjoyed it, but that flame had gone out. It had to be done, and he'd shed no tears for Serana and her Cult. She'd make no appearances among the faces that haunted his dreams. There was no pleasure in this. It was practical and cold, as killing should be. Do it, be done with it, move on.

After she was dead, he scrounged around the little cave, but found nothing to aid in their trip. All he found of any value was a small wooden jewelry box, probably quite fine at one time, but now closer to garbage than grandeur. Inside, there was a locket, containing a small painting of a family of six: the four wretches as children, Jarus still a bouncing baby in the lap of his mother, who looked like a kind woman to Sen. And then the father, stoic and grim, lip adorned with a wicked moustache, watching over the family. Behind them, Sen could see a lower mandible and set of teeth displayed on a countertop. So they'd been with the Cult for a long time. The father was probably an escapee of one of Sen's previous raids who thought he could dig a hole and hide his horrid little family from the world.

You couldn't save them, though, Sen thought. *You couldn't save them from this life. And you couldn't save them from me.*

He shook his head sadly, then tossed the jewelry box into the cauldron and left.

Chapter Seven

The Living Storm

Magic will betray you, in the end. Do not trust gifts given by the gods.

-Log of Dragonmaster Bragg, 78th Lord of Mun-Alin

Wik gripped her blade in sweat-slick hands and blew a stray lock of soaked hair from her face. Her eyes were trained on the man made of living shadow who stalked closer, every step crackling with lightning. His right arm was held low by his side, a longsword made of shimmering energy held tight in his hand. In his left hand, wind and lightning swirled, a tempest in his palm.

He stepped toward her with a sudden quickness, his blade coming toward her in an uppercut. She moved to block it with her own sword, realized too late it was a feint, and found her side left open. She tried to twist away from him, but she was too slow, and his left hand, still crackling with magical energy, caught her flush in the ribs. She heard bones crack as lightning shot through her body and a gale lifted her from the black marble ground and sent her sailing through the air to land in a heap thirty feet away. Her sword skittered off into the darkness.

She tried to rise, but she had no strength left. The fall had knocked the air from her lungs in a long wheeze, and she couldn't stand. The shadow man approached with careful steps, then touched her on the forehead with the tip of his blade.

"I think that's another point for me," Uanari's voice growled from the man, like an earthquake brought to life.

Wik felt her wounds stitch back together as she climbed to her feet.

"The magic was cheating," she said to the dragon's avatar.

"Your opponents will consider it an effective way of putting you down. You must understand—and be able to counter—its use."

Wik groaned as she propped herself up to a sitting position. "That's difficult, when it won't do anything *I* tell it to, but it makes a portable storm in your hand."

Uanari's avatar thrummed. "You are still seeing magic as a tool, to be controlled. You must realize, magic is not something you *use*. It is something you *are*."

Wik must've looked very unsure, because he continued after a moment.

"The truth Riders and other magic users like to ignore is, you can't control magic anymore than you can control the weather. Sometimes, you try to create a gust of wind from your palm, and it works. Others, you spew lava from your mouth." The shadow man inclined his head toward her, and Wik could've sworn she saw a smile in those swirling tendrils of night. "The key is *channeling* the force of the magic, and aiming it the right direction. Try too hard to force it into a certain shape, and it's likely to rebel."

Wik nodded along, but a question floated to the top of her mind. "What about experienced users? Can they control it more?"

Uanari gave a great *huff* and shook the very air around his avatar. "There is no such thing as an experienced magic user, Wik. There are just old ones, and dead ones."

"Oh," Wik said. "Pleasant."

The shadow man waved his hand and Wik's sword rematerialized in her hand. He gestured to it. "Let's get back to work."

They sparred again. And again. And again. In this lucid dream, Wik found she never tired, and though she felt pain, it was fleeting. Her wounds healed almost instantly, and she could try different types of weapons and styles of fighting with no delay. Uanari had carved this space out of her mind through the mental connection they now shared, and she was trying not to consider what he might have displaced by doing so. She had chosen not to ask after the specifics. Either way, this allowed her to train while her body slept and to practice her magic use without risk of destroying more statues.

As their training time was coming to an end, Wik was trying her best to parry a furious series of strikes from a halberd with a shashka—a longsword with a gently curving blade and no crossguard. Ideally, this weapon was more maneuverable than a traditional longsword, but Wik found it had little defensive capability, and she was thumped in the sternum by a hard thrust with the butt of Uanari's halberd. The blow sent her sprawling to her back again.

As Uanari stepped forward to tap her again and take his victory, she reached for her power, thrust out her hand, and exhaled.

The world exploded in a brilliant white light. Uanari's avatar stumbled back, shielding his eyes, weapon discarded. Wik seized the opportunity, brief as it surely would be. She leapt to her feet, sprinted forward, and caught Uanari full in the chest with a shoulder charge. Now he was the one sprawled on the ground. Wik flicked her falchion out, then lightly touched him on the top of his head and claimed her victory.

...or she would've, had he not swept her leg from under her, pinned her to the ground with his legs, then rapped her on the side of the head.

"My point," he said. "But you used your magic reflexively. This is good progress, Wik." He spoke with such little inflection, Wik had trouble deciphering whether he was serious. But when he extended a shadowy hand to help her up, she knew he'd spoken with legitimate respect.

"And I didn't even blow you up," she said with a laugh as she stood and dusted herself off.

Uanari paused, then looked at her. "If I'd actually been trying to kill you, could you have?"

She thought about it. "I'm honestly not sure. Meristofales says I have a vast well of power in me, but..." her voice trailed off as she stooped to retrieve the falchion. "...I don't think I could make it kill you one time and not another. It all seems to be luck."

Uanari nodded. "Many others find it to be similar. Some days you can blow a hole through a mountain, others you struggle to blow leaves from branches." He spun the halberd in his hand and adopted a battle-ready stance. "Thus, your martial skills will probably serve you better most of the time, lacking though they may be."

Wik felt her cheeks flush as she tossed the falchion aside and summoned a short-hafted battle axe. She looked at the weapon with a mixture of surprise and excitement. She hadn't meant to summon an axe, but the weight of it felt good in her hand. The handle was polished wood, stained dark and sanded to fit her hands perfectly, in either a one or two-handed grip. The head was bladed wickedly on one side, curved with jagged sawtooth running the length of it. The other side of the head was a round hammer.

She spun the weapon, then looked to her other hand, where she summoned a round shield, emblazoned with the sigil of the monastery. She looked at Uanari and found him sinking lower into his stance.

So he feels it, too, she smirked. *He feels the rightness of these weapons in my hands.* His training was paying off. She'd finally found a weapon worth wielding.

Uanari struck first, a lashing stab of the pointed tip of the halberd. Wik caught it on her shield, then batted the longer weapon aside, spinning to the inside of the blade to close distance. Uanari slid his feet back, came at her sidelong, using the weapon's haft as a shield and weapon simultaneously. Her first downward strike with the axe was caught on the halberd's grip. Uanari twisted his weapon, trying to disarm her, but she brought the shield up into his stomach. He reeled, spun, brought the halberd down in an overhead two-handed swing that probably would've cut her in half if she hadn't stepped to the side. The blade of the weapon impacted the ground, giving Wik an opening. She slammed the rim of her shield down, warping the metal haft and wrenching it from Uanari's grip.

Disarmed, the shadow man raised both hands to Wik and unleashed a torrent of flame. She raised her shield, caught the magical blast on the front of it, then spun to the side, dropped to her shoulder and rolled toward the avatar. As she came up, he was turning one hand toward her. This time, she ducked, shield over her head, and caught the gale of wind on its face. It still hurt, shoving her almost flat to the ground, but she kept one hand gripped tight around her axe.

Screaming with the effort, she brought the hammer side of the axehead into Uanari's knee. He yelped and went down, the gale finally relenting. As he rolled to his back, arm reaching toward her to set off another blast of magical energy, she was on him. She buried a knee in his chest, which was more corporeal than she'd expected, and put the blade to his throat.

"My point," she panted, a grin crossing her face.

Then he punched her. The force of it knocked her sideways, throwing the axe from her hand. Uanari calmly retrieved it, then stood over her.

"No hesitating," he growled, then buried the axe in her skull.

Wik's eyes shot open, a scream dying on her lips as she came back to reality. Glancing around, she took in the interior of her room at the monastery. The sun of early morning filtered in through her open window, wind playing with the curtain. Her leathers, polished and ready for use, lay on the room's sole table, a sheathed sidesword next to them. She smiled as she looked at the sword.

Guess I need to trade that in for an axe and shield, she

thought.

It would seem prudent, Uanari rumbled in her mind. She stopped herself from jumping, just barely. The dragon's presence in her mind still unnerved her. She'd not had the opportunity to bond a dragon of her own yet, and something about Uanari hanging around her thoughts uninvited felt violating.

Still, she reminded herself, the results were hard to argue with. In the two weeks since she'd begun training with the dragon, her skills had grown significantly. Training with weapons and magic in a safe environment made her less concerned about people watching, or what she might do if she lost control. Not to mention, the opportunity to train with varying types of weapons.

What else do you have planned for us today? she asked in her mind, somewhat tentative. She hoped he'd give her the day off, but she knew how he was. Since he'd taken over her training, she'd barely had time to eat between lessons.

Is there something you had in mind, young one? The dragon's voice had an inquisitive quality, like a raised eyebrow.

Wik hesitated. She hadn't asked him for anything to this point, simply listened and tried to do her best with his lessons. But, well, she'd done well with that, right? It was time for her to push the boundary a little, and see what she could get from Uanari the Black.

I want to fly, she said, as confidently as she could.

A rumble emanated through her mind, but the dragon didn't respond right away. Just as she was about to relent and change her mind, he spoke.

Aye. You should have been on a dragon two years ago, if this order had anyone left willing to teach you. Wik stopped herself from screaming with joy. *Eat,* Uanari continued. *Then find me in the stables.* As she was about to grab her boots, he added, *Bring Eoradon.*

That gave her pause. She was about to ask, "why him?" when Uanari retreated from her mind, leaving her alone. The solitude was welcome, after so much time spent training.

Wik dressed in her leathers, tied her boots, and grabbed the now-pointless sidesword from the table as she left her room. The halls of the monastery were quiet, as always. As she walked to the mess hall, she couldn't help but reminisce on the times she'd spent in these halls over the years.

Her first memories were of running between the various Riders moving around the dormitory halls, playing with their cloaks, trying to stay ahead of her caretaker, Hilod. Wik smiled at the thought of her. Hilod was the closest thing to a mother she'd ever had. Of course, that was similar for most Riders, being orphaned foundlings or younger children, given to the monastery because their parents could no longer feed them.

Wik didn't know exactly what the circumstances were that led her to this place, but she knew she'd only been a baby at the time. Meristofales was reluctant to talk about it. The only thing she knew for sure was that the order to sequester came not long after her arrival. Thus, she was the only trainee in the monastery, and the youngest person there by at least ten years.

Of course, that hadn't helped her make any friends. Most Riders became close with the other members of their training cohort. But Wik was a cohort unto herself, and her unpredictable powers had caused her to be a pariah from the moment she'd begun training in earnest. Nevermind that Meristofales had deigned to train her himself; she'd been enduring stares and whispers from her fellow Riders for years.

The mess hall was crowded, compared to most mornings. Wik counted ten decrepit old Riders sitting around the stone tables, reminiscing about better days. She retrieved her breakfast of hard bread with jam, choosing to forego any meat this morning. Her stomach was rolling, wondering why Uanari wanted Eoradon to accompany them. For having lived in close quarters with him her entire life, Wik barely knew the man, other than his well-known royal heritage.

Eating slowly, Wik waited. Royal or not, he had to eat, right? After a half-hour of nursing her breakfast, the heir to Ir-Anan made his entrance. Wik took the opportunity to examine him. He was tall, long blonde hair pulled into a tight bun at the back of his head, though a few stray locks found their way to hang in front of his ears and frame a face that looked like it belonged on a statue, rather than a man. Eoradon was the picture of princely displeasure, a regal scowl fit across his brows and sank them down over bright green eyes. His high cheekbones were made even more striking by the slight frown adorning his lips. He did not wear riding leathers or his cloak, instead opting for a loose-fitting white shirt, tucked into cloth pants, ending in laced-up leather boots.

Interesting, Wik thought. *He has no idea about Uanari's lesson.*

She stood and moved toward the prince, patting an old Rider named Wulf on an aged shoulder as she passed by him. She knew how many of the Riders felt about her, but Wik had enjoyed the time she'd spent with the monastery's older Riders. They didn't act as though they feared her or remind her how utterly alone she was as the only trainee. Instead, they talked with her. And for her part,

Wik found their stories riveting, allowing her to imagine a time when the Riders had done more than sit in the monastery and reminisce about old glory.

Though in truth, she had come to understand that the Riders, even before the order to sequester, hadn't faced a threat requiring their immense abilities for many generations. Their histories told of a time they clashed in the skies with other magical warriors, the lives of thousands hanging in the balance. But much of that time had been lost to myth long before anyone currently alive had been born. At the time of the sequester, they'd spent most of their time as security to nobles who needed some extra muscle, or providing transport for diplomatic missions. Of course, there was always the threat of the Kerani raiding parties to the far south, but a quick show of force was normally enough to dissuade their halfhearted attacks, according to Meristofales.

She liked to think about those times when the Riders faced truly consequential threats, wielding their powers with wild abandon. Wik wondered if she'd have been more readily accepted by the order as it was then, as a source of power, rather than frustration.

She shook herself back to the moment as she approached Eoradon, who was moving to retrieve an apple, before apparently changing his mind and tossing it back into the basket.

"Excuse me," Wik said, stepping up to the prince and quashing her own nerves in the process.

He glanced at her over his shoulder, his eyebrows climbing higher in surprise as he saw her. He got them under control quickly, though, and resumed his scowling. Though Wik thought it was perhaps less severe.

"Wik, right? The girl who melted the statue?" He smiled so slightly Wik barely registered it. "What can I do for you?"

Wik cleared her throat, pushing down her annoyance. "Uanari says—"

Eoradon's brows creased in confusion and surprise as he turned to look at her. "Uanari spoke to you?"

Wik blinked, unsure if she should take the question as an insult. "He is providing additional training for me, as a favor to Merist—"

"*The Dragonmaster,*" Eoradon said, his voice growing colder. "I know you feel as though the two of you are old friends, but that man has lived more lifetimes than you can comprehend. Do not make the mistake of thinking yourself his equal." Wik was taken aback, but was that a hint of pain in his voice? Warning, even?

Heir to Ir-Anan, she thought, a little pity seeping past the anger she felt building in her gut. *What are you thinking about right now?*

Wik coughed, tripping over her words in the wake of his rebuke. "Right, the Dragonmaster, yes, well, he—" She stopped, took a deep breath, and spoke as clearly as she could. "Uanari has requested both of us report to the stable."

Wik couldn't help but notice Eoradon clench and unclench his fist three times in rapid succession. After a few tense moments, he spoke.

"After I eat, we'll go to see Meristofales and figure out—" A deep thrum cut him off, vibrating the floor and walls, knocking plates of food from the old stone tables, and nearly putting a geriatric Rider on his backside. Eoradon cleared his throat and groaned slightly as he put his bowl of porridge down on a table and grabbed a piece of hard bread. He didn't speak as he brushed past Wik and through the door of the mess hall. She looked after him, unsure of what to do. After a beat, she heard his voice call from the hallway beyond the door. "Come on, then. Best not to keep him waiting."

Eoradon let his long stride carry him down the hall, his heart pounding in his chest.

What could Uanari want from me? he thought to Iaxal, who was herself in the stable. *And why at the stable?*

I think he means for you to fly, came her simple response. Did he detect a hint of a *smile* in her voice?

I think he means to humiliate me by forcing me to train the untrainable girl, Eoradon groaned. *If Meristofales can't get her under control, what am I supposed to do?*

Perhaps Meristofales and Uanari think you need some motivation.

Perhaps? Eoradon made sure she could feel his frustration and anger at being apparently kept in the dark to a scheme she was already aware of. *And how much do you know of this plan to motivate me?*

She chortled. *Dragons talk to each other, you know. I have known Uanari all my life.*

Dragons, he thought in frustration. She said nothing in response, but he could *feel* her smug satisfaction radiating through his mind.

Eoradon was unsure about training Wik, but he had to

acknowledge a small part of him was excited to have a reason to fly again—a reason to do *anything* again.

Wik caught up with him as he turned down another corridor, his mind still thinking about what awaited him at the stable. He snatched bites off his piece of hard bread like an animal snapping at its prey.

"I need to stop by the Quartermaster, if we have a moment," she said as she closed the distance to him.

"Do as you wish," he said around a bite. "But if you incur the rage of Uanari the Black, I'll not be interceding for you." She faltered briefly as they passed the turn to the forge, but relented after a moment's consideration, and tried to keep stride with Eoradon.

They arrived in the stable a few minutes later, Eoradon carried in on long strides, Wik taking nearly two steps for one of his. He tossed the heel of his bread to Iaxal as he passed her, and her massive jaws snapped out and took it from the air. Uanari, impossible to miss, was curled up, lounging in the middle of the enormous space with his gargantuan head resting on crossed forelegs. Eoradon stole a glance at Wik and saw the color drain from her face. He wanted to laugh at her, but in truth, he was nearly as uneasy around the incredible creature.

Uanari was myth made legend, and legend made real. His exploits had been well-known throughout the empire for a hundred years before Eoradon had even been born. The stories some Riders still told about him and Meristofales would make even Eoradon question their validity. Though he had sparred against the man himself thousands of times now, the prince could count his victories on a single hand, and all of them after age had begun to catch up to the former First Ranger.

To hear the older Riders tell it, those two had been a living storm at one time. Wherever Uanari flew, he blocked the sun, and Meristofales was adept enough at magic usage to conjure lightning and gales from his fists. He was so deadly in this way, sometimes he apparently eschewed traditional weaponry to fight hand-to-hand. And even still, he could fight ten men at once, if the stories were true.

Eoradon doubted their truth, but ultimately it didn't matter. Truth was only what people believed, and people believed Meristofales to be the living storm, Uanari a punishment from the gods for the world's wickedness. And the old man had ridden his legend all the way to his current title of Dragonmaster.

Eoradon stood in front of Uanari's snout and waited, taking in the King of Dragons. Uanari was all bulk and brawn, thick ropes of muscles running the length of his legs and torso. On his huge head, a ring of spiky horns sprouted from his skull, just above the ridge of his brow. The beast looked to be asleep, but Eoradon didn't dare try to wake him. After a few minutes, he reached out to Iaxal.

Is he asleep? he asked.

I am not, came the response, an unfamiliar pressure and intensity pushing on Eoradon's mind. He recoiled from it, feeling violated and uneasy. Iaxal's presence was still there, too, just so much *smaller* than the immensity of Uanari's mind. Eoradon hated the feeling of someone else in his mind, other than Iaxal, of course. It made him feel weak, and small, and some part of him understood Rialin's reluctance to fully accept the bond.

Lord Uanari, Eoradon forced out. *You summoned me?* He did his best to keep the annoyance from his tone, but of course some still seeped through.

Uanari thrummed lightly, though it still shook the floor a little.

You will train Wik in flying.

Eoradon fought his instinct and managed not to sigh. *I thought Dragonmaster Meristofales was training the girl?*

He is.

Eoradon waited. No further reply came. He rubbed his eyes, and resigned himself to the task.

Understood.

Uanari gave him no further response, and the suffocating presence withdrew from his mind. Eoradon turned to Wik.

"Get Iaxal's saddle and meet me by her nest," he said, then pushed past her and strode over to his partner.

Wik hefted the enormous saddle on her shoulders, took one wobbling step, and fell over like a drunken turtle. Her second attempt was more successful, and she managed to carry it back to where Iaxal lay, coiled in her nest of scavenged timber, fortified with hay, straw, and rocks. The green and gold dragon eyed her, then emitted a *click* from her jaws, several times in rapid succession. Wik looked at her, confused.

What did that mean? she asked herself, though part of her thought Uanari might be listening. If the great dragon was aware of her question, he did not deign to answer it. Iaxal made the noise again, with no more indication of its meaning than the first time.

"It means you did well," Eoradon spoke as he approached

from behind her, making Wik jump. "Dragons do that when they're pleased with you, but aren't in your mind." The older Rider hefted the saddle onto Iaxal's back.

"Oh," Wik said, feeling her face flush. "I didn't know. I haven't really spent much time around the dragons."

"Yeah," Eoradon said, looking over the saddle before settling into the straps and buckles. "I had my first taste of flight at sixteen, but before that, they were essentially off-limits."

A question occurred to Wik. "Why is that? Shouldn't we be more versed in how to handle them *before* we're airborne?"

Eoradon turned to her and shrugged as he wiped sweat from his brow and tucked a stray hair behind his ear. "From what I understand, making physical contact with a dragon is what opens you up to being bonded. They don't want you having that connection too young. I guess it's too hard to control, and they only want people with some measure of control over their abilities." The prince eyed her hesitantly. "Can't say why Uanari chose this time for you."

Wik looked down. "You...make a good point," she forced out as she fiddled with her belt. "But I'm getting better. I think."

Eoradon gave a sad smile. "Give it time. Truthfully, my doubts are meaningless. If Meristofales and Uanari believe in you, I'm sure there's a reason for it." He beckoned her closer. "Now, get over here, and I'll show you how to strap on these saddles."

Over the next hour, Wik watched as Eoradon walked her through each step of affixing a saddle to a dragon's back. The straps, buckles, and harnesses seemed to form an endless roadway of oiled leather, all leading back to the Rider. After he'd finally gotten it seated properly, he pulled a singular strap by the leg and the whole thing popped loose again.

"Now you do it," he said, and Wik thought she detected the hint of a smile in his voice.

She replicated his movements as best she could, though she worried it wasn't as tightly seated as Eoradon's had been. When she was done, he inspected every inch of the saddle and straps. Eventually, he nodded satisfactorily, then promptly pulled the strap near the leg again, popping it loose.

"Again," the prince intoned. They did this five times, in all, before he finally relented and told her to hop on. Then he climbed on in front of her.

"You're not going to wear leathers?" Wik asked, trying and failing to hide the nerves in her voice.

Eoradon shook his head. "I doubt I'll need to protect myself from enemy arrows."

Wik thought tempting fate was foolish, and she was glad her own riding leathers were fastened to her now. She strapped her legs into the saddle's back seat, then gripped the handles she found by her hips. Eoradon nodded, and Iaxal, who'd been absolutely placid as they had maneuvered the bulky saddle into place, stood and turned toward the stable's massive exit to the sky.

I can't believe you're doing this, Iaxal said in Eoradon's mind. He didn't like the smugness tinging her voice.

I wasn't given much of a choice, he responded, sounding more irritated than he truly was. *Uanari made it pretty clear.*

Iaxal didn't respond, but he felt her glowing pride growing in his chest as she took off for the exit in a bound. She covered the floor of the stable in less than five strides, then leapt into the empty air. Eoradon smiled, the sun kissing his face as he bathed in her warmth. Iaxal hovered a moment in the air...

...then fell.

Chapter Eight

Sundered

I envy those who've never seen what dragonflame can do to the body of a man. Or a child.

-Log of Dragonmaster Bragg, 78th Lord of Mun-Alin

Rialin turned over a shattered shield with his boot, then bent and examined yet another corpse. This one was drawn, decay fully set in. All around him, the field surrounding Aneving Keep had been transformed into a slush of mud, blood, and bile. The Keep itself was brutalized. Massive swaths of black scorched the front and top of the Keep, the stones themselves warped and melted. Windows were shattered in deformed panes. The main building of the Keep looked ready to fall in on itself. The cause, however unlikely, was obvious to Rialin.

Dragonfire.

He knew of no weapon of man capable of such destruction. An airborne examination of the battlements told the same story.

The dragon had swept down, obliterated the men on the walls, nearly destroyed the Keep, and made pass after pass, burning out anyone who remained inside. He spied clawmarks scoring the stones on the wall one level up, where it was clear the beast had perched during the slaughter. Any men trying to flee the carnage on the walls would've run straight into its maw.

Rialin's stomach turned, his heart racing. This was *wrong*. Not only were all the Riders accounted for at the monastery, he had never even seen a wild dragon. As far he was aware, there hadn't been any untamed dragons in millennia, since their order had been formed.

Rialin could see the tracks left by the army that had besieged the Keep. They led down from the northeast. *Meloran,* Rialin thought, grimacing. The eastern kingdom had always been a concern, especially to its neighbors. But if they'd managed to somehow get a full-grown dragon on their side, there was more at stake than just Aneving Keep. The army had left the Keep, heading west through the Great Eastern Forest. They clearly had a head start on him, but he could catch up if they flew hard.

He shook himself. *First things first. I need to inform Meristofales.* His mount's head turned slightly toward him, and not for the first time Rialin wondered if the creature could hear his thoughts. But, no, the dragon wasn't looking at him. It was looking over his shoulder, to the sky.

Rialin turned, just in time to see the monstrosity in a full dive. A massive dragon, scales shimmering silver and red, sped toward him. On its back sat a Rider clad in full plate armor, massive blue cloak flowing out behind him. In his hand, he gripped an enormous Rider blade, such a deep black, it seemed to swallow the light around it. Rialin felt his miniscule magical reserves sitting there, but dared not call on them. It would take everything he had to even inconvenience the dragon, and then he'd be emptied out. With a grimace, Rialin spurred his mount to motion, and they sped off, past Aneving Keep and low over the treetops of the Great Eastern Forest.

The other dragon was huge, and the beats of its massive wings leant it significant speed, but Rialin's mount, though smaller, was more agile. As the great beast closed the distance, Rialin moved in unpredictable patterns to slow down its approach. Still, he knew outrunning it would be a matter of endurance, and his mount was slowing already. It was too young, too immature for a pursuit such as this. Seeing little choice, he forced the dragon down, beneath the thick cover of the trees.

The world darkened as they went under the canopy. There was almost no room to maneuver down here, but Rialin was confident the larger dragon couldn't follow them. He brought his mount to the ground, where they ran on foot with loping strides through the trees, back the way they'd come, toward Aneving. The larger dragon was circling overhead, Rialin knew, but it and its Rider didn't seem to know where they were.

All at once, the monster screamed, a sound so loud it shook the trees. Scores of birds took flight from the canopy as leaves, sticks, and some unfortunate small animals fell to the forest floor. Then, a plume of flame punched through the tree cover a hundred yards behind them.

They're trying to burn us out, he thought, trying to stem the panic flooding his mind. He leaned low to his mount and urged him on. Trees flew by in a blur of wood and leaves, fire raining from the sky all around him. Above, the monstrous dragon was screaming and raging, shaking the world with its fury.

Pain exploded through Rialin's arm as he was ripped from the saddle and launched through the air. He impacted a tree, light flashing in his vision, nearly blinded. His ears were ringing, deafening him to all other sounds. The pain in his arm was immense, and only after a moment did he realize he wasn't falling to the ground. He was pinned to the tree, a black-bladed sword pierced through his shoulder and buried deep in the wood.

Leaves crunched behind him, signaling someone approaching. Rialin couldn't turn his head, and at the moment he was so dazed, he didn't care to. The sword slid free from his shoulder, and he dropped the foot or so to the ground, where he landed in a crumpled mess. Somewhere, he vaguely heard his dragon calling out.

Be quiet, Rialin thought dumbly. *They'll know where we are.*

An armored hand cupped Rialin's chin and turned his head up. A fully-armored warrior stood over him, smoke curling from his thin visor.

"Hmmmm," the Rider hummed, sounding tinny inside his helmet. "Not the one I expected." When he spoke, his voice was a grinding, grating thing, like a tomb being opened. He leaned close. "Consider this your second chance. Go, speak of me to those who hold your leash. Bask...in my mercy."

And with that, he dropped Rialin back to the ground and turned, crunching leaves under his armored boots as he walked away. Before darkness took Rialin, he saw the enormous dragon dip just low enough in the trees to take the Rider in its claws and carry him up, through the canopy and into the light.

◆◆◆

Meristofales stretched his neck from side to side until he elicited a satisfying *crack*, then took up his sword and whipped out a series of quick strikes against the training dummy, sending it spinning from one direction to another. Swing, counter, swing, counter, dodge, duck, spin, swing, chop, overhand—on and on and on until he felt a sheen of sweat on his forehead and his breath came in hard-earned puffs.

As he slid the sword back into the sheath, he felt his knees and back scream in protest. As always, age was the opponent he could not counter. Gingerly, he dried himself off and replaced the training equipment. Exiting his private training space, he sat at the writing desk in his study. Outside, a moonlit night had descended on the monastery, bringing with it the calm, breezy cold he enjoyed so much.

He pried open the massive, leatherbound volume of *The Dragonmaster's Account* laying on the desk, dipped a quill in ink and began writing the day's events. These days, he found more and more often, his entries in this book were only a few sentences. Prior volumes would have pages and pages, sometimes broken down into chapters, to cover singular days. They told of great battles, death-defying feats of heroism, and warriors whose names should be committed to grand mythos.

Of course, their being completely secret kept all that from happening. Over a thousand years of history resided in these chambers, all of it kept from the outside world. Meristofales remembered the days following his ascension to Dragonmaster, when he'd ached to show the world these books.

You cannot, Uanari had told him, voice concerned.

What did they show you? he'd asked the dragon.

Silence, save the rumbling. *You cannot tell them what their gods are.*

Meristofales, still giddy with the knowledge he'd received, thought Uanari was being foolish. Of course, as he'd gotten older, he'd come to learn the truth. The people might be upset to know their gods' true identities. But it was the gods themselves who could not withstand the exposure.

But of course, some things were beyond even the gods' eyes.

A crash of stone came from beyond the door to his study, followed by shouting. Meristofales stood, hand reflexively forming into a fist as he reached for his power.

Uanari?

A pause, then a low rumble. *I do not know. Some commotion in the courtyard.*

Meristofales was out the door, sidesword in hand. Softly glowing lanterns of dragonflame lit the way to the monastery's main courtyard. A young red dragon had crashed down, ripping up stones as it came to a shuddering stop. It laid on its back now, heaving enormous breaths that misted in the cold night's air. Meristofales knew the poor creature immediately.

"Where is Rialin?" he boomed as he ran toward the small group that was now forming around the crash. They parted at his approach, and he found Ferao pulling a lifeless form from underneath the dragon's bulk. The shaggy dark hair and scruffy beard immediately confirmed the figure as Rialin. His skin was waxy, blood was caked around a wound in his shoulder, and the leg his dragon had landed on was crushed and facing the wrong way.

Meristofales knelt by the Rider. "Rialin?" he said, patting the younger man on the face. "Rialin, can you hear me?" A slight moan escaped his pallid lips, and Meristofales sighed with a slight measure of relief. He turned to see Eoradon arrive. The prince's eyes widened as he took in Rialin's condition. "Help me get him to Feordan."

Together, Meristofales, Eoradon, Ferao, and Virsk, a big, burly Rider hailing from Wulthoff, carried Rialin's shattered form to Feordan's infirmary. The monastery's primary healer was wearing a long nightdress, belted at the waist, and no shoes.

"Come in, come in," she beckoned, waving one arm to a flat stone table she'd cleared and readied with various tonics and salves.

The group gingerly placed Rialin on the slab, then stepped back as Feordan sidled up to him, deftly sliding a set of spectacles onto her nose. Through them, she looked down at the broken Rider on the table. After a cursory examination of his injuries, she turned to Meristofales.

"What happened?" she asked.

Meristofales rubbed his face. "I don't know, Feo," he said earnestly. "His dragon crashed into the courtyard, and this is the condition he was in when I got to them."

"The dragon was exhausted," Ferao spoke up, and the group turned to look at him. "He pushes them too hard, I've told him a thousand times—"

"No," Eoradon said. "This wasn't Rialin's doing."

Meristofales was surprised to see Eoradon, of all people, coming to Rialin's defense, but he agreed.

"Aye," he said, then pointed to the wound on Rialin's

shoulder. "That's from a blade. And it's getting infected. The dragon must've made the flight back on its own."

Feordan continued her examination, poking, prodding, and manipulating Rialin's injuries to examine them. She removed his leathers and cut away the pants and shirt he'd worn under them. In the naked light, even Meristofales stifled a wave of nausea at the sight of Rialin's leg, which more closely resembled a bag of broken pottery than a limb.

The wound on his shoulder was pink and puffy around the edges, dried blood and pus caking the edges of the gash. Feordan clicked her tongue in disapproval as she examined each injury. Finally, she spoke.

"I think I can save the arm," she said, removing her spectacles and rubbing her eyes. "The leg is more complicated. I can try to knit the bones with magic, but there's a chance he'll never properly recover, or at least will never walk without a pronounced limp."

Meristofales ran a hand over his face, scratched at his beard. "Do what you can," he said finally. "Try to save the leg."

The master of the infirmary nodded, then turned back to her patient.

"All of you can go," she said matter-of-factly. "You can check on him tomorrow."

As Eoradon, Ferao, and Virsk trailed out, Meristofales remained.

"Feo," he said, his voice a hushed whisper. "When's the last time you treated an actual blade injury?"

She didn't look at him as she spoke. "One that didn't come from a training bout or a flared temper?" She let out a low whistle and shook her head and glanced at him, worry creasing her brow. “What are you thinking?”

Meristofales sighed. “This blade ran him through like a spear, from the back. You can see the bruises on his face, too, I know you can.”

“From the crash—”

“No,” he cut her off. “And you know it. Rialin’s a talented warrior. But he was *running away*.” Meristofales held her gaze, trying to impart to her the importance of his words.

“What would make him run away?”

Meristofales shook his head, then shrugged. “I don’t know,” he admitted. “But I need him awake, and soon, so he can tell us.”

Chapter Nine

The Stone Plains

The southern border with the Badlands of Kerana is flush with activity. That harsh landscape is home to a people even harsher still.

-Log of Dragonmaster Jair, 506th Lord of Mun-Alin

Gradually, the trees of the Great Eastern Forest thinned as the road widened. The muggy heat of the forest gave way to a brutal wind that cut through Sen's cloak and layers of shirts, hot and arid by day, frigid by night. The Stone Plains, where the Empire bordered the deserts of Kerana to the south, were an unforgiving place.

Sen and Erick had bundled their cloaks tight to ward off the winds. By day, the wind carried a dry heat that robbed the air of its moisture and did much the same to the travelers' skin. After a few days in the unobstructed gale, Sen found his lips cracked and bloody, and his hands quickly following suit. The boy was faring even worse. The lack of any discernible food source was taking its toll on him. He looked wrung-out, like old cloth. His skin had grown ashen and his eyes drooped. With each passing day, the boy's feet drug the stones a little more, scraping down the road with a cadence Sen found uncomfortably reminiscent of things he'd seen from soldiers during difficult marches after lost battles.

On their third day shambling through the barren wastes, Erick collapsed.

Sen dropped to his knees beside the boy's small form, his heart pounding in his ears as he pressed two fingers to Erick's neck and checked for a pulse. It was there, but weak. Sen retrieved his waterskin, with barely anything left in it, and put it to the boy's lips.

"Come on, son," he whispered. "Come on, now. Drink for me." Sen couldn't stop his hand shaking as he dribbled water on the boy's bleeding lips. He swallowed. Sen took in their surroundings. What road there was in this place was elevated from the plains themselves, built up slightly on an incline from the cracked and broken stones below. Desperation gripped Sen, but he'd survived worse.

Frantically, Sen moved to where the dirt had been compacted into the slight incline that separated the road from the plains, and began to dig. At first, he clawed at the earth with his fingers, but he'd lost most feeling in his fingertips a day past, so he used his sword hilt. It was hard, backbreaking work, and Sen could feel his muscles crying out in protest. But he pressed on, sweat beading on his forehead. Or, what sweat there was left in him, which was precious little. When he'd dug an alcove out of the small hill, he rolled the boy inside, then strung his own sleeping roll up like a curtain to keep the biting wind out.

He dug through his pack and found what meager rations were left, then took both his and the boy's portions and cut them into small pieces. In all, it was four strips of jerky from a fat rabbit he'd killed in the forest, and some dried pears. Hardly a feast, but it would have to do. He gave Erick some more water, and managed to get him to swallow a couple bites of food before he drifted back off to sleep.

Sen propped himself outside the improvised alcove and tried to watch for any small game. He knew the deserts to the south would have lizards and other sorts of little animals. But here, nothing cared enough to battle the winds.

Stupid old fool, Sen thought to himself. *Should've waited. Prepared. Hunted some more.* He'd let his task from the Duke drive him, and hadn't stopped to think if he was pushing the boy beyond what he could handle.

Sen was snapped from his thoughts by some commotion on the road, back the way they'd come. It sounded like wood grating on stone.

Wagons? Sen thought. The sun was beginning to sink below the horizon, and the world was bathed in a hazy sort of half light, the constant swirling dust that seemed a permanent fixture in the air making it hard to see more than a few feet in any direction. Sure enough, after a few minutes of listening to them, the wagons emerged from the dusty haze, heading straight toward him.

Sen dropped to the ground, laying prone to avoid detection. The first wagon rolled by without incident, but there were several more behind it, and soldiers walking alongside. He couldn't make out their coat of arms, but it wasn't safe to assume anything about old loyalties at this point, anyway. With Aneving reduced to ashes, the various city-states around the Empire would be in political upheaval as they tried to decide how to respond.

Sen glanced to the alcove where Erick rested, then back to the wagon train passing above him. He had no idea how far they would go before reaching a town, and he had less than no confidence he could keep the boy alive until they did. The old man let out a withered sigh, then tossed out all his collected knowledge and instincts, stood up, and began to wave and yell.

The wagon rattled down the stone path, bouncing and jumping at every crack or rock in the path. Sen's left hand rested on Erick's chest, which was still rising and falling with regularity. His right hand held a canteen full of water, which he lifted to his lips and drank greedily. When he was done, he poured some water in Erick's mouth, and the boy's tongue shot out to lick the excess from his lips. Sen replaced the stopper and patted the boy's chest.

"That's good, son," he said, voice barely above a whisper. "That's good."

The soldier who'd seen him waving like a lunatic by the side of the road had told him the group was heading to Kanavar, a small city situated on the border with Kerana, servicing mostly traders and merchants traveling between the Empire and the desert nation to its south.

"It's a decent little spot," the soldier had said when Sen asked about the town.

"Is it imperial or Kerani?" Sen had asked as he climbed into the wagon at the very back of the train. His mind was struggling to recall ever hearing of a town called Kanavar, which surprised him.

The soldier shrugged. "It's Kanavar. Lady Brynne runs things there."

Sen's brows had wrinkled in confusion. "Lady Brynne?"

"She's in charge in Kanavar," the soldier said "That's all I know. What do I look like, a fucking courtier?"

Sen's mind landed on a town he remembered in the general area. "Is it near Nuruk?"

The soldier grinned. "It used to *be* Nuruk." He chuckled. "That was probably ten years ago, old timer. It's changed a lot since then, as I understand it."

Sen nodded. *I bet it has,* he thought.

The soldier, whose name was Jund, Sen learned during their second conversation, had brought the canteens of water a little later on.

"No food, though," he said. "Captain says we don't have enough to spare." Upon seeing the look flash across Sen's eyes, he put his hands up. "Don't worry, old timer. We'll be in Kanavar tomorrow afternoon. You and your...grandson?" Sen made no comment, and he shrugged. "You'll be fine 'til then."

And since then, Sen had let the wagon carry the two of them down the road. It even rocked Sen to sleep for a few minutes before he realized and forced himself awake. He still didn't know who these soldiers were, or what might await them in Kanavar.

The wagon came to a shuddering stop for the night, bringing Sen back to the present. He could hear soldiers dismounting and setting up camp outside when Jund returned and tossed him a rolled up tent.

"This ain't a charity," he said with a smile. "You can help pitch camp."

Sen flicked his eyes to the rolled up bundle of canvas and

sticks, then back to Jund. "We're fine in the wagon for the night," he said.

Jund chuckled. "Not an option. Captain says everyone helps."

Sen grunted, covered Erick with a blanket, and climbed down from the wagon with the tent in hand. Outside, on the smooth stone surface of the plains, the wind was blowing ice cold across the face of their encampment. The group had pulled the wagons into a circle to shield the tents from its bite, leaving them free to make fires. In the circle of wagons, Sen could see multiple small campfires, and one large cook fire in the middle, from which wafted the smell of cooking meat.

"Over here," Jund said, pointing to a patch of bare ground. "Just pitch the tent there, and we'll see if the Captain is feeling more generous about the food."

Sen got to work, and managed to only grumble a little while pitching the tent. Soon enough, the little bundle of wood and canvas had been erected into an actual tent, and Jund was smiling widely at him when he turned around.

"Good job, old timer," he said, clasping Sen on the shoulder. "Let's go see about that food."

Sen followed Jund through the little tent city they'd erected. Along the way, the soldier nodded to his compatriots, slapped backs, laughed at bawdy jokes.

"You're popular," Sen said quietly when he had stepped close to Jund.

Jund shrugged. "It's not hard for most of us to not be an asshole all the time."

Sen grunted, then resolved to stay quiet. As they moved

through the throng, Sen tried to discern this group's allegiance, but their coat of arms—a crescent moon bisected by a spear on a field of blue—was unfamiliar to him. Not wanting to give away his own connections, he chose to forego asking them about it.

As they approached the cook fire, Sen's stomach began to rumble. He hadn't had any real food in days, and his belly had grown soft on the pleasures of palace life the last few years. Even in the forest, there had always been something to hunt once fear of the dragon had abated somewhat. But on the plains, there'd been nothing. Food was running low, and what little there was tasted more like boot leather than meat.

Of course, in his younger days, Sen had boiled strips of shoe leather more than once and eaten it happily. Then again, as Sen remembered it, his younger days had mostly been total shit.

"Stay here," Jund said, gesturing to Sen with his palm. Sen did so, then watched as Jund moved over to speak in quiet tones to the man who must be the Captain. He wore a saber at his hip, not a longsword like most of these men. His uniform consisted of a knee-length dark blue coat over riding leathers, cloth pants, and laced-up boots. A wide-brimmed hat sat next to him on the ground. He and Jund spoke for a moment, each of them glancing his way more than once. When Jund returned, a smile on his face, he gestured to the pot over the large fire. "Dig in! Get food for you and your boy."

Relief washed over Sen for the first time since he'd flagged down the wagon train. He still wasn't sure of this group's connections or intentions, but at least they now had food. *Erick* had food.

As Sen ladled the hot meat stew into two wooden bowls for himself and the boy, he listened to the chatter floating up into the night air around him. Soldiers talked about anything and everything, Sen knew, and he thought he might be able to glean some information.

"Come on, now," one light voice was saying. "No one will get hurt, we just—"

"You look white as a ghost," a rough-sounding voice said. "Like old Vallos himself is gonna walk out of the night and—"

"You see Jund's pets? The old one is a big fucker—"

"I can't wait to be back in Kanavar, in Lady Brynne's court." Sen tried to focus in as he heard the name of Kanavar's enigmatic leader. "She's the only ruler I've ever seen who invites her soldiers to balls."

Sen lost the voice as it was drowned out by a dozen more, but it told him one thing: these soldiers belonged to Lady Brynne. And Jund knew more than he was letting on.

After Sen had filled two bowls from the cookpot, he turned and found Jund talking jovially to two of his fellow soldiers, and looked the man over for the first time. He was a few inches shorter than Sen, but stocky, with thick arms and legs. His hair was cut close and his face was clean shaven, save the stubble one accumulated on a march with no shaving implements. He was unarmored, wearing only a cloth shirt under his dark blue coat, the group's coat of arms stitched on the garment over his heart. His only weapon, from what Sen could see, was a dagger, sheathed on his belt. When he noticed Sen walking toward the group, he bade the other soldiers goodnight and turned back to the old man.

"I see you've got yourself some food," he said, pointing to the bowls in Sen's hands. "I'm sure you're tired. Ready to head back to the wagon?"

Sen glanced around. He was vastly outnumbered here. Sometimes, the only move is no move at all.

"Aye," he said. "Back to the wagon."

Jund nodded, then turned on his heel and headed back toward the wagon Erick was sleeping in.

Nothing rash, Sen told himself. *The boy must be safe.*

As Sen fought every instinct in his body and turned his back on Jund to climb into the wagon, he was relieved to see Erick was at least looking better. He considered the boy, who was finally getting some color back in his cheeks. Maybe he'd been wrong. Jund *had* helped them out, after all. Sen turned to thank the soldier to find him slamming closed the back of the wagon.

"Hey!" Sen roared. He threw himself into the now-latched drop-down gate covering the wagon's rear exit. It rattled from his weight, but didn't budge. "What are you doing?!" Sen pressed his face against the iron bars and stared at Jund as best he could.

"I'm sorry, fella," Jund was saying, refusing to meet Sen's gaze. "Captain's orders." And with that, he turned and walked away, back to the cookfire.

Sen screamed, raged, thrashed at the gate, but it was no use. Behind him, Erick was stirring.

"Sen?" he asked weakly. "What happened?"

Sen fought to stifle his anger, shove back the beast. He took a deep breath through his nose, blew it out his mouth. Then he did it again, struggled to unclench his fists, and rubbed his shoulder, now sore from where he'd rammed the gate.

"We're in a wagon," he said. Carefully, he retrieved the one bowl of soup he hadn't spilled in his anger. "We have soup. Here, eat." And he began to spoon soup into the boy's mouth, doing his best to stymie the rage that shook his hands.

Chapter Ten

Kanavar

The Kerani slave trade is a blight on this continent. The Emperor should march south and scour Tau Keran from the face of the world!

-Log of Dragonmaster Korvo, 507th Lord of Mun-Alin

Sen passed the time in the jostling wagon by imagining new, creative ways he could kill Jund the next time he saw him. The stocky soldier hadn't been back since he'd locked Sen and Erick in the back of the wagon two nights before.

We'll be at Kanavar tomorrow afternoon, Sen thought bitterly, remembering Jund's words to him. *Fucking liar*.

Sen looked over at Erick, who had recovered enough to sit up. In spite of everything, he couldn't say he was angry he'd flagged down this caravan. It had been his only choice, he knew. It was either that, or let the boy die.

"Sen," Erick said, his voice still a light rasp. "Where are we going? Are these men taking us to…to…" His brow furrowed as he fumbled for the words. "…the city where we're going?"

Sen smiled. "Ir-Anan. And no, they're not. They're taking us to a different city." He tried to keep the venom from his tone, and only somewhat failed.

"Oh," said Erick, and Sen couldn't help but notice he didn't seem sad. "What city are they taking us to?"

"A place called Kanavar," Sen said, leaning back against the side of the wagon and putting his right hand on top of his upraised right knee, then peering over both to look at the boy. "I don't know much about it. Never been there, truth be told. Not really. It was called Nuruk when I was still running errands for the Duke." He sighed. "There's been a change in leadership since then, apparently."

Erick moved right past their predicament to ask, "Have you been to lots of places?"

Sen laughed. Genuinely, this time. "Too many by half, son."

A shadow fell across Erick's eyes and he looked down. "Why do you call me that sometimes? I'm not your son."

Doing his best to ignore the surprisingly sharp pang that sent through his chest, Sen cleared his throat. "No, that's true. But I'm an old man and you're a little boy. So that's what I call you." He could tell this explanation didn't work for the boy, so he went on. "Do you not like it?"

Erick looked up at him suddenly. "No, it's not that!" he cried. "I just…don't want my parents to be mad at me."

"Ah." Sen took a deep breath. "Erick, look at me. Your parents are not mad at you. Wherever they are, they're just wanting you to be safe."

Tears welled at the edges of the boy's eyes. He blinked, sending them tumbling down his cheeks. "How can they keep me safe if they're dead?"

"Oh, that's easy," Sen said, and his voice dropped low, so low no nearby ears could've heard it. "They sent you to me."

The wagon bounced along the stone road for the better part of the day before the caravan camped again, sometime around dark. When Sen and Erick's food arrived, this time it was brought by Jund. Anger flared in Sen's chest at the sight of the man. The soldier must've noticed, because he sat the bowls of stew down just inside the bars of the cage and backed away. Sen retrieved the food and handed Erick his bowl before turning back to Jund.

"Look," the stocky soldier started. "This was nothing personal, old-timer. It's just—"

"Business?" Sen interrupted. Jund was momentarily surprised, then sighed.

"Should've known you'd piece it together."

Sen barked a humorless laugh. "Typically, groups of soldiers don't need hidden drop-cages in their wagons." He hardened his gaze, fixed it on Jund. "That's a specialty of *slavers*." He injected as much venom into the last word as he could manage.

Jund sighed again. "You know how this goes, then. Big battle? Keep falls? Lots of people scattered, no home to go back to, running every which way. Running right into us."

"Yes, I'm familiar with how your ilk kidnap innocent people." Sen looked at Erick, then back to Jund. "*Children*."

Jund grimaced like it hurt him to consider. "It's not a pretty business, fella, but it puts food on the table for my own children."

Sen looked him up and down. "Bullshit," he said. "You don't

have any children. You're a fat little worm, gorging himself on the leftovers of people who wouldn't piss on you if you were burning."

Jund's face flushed at that. "I am *not,*" he exclaimed. "I am an officer in this company, and I—"

"You're expendable," Sen said flatly, spooning stew into his mouth. "And I've seen more than one slaver end up in their own cage before all is said and done."

Jund's fists were clenched by his side now, knuckles white. "I came back here to try and talk to you about this like civilized men —"

"Then you're wasting your fucking time." Sen spooned more stew, his eyes never leaving Jund's. He swallowed. "There aren't civilized men back here. Just slavers, and *me.*"

Jund laughed a little, then coughed a bit as he looked away from Sen's gaze. "And what exactly are you, old timer?"

Sen smiled. "Let me out of here and I'll show you."

Jund took a little step back, his hand falling to the dagger on his belt. "Fantasize about killing me all you want, but you'll be in that cage 'til we reach Kanavar."

Sen nodded. "You said what you came to say." He slurped stew. "Now get the fuck out of my sight and let me eat."

Camp was quiet through the night, but Sen remained on edge. He kept watch as the moons rose into their crisscross arcs through the dark sky, snatching only fitful and frustrating bouts of twilight sleep. The company struck camp just before sunrise and were moving as morning took over. A different man had brought Sen and Erick their breakfast, which consisted of a lump of hard, moldy bread.

I suppose that's the punishment for slaves who talk back, Sen thought, and wondered briefly if he'd made a mistake by challenging Jund. Ultimately, he decided, men like these needed to be humbled. And if he was the one who had to do the humbling, so be it.

The wagon rumbled along, and Sen noticed the wind finally dying down, the acrid heat replaced by a sort of general warmth. They were moving out of the plains, he figured, into the calmer sections of the Empire's southern border.

Sure enough, before lunch had been served, he heard the call.

"Hold!" came the booming voice from somewhere further up in the caravan. The wagon came to a grinding, shaking halt, pitching Sen back and causing Erick to start.

"Shhh," he comforted the boy. "Shhhh, it's alright. Just focus on me." He guided Erick's face up and looked into his eyes. "You do what I say when they let us out of here, you understand? You do exactly as I say, and don't question it." The boy nodded, big round eyes wet and full of fear.

Sen tried to stretch his sore muscles. The best opportunity to break away would be as soon as the gate opened. They'd confiscated his weapons. Or at least, the ones they knew about. No one had been brave enough to pat him down, so he still had two long daggers, strapped to his thighs, and two throwing knives on his sleeves by his wrists.

Sen couldn't see the city as they entered it, but he heard the creaking of large wooden doors being opened, shouting in both Kerani and Imperial, and then the wagons were moving again. As they rolled through, the smells of the city overwhelmed the senses.

After some time on the road, Sen had forgotten how cities smelled. People from the country never got it right. Yes, there were the familiar clichés like sweat, urine, and stinking shit. But more than that, there were the smells of *life*. Food roasting in carts along the street: pork, chicken, beef, lamb, spiced heavily in the Kerani style and served skewered on long, thin sticks. Cooked fruit, made sweet or savory to the taste of the customer. Fried bread, served topped with various curries. Flowers filled the streets, spilling over their boundaries, giving the air a soft quality, easy on the nose where the spices had been more assaulting.

Sen looked at Erick, whose eyes had gone wide the way country folk tended to do when they saw a real city marketplace for the first time. Of course, the Kerani did things their own way, and this would be even more baffling to the boy who'd been raised in a Keep in an Imperial forest.

But then, Sen noticed this was not, strictly speaking, a Kerani city. There was plenty of Imperial being spoken, and wares being hocked. Mostly clothing, from what he could hear.

Well, he thought. *It* is *a trading outpost of sorts. Last stop, if you're venturing south to Tau Keran.* Still, he knew the sorts of goods this place chose to trade in, and he couldn't believe the Empire had let this continue. Slavers, openly operating on the border, stealing Imperial citizens. He shuddered, which was a bit strange, given the heat and Sen's hard-won experience. *This is what you get when there's an Empire with no Emperor, I suppose. A nation of fools.*

The wagon train turned off the main market thoroughfare, then came to a shuddering stop in a shaded corner. Sen could hear other wagons being unloaded, cries of "no, stop, please!" and "don't you know who I am? I'll have you hanged for this!" and one particularly agonizing "no, please, don't take her, she's only a girl!" followed by a thud and a scream. He clenched his fists so hard his knuckles cracked.

"Remember," he said, speaking low and quiet. "You stay with me, you keep your head up, and if I tell you to run, you don't wait for me. You run until you can't run anymore." He didn't look at Erick, but he thought he felt the boy nod his head.

Sen could hear them now, a group of soldiers approaching their wagon. When they came around the back, he counted four, but Jund wasn't among them. As they deliberated who was the unfortunate soul tasked with retrieving Sen, he looked for weapons. Pretty standard fare, he decided. Three longswords, one shortsword, and a dagger, from what he could see. Two of them wore light chainmail, the other two only leathers. No one bore a helmet, the heat too oppressive for a head covering, apparently.

Sen felt the daggers resting on his lower back, and he was thankful for the comforting presence. He slid one of the throwing knives down into his palm. When they'd chosen which of them would be opening the gate, Sen readied himself. He was a young man, maybe early twenties. His face bore the untreated, patchy growth of a young man, and his skin was pockmarked and splotchy. A wet mop of red hair stuck to his head and he brushed it back out of his eyes.

"I'm just gonna unlock you," he was saying, not looking at Sen. "Let's just get out, nice and—" As the gate slid up, the throwing knife sprouted from his eye, buried down to the hilt. It put him down instantly, and he dropped like a sack of rocks. Before he hit the ground, Sen sent the other throwing knife toward one of the armored ones and caught him in the mouth as he opened it to yell about his fallen compatriot. His scream turned to gurgled blood as he choked on the knife and fell staggering back.

The other two—one armored in chainmail and one in leathers—were turning to face him now. One had his longsword halfway drawn, so Sen went for him first. He sprang from the back of the wagon, arms outstretched, and tackled him into a roll. When they came up, Sen was on top, dagger already drawn. The soldier's longsword was forgotten in the bloody sand, and Sen drove his dagger down, straight through the man's fleshy nose and into the brain. He twisted as he pulled it out, then spun to see a shortsword coming for his neck. He dropped low to the body he was still straddling, then rolled over, pulling it on top of him to catch a dagger thrust in its fleshy back. Sen rolled the corpse off of him, just in time to see the shortsword scything down at him in an overhand chop.

Sen caught it on his long dagger, right at the crossguard. He kicked out with his feet and managed to sting the soldier enough to make him back off for a split second. Then, Sen was on his feet, dagger held close, crouched down and readying himself. The soldier looked up, realized his mistake, then slid into an effortless stance, from which he stabbed out with his sword and tried to give himself a little more room.

End this, Sen thought. *End it now!*

He rushed the soldier, then dropped and rolled beneath a sweeping attack. As he came up inside the soldier's reach, he buried his dagger in the man's belly. Then he ripped it to the side, causing guts and gore to spray onto the sand.

As Sen stood there for a moment, trying to get his breath, he heard a muffled cry from the wagon. He spun, blood-soaked dagger cocked and ready to fly, just to find Jund, his arm around Erick and hand clamped over his mouth, a wicked serrated knife in his hand and pressed to Erick's neck lightly.

"Just throw down the knife, fella," Jund was saying. Sen barely heard him. His eyes were locked on Erick, trying to make him understand, to remain quiet. He wanted to say that it would all be okay, that he would come save him. But the knife in Jund's hand caught the sunlight and glimmered along its serrated edge. Then Sen saw the fear in Erick's eyes. The boy was shaking. A wet spot had spread across the front of his trousers. Sen knew in that moment, there was nothing more to do. With a sigh, he dropped his dagger to the ground.

"Hurt him, and I'll make damn sure you regret stopping for me." Sen was shaking with rage, his voice coming out as a low growl.

Jund grimaced. "Always with the threats." His eyes took in the carnage of the fight. "I suppose you *do* know something, though. Gods above, you looked like Vallos, stepped out of legend and onto the streets of Kanavar." He sighed, gestured to another nearby soldier with his head. The other man approached Sen with trepidation, metal bindings in his hand. After a moment's hesitation and another look at Erick, Sen allowed himself to be bound. Jund released Erick, replaced the knife on his belt, and moved on with the smug satisfaction radiating off of him, paying no mind to the bodies of his fellow soldiers lying in pools of blood.

Sen swallowed fury and bile and blood. His heart was pounding, blood thundering in his ears as he watched Jund glide gleefully away. *Kill him*, his mind whispered, a voice from years ago. *Kill him,* it repeated. He'd known this voice for many years, and closed his eyes to block it out. It only grew louder. *He was going to hurt the boy. Kill him, kill him, kill him, kill him, kill him, kill him...*

"Sen?"

A small voice snapped Sen back to the moment, and he looked down to see Erick clinging to his leg. He tried to muss the boy's hair, comfort him somehow, but the jingle of the foot-long chain between his wrists spoiled the effort. Instead, he knelt on the compacted dirt of the street and smiled at him.

"Do you trust me?"

Erick nodded.

Sen smiled. "Good. You stay with me. I'll keep you safe." Erick's small body practically melded to Sen as they were prodded into motion by the slavers. Sen took a breath of macabre delight in hearing the last bloody gurgles of the men he'd left in the street.

Sen, Erick, and about thirty other people in varying states of filth were marched from the market to a warehouse a few streets over. Crowded as Kanavar was, it took time to make the trip, and afforded Sen a chance to see the city for the first time.

Kanavar was situated on the Vinube River, which bisected the continent and ran north to south from the Great Bay of Ir-Anan all the way to the Eternal Lake in southern Kerana. The city was built on both sides of the river, Sen realized as he was marched across a sandstone bridge that put him some thirty feet above the rushing waters below. The last time he'd been here, the place had been called Nuruk, and was little more than a marketplace and a tavern. Lady Brynne had apparently valued expansion and industry more than the city's former leaders.

The buildings were growing taller everywhere Sen looked. In some places, the towering stone monoliths wouldn't have been out of place even in Ir-Anan. He could see firelamps dotted throughout the city, in little carved-out alcoves in the walls, or hanging from tall poles, which took to burning as the sun set and evening descended upon them. This city didn't sleep, apparently.

As night engulfed the city and the little dots of firelamp light sparked to life across the darkness, the convoy of slaves was led through winding streets and alleys until they reached a staircase leading under the empty warehouse. They descended the steps to a thick metal door. Jund disengaged the door's bolt, then clumsily hauled it open, clearly more exerted by the effort than he'd like them to know. But Sen could see the sheen of sweat on his forehead as the door squawked open on rusty hinges.

Sen watched the would-be soldier strain as he pulled the door open, thinking back to his decision to drop the dagger. There'd been no choice, he knew. Not really. If he'd missed, the boy would be dead. And if his aim had been true...then what?

The boy would still be dead, he thought bitterly. *I was outnumbered five to one.*

Sen sighed. He felt so *old* of a sudden, his bones seemed like rotten twigs, ready to snap at the slightest provocation. His muscles protested at every movement, and he was sore from the fight and the days cooped up in the wagon.

There had been a day he'd have let that dagger fly. When he was young and strong and terrible. But the sun had set and risen ten thousand times since then, and the darkness of its passing had left him old and slow and tired.

Sen and Erick passed through the heavy iron door and the old man gripped the boy's shoulder tight as they glimpsed what lay beyond for the first time. A hall, so long it ended in nothing but darkness, as far as Sen could tell. Evenly spaced along the wall, wrought iron cage doors, one after another, off into the black. Panic gripped Sen's heart as his breath caught in his throat, and he knew what was coming next.

One of the guards grabbed his right arm. Reflexively, he brought his left up for a punch, but another guard seized him by the elbow, wrenched it back down.

A scream. High and shrill. Terrible in its youth and the fear that tinged it.

"Sen!" Erick screamed. *"Sen, help me! Sen!"* Sen struggled, growled, snarled, pulled with all his strength. He managed to free his right arm and elbow one of the guards in the mouth, thought he felt some teeth give way as he did.

"Leave him!" he bellowed. But when he managed to turn his head, he saw Jund dragging the boy roughly away, ignoring their pleas.

"Sen! Help! Please! I'm afraid, please!" Erick kicked and clawed at Jund, but the slaver's grip was iron, his meaty forearm wrapped around the little boy's chest, pinning his arms down.

Sen tried to take a step toward them, but someone had him by the midsection now, and he felt arms wrapping around his chest from behind. He whipped his head back, felt a nose break.

"Fuck!"

Someone punched him in the ribs and he felt something give, but he struggled through another step. They were vanishing, the darkness enveloping them. *No no no no,* Sen's mind raced. Flashes of another child, ripped from his arms. *No, no, NOT AGAIN.*

More hands grabbed at him from whatever hell lay behind, keeping him from whatever hell lay ahead. He kicked back, felt the meaty flesh of a groin, someone tumbled away. His left arm was still being wrenched back, and he strained until he felt his own tendons giving way, his restraints cutting into his wrists. He whirled with his right hand , caught the slaver who held him by the throat. Sen's fingers dug in, looking for purchase. Panic gripped the man's eyes as he realized he had no escape. His compatriots and the other slaves formed a press behind him, and in front of him there was only Sen and the interminable dark.

That's right, Sen thought hazily, blood pounding in his head and threatening to blind him. *Draw your blade.*

The slaver released Sen's arm, went for his dagger. No sooner was it drawn had Sen grasped the man's wrist, twisted, felt the wet *pop*, and taken the blade. He plunged it into the slaver's stomach, dug around in his guts for a moment, then dropped him. The other slavers went for his right arm, which held the knife, while he laid about with his left.

But in the end, he was old and slow and tired, and vastly outnumbered. The knife was ripped from his grip as someone landed a punch on his face and snapped his head back. Another blow to the stomach drove the wind from him. Still, he fought, swinging wildly, not caring, just trying to cut free from the vines of human hands that held him back from pursuing Jund. It was sticky, hot chaos, the smell of blood and sweat nearly enough to make him sick. His breath driven from him, Sen lost his footing and went down. In a moment, five other men were on his back, tightening the restraints on his wrists until he could barely move. Ahead of him, he could just see Erick's terrified face disappearing into the shadow as his eyes closed and the same silent darkness took him.

Part Two

March to War

Chapter Eleven

Flight Through Memory

My dreams are alight with the flame of inspiration. Each night, I soar above the world, and see it finally put right. They have shown me the truth, and I can finally see.

-Log of Dragonmaster Horus, 873rd Lord of Mun-Alin

Wik wandered the monastery, aimless. Meristofales had ordered regular patrols of the surrounding area, sky and ground, since Rialin's return over a week ago. It didn't help that they had no idea what to look for, but the Dragonmaster was exercising extreme caution. She understood it, but it left her with little to do. All three of her mentors were now busy with other tasks. Meanwhile, the ache in her chest to help, to do *something* was greater than ever.

A dull, gray sky lingered above as she crossed the empty courtyard. Somewhere overhead, Eoradon and Iaxal were lingering, watching out for...something. Whatever could come for them.

"We will take no risk when it comes to the safety of this monastery," Meristofales had said at the emergency meeting he'd called the day after Rialin's crash landing. He'd added, so low Wik had to strain to hear, "I will not lose any of you."

Wik found the corridors of the monastery's interior a welcome sight, compared to the gloom of the windswept outdoors. She followed the passages through their winding path, acutely aware of the sense of *tightness* lingering over the place, like the entire world was holding its breath. The older Riders had taken to telling stories of days gone by, when the order had most recently had to draw steel, and Wik found herself almost *wishing* for the opportunity to defend this place. She banished the feelings immediately, but she couldn't deny their truth: she was ready to fight, kill if need be.

And she'd be doing it with her new weapon, which the Rider smithy should now have ready. This is where her steps through the winding passages led her, and she arrived to see Melysta stoking the forge. The Riders' head smith, Melysta was lean and strong from years of working metal into weapons and armor for the Riders, though in recent years, she'd spent more time forging eating utensils than weapons of war. Not a Rider herself, she was still known to be the most adept among them. Though only a teenage apprentice at the time, she'd chosen to stay when Meristofales had closed the monastery to the outside world.

"Mel!" Wik shouted over the sound of the forge. The smith made no move to indicate she'd heard, so she tried again. "Melysta!" This time, she snapped her head up and looked at Wik through thick goggles, tinted to save her eyes from the flames.

"Wik! Sorry, lass, I can't hear shit over these beauties," Mel gestured to the monastery's forges as she spoke. She pulled the goggles over her head, exposing two rings of skin, untouched by the soot that was ever-present in this place. In the center of said rings were two bright green eyes.

Though she'd never have been called a beauty, Wik thought Mel was far from ugly. Now in her late thirties, she was tall and well-muscled, her auburn hair cut short and almost always kept under a cap. Wik assumed long hair could be a hazard when one spent as much time as Mel around open flame. She absentmindedly wondered what she might look like if she cut her own dark locks short, then was brought back to the moment by the smith's even stare.

"I was hoping you might have my order ready?" Wik asked.

Mel's eyes brightened even further. "Aye! I do!" She turned to walk to the back of the forge, and beckoned Wik to join her.

Together, they walked between the various implements of smithing, about which Wik knew less than nothing. A fire here, a metal clamp there. It was nothing to her. But as they navigated to the back wall of the forge, they arrived at a table, upon which Wik saw a long object, wrapped in canvas. The shape instantly gave it away as an axe. Wik's heart threatened to leap out of her chest as Mel peeled the cover away.

The haft of the weapon was carved from oak, stained to a deep red, and wrapped in boiled leather down to the pommel, which was a heavy round metal ball. The blade was double-sided: On one side, a wicked axe blade, large and curved. On the other, a hammer head, brutal in its efficiency. As Wik took it in trembling hands, she noticed the intricate carvings on the haft. Dragons in flight adorned the weapon above and below the grip. On the head, she saw the etched sigil of a dragon's eye, surrounded by flames. The monastery's sigil.

Wik tested the weapon with some easy swings, and found it felt like an extension of her own arm. Easy and effortless, perfectly weighted. She had no doubt she could throw it with good results, too. She turned to Mel, saw the smith sporting a wry smile.

"I knew you'd like it," she said.

Wik caught her in a hug. "Thank you," she said. "It is more than I could've ever hoped."

Mel patted her on the back and removed herself from the embrace, clearing her throat. "Aye, it's a good one," she said. Then quickly added, "Once you bond a dragon, bring it back and we'll see if we can get it functioning like a Rider blade."

Wik's eyes widened. "That's possible?"

Mel shrugged. "Truthfully, I don't know. Normally, anything with a finer edge than the huge greatswords breaks down when we add the blood from the bonded Rider and dragon in the smelting process. But we have some records to indicate ancient Riders could use weapons other than swords, and I want to find a way."

Wik nodded, running a finger along the blade. "That makes sense." She yelped and pulled away as a small droplet of blood welled on the tip of her finger.

"It's sharp," Mel said with a stifled laugh. Wik nodded, sucking the blood from her finger and replacing the canvas cover on the axe.

"It's beautiful," Wik said, turning to Mel. "Thank you."

The smith smiled as she looked at the bundled-up weapon. "Just keep it close," she said sadly. "It seems all sorts of things are turned upside down nowadays."

Wik nodded solemnly, then patted Mel on the shoulder as she made her exit, with promises to report back once she'd had a chance to put the weapon through its paces.

As she strode past the infirmary, Wik was nearly bowled over by Meristofales and Feordan, heads down and deep in conversation. As she stumbled clumsily out of the elder Riders' way, they both looked up and gave apologetic nods before continuing down the corridor toward the mess hall. Wik had turned to leave, continue on her way to find a training dummy, when she noticed the door to the infirmary standing slightly ajar, a thin ribbon of light pouring out onto the stone of the hallway. She moved to close it, but caught sight of a stone table and a mangled foot.

She hesitated only a moment before her curiosity overcame her and she ducked inside. The front of the room was lined with all of Feordan's implements of healing, but just off to the side stood a stone table, upon which laid a man who looked closer to dead than alive.

"Rialin," Wik whispered. She'd met the man, of course, but only knew him in passing. From all her accumulated knowledge about him, she could only confidently say most people in the monastery thought he was an asshole. Still, she wondered what some of those people would say if they were standing here, looking down at his broken form.

She'd heard his leg was gruesome from Ferao and Virsk, but this was beyond any injury she'd ever seen. The leg looked like a sleeve of loose rocks, and it was barely held together in its shape by the metal screws and plates Feordan had set up here. Wik knew better than most the potency of Feordan's healing abilities, but she doubted even she could fix something so deeply broken.

The rest of Rialin's injuries were in various stages of healing, and Feordan had clearly applied several salves and poultices, if the smell was anything to go by. His face, clean-shaven by the head of the infirmary, was twisted in a mask of pain, but he did not wake.

Wik jumped as the infirmary door squeaked open. Spinning, she found Feordan and Meristofales watching her. Feordan's face bore a disapproving scowl, but the Dragonmaster wore a wry grin.

"You know, Feo," he said in that gravelly bass of his, and Wik felt her stomach drop. "You *did* just tell me you could use some assistance with Rialin's care."

Eoradon sat astride Iaxal, hovering on the wind current flowing around Mun-Alin, and surveyed the skies. The monastery was hundreds of feet below, and the winds up here whipped violently at the Rider's cloak and hair. His eyes were only saved by the mask he wore to shield them.

I don't see anything, he told Iaxal.

Me either, she responded. She sniffed. *Nothing on the wind, either*.

Eoradon nodded, then relaxed slightly in the saddle. *I doubt whoever attacked Rialin would make a direct assault on the monastery, anyway.* Iaxal said nothing, but he felt her agreement. Wordlessly, Eoradon sent her a series of mental cues, directing her where to go. She folded her wings and they dropped into a short dive before she spread them again and they soared down past the monastery, then banked and sliced around the surface of the next peak over, coming up on the other side and getting a good view of the land at the base of the mountains as they leveled out.

I missed this, Iaxal said, contentment flashing in Eoradon's mind.

I know, he said. *I'm sorry for keeping us grounded all that time.*

She thrummed happily beneath him. *You did what you thought was best.*

I know, he said again, but he didn't feel it. *It was still the wrong choice. You were never to blame for what happened.*

A red flash in his vision, a feeling of bubbling rage, an aching in her missing forefoot. *No,* she said icily. *He was.*

Eoradon said nothing. He knew why she felt this way, but he couldn't argue it. There was no point. He returned to scanning the horizon, but there was nothing to see but idyllic farmland all the way to the distant shimmering point he knew to be Ir-Anan.

Cold marble, slick with hot blood. A rough hand scooping him up, so stunned he couldn't even cry.

Eoradon shook his head, tried to clear the cloying thoughts. *Not yet,* he thought.

What? Iaxal asked, and Eoradon's heart surged with panic. She had heard him. She'd never heard *those* thoughts before.

Eoradon was caught wrong-footed and unsure of how to respond. He stammered about before finally saying. *What did you hear?* Though he couldn't keep the panic from his thoughts.

I didn't hear it, Iaxal said, seeming confused. *More like I* saw *it. You, as a boy? And the blood—*

Don't, Eoradon cut her off. *Please.* He tried so hard not to sound pleading, but it wasn't the man of over forty years who said the word. It was the boy of six, being dragged from his home on the night the Empire fell.

Rodo, Iaxal said, compassion flooding his mind. *You've carried this without me all this time?*

Eoradon suppressed a chuckle. *I've carried it for as long as I can remember, Iaxal. But you feel what I feel, and this is more than I ever wanted to burden you with. One day, maybe. But not now.*

Rodo, she began again.

No, Iaxal. I can't. His eyes were wet with tears behind the face shield. He drew in a deep breath. *When I can, I will. But right now, I just can't.* More compassion flooded his mind, but she let it drop. And for the rest of their flight, they had only the wind's song for company.

Chapter Twelve
The Fraying Rope

22 Years Ago

Steel rang as the swords collided. Eoradon wheeled, caught another sword on his blade, turned it away and sent its wielder stumbling. The sound of a boot scuffing stone alerted him to another opponent moving in behind him. He ducked, swept out his leg, and sent the attacker—Ferao?—onto their back. When he rose, he found Virsk stalking toward him, shortsword in hand.

The big northerner spun the sword once, then darted in with an overhand strike. Eoradon blocked, but the strength of the attack broke his guard and set his arm to tingling. His sword clattered to the stones, where Virsk kicked it away. Eoradon stumbled back, trying to shake feeling into his right arm, but it was all pins and needles. Another downward chop came and Eoradon slipped to the side. Virsk brought his sword up in a sideways swing, aimed right for Eoradon's midsection. The prince danced away as feeling began seeping back into his arm.

Motion in his periphery caught Eoradon's attention. A glance showed Rialin, breathing hard, bearing down on him. Virsk from the front, Rialin to the side, no sword. Eoradon's heart was pounding, his hair plastered to his forehead and soaked with sweat. Without thinking, he lifted his palm to Virsk and screamed. As he did, he reached within, to the immense well of power he held. He took only a small amount of that force and channeled it through his arm, as he'd been instructed. Or rather, as he'd been instructed *not to do,* unless there was no other choice.

A gust of wind exploded from Eoradon and threw Virsk into the air like nothing more than a child's plaything. He cartwheeled, end over end, landed hard on his back and skidded to a stop, his sword careening off the side of the mountain. For a moment, Eoradon stood in stunned silence, shocked both that it had worked and that he'd actually unleashed his magical abilities in a training bout. Dread immediately weighed on him when Virsk continued to lie on the stones, unmoving.

Eoradon held his breath as he watched, along with, he knew, Meristofales, Liran, Feordan, and the other instructors.

Rodo? Iaxal's voice echoed in his mind, quiet and far away in the stable. *What just happened?*

Eoradon swallowed. *I think I might've killed Virsk,* he said. *I used magic during our training fight–*

Eoradon! She cut him off. *You know how volatile magic is.*

I know! he snapped. *I didn't mean to–well, I* did *mean to, but obviously not enough to hurt him.*

To his endless relief, Virsk stirred and rolled himself over, rubbing his midsection, where he'd taken the blunt of the blow.

Eoradon sighed, then rubbed his eyes.

Rialin crashed into him at full speed, taking both trainees off their feet and to the ground in a rolling, screaming mass of snarling faces and swinging fists. Somewhere in the midst of it, Eoradon noted Rialin could've tapped him with his sword and ended the bout. He'd *chosen* to attack him like this. They were locked, snarling and growling face to face like animals, each having landed punches on the other, when Meristofales and Liran arrived to break it up.

Held back by Meristofales, Rialin was still straining like a mad dog on a leash against the First Ranger's superior strength.

"You could've killed him!" the commoner bellowed, spittle flying from his mouth. "You pompous, stupid fool!"

Eoradon felt his face flush as he spun to fire off a retort, but Liran's arm snaked around his neck, then tightened.

"Shhh, prince," Liran half-whispered, half-seethed into his ear. "Easy now."

Eoradon felt the lights of his vision going out, and put up his hands in a show of surrender. Liran released him, giving him a little support to prevent the heir of Ir-Anan from falling on his ass.

Rialin was being dragged away by Meristofales now, but he was still fighting to be free, still screaming at Eoradon.

"You damned fool!" he yelled. "You're a prince of *nothing*, Eoradon! A *prince of nothing*!"

Eoradon couldn't help but notice Meristofales made no attempt to prevent Rialin from speaking as he dragged him away.

Liran took Eoradon by the arm and escorted him away from the training area. Once they were out of earshot of the other trainees and instructors, the Rider crossed his arms and looked at Eoradon from under a brow creased with frustration.

"What," he began, "was *that*?" A note of fury tinged his voice, kept carefully in check.

Eoradon sighed and rubbed his face again. "I don't know," he said honestly. "Reflex, I think. I saw Virsk coming at me from one side, and Rialin from the other, and I just...reacted." He hung his head.

Liran sighed and ran a hand over his jaw as he turned to look at Virsk, now sitting up and being tended to by Feordan. "You really could've killed him, Eoradon."

Eoradon took a deep breath, looking for words. "I know," is all he could come up with. "I'm sorry; I wasn't thinking."

Liran nodded. "That feels like an understatement." He turned back to Eoradon. "The truth is, you're nearly a fully-vested Rider, Eoradon. Iaxal is almost fully-grown, and then you'll be out there–" He pointed off into the general distance, but Eoradon knew it was the direction of Ir-Anan. "–on your own. And you can't afford to 'not think' when you're dealing with ordinary people. Are you going to obliterate everyone who crosses your path with magic you can't control?"

Eoradon's face flushed again. "No, I could never–"

"You certainly looked capable enough just now!" Liran was trying to stop himself from yelling, and barely succeeding. "You were *lucky* you didn't do more than shove him back. You know there's no real controlling those powers, no matter how experienced you are."

Eoradon sighed, tiring of the lecture. "I've heard Meristofales uses—"

"Meristofales!" Now Liran *was* yelling. "That brute goes into every situation *looking for a fight*, Eoradon! You have no idea the damage he's wrought."

Eoradon regarded Liran with a shocked expression. The Rider, seeming to remember himself, took a deep breath and smoothed his hair back from his face. Eoradon couldn't help but realize how tired his eyes looked, ringed by purple circles.

"You are not the First Ranger," he said after composing himself. "You are a promising trainee and the *Prince of Ir-Anan.*" He placed particular emphasis on Eoradon's title. "You cannot go off half-cocked, throwing around magical attacks, because it will backfire on you. We do not need you to be a killer, Eoradon. We need you to be a ruler."

Eoradon was taken aback. He'd never heard Liran speak so plainly of his heritage before. "A Rider," he said.

"What?"

"You need me to be a *Rider*," he said again.

Liran waved it off. "Yes, obviously. That's what I said."

Eoradon regarded Liran carefully. "You said you need me to be a ruler."

Liran sighed. "I'm exhausted, Prince. I misspoke." He rubbed his eyes to drive the point home. "Go throw yourself at Feordan's mercy. Do whatever she asks of you, until she releases you." And with that, he turned and swept away, his purple cloak trailing across the stones after him.

As the sun descended and the twin moons rose, Eoradon was finally released from Feordan's service. He'd helped her move Virsk to the infirmary, retrieved ingredients for her, applied a salve to his cuts and scrapes and, in a moment Eoradon swore was necessary for nothing more than his humiliation, he'd been made to prepare refreshments for both the elder and the younger Rider.

In the end, he'd actually found the simple work refreshing. And it had given him the opportunity to apologize to Virsk in full.

"I'm sorry," he'd said, quiet and simple when Feordan had stepped away.

Virsk looked up at him from beneath his thick black brows, regarding him seriously for a moment. Then, he laughed. The northman laughed low and long before clapping the heir of Ir-Anan on the shoulder.

"It's alright," Virsk said, his Wulthoff accent faded after years at the monastery, but still there on the periphery in the form of a slight roll to his R's. "I mean, it was crazy, but I can't deny, it was impressive."

Eoradon allowed himself a small smile. "I really *wasn't* trying to hurt you, you know."

Virsk returned the smile with one of his own. "I know. But if I'd really been trying to kill you, I think it would've been the right choice."

Eoradon nodded. "Probably," he agreed. "But I don't think I'll be doing it in training again anytime soon."

Virsk laughed again. "Probably for the best."

When Feordan had released Eoradon for the night, he'd clasped hands with Virsk, and left feeling closer to the northman than he had in all the years they'd known one another. He was used to the other trainees viewing him with trepidation, but Virsk didn't seem to care about his lineage or where he'd come from. It was a refreshing change.

Eoradon crossed the courtyard under the light of the twin moons, one silver and one pale green. He was admiring the way the moonlight bathed the stones in that easy light when he noticed two figures standing on one of the meditation platforms that jutted out from the mountain to hang over the dizzying drop off the side of the monastery. As he drew closer, Eoradon realized the two figures were Liran and Meristofales, seemingly deep in conversation. He looked around, but there was no easy exit from the courtyard without being seen. As he drew close, he caught their voices, if not their words.

They were speaking in harsh, hushed tones, gesturing to one another, seemingly angry. After a moment, Meristofales shoved a finger in Liran's face, said something in a clipped tone, then turned and swept away into the night. Liran's head dropped, then he turned and stalked in the other direction. He passed Eoradon as he went. Their eyes met, and Eoradon noticed Liran's eyes were dark, with a wild tinge, his dark circles having grown even more pronounced. The mentor fixed the trainee with a hard stare, then grinned slightly and inclined his head.

"Prince," Liran said, his voice nearly a growl. "Feo has no more need of you tonight?"

Eoradon swallowed hard, suddenly uncomfortable beneath those large dark-rimmed eyes. "No," he managed. "Virsk is feeling much better."

Liran's gaze flicked away as he nodded. He looked up at the green moon and drew in a deep breath, then exhaled it slowly. He didn't look back at Eoradon right away, instead keeping his gaze fixed on the star-filled canvas of dark blue and purple.

"Your instincts were right today," he finally said, so quiet Eoradon had to lean forward to hear him. "But you have to be careful. No one will follow you if you murder your fellow trainees by accident. And then there's Rialin..." Liran's voice trailed off as he turned back to face Eoradon, who'd barely moved since the strange encounter began. "That one is going to be trouble. Keep an eye on him."

And with that, Liran turned and walked away, his boots *clack*ing on the stones as he went.

The next morning found Eoradon groggy after a fitful night of non-sleep. He couldn't shake Liran's strange demeanor. And what had he been arguing with the First Ranger about? It all seemed so strange to Eoradon.

When the sun rose and he'd barely slept, the heir of Ir-Anan gave up. He dressed, then headed to the courtyard, hoping to find someone he could spar with. But, early as it was, no one had made their way out yet. Iaxal was off hunting and doing some flight training of her own, so the young Rider found himself with a rare moment of free time. He wandered the ancient monastery, until his feet carried him, unbidden, to the infirmary door. He knocked, still not sure why he'd come here.

Feordan's lined face failed to contain her surprise when she opened the door and found Eoradon standing there.

"Ah, good morning, Eoradon," she stammered. "What can I do for you?"

He looked around and shrugged. "I'm honestly not sure," he said after a moment. "No one is sparring, I haven't seen Meristofales or Liran, and..." He trailed off, turning to look at her. "Is there anything I can help *you* with?"

The older Rider suppressed a look of surprise, then smiled.

"Of course, prince. Come on in."

Now

Wik watched closely as Feordan applied the salve to Rialin's shoulder wound. The sleeping Rider had been unconscious for almost two weeks now, and showed few signs of waking. His leg was starting to stitch back together, Feo had told her, and the shoulder wound was looking better. But he still slept.

Feordan had spent the last couple of days showing Wik the various poultices and salves she was using for Rialin's wounds, and how to make them. Wik had then spent several agonizing hours grinding and mixing the concoctions. The healer had told her she was a natural when she only vomited twice from the smells.

Feordan moved away from Rialin's shoulder to check his leg. Wik slid over to stand by the Rider's head. She leaned down and examined his closed eyes. They moved rapidly under the lids—back and forth, up and down. Curious, Wik placed a hand on Rialin's chest. Her eyes widened; his heart was hammering on the inside of his chest and his breathing was fast and shallow.

He's panicking, she thought, unsure of what to do. She turned to Feordan, saw the older woman had noticed the same thing she had. The healer moved to the other side of the prone Rider's head and placed a hand to his forehead.

"Clammy," she said in a clipped tone. "but not fevered. Quick, fetch me that—" She was cut off as Rialin's eyes snapped open and he drew in a ragged, gasping breath. With one hand, he shoved Feordan away, knocking her into the wall and driving the breath from her lungs, while the other hand shot out and clamped down on Wik's wrist, shocking her with its strength. With seemingly no effort, he pulled her toward him, until their faces were inches apart and she could feel his hot breath on her.

"Meristofales," he rasped. "Now."

Chapter Thirteen

The Larger World

The people think we Riders feel no fear. They are wrong.

-Log of Dragonmaster Horus, 873rd Lord of Mun-Alin

Rialin gulped water from the basin the girl had given him. His throat ached like it was full of knives, and his body was broken, but the simple pleasure of cool water still soothed him. From what little she'd said, his leg might be beyond saving. He'd still not let himself worry about that, instead preferring concern over the madman who tried to murder him.

Go, speak of me to those who hold your leash, he'd said. His tinny voice and smoking eyes still haunted Rialin's mind, as fresh as they were on the forest floor. *Bask in my mercy.*

Fuck your mercy, Rialin thought, trying not to shift his ruined leg or aching shoulder.

The door to the infirmary burst open and the Dragonmaster thundered through, trailed by Feordan. He brushed past Wik with barely a glance, then took a knee by the place where Rialin's head was propped up on pillows. As the older man looked over Rialin's face, in his eyes, the younger Rider thought he saw moisture gathering at the corners of his slate gray eyes.

"My boy," he said, so quiet Rialin struggled to hear him even this close. Then the Dragonmaster surprised his pupil by wrapping his arms around him and pulling him into an embrace. "I thought we'd lost you."

Rialin's instinct was to shrink from the touch, but in the arms of his mentor, he found comfort, and was surprised again to find tears welling in his own eyes. He embraced Meristofales with his good arm. For a while, they leaned on one another. Meristofales broke away first, then held Rialin at arms' length, cupping his callused hands around the Rider's face for a moment before releasing him.

Meristofales cleared his throat to speak. "When you're more rested, we can discuss what landed you here in this shape."

Rialin shook his head. "We need to talk now." He was surprised at how whingey his voice was, but he fixed the Dragonmaster with his most serious stare and pressed on. "None of us are safe."

Meristofales hesitated a moment, then nodded and pulled up a chair to the bedside. He sat there, fingers steepled in front of his face while Rialin recounted the story of his attack and subsequent flight home. When he'd finished, the old Dragonmaster exhaled and rubbed his eyes.

'Thank you," he said after a moment. "Now rest." As he rose, Rialin made to sit before he was forced back by the pain, still ever-present throughout his body. Meristofales put up a hand to still him. "Rest, Rialin. I will think on this and decide our next move."

"I need to help," Rialin said between panting breaths as he tried and failed to adjust his position on the table.

Meristofales patted the Rider on his good shoulder. "I promise," he said, his eyes fixing Rialin with that gray stare he used so effectively. "I will make no moves without your knowledge." Then he turned and swept from the room, beckoning Feordan to follow.

"Is there anything you need?" The girl Wik spoke, reminding Rialin of her presence. He sighed.

"No," he said, feeling suddenly very tired as he rubbed his eyes and laid his head back. "I'll just sleep for a while, I think."

The girl nodded, then extinguished the flame nearest to him, plunging Rialin into a comforting darkness.

Meristofales fumed in the hall as Feordan closed the door to the infirmary behind them. His fists were clenched so tight, he felt his knuckles pop.

"Meristofales," Feordan spoke from behind him in the voice she used when she was trying to calm him. "Take a breath. Don't do anything rash."

The touch of her hand on his shoulder served to stem the tide of his bubbling rage, if only a bit. Meristofales rolled his neck from side to side, eliciting a few cracks, then turned to face her.

"I won't," he said, knowing it would probably be a lie. "But action must be taken."

"What are you going to do?" she asked, lines of concern crossing her face.

Meristofales breathed deep, then exhaled. "We need to have

a meeting."

She nodded. "Do you want everyone?"

He shook his head. "No. That would only complicate things. I will notify the ones I need." He turned back to Feordan and gestured to the room where Rialin lay recovering. "Can you get him well enough to attend? Others will want to hear what he has to say."

She glanced toward her door, hesitated a moment, then nodded in ascent. "I can get him there, but he won't be whole for a long while yet."

Meristofales nodded. "It'll do. Thank you, Feo."

She smiled slightly and inclined her head. "Of course, Dragonmaster."

Normally he would've laughed at her playfulness. But he was all storm and fury now as he turned and stalked away.

As he walked, he reached out with his mind. *Uanari.*

Yes, Meristofales? The reply came almost instantaneously.

I need you to reach out to a few people for me. Call a meeting. Need-to-know basis.

Agreement flooded his mind. *Of course.* After a moment's hesitation, the dragon continued. *I heard what he told you. This feels like a moment of import, Meristofales. We must step carefully.*

Aye, Meristofales said.

Uanari wavered for a moment, unlike him.

Meristofales, the dragon Rialin saw—

I know, Meristofales cut him off. *Dyraxian.*

He's mentioned in the records. Why would he be here? And with a Rider? Uanari huffed, so much as he was able. *It makes no sense.*

I agree, Meristofales said. *But I intend to* make *sense of it. Now, about that meeting...*

An hour later, Meristofales found himself sitting at a large stone table in a council chamber that had sat unused for many years. The Dragonmaster sighed as he wiped a layer of dust from the table.

I've failed them, he thought. How many years had he kept the Riders here in these walls? Safe and secret...and weak. And now, an actual threat had risen, and who was there to meet it?

We did what was necessary, Uanari thundered in his mind.

No, Meristofales retorted. *I did what was easy.* He balled his hand into a fist. *I was afraid, and I cowered in this place. But I've made us vulnerable.*

You bought time, Uanari said. *You have given them a chance.*

"Bah," Meristofales waved the notion away, then continued the conversation in his mind. *Lot of good it will do if they're all too inexperienced to make a difference.*

A beat of silence lingered between dragon and Rider.

Meristofales, Uanari probed. *What are you thinking?*

Before the Dragonmaster could respond, the door to the chamber creaked open, and the first of the called Riders entered. Virsk was a big man, a long black braid cascading down to the middle of his back and a thick beard of the same shade adorning his face. His nose was pierced by a large metal ring in the custom of his homeland, the fierce north of Wulthoff.

"Aye, Dragonmaster," the northman inclined his head to Meristofales. "I hear Rialin's back from the dead." A broad smile split the Rider's face. Meristofales tried to return it with one of his own but only mustered a small grin.

"He is, at that." Meristofales sighed, closed his eyes, and stretched his neck for a moment. "I'll have more to say when everyone else arrives."

The others made their entrances one by one over the next few minutes. Ferao came next, clapping Virsk on the shoulder. Then, there was Feordan, pushing Rialin in a modified rolling chair, his leg laying elevated on a stiff board. He got the warmest reception by far, as his fellow Riders crowded around him with firm clasps of forearms, and good-natured jibes about forgetting how to fly. Finally, walking in with what looked like a physical weight on his shoulders, came Eoradon. The prince caught Meristofales's eye and nodded. He and Rialin exchanged a glance, but neither spoke.

"Now that we're all here," Meristofales began, calling the attention of the others to him. "Everyone sit. Rialin has something to tell you all."

For the next while, the room sat still while Rialin recounted the tale. When he finished, no one spoke for a long moment. Finally, Virsk broke the silence.

"What are we going to do?" he asked, turning to face Meristofales.

"We have to go hunt the bastard down," Ferao added. Virsk nodded.

Meristofales held up a hand to calm them. "Yes, something must be done." His eyes cut to Eoradon, where he found the heir to Ir-Anan already looking at him, brows furrowed. As his words settled, he saw realization cross the prince's face.

"You're not considering what I think you're considering," he said, a warning in his tone.

Meristofales remained silent. Feordan's hand went to her brow. Virsk and Ferao exchanged confused glances.

"What?" Virsk asked. "What is it?"

"He's going to go himself," Rialin added, his voice a hoarse whisper as he locked eyes with Meristofales.

"He's going to get himself killed." Eoradon's fist was clenched on the stone tabletop. "It's a fool's errand, Meristofales."

Virsk and Ferao lodged noisy complaints at the same time, speaking over one another in an effort to be heard.

This feels rash, Uanari rumbled. *Though I cannot say I would've chosen differently.*

Meristofales allowed himself a smile. *I knew you'd be on board, old friend.*

"Quiet!" The Dragonmaster's voice boomed in the small chamber, stilling the Riders. "I've made my choice." A steely quiet settled over the group, Eoradon's fuming nearly audible. Meristofales took a deep breath, calming himself before he continued. He balled his hands into fists and settled them on the tabletop as he spoke. "I've brought you here because I trust your abilities to oversee the operations of this monastery in my absence. You possess the necessary experience—" he inclined his head to Feordan "— skills—" he acknowledged Virsk and Ferao "—and leadership—" his eyes settled on Eoradon and Rialin "—to ensure our home remains a sanctuary."

After a moment, Ferao nodded. "Alright, then. If I cannae convince you to stay, I'll do as you ask."

"When will you leave?" Virsk asked, his fingers drumming a nervous beat on the table.

"Dawn," Meristofales said. "Uanari and I will track down this foe, defeat them, and find out where they came from." The Dragonmaster locked his slate gray eyes on Rialin. "And when I return, I intend to lift the order of seclusion and admit new pupils."

Rialin perked up at that, and he nodded in agreement. "See to it you come back, then." He flashed Meristofales a smile, which the older man returned.

Meristofales cleared his throat before continuing. "I'm naming Feordan as Dragonmaster in my stead. She—"

"Absolutely not!" The head of the infirmary had a finger leveled at Meristofales, who found himself without words. "There is no one else to run the infirmary, and Rialin isn't healed yet. I will assist and advise in any way you want, Meristofales, but I will not sit in your chair." And she sat back, making it clear there would be no debate.

"Ah," Meristofales coughed into his hand. "Very well, then." He scanned the others gathered in the chamber and considered them. Virsk and Ferao were too emotional, too prone to outbursts. Which left two options. And given Rialin's condition, only one. Eoradon hung his head slightly as Meristofales's gaze settled on him. *Of course,* Meristofales thought. *It was always going to be Eoradon.*

The prince nodded ever so slightly. "I'll do it," he said as he straightened his back. "But don't get any ideas about retirement. When you get back, this mantle passes back to you."

Meristofales smiled. "Aye, prince. The crown will only be yours for a short time." He turned to the rest of the gathered Riders, and allowed himself a moment to take them all in.

They'll be fine, Uanari said in his mind. *You trained them.*

The Dragonmaster sighed. *That's what concerns me.*

As Feordan pushed Rialin from the chamber in his wheeled chair, Eoradon hung back and found himself alone with Meristofales.

I cannot believe he's doing this, Eoradon said to Iaxal through their mental link. *He's going to get himself killed.*

Don't be so sure, Iaxal said. *Uanari is a force to be reckoned with, and I've always understood Meristofales to be of similar stock.*

He's old, Iaxal.

She snickered. *Don't let* him *hear you say that.*

The Dragonmaster sighed. "I assume you would have words?"

Eoradon scoffed. "Yes, I would. Why are you doing this?"

Meristofales rubbed his brow. "We cannot allow a rogue dragon to roam the countryside, incinerating castles."

"You know what I mean, Meristofales." Eoradon lowered his voice, stopping himself from yelling. "Why are *you* going?"

Now it was the older man's turn to scoff. "Who would you have me send?" He flung his arm out to gesture at the rest of the monastery beyond the chamber's door. "None of the rest of you have ever fought from dragonback."

"We've trained—"

"Bah, trained!" Meristofales swatted the argument away as if it were nothing. "It's my fault. I made you all so safe, it turned you soft." The Dragonmaster shook his head. "I should've listened to Rialin and lifted the order. We could've met this threat together. But now..." he trailed off, seeming to talk to himself more than Eoradon. He looked back up and met Eoradon's eye. "Besides, what if he circumvents me? What if he comes here?" He shook his head.

The prince had bristled at being called soft, but he knew in his bones the truth of the words. He shook off his pride and approached Meristofales, putting a hand on the older man's shoulder. "We can still meet it together. Let me come with you. Iaxal and I can help." *That would be something, at least,* Eoradon thought.

Meristofales seemed to consider it for a moment, and Eoradon felt hope rise in his chest, only to be dashed a moment later as the Dragonmaster shook his head. "That would just give me something else to worry about." He rose to his full height and straightened his shoulders. And for a moment, he looked every bit the fearsome First Ranger Eoradon remembered. "I will meet this foe as the living storm, and wipe them from the world." He turned and fixed his gray eyes on the new Dragonmaster of Mun-Alin. "And I *will* come home."

Dawn found Eoradon standing in the courtyard, watching as Meristofales checked and double-checked his supplies. The old Rider had outfitted himself in the armor he'd worn when he was First Ranger; dark riding leathers over a thick woolen shirt and pants tucked into leather boots, accented with black armored pauldrons and bracers. A thick, black cloak hung around his shoulders. Eoradon thought the old man would probably be nearly invisible at night, on Uanari's back.

I'm sure that's his goal, Iaxal said. Eoradon turned to where she sat on her haunches behind him. She wasn't the only one; nearly all the dragons were out to see the Dragonmaster off. Their scales leant a shimmer to the morning as the sun rose higher into the red-tinged sky.

Feordan stepped up beside Eoradon. Her dragon, Visyn, glittered gold and silver in the early-morning sunlight, and the prince was reminded why the dragon usually kept himself to the lower levels. He was almost blinding to look upon. It lent him a mystical quality, even among the Riders. The dragon of Feordan Bonestitcher was a rare sight, indeed.

"How are you feeling, Dragonmaster?" The old healer punched Eoradon on the arm playfully.

Eoradon managed a weak smile. "Would it be undignified to vomit in front of everyone as my first act?" He adjusted the steel circlet on his head, but couldn't find a comfortable position for it. Feordan noticed and smiled. "I swear it's already chafing," he said.

She gestured to Meristofales, who was clasping various Riders on the back now. "He said the same thing."

Eoradon stifled the urge to flee as Meristofales made his way over to them.

"Dragonmaster," Meristofales inclined his head and gave a wry smile.

Eoradon forced a smile and nodded in return. "Dragonmaster."

The old man put his hands on his hips and regarded the two of them. "I know where everything is in that office, and if I come back to any changes—" he shook a fist at Eoradon "—we'll see who the better fighter is."

Eoradon's smile was genuine this time as he put his hands up in feigned surrender. "Don't worry, it'll all be as you left it." He hesitated a moment, then pulled the old Dragonmaster into a tight embrace, choking back tears. "Just come back, and you can kick my ass as much as you want."

Meristofales chuckled from somewhere in his chest and slapped Eoradon on the back before sliding his eyes to Feordan. The head of the infirmary opened her mouth to speak, but Meristofales grabbed her by the waist and pulled her to him. She gave out a squeal before their lips met. Her eyes showed a moment of surprise before they closed and she melted into Meristofales's embrace.

A chorus of whoops went up from the assembled Riders, and Eoradon even sensed shock from Iaxal. He couldn't help a laugh escaping his lips.

The two of them broke apart, but stood with their foreheads touching for a long moment before Meristofales turned wordlessly away. Eoradon saw Feordan wipe a tear from her cheek before she smiled and looked back up at the assembly.

Meristofales cleared his throat and spoke as he returned to the front of the group.

"I know many of you are worried for my safety," he began, his rough voice still thick with emotion. "But I would tell you to sleep soundly. I have met foes on the battlefield before and come away safely." He let the moment settle as stillness overtook the gathered Riders. "And let us not forget the one who accompanies me."

Impossibly loud beats of wings preceded Uanari's arrival. His enormous onyx head crested the lip of the monastery, and a golden eye the size of a horse took in the crowd. He huffed, and hot air cascaded across the stones. His enormous claws bit deep into the stone of Mun-Alin as he clung to the side of the mountain, and for a moment, Eoradon felt a pang of concern that he might topple the entire thing.

Meristofales's sharp gray eyes took in the crowd as some Riders took a small step away from the incredible black dragon. The Dragonmaster smiled, then walked over and patted the beast affectionately on his great snout.

"The Guardian of Mun-Alin is not easily defeated," Meristofales said as he stepped up onto Uanari's head and strode toward the creature's back and, Eoradon assumed, the saddle that rested there. The old man turned and regarded the gathered Riders one more time, and Eoradon noticed his eyes settle on the girl, Wik. The old man nodded to her, and she returned it, eyes brimming with tears, but a hopeful smile on her face. Then, with a singular wave, Meristofales dropped over Uanari's back and out of sight. At the same time, those wings unfolded and beat once, twice, three times, forcing Riders to steady themselves or be blown off their feet. As Uanari the Black took to the sky, Meristofales could be seen on his back, hunched low against the wind.

And then they were gone, taken off around the curve of the mountain and out of sight, off to an unsure future.

Chapter Fourteen
Beneath the Mask

Apparently, there is a young warrior in the Aneving militia who is turning heads. The Duke even asked the Emperor for permission to have him trained as a Rider. But of course, he is far too old. Still, though, he must be a demon with a blade.

-Log of Dragonmaster Rykas, 874th Lord of Mun-Alin

Sen couldn't say for certain how many days had passed in the dusty cell. There were no windows, no way for light to get through. So he sat in the corner and drew circles in the gathered dirt on the floor. The slavers had taken his weapons and armor, so he wore a pair of roughspun pants that ended three inches above his ankle and a similarly-fashioned tunic that refused to fasten across his broad chest, making it more of an ill-fitting vest than a shirt.

Every so often, there would come three heavy knocks against the metal door that shielded him from the rest of the world. After the knocks, a slit in the door would bang open, and a tray of slop would slide through. Often, the guard on the other side pushed the tray through with such force, it spilled immediately. Then Sen would hear their laughter from the other side of the door as the slit closed again and left him in his dusty silence.

The first few times, Sen had tried to reach his hand through the slit and grab the guard on the other side. That had ended with his fingers smashed in the slit or smacked with a club, and he'd realized the futility of it. So now he sat in the dark, his finger dragging circles through the dust as he waited for his opportunity.

Eventually, he thought, *they'll have to do something with me. They won't let me sit here forever, now they know I can fight.* Sen was sure he'd killed at least one man the night they dragged Erick from him, and he'd broken a couple limbs besides. He expected to be forced to fight in a Kerani slave pit, or perhaps conscripted to some wealthy family as security.

And then they'll give me a weapon, and I can begin to put things right.

Sen seethed in the dark. For however much the dark and dust dulled his senses, his anger still burned white hot. So he waited.

Until one day, the knocks came on the other side of the door, but the slit never opened. Instead, the heavy metal door swung open, and three of Lady Brynne's men entered. The two on either side carried short swords, but the one in the middle was unarmed, save the stupid grin he wore on his face.

"Hello, old timer." Jund was positively radiating with glee. Sen clenched his teeth so hard, he feared they would crack. "How're you liking the...*accommodations?"*

Sen tightened his hands into fists to keep himself from launching at the fat slaver.

"A little dirty, if I'm being honest." Sen forced the words through his gritted teeth.

Jund chuckled. "I'm sure. Let's see if we can make other arrangements." He took a step forward, removing a small folded piece of paper from his belt. He unfolded it, then extended it to Sen, who took it in hands still sore from throwing punches as he was dragged to this place. He could still see Erick's terrified face vanishing into darkness, carried away by this man.

Sen forced his anger down, swallowing bile. He unfolded the paper, reading it by the light of a torch flickering in the hall outside the door. It was familiar to him, as it had been thrust into his hand by the Duke of Aneving just before he'd attempted to parlay with a dragon.

The bearer of this writ serves as an official envoy of the Province of Aneving, and may barter, negotiate, and otherwise speak on behalf of the Duke.

The official ducal signet was stamped into wax at the bottom of the page, signifying the document's legitimacy.

"So," Jund said, "do you know anything about this?"

Sen looked over the paper for another few seconds before nodding and handing it back to the slaver. "Looks like paper to me."

The backhand surprised Sen with its speed and caused his head to crack against the hard stone wall of his cell. Light flashed in Sen's vision as his head pounded and his ears rang. But the fury quickly replaced those feelings as he spun toward where Jund had been crouched down to look at him. Instead of the stocky slaver, though, Sen found himself staring down two sharpened points of steel as the guards had stepped in front of their officer. But Sen made sure his eyes never left Jund's, who was now dabbing blood from his hand with a kerchief.

"Doesn't much matter what you say," Jund said, straightening himself. "The Lady has asked to see you and have you explain in person."

Sen's brow narrowed in confusion. "She wants to see me?"

Jund sighed. "Yes, try though I might to dissuade her." He replaced the kerchief in his breast pocket and smoothed the front of his uniform. "You'll be made presentable and given an audience with Her Ladyship. At which point, *she* will decide what is to be done with you." As Jund stepped away, guards in tow, Sen shook himself and sat up straighter.

"Wait, wait—" Jund stopped in the door and turned to regard him. Sen licked his lips before continuing. "The boy—is he safe?"

Jund sighed. "He's safe. That's all you'll get from me until the Lady decides what is to be done with you." And with that, the three men turned and left, slamming and locking the door behind them.

Sen sat back, forcing himself to breathe.

Erick is safe, he thought. But doubt crept in. *There is no safety in the hands of slavers.*

Of course, Sen knew now he would have an opportunity. Lady Brynne had invited the devil to dinner. He cracked his knuckles and allowed himself a smile.

I will show them the error of their ways, he thought. *I will remind them who it is they have captured.*

It wasn't long before Sen was retrieved from his cell and marched through the winding halls of the slavers' prison—or maybe it was more of a holding area? It didn't matter. Sen didn't intend to return.

He was taken up a set of stairs leading out of the basement and the cells. His hand reflexively came up to guard his eyes as he emerged into a well-lit space. As his eyes adjusted, he saw he was in a spacious room, lushly furnished and scented with the soft perfume of flowers. It looked like a luxurious office space to Sen, at which point he realized where he was. The cells were down below, so this must be where the deals were made, where human lives were bought and sold in the name of profit.

Sen forced himself to calm as he was led through the plush offices to a luxurious wash room, dominated by a massive porcelain tub in the center of the room. Steam rolled from the surface of the water that already filled the tub. It, too, was scented with flowers. His guards released him and unshackled his hands. Sen rubbed his wrists absentmindedly as he looked around the space.

"Get in the water," came the order from one of the guards. The man was Kerani, if Sen had placed his accent correctly.

"We'll be right outside, so don't get any ideas." The other guard—an Imperial—was speaking now.

Sen nodded. "Don't worry," he said, painting an easy smile across a face he was sure had to be caked in dirt and blood. He hadn't been cleaned up before being deposited in the cell, so he was still wearing the blood of both himself and his victims. "I'll be good."

The Kerani guard grunted, but he backed away and left through the room's only door. Sen took in the space. Only one entrance, no windows, so there would be no escaping. No weapons of any kind, not even a hairbrush. *They must bring all the accouterments in with them.* His eyes rolled over the tub of steaming water. *Of course, weapons exist in places people would never expect.* He banished the thoughts. Any killing now would keep him from getting to his real prize.

He stripped, removing the threadbare slave's clothing. As he removed the shirt and pants, he realized yet again how sore his body was from the fight on the night of his imprisonment. He knew for sure one of his ribs was broken. A healer had seen him after the fight, but it had been determined his injuries were not life threatening, and thus not worth the trouble or the cost of his services.

Gingerly, Sen lowered himself into the steaming tub, letting the hot water come up to his neck. He was a big man, but the tub was enormous, so he was surprisingly comfortable. He hated himself for his comfort.

How many are still down there? he wondered. *Still knee-deep in shit and blood, waiting for salvation that won't come?* His anger rolled up from his stomach and he had to stamp it down forcibly by submerging his head in the water and holding his breath. When he emerged a moment later, he was surprised to find two young women, the oldest having seen maybe eighteen winters. They stood in front of the tub, one holding a tray full of the instruments of bathing; soap, sponge, perfume, razor. The other held a stack of men's clothes that appeared far too fine to Sen's eyes.

Sen sank further below the water as the two girls went to work. They never spoke to him, but communicated fervently with each other in Kerani. He didn't speak the language, so they mostly pointed to where he needed to be. After a stretch of time that felt far too long, Sen's head was shaved close, his beard was trimmed from a bushy mess to a short, regal length, and the grime was washed from his body. They gave both his body and the stack of clothes a light spray of perfume before making their exit through the room's only door.

Sen sighed, loath to leave the warm bath, and climbed free. They had even manicured his finger and toenails, leaving his hands feeling softer than they had in his life, so far as he could remember. He dressed himself in the fine silken doublet and pants, tucked into plush leather boots. Finally, he fastened the cloak around his neck—black silk, linked in the front by a gold chain. When he regarded his reflection in the mirror, Sen didn't see himself. He looked like a dandy of the court, the sort of sycophant he'd grown to hate in his time at Aneving Keep.

She wants me to look fine for her guests, he thought. *But she will see soon enough what so many others have already learned; fine clothes may look pretty, but they do a shit job hiding the monster who wears them.*

Sen knocked on the heavy wooden door, and it swung open. The two guards took him by the arms, one on each side, and led him from the bath chamber. He noticed they didn't replace his irons.

The guards led him back through the office space, out a door made of glass, and into the street outside. Sen was surprised to find a coach, led by a striking black horse, waiting for him with the door open.

"Sir," said the footman, gesturing to the interior of the carriage with a gloved hand. The guards gave Sen little choice, hoisting him up into the vehicle. The Imperial guard climbed in after him and sat on a maroon, pillowed bench opposite Sen. The Kerani guard moved to the front of the coach and, Sen assumed, sat next to the driver. The footman closed the door, and within a moment, they were off, rolling through the streets of Kanavar like a fine gentleman taking a turn about the city.

Sitting in the chariot, Sen's mind reeled. Kanavar had gone from an out of the way trading post to a center of industry and trade in less than thirty years. How had this been done? Surely the money from slaving wasn't this good. The city rivaled even the wonders of Ir-Anan, a city that had stood for thousands of years, if the histories were to be believed.

Sen shook his head slightly, refocusing himself. His heart was pounding, and he felt the familiar touch of fear crawling up his back as the chariot rolled through the city. He looked up to find the guard's eyes on him, brow furrowed.

"Yes?" Sen asked, sighing.

The guard grunted, then turned away, looking out the window where Sen noticed the sun was setting, emblazoning the sky and city with reds and purples.

Sen laid his head back against the headrest and closed his eyes, and soon enough, the chariot came to a stop. The door swung open, revealing the footman, who again gestured with a gloved hand to Sen. He climbed out first, fighting his instinct and letting the guard see his exposed back.

They need to believe it, he reminded himself. This was a play, and he was merely an actor. Soon enough, Sen would need to fall away, and another, more terrible man take his place. *But not yet.*

As Sen set his foot down on cobbled stone, instead of dust or dirt, he looked up and nearly gasped. The palace was *enormous*, large enough to rival any Kerani king, second only to the Imperial Palace in Ir-Anan. Though that throne sat vacant. *This one* was very much occupied, and the woman sitting on it held the key to Sen and Erick's freedom.

She'll never give it willingly, Sen thought. *Don't fall for her lies. Don't play her game. Remind her of her sins.*

Sen, still flanked by guards, breathed deep as he ascended the staircase, to the massive ornately carved wooden doors, which stood open to the warm night air. His boots made a *click-clack* sound as he proceeded from the cobblestone onto the tiled floor of the palace. His guards led him to another massive, carved wooden door. On the other side, Sen could hear the sounds of revelry.

A ball, he thought in disgust. *She throws parties while children starve in those cells*. His fists clenched and he forced them to open, an action he found palpably difficult. *I will take nothing this snake gives,* he thought. *I will wrench it from her cold fingers*.

He closed his eyes and breathed deep as his guards placed their hands on the doors and pushed them open. His eyes opened as he let the mask fall away, and the real man emerged.

He stepped through the door to the great hall beyond.

Lady Brynne de Montilliard giggled as she separated from her dance partner. The music slowly faded, the dancers gave each other short bows—well, all except for Brynne, of course—and the great hall devolved into a general din of chit chat again.

Her dance partner, Baron Wilhelm Serengard, was a well-to-do man in his late forties. By all accounts, he'd been a damn good fighter in his younger days, but now his paunch overtook the sword belt, upon which he wore a ceremonial saber. He'd apparently been gifted the blade from the Emperor of Ir-Anan himself for bravery in the field. Of course, the Emperor was long-dead, and now the strapping young man who'd vanquished the enemies of the Empire was wiping sweat from his forehead and excusing himself to retrieve a cup of wine after a single medium-tempo dance.

"Of course, Baron Wilhelm." Brynne flashed the fat, old man a practiced, toothy smile as he retreated. She had to forcibly stop herself from harumphing at the lack of eligible men in attendance tonight.

Some ball, she thought. *Looks like I'll be sleeping alone.* Her eyes fell on a young man of seemingly good stock, holding a serving tray. He was one of the new servants, brought in by Tovin's company. She snatched a goblet of dull red wine from a passing tray and eyed the man up and down. He was still very green—fighting to keep his hands from shaking. She noticed the scars still present on his wrist, the makeup applied to his face to cover bruises. She sighed. *He'll do, I suppose.* She was attempting to get the attention of Guard Captain Ren when the doors to the hall slid open. As she turned to see who the newcomer was, a voice spoke by her ear, the breath hot on her neck, causing a tingle she had to suppress.

"This is the slave who had the writ from Aneving, my Lady." The voice was high and singsong, meaning it had to belong to Byron, the court eunuch.

Brynne turned to the eunuch and nodded, trying not to look at his hairless face for too long.

"Shall I move him to a private chamber?" Byron asked, not seeming to care either way.

Brynne considered it, then shook her head. "No, this party is too dull as it is. I'll meet with him here, from a position of power." Byron nodded and silently reached up to adjust her tiara before moving away to create some space for them. Within a moment, the band had stopped the dancing tune they were playing, and shifted to a more ambient piece, better for background noise.

As she ascended the steps to the dais where her throne sat and the dance floor began to thin of people, Brynne finally got a good look at the man they'd brought to her.

He was tall and broad-shouldered, and he carried himself confidently, an ease to his steps that showed Brynne he was almost certainly lighter on his feet than people would think. He was older than she'd expected; his head was shaved bald, and his short gray beard cut to a refined point, squaring a jaw she expected didn't need much help. He was dressed in finery, as she'd requested, but his eyes made her breath catch; piercing blue, like staring into the clearest sapphire she'd ever seen. As she watched, he came to a stop ten paces from the dais and an easy smile split his beard. He bowed, though not as low as he should've.

"Good evening, my Lady." His voice was deep and rough, like stones tumbling down a mountainside.

Brynne cleared her throat. "You may rise," she said in her best royal affect. Even after all these years, the accent was the hardest part of pretending to be someone of means. The big man returned to his full height, the dark cloak around his shoulders flourishing slightly. Before he could speak, Brynne plowed forward, suddenly aware of all the eyes watching this conversation. The rest of the hall had gone eerily silent. "My men tell me you carry a writ, designating you as an envoy for the Duke of Aneving."

"Aye, my Lady," he said, his eyes never leaving hers.

Brynne cleared her throat. "Why?"

He shrugged. "The Duke of Aneving gave it to me because he wanted me to serve as his envoy." A chuckle erupted somewhere in the hall and was stifled, presumably by an elbow to the perpetrator's ribs.

Brynne smiled. "I would assume he entrusted you with a task of some sort?"

The big imperial smiled again, that easygoing, disarming smile. "You assume correctly."

"And what was it?"

"Private." No chuckle this time.

Brynne swallowed the bile she felt rising. "Good sir, I have no doubt of your honor, but—"

"Now *that* is a bold assumption," he cut her off.

"I'm sorry?" Brynne was fighting to keep control now, the instincts she'd sharpened on the streets of Tau Keran screaming at her to have this man's head lopped off before he could speak again. That was fine for a Kerani street rat; not so much for Lady Brynne of Kanavar. "Are you not honorable, Sir..."

"No 'Sir,'" he said, moving his shoulders ever so slightly and clasping his hands in front of him.

Brynne sighed. "Fine, then. What is your name?"

"Sen."

Commoner names, Brynne thought with a huff. "Fine then, *Sen—"*

"Senran."

Brynne's eyes snapped up to the man's blue pools as the words caught in her throat. "Senran?" she coughed out. *No, no, no.*

Not possible. Her mind was reeling. *It can't be.*

The big bald man smiled again.

"Senran *Vallos.*"

The room exploded with sound. The collective gasp of the gathered guests didn't come close to the reactions of the soldiers and guards lining the walls, as hands reached for swords, but curiously did not draw them.

Brynne couldn't speak. Her breath wouldn't come, her heart pounding on the inside of her chest. *No no no no no.*

"Senran Vallos," she finally squeaked, "is dead. He died at Aneving."

Vallos's smile never moved as he took a step toward the dais. "Unfortunately for us both, my Lady, he did not." He stopped five strides short of the dais' first step. Brynne cringed back from him, then caught herself and smoothed her skirts.

Brynne's eyes moved to her guards, still standing against the walls lining the room. "A fortune to whichever one of you kills this man!" She called out, expecting the men to rush forward. No one did.

Vallos turned his back on Brynne and faced the crowded hall, his arms spreading wide.

"Aye, boys—which of you wants to take your shot at old Vallos?" One soldier—a new recruit, aged no more than seventeen summers—stepped forward, hand falling to the hilt of his sword. Before he could draw the blade, a greybearded veteran standing next to the boy yanked him back by the collar of his gambeson. Vallos nodded. "Wise choice." He turned back to Brynne, his smile never having moved and let his arms drop, again clasping his hands in front of him. "Well, you're *very* popular," he chuckled.

Brynne realized her hand was shaking and wrapped it in the material of her skirts. "Will none of you fight for your Lady? Is my guard full of cowards?"

"Don't be so hard on them," Vallos said with a shrug. "Every man in this room was told stories of me when they were children; told I'd come and take them away if they didn't listen, or do their chores, or what have you." Vallos's tone dropped. He was deathly quiet now, his smile fading to a menacing grin. "Then they grew up, became enlisted men, and learned the truth." He took a slow step forward. "They were not stories. There is no exaggeration." Another step.

"I am Senran Vallos."

Another step.

"The First Blade of Aneving."

Another step. Brynne couldn't breathe.

"Knife in the dark."

His booted foot landed on the bottom step of the dais. Brynne was against the wall. No one was coming. She felt her chest constrict as she struggled to breathe. Those horrible blue eyes never moved from her, and she couldn't look away.

"Tip of the spear."

He was one step away now, so close she could smell the perfume he'd been given. Vallos came to a stop not a foot away from her.

"And I have been given a sacred task by *our* Duke, may he dine with the Six."

Brynne waited a moment. She wasn't dead. His hands had never moved, still clasped in front of him. His eyes bore through her, and she feared he could see her thoughts, know all of her mind.

You're being foolish, she chided herself. *He's just a man.* She straightened, smoothed her skirts. Maybe she could still get out of this alive.

"Surely, we can come to an amicable agreement that sees you on your way." She should've felt ashamed, letting one old man dictate terms to her in her own throne room, but this was not the time to worry about that, not with the most dangerous man on the continent a foot away from her.

Vallos's smile returned as he stepped away from Brynne and leaned against the throne. "I daresay we can, my Lady." He sat on the throne and crossed his legs, forcing her to move around in front of him to continue speaking.

Brynne forced herself to keep her composure, keep her voice steady as she spoke. "What do you need?"

Vallos cleared his throat. "I need a wagon, loaded with enough supplies for a two week journey, along with two fresh horses —strong ones, I don't want them collapsing a day out of the city for your people to ride me down." His eyes darkened and Brynne thought for a moment he might kill her anyway. "And the boy," he said, his voice so low she had to strain to hear him.

"Boy?" she asked in genuine confusion. "What boy?"

Vallos raised his chin to her. "My grandson. He was with me when I was captured by your men. Oh!" Vallos snapped his fingers as he exploded to his feet, much faster than a man his age or size should've been capable of. He pointed out into the crowd, to a stocky man trying to slide unnoticed through a side exit. "And that fat fucker. He comes, too."

"Done." Brynne didn't even need to consider it. *Give him whatever he wants, get him out of the city, and then we can deal with him somehow.*

Vallos's eyes rolled back to her. "We will leave as soon as the wagon is ready. When we're three days from the city, *you* will be free to return."

Brynne was nodding along until she realized what he'd said. "Wait, what?" she nearly squeaked. "*I'm* to come with you?" Fear gripped her heart again.

Vallos smiled again. "Of course. How stupid do you think I am, Lady Brynne? You'll serve as assurance I won't be pursued."

Brynne huffed as her frustration finally boiled over. She paced away from Vallos. "So you come in here, take my men, my provisions, and now my dignity? Who do you—"

He rose and stepped toward her, so close she could see his pores. Her breath caught as she realized her mistake.

"Yes," he seethed, his smile long gone. "I will take your men, and your provisions, *and your fucking dignity*. And you will thank me, for I have not taken your life." He bit off the words as he spoke, as if trying to contain himself, as if the effort of not killing her then and there was so strenuous it was causing him pain.

No one spoke for a long moment. Finally, Brynne's breath returned to her.

"Yes," she said in a quavering voice. "Of course."

Vallos nodded and returned to the throne.

"Be quick about it, Lady Brynne," he said, nonchalant. "The sooner you ready my wagon, the sooner this is over."

She signaled Byron to make preparations, then stood awkwardly by her own throne as the gathered nobles of Kanavar looked at her. She noticed there was no fear in their eyes—they knew Vallos would be satisfied. No, they looked *hungry*. And their collective gaze was fixed squarely on her.

As the moments dragged by, Sen found it harder and harder to keep himself going. He'd spent a long time living in relative anonymity, the deeds of Senran Vallos resigned to the whims of history; bringing him back to life had been more taxing than Sen had expected.

Though he had to admit, part of him enjoyed it. It had been a long time since he'd seen fear like that spread through a room at the mention of his name.

The great hall was deathly still as Sen sat on Lady Brynne's throne, one leg draped haphazardly across the other. The minutes seemed to creep by.

What is taking so long? Sen wondered in his mind. This act wouldn't hold forever, and he didn't need the guards around the room to suddenly remember their courage.

The large doors at the far end of the hall banged open, and Sen let himself exhale a bit. Erick's eyes met his and a broad grin split the boy's face.

"Sen!" He screamed, and took off toward the old man in a sprint. He was dressed finely, Sen noticed.

They must have had him working as a serving boy, Sen thought. But that thought, and all others, abandoned him as he rose and caught the boy in a tight embrace.

"I was so scared," the boy whimpered, tears falling down his face and wetting Sen's shirt. "I thought you were–"

"I'm not." Sen tried to cut through the boy's fear, but didn't think he succeeded. Still, Erick clung to him.

"Do we have to stay here?" Erick whispered.

Sen took him by the shoulders and locked eyes with the boy. "No," he said. "They're readying a wagon for us, and we'll be on our way."

Erick nodded and wiped his tears away. Sen took him in his arms again and cradled him.

"Sir." Sen searched the crowd for who was speaking to him and eventually landed on a baldheaded, smooth-skinned man of an age he couldn't decipher. "Your wagon is ready."

Sen scooped up Erick, then turned to Lady Brynne. He fixed her with that practiced smile that always seemed to unease people. "My Lady." He held an arm out, indicating he wanted her to lead. She nodded sadly, then did as instructed.

The strange group proceeded through the palatial halls until they emerged at what looked to be a servants' loading area. There, Sen saw a fully stocked wagon with two horses. A quick check of the provisions showed it was all real, and there were no dummy boxes. He nodded to himself.

"Also," the eunuch spoke in that singsong voice from the front of the wagon. Sen stepped around to where he stood and found his heavily powdered perfumed hands holding out Sen's longsword and bow, along with his knives and other various accouterments. "I apologize—it took me longer to locate your belongings than I thought. But I hope you'll find these to be sufficiently undamaged."

Sen took the bundle of weaponry and tossed it up into the front of the wagon. "If they still kill, they're as good as new." Then he smacked the Eunuch on the arm. "Appreciate it, No-Nuts." To the man's credit, he did not shrink from the touch or the quip, but only bowed his head slightly.

"I live to serve."

Sen helped Erick up into the wagon and situated him among the various foodstuffs and supplies. He eventually got him into a comfortable-enough little nook with a blanket and pillow, and the boy quickly settled in. He found Lady Brynne already sitting in the front of the wagon, hands in her lap.

"There is a change of clothes for My Lady in the supplies," the eunuch said. "For the ride back."

Sen nodded at that.

"There's still one thing missing, though." Sen turned his gaze to the hairless man. "Jund."

The eunuch smiled again, and this one looked genuine. "I took the liberty of providing him special quarters."

Sen lifted an eyebrow as two guards rolled a small, wheeled cage out of the palace. Inside the cramped space sat Jund, bloodied and bruised, feet dangling out of the cage between the bars. Sen couldn't stop the laugh that escaped as he took in the slaver.

"Well, isn't this grand." Sen knelt down by the former officer. "I told you, slavers often end up in their own cages."

"Fuck you." Jund spat through the bars of his cage at Sen's feet.

Sen smiled as he strode away from the man. His rolling cage was hooked to the back of the wagon. Sen climbed into the driver's seat and took the reins.

"She'll be back in a week, if she's any use on a horse."

"Of course," said the eunuch.

"I'm not to be followed, or else I kill her and dump the body beneath the horses' hooves." Sen gave the man a hard stare.

He smiled. "Of course."

Sen couldn't pinpoint why the man's smile unsettled him, but he snapped the reins anyway, and the horses took off at a trot. They passed the city's western gate unmolested, though guards watched them all the way. Word would spread soon, Sen knew. Lady Brynne's time as the ruler of Kanavar might very well be over when she returned to the city. As if she could read his thoughts, the woman spoke.

"You've ruined me," she said, choking back tears. "They'll never have me back."

"You built that city on the backs of slaves," Sen spat. "Whatever station you achieved there was from *their* work, not yours."

She barked a humorless laugh. "Easy for you to say. You've never built anything." She turned to face him. "All you've ever done is kill and burn. You have no idea what it took to wrangle that place into submission. The slaves are the price I paid to build a piece of civilization, a bridge from Kerana to the Empire."

Sen didn't respond. Her words held more truth than he wanted to admit. He'd never built anything, and any time he'd tried, it had been taken from him. None of that excused her actions, but it wasn't his job to convince her. His place was at Ir-Anan now.

As they crested the first hill along the western road, a group of torches shone in front of the wagon.

"Oh, shit." Brynne groaned.

Sen brought the wagon to a stop as they entered the ring of torchlight. He could see now—eight men, all armed and armored. The one in the front wore a wide-brimmed hat, a black feather tucked into the hat's band. Heat flared in Sen's stomach. He knew this man. He'd seen him speaking to Jund by the cook fire, just before the slaver had turned on him.

Anger bubbled in Sen's veins as the captain stepped into the light.

"My friends," the man began. He had a pompous air, as if he always expected the undivided attention of everyone around him. "I am Trajar Sylvano, Captain under Lady Brynne of Kanavar." He still wore that wide-brimmed hat on his head, but he removed it now to sweep it in front of himself as he bowed far too deeply. He replaced it on his head and drew the saber at his side. It was a fine blade, and shone in the torchlight. A slight curve ran down the blade, built for finding the points between armor, rather than cleaving through it.

Sen couldn't help but notice that Sylvano's boots looked freshly polished, his uniform pressed. Not a stitch was out of place.

"Sylvano, stop this," Brynne called out to him. "Let us pass, and I will return in a week. Do you know who this is?" She glanced at Sen, her eyes still full of trepidation.

"Aye, my Lady," Sylvano replied, one gloved hand tracing his mustache and goatee. "This is the famed Senran Vallos." A devilish grin spread across his face, exposing a mouth of glimmering white teeth. "But I think he looks like an old man, long past his prime."

Sen laughed. "You're not wrong, Captain." He looked at the reins in his hand, and thought for a moment about just plowing through the group. But no, that was too risky to Erick, who was probably asleep by now. Sen let the reins fall and took his sheathed longsword in hand. Before he jumped down, he turned to Brynne. "If you do anything—*anything*—to jeopardize mine or the boy's lives, ensure you kill me. Because if you don't," he paused to leer at her. "You'll die slowly."

As Sen jumped down from the wagon and approached the captain, the other gathered guards drew their swords. Sen regarded them, then turned his gaze back to Sylvano.

"I've no quarrel with your men," he said. "You and me, single combat. I win, they let us pass."

Sylvano barely thought a moment before agreeing. "You heard him," he told his men. "If he wins, you stand aside." Then he turned back to Sen, grinning. "Something tells me it won't matter."

Sen nodded, then drew his sword. It came ringing from the scabbard, which he tossed away. After a couple practice swipes, he determined it was still perfectly weighted and sharpened. He bounced on his heels, feeling his muscles straining from his time in the cells. But he also felt his body crying out for action. It had been too long since he'd had a good duel. All this skulking about, killing people from behind or in ambushes—it was fine, when necessary. But Sen still preferred to look people in the eye when he fought them. That was his one concession to honor.

Across from him, Sylvano was saying a prayer to the Six. When he finished, he settled into a fighting stance, crouched with his left arm behind him and right elbow bent into his ribs. His sword was held in what looked to Sen like a loose grip. The captain nodded, beginning the fight.

Sen didn't move. Sylvano bounced on the balls of his feet, clearly anticipating him to attack first. But Sen was content to wait. He stood straight, tip of his sword pointing down. After a few seconds, Sylvano grunted.

"Damn cur," he snarled. "If that's how you want it—" He came at Sen midsentence with a thrust aimed at his stomach. Sen whipped his sword up and deflected the strike with a ringing of steel. As the captain tipped ever so slightly off-balance, he slid inside Sylvano's reach and shoved the tip of the blade up through the man's belly, into his chest. A gasp escaped his lips, his eyes going wide with fear and realization.

"Fucking slaver," Sen seethed the words in Sylvano's stunned face, then ripped the blade free, spraying blood on the ground. The captain stumbled back, then dropped to his knees, ornate sword forgotten in the dust, hands going to his rapidly emptying midsection. Sen strode forward and kicked Sylvano in the face, sending him sprawling to his back with a pained grunt. Then he strode easily around to the man's head and plunged the sword through his eye. He felt the back of Sylvano's skull give way as the sword stabbed into the dirt beneath him.

Sen let himself breathe a moment, then ripped the blade free and strode back to the wagon, where he climbed up and took the reins back in his hands, handing the sword, still dripping with gore, to Brynne. She took the sword, her skin even more pale than usual, but managed not to say anything.

In stunned silence, the remainder of Sylvano's men parted in the middle and allowed Sen passage. He made sure to drive the horses directly over the captain's body.

Chapter Fifteen

The Hunt

There is so much I wish I'd done differently.

-Log of Dragonmaster Meristofales, 875th Lord of Mun-Alin

Meristofales stoked the meager fire he'd built and looked out at the expanse of green fields awash in moonlight. He'd settled onto a rocky outcropping overlooking the lush grass fields of the endless plains, ostensibly because it put his back to a mountain and allowed him long sightlines in all directions. That was half-true. It *was* a strategically advantageous position, but in truth, Meristofales couldn't stop looking at the ocean of waving grass.

It's been too long, he thought. He'd spent decades cooped up in Mun-Alin, fearful of what was coming for them, convinced he'd made the best choice he could. But cowardice hadn't saved them; it had just killed them more slowly. A blade of steel cuts flesh, but the blade of time rends souls. And Meristofales had let his fear of one run him straight into the other.

The old Dragonmaster sighed and tossed a pebble off the cliff face, listening as it clattered down the rocks and disappeared below. In the distance, he could make out the edge of the Great Eastern Forest, which made up the majority of Aneving Province. They would arrive at Aneving Keep early in the morning, and the search for this rogue Rider would begin in earnest.

A trill of fear and excitement ran down Meristofales's spine. He shook his head to clear it.

No point in fear, he thought. *It's why we're out here, after all.*

Fear rarely has a point, Uanari rumbled. Meristofales startled at the dragon's voice.

I thought you were asleep, he said.

Uanari thrummed, shaking the ground from his perch higher up the cliffs. *I know.*

Meristofales smiled to himself. As much as everyone feared the enormous dragon, he knew a softer side to Uanari; a playful side, like all dragons seemed to have. Of course, most dragons weren't the size of buildings and pure black. The creature *looked* evil, to be sure. Meristofales had always liked it that way, though. If people thought the dragon was a cruel beast, they usually gave him the same deference.

The Dragonmaster settled back, laying his aging head on his rolled up pack and gazing up at the stars.

Get some rest, he said. *Tomorrow could be a big day.*

The next day proved more uneventful than Meristofales had hoped, though. They made it to Aneving Keep, but found little beyond the death and decay Rialin had already described. They'd waited for some time, hoping their opponent might make it easy on them, but there was no such luck.

The next few days were spent in search of the army that had sacked Aneving. Meristofales found it odd that they'd not struck anywhere else in the intervening weeks. But of course, he quickly found that wasn't the case.

The army had cut a river of dirt from Aneving, burning farms and villages as they moved north and west. They were slow, as are most armies, but it was clear they were far from sated with one victory. From what Meristofales had gathered from the land around Aneving Keep, they'd come from the east, on the other side of the forest, and continued west.

Meloran, Meristofales thought as he adjusted his flight mask to be tighter to his face.

Uanari waited a moment before responding as they banked north, skirting a thunderstorm. The winds from the storm would've made it hard for a younger dragon to navigate, but Uanari had plenty of experience handling storms.

The Vicar has finally made a move, he finally said. *Meloran has coveted the Empire for hundreds of years. Now, with the throne vacant and the region constantly scuffling amongst themselves,* does *seem the perfect opportunity.*

Hmmmm, Meristofales fiddled with the horn of his saddle as he thought. *But how would Dyraxian fit into Meloran's schemes? And who is this Rider? Is it possible we're wrong about the dragon? Maybe Meloran got an egg somehow. Produced their own Rider.*

Perhaps, Uanari said, though Meristofales sensed doubt in

his words. *But, Meristofales, you know what this could be.*

Meristofales sighed. *I know. But we cannot ignore Meloran's move to outright war when they've been content to remain in their borders and conduct operations from the shadows until now.* He lowered himself closer to Uanari as the dragon dropped below the blanket of clouds. Meristofales leaned over to look below them. Of course, more evidence of the army's movement. Here, they'd plundered a small city and left it burning. *This is not Meloran's way.*

No, Uanari rumbled, anger flashing through the bond as he dropped lower to survey the devastation. *But we know whose way it is.*

Meristofales sat with the truth of Uanari's words. Of course he knew who operated this way, provoking nations to war and reaping the benefits. But that road held a peril far greater even than one rogue Rider. He shook his head to clear it.

Let's focus on finding the Rider. Then we can plan our next move.

A couple more days following the army's trail eventually proved fruitful.

Uanari had been smelling the smoke for at least two hours when Meristofales finally spotted the plume. They dropped low, beneath the clouds, and saw an open field, dotted with destroyed siege equipment, crushed and mangled bodies beneath massive hunks of stone. At the end of the path of destruction sat the city of Iannivar, the Empire's largest port, situated midway around the ring of the Bay of Ir-Anan.

The city was in flames, massive plumes of smoke rising into

the clouds from behind its walls. Like Aneving, Iannivar had been cracked like an egg from the top, fire reigned down on the city from the sky. They had put up a good fight, if the killing field was any indication, but there were few weapons known to man that could stop a fully-grown dragon. And the few ballistae adorning the walls, now little more than melted slag, had been targeted first, by the looks of it.

Meristofales wrapped his cloak over his nose and mouth, shielding him from the bitter smoke as they descended. He noticed a clump of Melorani soldiers down on the battlefield, presumably looting corpses, and anger roiled his guts. His fingers flexed instinctively as he drew on his power.

Let's draw him out. He need not explain further, as Uanari evidently felt his revulsion across the bond. The dragon banked hard, dropping from the sky like a meteor. Just before impacting the ground, he unfurled his enormous wings, blotting out the sun as Meristofales leapt from the dragon's back and landed in front of the soldiers. Uanari dropped to the ground harder than was probably necessary, shaking the very dirt under their feet.

Meristofales could picture it from their point of view: his cloak billowing behind him, outlined by the angry red sun as it set over the water of the bay, the smoke in the air, swirling from the beating of the monstrous dragon's wings. He knew, to these men, he was more than a man, or even a Dragon Rider.

He was an apocalypse given form.

A circle of soldiers was closing in around Meristofales. The Dragonmaster didn't miss the nervous glances they threw toward one another as they approached.

"State your business!" one of them was brave enough to call

out.

Meristofales stretched his neck one way, then the other, feeling the cracks and pops within. The soldiers watched him warily as the air grew thick with moisture. Meristofales could feel the power roiling in his veins, calling out to be unleashed.

One of the soldiers took a step forward.

He extended his hands to either side as he drew from his reserve of power and prayed it would respond. He smiled as he felt the familiar strength fill him, the very essence of the world bending beneath his will.

Lightning crackled across his arm as a gale formed in the palm of his left hand. The fingers of his right hand wrapped around the hilt of his enormous eight-foot sword, which floated down from the saddle on Uanari's back. The circle of soldiers around him backed five steps away instinctively.

It would not be far enough.

Meristofales extended his left hand and sent a blast of wind toward half of the group, launching them through the air to land in a broken heap. One man found his courage and took a step toward him, axe raised. But The Living Storm was awake now, and a flick of his index finger arced lightning through the man's skull, dropping him to the ground as the smell of cooking meat joined the acrid odor of smoke to linger in the air.

Three of the men on his right side tried to attack at the same time. He whirled, the Rider blade light as a feather in his grasp, slicing the first one across the middle, separating his legs from the rest of his body in a spout of blood, painting the ground red. Using his momentum, he spun fully around and thrust the huge blade forward, skewering the next attacker straight through the chest. The third man had slowed his charge as he met Meristofales's eyes. The Dragonmaster thought he could actually *see* the moment the fear overtook the man as he turned and ran. Spinning again and taking the sword in a two-handed grip, he whipped it around and flung the body of the soldier, still skewered on its length. The corpse spun over and over in the air, crashing into the fleeing man and bowling him over.

Meristofales released the sword, sending it off at speed with his telekinetic link, catching the man just as he rose to his knees, stabbing straight through his head and pinning him to the ground.

And then he was alone on the battlefield, all the other combatants choosing to run for the safety of the walls.

And what safety will they provide? Meristofales seethed in his mind as he watched them run like rats from a sinking ship. *What quarter did you give the people of Iannivar when they hid behind their walls?* He took a step toward the city.

Meristofales, Uanari's voice was thunder in his mind. *Allow me.* With two massive beats of his wings, Uanari was airborne, flying toward Iannivar. Meristofales watched as the dragon's jaw opened. There was an audible intake of air as Uanari breathed deep. Sparks crackled along his body, deep orange and red contrasting brightly with his black scales. Then, he erupted.

A spout of flame as thick as three men across exploded from Uanari's maw. The fire impacted the ground with the force of a crashing wave. It was concussive, the very air being burned as the fleeing men unfortunate enough to be caught were instantly incinerated. Meristofales saw them, not even with enough time to cry out before they exploded, their blood and organs like water left too long on a stove. It was gruesome, but he found he couldn't look away. The world may have forgotten the fury of dragons, but anyone who saw Iannivar would always remember.

Uanari made two strafing runs, dousing the blood-soaked killing field in flames. As the massive dragon settled back to the ground by Meristofales, he thrummed happily.

It has been too long since we fought for something, Uanari said.

Meristofales nodded, bidding his blade to return to its scabbard, fastened to the saddle on Uanari's back. He had released the power of the storm, and he felt like he'd aged twenty years in a moment. The lure of power is seductive, he knew. But he'd forgotten how strong a pull it could have.

What now? the dragon asked, lying his gargantuan head on his forelegs and staring at Meristofales with a massive yellow eye.

Meristofales crossed his arms and leaned against Uanari's bulk.

Now, he said, scratching absently at his partner's jaw. *We wait.*

It didn't take long. The sun had barely sunk below the water of the bay, leaving the flames of the still-burning city to light the sky. A glint of firelight in the sky caught Meristofales's attention.

Wake up, he called to Uanari. *I think he's here.* The dragon rumbled, shaking himself to wakefulness.

Sure enough, the glint drew closer as they dropped toward the ground, and Meristofales was able to pick out more details. The dragon was huge, the closest he'd ever seen in size to Uanari. Silver scales accented with red patterns throughout shone bright in the firelight as the monster's huge body writhed through the sky. This dragon was long, easily over fifty feet from nose to tail, making it longer than Uanari by ten feet at least. But the black dragon made up for that in sheer bulk. Meristofales squinted as they drew closer, trying to make out the dragon's face. An impossibly wide mouth, as broad as its head was long, split into a snarling grin beneath eyes of stark red and yellow. The Dragonmaster suppressed a shiver and looked at the Rider.

He wore full plate armor, as Rialin had described. A massive shock of blue fabric made up his cloak, twisting off into the darkness as they flew. Meristofales was surprised to see no saddle. Riding a dragon without a saddle was more than most could handle, but this man sat astride that behemoth as easily as if he were riding a docile pony.

Something isn't right here, he said to Uanari. The dragon thrummed in agreement, but said nothing.

The impossible Rider and dragon came to a hovering stop about twenty feet above Meristofales and Uanari. As the monster beat its wings, the Rider stood and walked to the crown of the dragon's head to speak down to them.

"Hello, *Dragonmaster*." The Rider spoke evenly, not shouting, but easily heard, even with their distance and the beating of wings. The man's voice was like rock sliding against metal; it almost hurt Meristofale's ears, but he stopped himself from flinching, with some effort.

"I heard you were looking for me," Meristofales said. "Thought I'd save you the trouble."

The Rider laughed, and the sound nearly made Meristofales retch. "I see that. But killing a few soldiers is a far cry from ending *me*."

Meristofales shrugged. "Still figured I ought to give it a try."

A beat passed in silence.

Be ready to pursue them, Meristofales warned Uanari.

"If it's all the same to you," the Rider said, finally breaking the silence. "I think we'd prefer to continue the war effort." And with that, the dragon's wings beat again and they took to the sky at speed.

Meristofales cursed, climbing onto Uanari's back as fast as he could. He was still making his way to the saddle when Uanari's wings unfurled and beat down without hesitation, sending them airborne.

They climbed into the darkening sky, the burning city falling away below them as they crested the clouds and confronted an ocean of stars, the dragon and Rider silhouetted against the carpet made of a million shimmering points of light.

The dragon, Uanari said in Meristofales's mind. *There's no doubt: it's definitely Dyraxian.*

Meristofale's skin crawled at the mention of the ancient dragon. *How is he here now?* he asked.

Unease flashed through the bond before Uanari spoke again.

I do not know. It shouldn't be possible, and yet... he trailed off. Nothing more need be said. Meristofales leaned closer to Uanari, bending over the saddle horn as he pulled his flight mask on.

It doesn't matter, he said. *He's here. We have to kill them.* Agreement flashed from Uanari, along with resolve, and Meristofales knew they were together on the issue. Not that it was in doubt. They'd been in lockstep since they bonded.

Meristofales allowed himself a smile at the thought of Uanari as a hatchling, able to be held in his arms. It was so long ago now.

Up ahead, Dyraxian banked hard to the south, heading back toward land. Uanari followed. The rogue pair had to know they had little chance of running far enough away that Meristofales would not pursue. And given Dyraxian's size, there was even less chance one of the two dragons would outlast the other.

Where are you going? Meristofales thought.

His answer came within a half-hour. Dyraxian dropped beneath the clouds and Uanari followed. As they dropped below the cloud cover, Meristofales was surprised to find himself staring at a volcanic emergence. And suddenly, as his stomach dropped, he knew *exactly* where he was.

The three volcanoes were clustered together like fingers on a massive hand pushing through the dirt. Smoke billowed from their open mouths, compounded by burping gas, spouting arcs of lava hundreds of feet into the air. The rotten stench of sulfur hung thick in the air, stinging Meristofales's nose every time he breathed, threatening to force his stomach to empty. At the base of the volcanoes, Meristofales could make out the detritus of the villages, eviscerated during the emergence, and his stomach turned for a reason unrelated to the sulfuric air.

Dyraxian and his Rider banked low and close to the volcanoes, daring Uanari and Meristofales to follow them into the plume of pyroclastic ash. Caution flashed across the bond; no time for words. But in the fires of those mountains, Meristofales saw not just the lava and ash and flames of the volcanoes; he saw Aneving, shattered and ruined. He saw Iannivar, its walls turned to prison bars as its people cooked in their homes. He saw Ir-Anan and the monastery, blasted away to nothing as Dyraxian laughed and his Rider finished what he started. He saw the blade pierce Rialin's chest. Anger roiled in his stomach. Reflexively, he reached for his well of power and found it, too, rolling like boiling water, and so he sent his feelings across the bond, along with one word.

Pursue.

And Uanari did. Meristofales again tied his cloak over his mouth and nose, shielding himself from the smoke, for all the good it did. It was overwhelming, like moving through carpet. It burned his throat and eyes, despite the flight mask. They followed Dyraxian as the dragon banked, dropped, climbed, even managing to keep up as the beast corkscrewed and flipped underneath them, only to reemerge going the opposite direction. Uanari's flying was masterful, and Meristofales was more than a little proud of himself for holding on through it all. Truthfully, he had no idea how the other Rider managed to stay on Dyraxian's back. As he considered it, an idea occurred to the old Dragonmaster.

Give me a clear shot, he said to Uanari.

Why? Uanari sounded exhausted; he couldn't keep this up.

It's time to take this to the ground. Uanari flashed agreement through the bond, then beat his wings in double time, giving him a temporary burst of speed.

Meristofales could feel the dragon's exhaustion and knew he wouldn't have another opportunity. He stood up in the saddle and called on his power. It responded, coursing through his body and imbuing him as The Living Storm. Taking his power in both hands, he formed a spear of pure air. He doubted he could kill either the Rider or the dragon from this distance, but he needed to upset the balance somehow.

With a scream, he unleashed the blast. It careened off into

the night. Meristofales thought he must have missed, but after a moment, the Rider rocked, waving his arms wildly, and fell.

Meristofales released the power and clapped his hands together. He could already see Dyraxian slowing, turning to go back for him.

Take me to the ground, he called to Uanari, who responded with relief. As they approached the ground, it was clear the dragons would arrive at virtually the same time.

I'll take the dragon, Uanari said, fatigue coloring his usually vibrant voice. *I can't kill him in this state, but maybe I can buy you some time.*

Meristofales nodded. He could see no other way. *Kill the Rider—*

—kill the dragon, Uanari finished. And with that, the pair had hatched a plan. Meristofales stood, readying himself. Uanari diverted course; instead of going to the ground where the Rider was, he was going to ram straight into the other dragon. This was his only opportunity.

Meristofales leapt into the night air. The drop was longer than he'd realized. The night sky, smoke, and light of the volcanoes was playing havoc with his vision. He was in free fall, calling on his power to buffer his fall. This time, it did not respond, and he crashed to the ground in a heap. He laid there for a long moment, until he heard the deafening crash of two massive dragons hitting the ground a hundred yards away.

He sat up as pain coursed through his side—not from his own fall, but from Uanari's. The two dragons were engaged in a snarling, spitting wrestling match. On their best day, he'd have taken Uanari in that fight ten times out of ten. But today? Fatigued and hurting, he knew he had to finish the Rider quickly.

Meristofales rose, calling his blade to him. It came whistling through the air from where the dragons fought and settled gently into his palm. The Rider was nowhere to be seen. Had he gone to aid Dyraxian?

As the Dragonmaster considered the question, he heard another whistling sound. His arm darted up just in time to deflect the Rider blade that appeared out of the darkness. If not for the slight glint from the still-present light of the volcanoes, he thought he might've been speared right through. But he sent it careening away with a ringing of steel and spun, searching for his attacker.

The sound of plate mail boots stamping on dirt gave him away. Meristofales wheeled to find the Rider approaching him from behind, Rider blade back in his hand. From this distance, Meristofales could see the unsettling, glowing purple smoke emanating from the eye slits of the man's helmet.

Is he a man at all? Meristofales wondered. He chastised himself. It didn't matter. Man or no, he would die tonight.

"That was a good shot," the Rider said, his horrible voice grating on Meristofales's ears. "We'd hoped to lead you on for a while yet."

Meristofales took his sword in a two-handed grip, keeping the tip up and pointed toward his opponent. "Thought that might've been the plan," he said, as the two men rounded each other in careful steps.

The Rider struck out with his sword in a one-handed grip, just a probing strike, and Meristofales was careful to deflect it, but a little slower than was strictly necessary. The Rider came again, this time with three strikes. Meristofales feigned difficulty with them, and the other man settled back, getting some distance.

"Don't play with me, Dragonmaster." His voice was harsher now, angry. "I know you're holding back."

Meristofales didn't respond with words, instead striking out with his sword, much faster. The Rider brought his blade up, deflecting three successive strikes and parrying the fourth. Meristofales twisted out of the way of his thrusting riposte and swung viciously, aiming for his head. The Rider was too quick, ducking under the swing and kicking out, catching Meristofales in the stomach and sending him stumbling back. He caught himself and looked back at the Rider.

He was nodding to himself.

"Good, good," he said, more to himself than to Meristofales. "I was hoping you'd still be in fighting shape." Without warning, he whipped his hand out and sent his blade streaking toward Meristofales, who managed to knock the strike away, only to find the Rider rushing in behind his blade, a sidesword drawn and aimed at the Dragonmaster's neck. Meristofales cursed, dodging to the side. The Rider followed up his charge with a vicious sidesword combination, forcing Meristofales to stumble back as he clumsily blocked the attacks. As the Rider finished his onslaught, the telekinetic blade appeared from the darkness again, spearing down from the heavens.

This time, Meristofales released his own blade, sending it up to meet the other, lighting the night in a cascade of sparks. As the two massive swords attacked, blocked, and parried independent of their wielders, Meristofales drew his own sidesword. It was much shorter in reach than his Rider blade, but also more maneuverable in close proximity.

The Dragonmaster chose to go on the offensive and see what his opponent was made of. They met in a clash of singing steel as Meristofales pressed his attack. But no matter how fast, how vicious the onslaught, the Rider was always just out of reach, barely able to block or parry or dodge. Frustration grabbed at Meristofales, and he broke off the attack, summoning his power as he did. But the Rider pressed him, attacking again and again and again. Meristofales was struggling to breathe; there was no way he could control his power now. The volcanoes surrounding them were proof of the consequences of using magic without taking the proper precautions. He hesitated.

White-hot pain lanced through his leg. Meristofales screamed as Uanari's pain became his own and dropped to a knee. A glance up told him the Rider was almost on him, raising his sword. There was no time. Meristofales channeled his pain and rage and frustration into his well of power and *let go*.

The air itself exploded. He'd managed to contain the blast somewhat, but everything in a twenty-foot radius of the two combatants was scoured to bare stone. Meristofales laid flat on the ground, his head resting on the hot stone beneath him, his ears ringing so loud, nothing else could get through. His vision was nothing but white for a long moment. Slowly, it came back to focus. He breathed deep, letting himself relax.

Nothing could've survived that, he thought, immensely proud of himself for not causing another emergence. *Uanari, are you–* he was cut off by another pain lancing through his hand. He rolled over, gripping his hand as it seized and locked up. The pain lasted only a moment, but it left him feeling even dizzier than the explosion.

His vision now clear, Meristofales looked around, and his heart sank when he saw the two dragons, still locked in battle. They rolled over and over, flattening whatever vegetation dared to grow in this place. A sound of metal shifting promptedMeristofales to turn. The Rider was rising to his feet.

Pain flashed through his bond with Uanari. Pain and rage. It was a message that needed no words. Meristofales embraced his anger and drew again on his well of power.

"Alright then, you shit." The Rider blade settled into his right hand as his left crackled with lightning, arcing and running up the length of the sidesword it still gripped. "Let's have you."

The two fighters rushed each other and met in a cacophony of blades. Meristofales's sidesword arced lightning with every blow as the Rider blades met in whirling patterns. The fight was poetry. But it was a dance Meristofales was losing. He could feel it. He wasn't quite fast enough, not quite strong enough.

I'm not sure I can win this, he said to Uanari.

Uanari sent resolve through the bond, and Meristofales felt a moment of strength as he was buoyed by Uanari's belief. *You are The Living Storm.* We *are The Living Storm.*

Meristofales redoubled his efforts, and he felt Uanari follow suit as he wrestled Dyraxian. He stabbed out with the sidesword, arced lightning through the blade that scored the Rider's chest, then moved in with an overhand swing from the Rider blade. The metal-clad Rider stumbled back, but still managed to avoid the sword's bite before returning with a vicious combination of both of his own swords, used in twisting spins that Meristofales wasn't fast enough to block or avoid. The Dragonmaster leapt backward, his jump aided by a small burst of wind released beneath his feet.

As he landed, he called on flame, and the power within him responded, coiling along his left arm and down the blade of his sidesword, then extending further, forming a whip of solid fire. Lightning still arced and crackled along his arm as he cracked the flame whip, sending tendrils of fire into the night's sky. The Rider cocked his head, but Meristofales gave him no time to plan.

He sent his Rider blade off in a streak toward the other fighter. As he lifted his own sword to knock the blow away, the flame whip shot out, scoring a hit against the Rider's armored side at the same time the two blades met. The Rider stumbled, then righted himself, but Meristofales could feel his reserve nearing its end, and so pressed his advantage.

He stepped in, cracking the whip again coiling it around the Rider's leg. His Rider blade returned in a flash, and he caught it from the air, hand already forming a thrust that would pin the traitor to the ground. The Rider's smoke-filled visor snapped up to meet Meristofales's eyes.

I've got him. Meristofales felt elation pass through his bond with Uanari.

His reserve ran dry.

The flame whip disappeared in a puff of smoke, leaving behind the melted and charred form of his sidesword. He pitched off-balance, and the Rider slipped away from the attack. Pain exploded through the Dragonmaster's side as he felt the Rider's sidesword slide between his ribs.

Meristofales stumbled away for a few steps, then dropped to one knee. He tried to call his blade, but there was nothing left in him. He tried to push himself to his feet, but only succeeded in falling back down to his knees.

Uanari, he said. *Uanari, I can't...I can't stand.*

He knew his breathing was coming faster now than it should be. *A lung, probably.* Pain exploded through his abdomen when he breathed, and he knew he would not rise again.

I'm sorry, Uanari, he said. Tears mingled with the curtain of blood running down his face as he reached out to his oldest friend. *I'm sorry, I couldn't beat him.* The two dragons were quiet now. No fighting. No victory there. Uanari had done his part, and battled to a draw.

Don't be, Uanari said, his voice low and quiet, the fading, distant thunder of a storm running out of fuel. *All things end, Meristofales. I am proud to have known you, and to be with you now.*

Thoughts rose unbidden to the front of Meristofales's mind as he watched the Rider take slow strides toward him. He thought of Eoradon, Rialin, Feordan—oh, there was so much he should've said to all of them. The enormity of the Dragonmaster's failure crashed into him now.

I've failed them all, he said, panic rising in his chest as he struggled for air. Darkness tinged the corners of his vision and he knew his time was growing short. *Oh, Uanari, I've doomed them all!*

The Rider came to a stop in front Meristofales and rammed his sword into the ground. It struck the Dragonmaster as strange, since he could've simply let it float. But his mind was hazy now, and he found it difficult to focus.

The Rider squatted down, bringing him even to Meristofales's face. A gauntleted hand took Meristofales by the jaw, and the pain jolted him back to consciousness for a moment. In that clarity, he took in the helmeted face of the Rider. The purple smoke curled lazily from the eye slits of the helmet, and a rotten stench overtook the Dragonmaster. He coughed, tried to pull away, but he was too weak, and the Rider held him fast.

"I have waited for this day." He spoke in a grinding whisper, so quiet it was hard to hear, even from this close proximity. "Meristofales." The Rider spoke his name with such venom, it took the old man off-guard.

Who are you? he thought, not for the first time. The hatred in the man's voice was palpable.

"My masters will set right what you have wronged," he said, squeezing Meristofales's jaw even tighter, pain lancing up through his head as the gauntleted fingers cut him and drew blood. The Rider cocked his head, reminding Meristofales for a ridiculous moment of an inquisitive dog. "Pity, you will not be there to witness it." Meristofales could've sworn he heard a smile in that horrible, grating voice. And then he was thrown to the ground, his head smacking hard against the stone and causing his vision to flash white.

Breathing was an act of defiance now. It burned and seared his abdomen, just to keep refilling his lungs. He felt underwater, like he was breathing in pure salt. He reached for his power, but there was nothing left—his body simply couldn't find the well of power anymore. He thought he'd be afraid, but what overtook him wasn't fear. He felt at ease. He knew he shouldn't, but he couldn't fight the feeling—didn't want to. So many things he hadn't done, hadn't said, but it was all as flimsy as wind now; just the far-away fears of a man long dead. Vaguely, he registered the Rider lifting his sword.

Meristofales's last thought was of his mother.

How strange, he thought. *I can hardly remember her face.*

In the depth of sleep, Wik felt the power call to her. She found herself standing at the edge of the massive glowing pool, wisps of light dancing off the surface. It directed her to something new, something she'd never seen before in this place of dreams.

A massive iron pillar stood in the dark, some distance away from her. As she approached it with careful steps, she saw it was not a pillar; it was two massive cords of iron, interwoven with each other, leaning on each other for support. The two made one.

As she watched, the column groaned and stretched, as though being ripped apart. It snapped, as though under stress from some outside force. One cord whipped away into the darkness instantly, so fast she barely saw it. The other one, though, lingered. Just for a second, just long enough to notice.

The power called to her, and she answered. With a wave of her hand, hardly more than a thought, she took hold of the two halves, and forced them back together. It was imperfect—where there had been two, there was now only one. But the cord of iron was restored, held together by the glowing tendrils of her power.

Chapter Sixteen

Voices

The most fundamental truth of the bond is this: if the Rider falls, so too does the dragon.

-Log of Dragonmaster Jarik, 14th Lord of Mun-Alin

Wik awoke to the sound of screaming. As her eyes snapped open and her hand went for the axe on the table by her bed, she realized the scream had been in her mind. She breathed deep, eyes glancing furtively around her chamber, making sure there was no intruder. As her waking mind caught up, the scream faded into the background, like a dream slipping through her fingers more and more, the longer she was awake.

She replaced the axe on the bedside table and sat upright. As her hands moved to fling off the sheets that covered her, she realized they were all wet. She moved a hand to her forehead and found it, too, was wet. Not only wet, she was soaked with sweat.

As she stood from the bed, Wik found herself unsteady on her feet, and she leaned against the wall for support.

Am I ill? she wondered. But no, she felt good—strong, even. After a moment, she managed to right herself and dress in a plain linen shirt tucked into pants, boots laced up tight. She affixed her axe to her hip and made her way out into the halls of the monastery.

Something was different. She could feel the cold of the monastery—winter was descending on the place, and it was crisp at the best of times—but there was something else there. A heat on her arms, an acrid smell in her nostrils. It felt somehow far away, but when she focused on it, it came rushing to the surface, overwhelming the cold.

She decided to skip breakfast and head straight to the infirmary.

Maybe Feordan will know what's happening.

As she made her way to the Bonestitcher's infirmary, she caught bits of hushed conversations, the older Riders trying not to be heard.

"The Prince isn't quite the leader we were led to believe."

"I don't know what Meristofales saw in him."

"It should've been Rialin."

"It should've been Feordan."

"It should've been me."

The last one caused Wik to stifle a chuckle. Wulf might've been a candidate for Dragonmaster long ago, but he was even longer in the tooth than Meristofales, and made Eoradon look like a child in comparison.

Wik rounded the corner and pushed open the door to the

infirmary. Inside, she found Feordan mixing a salve, surely for Rialin. The Rider was growing stronger, and was supposed to start walking with a crutch today, in fact. But his wounds still risked infection if they went untreated for too long, so most of Feordan Bonestitcher's time was taken up by mixing and applying various concoctions to ward off any sort of inflammation. She looked up as Wik pushed the door closed.

"Wik," Feordan said, peering over spectacles sitting low on her nose. As she took in the look on the girl's face, she must have perceived something was bothering her, because she put down her mortar and pestle and stood, gesturing to the stone slab that had been Rialin's bed during his coma. "Sit down."

Wik didn't argue, scratching at her arms, still waffling between uncomfortably warm and biting cold. Feordan looked her over, checked her pulse, put a hand to her forehead, listened to her breathing, then finished by looking deep into her eyes.

"What ails you, girl?" she eventually asked. "You look like you're seeing spirits, but I find no physical ailments."

Wik sighed, wringing her hands together. She could feel panic rising like a tide in her chest, but like the heat, it felt both far away and on top of her. "I don't know," she said honestly. "It's like I'm in two places at once; both cold and hot, and I feel panicked, but it's...not mine, somehow." She shook her head, long dark hair moving around her shoulders as she realized she forgot to tie it back in the chaos of her waking.

"Hmmm," Feordan hummed to herself. "Has there been anything else? Hallucinations? Nightmares?"

The mention of nightmares shocked Wik back to clarity. "Yes, I had a strange dream last night." She recounted the dream to

Feordan, how she'd repaired the shattering iron pillar and mended part of it. The older woman leaned back against her desk and listened intently, a hand cupping her chin.

"I don't know what's causing your discomfort," she said. "But my guess is you're worried about Meristofales, and it's somehow causing you to feel this panic and disconnect."

Wik was unsure. "Of course I'm worried about him—everyone is. But I hardly think my worry could cause *this*." She gestured at her body, though she knew Feordan couldn't see the alternating chills and sweats plaguing her.

The Bonestitcher shook her head. "Worry and anxiety can cause many physical symptoms. It's natural; don't beat yourself up over it."

"No, I—" Wik started to protest, but Feordan continued as if she hadn't heard. She thrust a vial of liquid into her hand.

"A mixture of poppy flower. It'll help you sleep and calm your nerves. Take this and rest today, and we'll see how you feel tomorrow."

Wik thought about arguing further, but saw it would be no use. Feordan was decided, and she'd learned in her time around the woman that she rarely changed her mind so easily. "Yes, ma'am."

Feordan nodded and turned back to the salves she'd been working on, while Wik stifled her frustration as she marched back to her chamber.

Wik shut the door to her chamber harder than she intended. But she couldn't help it; anger and frustration stirred in her belly, and unlike the panic she'd felt earlier, she knew these emotions were hers. Feordan wouldn't hear reason, Meristofales had abandoned her on some damn quest, Eoradon was Dragonmaster now—no one had time for her, all of a sudden. As she sank into her bed, the still-full vial of poppy across the room on the table, Wik's mind was turning over and over, debating how she should've stood up to Feordan, or maybe forced Meristofales to take her with him, or stay here himself, or—

Wik gasped as a wave of incredible, unspeakable sadness washed over her. It blocked out everything. The anger, the frustration, the embarrassment; it all vanished beneath the blanket of grief that stole her breath. Tears gathered at the corners of her eyes and she did not fight them. They fell down her cheeks, cascading across her pillow and making dark spots on her bed. The emptiness, the hollow horror that is true sadness overtook her. She curled into a ball, made herself as small as she could, and wept.

Rialin took a deep breath and blew it out. Feordan stood five feet away from him, but she might as well have been across an ocean. His sweaty hand gripped the crutch she'd fashioned for him, and he was forced to admit he felt fear rising in his chest.

His leg still ached, but Feordan claimed the bones were healed enough to attempt walking. Rialin knew he needed it—he was sick of being pushed around in that wheeled chair—but the idea of actually putting weight on his shattered leg made him want to vomit.

"You can do this, Rialin." Feordan flashed him an encouraging smile and nodded her head. "I'm right here, if you fall."

Rialin nodded, blew out another deep breath, and leaned on his crutch as he took a shuddering step. As his weight settled on the mangled leg, he screamed. His leg felt like a stack of rocks, unsteady and likely to break again if he pushed them. Agony exploded through his body like fire in his muscles. He tried to hop back to his good leg, but his balance was off and he fell unceremoniously to his backside.

Immediately, he discarded the crutch and started massaging his leg. He fought revulsion at how emaciated it felt, the muscle hanging limp from the bone, like bags of water hanging from tree limbs. He cursed to himself as Feordan settled down next to him and examined the leg.

"All good," she said after a moment. She turned and looked at him. "Time to try again."

Rialin huffed as she stood and extended a hand. Begrudgingly, he took it and allowed himself to be helped up. The next attempt went much the same, though he did manage to stay off the floor. And on they went like this for an hour. He'd grit his teeth and curse, and she'd continually put him back on track and make him keep trying. No matter what he did, how he raged, Feordan's advice was the same.

"Try again."

And he did. By the end of the hour, he was drenched in sweat, hair plastered to his forehead. His leg was on fire, pulsing and throbbing, enough to make him scream if he let it. He felt like he'd been in a fight against ten men; he ached all over.

He'd taken two steps.

A few minutes later, after Feordan had helped him to a seat and given him some water dosed with herbs to dull the pain, Rialin's thoughts turned to Eoradon—the Dragonmaster. He scowled. Even the tasteless water turned bitter in his mouth at the thought of it, so he spit it out in a basin.

He knew the truth of it, of course: Rialin's injuries kept him from being the choice. When Feordan rejected the position, Eoradon was the obvious choice to look after the monastery while Meristofales was away. The thought of the old man angered Rialin even further.

If I hadn't been caught unawares, he thought. *If I hadn't been defeated. Crippled. None of this would've happened.*

He set the water on a nearby table harder than necessary, sloshing liquid over the cup's brim. Standing, he hobbled to the wheeled chair and flopped down.

"Hey," Feordan said, looking up from where she was straightening supplies. "Where do you think you're going?" Alarm touched the edge of her voice.

Rialin sighed. "I need to be outside, Feordan. I'm not meant to be under all this stone." He gestured around the infirmary. "Besides, this is a place for the sick, and I am—" her flat stare cut him off "—getting better."

She sighed and rolled her eyes skyward. "Fine. Go get your fresh air." She lifted a finger to point at him. "But then you're coming back here and getting back to work."

Rialin smiled and nodded. "Aye, Bonestitcher. I'll be here." The use of her nickname caused Feordan to roll her eyes again and turn away from him, muttering. Rialin suppressed a chuckle as he clumsily navigated the chair through the door and out to the halls of the monastery. Slowly, deliberately, he pushed himself along until he reached the courtyard.

A chill had settled over the place, so he pulled his cloak, which he'd insisted on having draped over the back of the chair, around his shoulders to block out some of the cold. Rialin's eyes turned up, to the sea of rolling gray clouds, now spitting flurries of snow. He allowed that drab visage to carry his mind away, thousands of miles across Isthyl, to Aneving.

He replayed the day he'd met the rogue Rider again, for what had to be the thousandth time. *I should've been better*, he thought. *I should've been prepared.* But how could he have been better prepared? How could he have known? He shook his head, closed his eyes, and buried his face in his hands.

"Rialin?" A voice spoke from behind him. Rialin turned to look over his shoulder and saw Ferao approaching, concern written across his bearded face. "You alright?"

Rialin sighed and nodded. "Sorry, just—" Ferao held up a hand, cutting him off.

"No explanation necessary, my friend," he said, his thick midlands accent rolling over the words like water over stones. Rialin nodded gratefully. Then Ferao's face suddenly grew serious as he seemed to hesitate, looking for his next words. "Rialin, have you been to see him?"

Rialin's brow furrowed in confusion. "Him?"

Ferao sighed. "The dragon, what brought you home."

Rialin barked a humorless laugh. "The dragon who failed to escape Aneving and crushed my leg to a fine powder?" He shook his head. "No, Ferao, I can't say visiting it has been high on my list of priorities."

Ferao looked down, dejected. "He saved your life."

Anger exploded in Rialin's chest. He wrenched the wheeled chair around to fully face Ferao. "*He crippled me!*" He screamed. His face flushed as he panted, breath steaming in the winter air.

"*He* failed, Ferao, not me! If he'd been faster, or stronger, I'd never have been hurt to begin with!" His head pounded at the temples as blood pulsed through his veins.

Ferao's eyes snapped back up to Rialin, and there was a new fire there now. "He failed you?" Ferao stepped closer, his voice lowered to gravelly whisper. "He saved your sorry life, even though he could've left you there to die." Rialin started to speak, but the fight fled from him in a moment. Ferao noticed and used the opportunity to twist the knife. "Oh, you didn't think about that? You refused to fully bond, so you left him free to keep on living if you die." The broad, bearded Rider sneered at Rialin. "It goes both ways. But unlike *you*—" he shoved a finger in Rialin's chest "—he sees you as more than just a beast of burden. He did his *duty*, Rialin." Ferao settled back, but the fire never left his eyes. "Even though you refuse to do yours." Then he shoved past him and took off for the stable, long strides carrying him deeper into the monastery.

Rialin wanted to rage, call after him, *something*. But he couldn't. He was rooted to the spot, and not just because of the throbbing in his leg. Ferao had never challenged him like that. It made him feel uneasy, to be put on the back foot by someone he'd never thought of as a fighter.

Does he have a point? Rialin thought, pulling his cloak tighter around his shoulders. He hadn't considered it for a long time; the bond was dangerous, and he wasn't interested in putting his life in anyone's hands. But there was truth to Ferao's words. The beast could've left him there to die, but it chose to bring him home, even pushing itself to exhaustion and near death.

Unsettled and off-balance, Rialin slowly wheeled himself

back toward the infirmary. The air had grown colder, and he had tired of the gray sky's unblinking judgment.

The setting of the sun found Wik curled into a ball, swaddled in the still darkness of her chamber. She'd cried herself dry long ago, but the heaving sobs and shaking breaths hadn't ceased until just a few moments ago. Her body ached, her throat burned like fire, and sweat beaded on her skin in spite of the gathering cold of the monastery. But the veil of grief receded as suddenly as it had appeared, and she was finally able to move.

She stretched her body, untangling her sore limbs from each other as she tried to work feeling back into her extremities. Her fingers had been curled into fists so long, it felt like breaking them to open her palm. After a few moments of agony, she finally found herself lying stretched out on the bed.

Her mind was coming back into focus now, and it was reeling.

What was that? she thought.

The voice that responded was like the roll of thunder, the breaking of stone. It spoke from deep in the recesses of her mind. If not for its sheer presence, Wik might've convinced herself it was a dream. But she was wide awake, and it was all-encompassing.

He is gone. The grief came again, a wave breaking on a shore that was already beaten and bruised, threatening to overwhelm her. *He is gone, and yet I remain.*

She screamed, but could not hear it.

She heard a great and terrible roar.

Chapter Seventeen

Echoes of History

Eoradon shows significant promise, but he lacks the confidence to do what will eventually be necessary. I believe he will need to be forged into a stronger weapon.

-Log of Dragonmaster Rykas, 874th Lord of Mun-Alin

Eoradon buried his head in his hands and sighed deeply. He was leaning, propped up on his elbows on the ancient wooden desk in the Dragonmaster's chamber. His fingers brushed the edge of the iron circlet adorning his brow; he removed it, tossing it aside to land on the desk with a dull thud. He massaged his head, still sore from the adornment, and cursed silently at Meristofales.

In the two weeks since the old man had departed Mun-Alin, Eoradon had found leadership to be exactly the headache he'd expected all these years. Even in the monastery, where they'd been sequestered from the outside world for years, there was constant upkeep to oversee. Eoradon had been shocked when he thought, for the first time, about where their food came from. Apparently, there were some small fields at the base of the mountain, accessible via a tunnel system under the monastery.

And then, of course, there were the logs. Each night, he sat down at this desk and tried to come up with a few lines to write about whatever the day held. He'd glanced back through Meristofales's entries, only to find them achingly mundane.

No wonder he jumped at the opportunity to leave, Eoradon thought.

Iaxal, resting comfortably in the stable, chortled in response. Eoradon sent frustration through their bond.

Come now, Rodo, she said. *It can't be* all *bad. Have you looked through the older logs?* Her voice carried an excited tinge Eoradon wasn't used to hearing. He smiled.

No, I haven't.

She huffed. *Think of the history you could learn, Eoradon! Meristofales probably hasn't even read all of them.*

Eoradon looked around at the bookshelves lining the chamber's walls, and the hundreds of massive volumes. He gave a low whistle as he reclined in the chair.

No, he said. *I'd guess not.*

Then come on! she said, unable to contain her excitement any longer. *Pick one of the really old ones and see what you find.*

Eoradon rolled his eyes, but acquiesced. *Not like I have anything better to do.* He stood and walked to the shelves, running his finger along the ancient wood, bending under the weight of the massive tomes. After a moment's consideration, he plucked a volume at random and returned to the desk, where he flopped it down. The book's considerable heft shook the desk on impact, rattling an old stone cup to the floor, where it bounced once, then rolled a few feet away before coming to rest against the foot of the chamber's bed.

As Eoradon opened the book, he felt Iaxal's excitement through their bond. She was probably looking through his eyes—a trick she'd only picked up in the last few years.

This volume was from roughly four hundred years ago, written by Dragonmaster Jair, and mostly consisted of details of the Riders' day-to-day operations. At the time, they were assisting the Emperor with incursions at the southern border. Eoradon was surprised to find records of magic users among the Kerani warriors.

There are other people who can harness magic? he thought, incredulous.

I had no idea, Iaxal said, similarly stunned.

Other than that, he found little of note as he scanned the volume. Dragonmaster Jair seemed imperious, if her writing was anything to go by. She spent much time discussing the rules and regulations she used to govern the Riders, and decrying the various other rulers around Isthyl for their recklessness.

Eoradon replaced the volume and retrieved another, even older. This one was from six hundred years ago and consisted of multiple Dragonmasters. It seemed the monastery at this time was overrun by petty feuding. From what he could gather, the Riders of this era were warriors through and through, barely doing anything other than assisting the Empire in war efforts. When they weren't fighting for the Empire, they fought amongst themselves.

Petty fools, Iaxal said.

Aye, Eoradon said. *All that war; it can't have been good for the people of the Empire.*

Or, assuredly, anywhere else.

Eoradon suppressed a shiver and closed the book. This time, he moved to the oldest volumes, thousands of years old. But he was surprised to find them locked with chains, completely inaccessible.

Why are these locked, I wonder? he asked.

Iaxal responded with confusion. *I have no idea,* she said.

Eoradon ran a finger along the chains. They shimmered, not dulled by the passage of time. *They're new,* Eoradon said. *Or at least, much newer than these books.* He replaced the volume, running a finger over the spine. No title. No description. Just a book he wasn't allowed to open, even as the Dragonmaster.

"What are you hiding?" He asked aloud.

Something to ask him when he returns, Iaxal said. Eoradon nodded, but he couldn't shake the feeling that something was amiss. Why would Meristofales entrust him to serve as Dragonmaster, but not allow him to know the oldest histories of their order?

Shaking his head, he moved back toward the more recent volumes, choosing one from when he was a boy. He smiled as he read Dragonmaster Rykas's name, running his hand over the page. Eoradon remembered Rykas well; a kind man, dressed in robes, rather than the more practical shirts and leathers Meristofales favored. Eoradon still remembered him primarily as the man who first introduced him to Iaxal. For that, at least, he would forever be in the man's debt.

This volume was much the same as the most recent ones he'd read from Meristofales. But as he flipped through the waxy pages, one short entry stood out to him:

Horus was right. I hear them, too.

Horus? Eoradon had never heard the name. And who was Rykas hearing? *Iaxal, do you know anything about this?*

Iaxal thought for a moment before responding. *Uanari has mentioned a Dragonmaster Horus, I believe. From when he and Meristofales were younger.*

Eoradon looked back to the shelves, and moved back through the volumes written by Rykas. Sure enough, Dragonmaster Horus was mentioned a few times, but never in such cryptic terms. He came to Rykas's first volume, and—

Eoradon stopped. There was a gap. Right where Horus's final logs should be, there was a gap. *A volume is missing,* he said.

Iaxal sent concern and confusion though the bond. *Missing?* Her voice was low, conspiratorial, as if she could be overheard.

Eoradon's eyes slid back across the shelves, to the locked books at the end. *Locks, missing books, cryptic messages.* His fingers curled into fists as he fought to tamp down his frustration. He most certainly had questions for Meristofales to answer.

Wik dragged herself from bed as the sun rose. The voice had not spoken again, but she could feel *something* in the dark corners of her awareness; eyes, peering from the shadows. When she closed her eyes, she could see yellow pupils staring from the back of her eyelids. Sleep was out of the question.

So, as the red sun crested on the horizon and set the sky aflame, she moved through the halls of the monastery, a sweaty, crying mess. Her head pounded from the crying and heaving, and her eyes stung from the tears and lack of sleep. She was in a daze, unsure of what was real and what was imagined. Somehow, despite her stupor, as though someone were leading her by the hand, she found herself pounding on Feordan's door.

The door opened to the older woman, wrapped in a robe, sidesword in hand. "What the fuck do you—" She stopped cold when she saw Wik, leaning on the doorframe for support. "Oh my. Come in, girl."

Feordan ushered her inside and sat her on the stone table that had served as Rialin's bed for several weeks before he'd woken. She laid back when the room started to spin. Feordan moved around her at a frenetic pace; she checked her pulse, her eyes, both ears, joints, and affixed a device to her head to measure something about her magical connections.

"Tell me what's happening," Feordan ordered as she moved. So Wik told her everything that had happened since she left the infirmary the day before. For the most part, the older woman listened intently, her eyes fixed on Wik's face. When Wik mentioned the voice in her head, though, Feordan's eyes widened.

"A voice?" She asked quietly. "Did you know it?"

"What?" Wik was trying to focus, but she was so tired.

"The voice," Feordan snapped. "Did you know the voice?"

Wik wasn't sure. It was only a couple words, but...

"It was familiar," she said after a moment spent trying to refocus. Her vision was darkening. She was so tired. "Like... thunder. It was...everywhere." Wik's resolve failed. Her eyes fluttered shut as sleep took her. Just before the darkness overwhelmed her, she noticed the tears in Feordan's eyes.

◆◆◆

Eoradon was startled awake by a loud pounding on his door. He'd fallen asleep at the desk, still poring over Rykas's words. Nothing else had surfaced about Horus, but he knew something was wrong with the situation, and he couldn't stop digging now.

More banging. Eoradon rubbed his face groggily.

"I'm coming!" He called out. The pounding on the door persisted. He rose and crossed to the door, yanking it open. The sight shocked him to full wakefulness. For one thing, the sun was rising steadily into the sky, meaning he should've been awake an hour ago, at least. But far more urgent, Feordan stood in front of him, a panicked look on her tear-streaked face. Eoradon didn't know what to say; he'd never seen her cry. Before he had the chance to think of something, though, she pushed past him into the room.

"I think he's dead." Her voice was warbling, rough, as though it took effort to force the words past her teeth. Eoradon, still groggy from the night before, shook his head.

"What? Who?"

"Meristofales!" Feordan nearly screamed the word. Eoradon's blood went cold in his veins.

"What happened?"

Feordan flopped down in the desk chair. Her hands came together in front of her, wringing endlessly. "It's Wik. Something's wrong and..." She shook her head. "I don't know, Eoradon; it sounds like madness."

The heir of Ir-Anan pulled up another chair from the room's small, round dining table and sat opposite the healer. "Tell me," he said, looking into her eyes in a way he hoped projected confidence.

“We’ll figure it out together.”

Feordan returned his gaze, took a deep breath, and spoke. “I think Wik has bound Uanari.”

Eoradon had to stop himself from barking a laugh. Feordan’s red-rimmed eyes provided no levity, though.

“That’s impossible,” he said, lowering his voice. “Uanari could not be bound to a new Rider. And if Meristofales died, Uanari would also be dead.”

Feordan nodded. “I know, I know. As I said, it sounds mad. But...” She stood, pacing the floor. “Eoradon, she heard him in her mind. And she’s feeling emotions: intense grief, restlessness, debilitating levels of sadness. She said she can feel a presence in her mind.” Feordan buried her face in her hands. “I don’t know; I can’t shake this.”

Eoradon blew air out as he took the information in. “I don’t know how it would be possible. Uanari *did* help train Wik, so he was in her mind already. Maybe that could manipulate the bond in some way? Allow him to live, even if...” He trailed off, unable to give a voice to the potential of Meristofales’s death. “Does this... *presence* respond to her?”

Feordan shook her head. “She passed out not long after telling me. I haven’t had a chance to try anything like that.”

Eoradon nodded. “Let’s go see her, then.”

When they arrived at the infirmary, they found Rialin waiting by the door, looking uncomfortable in his wheeled chair. Iaxal rippled in anger at the sight of him. Eoradon realized she must still be looking through his eyes.

“There you are,” Rialin said to Feordan as they approached. His eyes passed over Eoradon with no acknowledgement. He turned back to Feordan. "I wanted to put in some extra work today." He absently rubbed his bad leg as he spoke.

Feordan nodded. "Aye, Rialin. It's good you're here. Come inside."

Eoradon tried not to bristle at her inviting Rialin in without consulting him. But Rialin nodded and the three of them moved into the infirmary. Eoradon was shocked by what he saw.

Wik lay on the stone table, pallid and sickly. Her skin was ghostly, but patches of red sunburn dotted her arms and legs. Sweat beaded on her skin, and deep purple bruising adorned her eye sockets. She twitched in her sleep, grimacing and baring her teeth.

Eoradon sighed, placing a hand on the girl's arm. Her skin alternated blazing heat and searing cold. Sweat would sprout from her flesh, then freeze into frost before melting back to liquid a moment later. He grimaced.

Iaxal, are you seeing this? he asked in his mind.

I am, she said, worry coloring her voice.

An idea occurred to Eoradon. *Can you enter her mind?*

A pause. *I can try. Uanari is usually the only one who does that sort of thing*.

Eoradon felt her presence recede from his mind. He was caught off-guard by how intensely lonely he felt in her absence. Even when they weren't actively communicating, Iaxal had been a presence in his mind since he was little more than a child. He felt suddenly very alone. But Wik needed her. He relayed their conversation to Rialin and Feordan. Feordan nodded, clearly still far away in her mind. Eoradon assumed she was caught up in worry for Meristofales, more than Wik's well-being, but he knew she had grown fond of the girl.

Rialin only nodded, his eyes fixed on Wik. There was concern on his face, but he seemed to be conflicted, like he was waging some internal war. Eoradon thought about asking him, but he knew there was nothing to be gained from it. Instead, he turned back to Wik and focused on her. After a moment, Iaxal's presence rejoined his mind, and he felt himself relax physically. He realized he'd been tensed since she left him.

Her mind is guarded, she said. *But not by her. There's no way Wik has the training to do this.*

So you can't reach her? Eoradon was confused. What did she mean by "guarded?"

It's not that, Iaxal said. *Her mind is closed off. Walled up. I can sense her, reach out to her, but she's actively fighting back against me.* She paused, then continued. *Or,* something *is.*

Eoradon felt goosepimples emerge on his arm and across the back of his neck. *So what do we do now?* he asked.

A flash of concern. *We can't do anything,* Iaxal said, her voice sad and nervous. *It's up to Wik now.*

Wik's eyes fluttered open. She was surprised to find herself lying, not on the stone table in the monastery's infirmary, but in a bed of tall swaying grass. She could feel the cool dirt beneath her as she pushed herself up to a sitting position. She dug her fingers into the ground, pulled up a handful of the cold, damp clay, letting it fall through her grip like sand in an hourglass.

A rumble of thunder drew her attention to the sky, where she saw an embankment of storm clouds a little ways off. Lightning flashed inside the roiling mass, crisscrossing its bulbous surface like a lattice.

She stood, looked around, but couldn't determine where she was. Mountains seemed to ring this verdant plain, but there was nowhere in Isthyl that she knew of a mountain formation like these. And that storm didn't feel natural. It still hadn't moved, despite the cool wind Wik could feel sweeping across her body. So that left only one option.

"I know what this is," she yelled, spinning and looking for any sign of other people here. "You cannot trap me in my own mind."

The wind ceased as an earthshaking rumble of thunder exploded from the storm clouds. Wik spun in time to see arcing lightning illuminate the thunderhead, and what lay inside. Wik gasped.

A face stared at her. A face made of lightning and wind and rain. A face of a dragon, enormous, large enough to cause her very body to tremble.

When the creature spoke, its voice was the breaking of trees, the shattering of armies. It was the torrent of rain. Its breath was an earthquake, its gaze the light of the rising sun. Wik gawped at the monstrosity, but could not turn away.

"I WILL DO WHAT I WISH," the creature thundered. The wind was back, a whirling, screaming gale that threatened to lift Wik off her feet. She hunkered closer to the ground, tried to lower her center of gravity. "YOU DO NOT KNOW MY TRUE POWER."

Wik didn't feel the need to object, so she let the creature continue uninterrupted.

"HE IS GONE," the voice boomed. "BUT I REMAIN." That inexorable sadness swaddled her again, but this time she was not overwhelmed. Slowly, Wik stood to her full height again. She tried to look at the storm beast, but couldn't hold its gaze, so she turned her eyes downward.

"Who is gone?" She asked. It was an innocent enough question, she thought. Just trying to understand.

The beast snarled, showing fangs of whirling winds draped from a maw made of the storm itself. Somehow it grew even *larger*, now blotting out virtually the entire sky, hanging right above Wik. She stared up at it, falling to her backside as she did.

"WHAT DID YOU DO?" It was an accusation, that was clear. The beast's voice was full of rage, full of fury. Lightning spit from its enormous mouth, impacting the ground around Wik, throwing bits of dirt and stone skyward.

Wik tried to think, tried to force her mind to work. But she couldn't think of anything she'd done that could cause this.

"I don't know!" She screamed over the storm. "Who is gone!?"

The monster growled, and Wik thought she'd made a mistake. Then, in a lurching instant, the world shifted, and she found herself on a very tall mountain, on a flat surface, like the top of the mountain was just shorn off, leaving this flat stone circle, maybe twenty feet wide. Wik tried to scoot to the center of the platform, but lightning scored the stone in front of her, stopping her movement.

The dragon face emerged again from the roiling pall to fill the sky, its eyes of clouds with lightning irises fixed on Wik. She felt suddenly very, very small.

"WHY AM I HERE?" The voice boomed, nearly knocking her from her feet.

"I don't know!" She screamed back. "But if you're going to kill me, just do it already!"

The winds quieted, allowing Wik's long hair to settle around her shoulders in a windblown mess. The thunder lowered to a rumble, instead of the all-encompassing earthquake from the sky it had been. And then the face vanished in a swirling of vapors and deposited itself in front of her.

She gasped. The form was a swirling mass of shadow in the shape of a man. And she knew him instantly.

"Uanari?" She whispered. He looked at her, and gone was the rage he'd been so full of a moment ago. His eyes told her of a deep sadness, an ache she could hardly comprehend. But she knew it. The tendrils of that pain had incapacitated her. Her mind reeled.

How is this possible? And then the grief overwhelmed her, too. Because she remembered his words. As if he knew her thoughts, he spoke them again.

"He is gone," the shadow man said, his voice a trembling whisper as he collapsed to his knees and buried his head in his hands, "and yet I remain."

Meristofales. Meristofales was gone. The sadness settled in her chest with a weight that felt physical. How could he be gone? The Dragonmaster, her mentor, their leader—gone. Her eyes slid back up to the simpering mess that was Uanari's form. The shades faded from the man, leaving the dragon. Small, shuddering with sobs, the King of Dragons looked so very scared.

He remains. Wik took a wobbling step toward him, trying and failing to hold back the sobs that threatened to choke her now. Tears rolled in rivulets down her face, so she let the sobs come, as she collapsed with Uanari, pulling him into a tight embrace.

Together, they wept.

Chapter Eighteen

Bonds

Rialin is also one to watch. Ideally, he would work with Eoradon. They could be unstoppable. Unfortunately, they seem intent on killing one another instead, to say nothing of Rialin's refusal to fully bond.

-Log of Dragonmaster Rykas, 874th Lord of Mun-Alin

Rialin's fingers drummed along the top of his knee, pounding out a rhythm as his eyes stared at Wik's still form. It had been hours since Iaxal's revelation about the girl's mind, and yet there had been almost no movement from her since.

Feordan slumped at her desk, having managed to fall asleep on top of her folded arms. Eoradon had spent most of the intervening time pacing the infirmary, and Rialin was sure the prince would wear a groove into the stone floor eventually.

Occasionally, he would pause, sit down, fitfully bouncing his legs until they forced him to move again, at which point he would stand and resume his endless trek from one end of the room to the other.

I wonder if he's been talking to the dragon the whole time? Rialin wondered. His mind wandered back to his own mount, currently recovering in the stable down below, as Ferao's words soared to the front of his mind.

"He saved your sorry life, even though he could've left you there to die," he'd said. The fury in his eyes took Rialin aback, even as a memory. Again, he found himself wondering if the Rider had a point.

Would I have done the same? Rialin wondered, knowing the answer even as he thought the words. He'd let three dragons die now, and he knew he would've let this one perish, too, if it had meant saving himself. Unease gripped him as his stomach flipped and roiled. Not for the first time, Rialin wondered if the dragon was more in his mind than he realized.

Of course, it hadn't always been this way. When Dragonmaster Rykas had handed him that first hatchling, he'd been so excited, just like everyone else who made it that far. But fear had stopped him from opening up to the creature; fear of letting something into the confines of his mind, fear of allowing someone to see his inner self.

Fear of death. Of course, that was the reason hovering over all the others. He was afraid of dying, and if he let a dragon in, became fully bonded, he would die when the beast did.

If I'm going to die, he'd thought on more than one occasion, *at least let me be the one who earns it.*

Rialin sighed and rubbed his eyes.

"What is it?" Eoradon's voice wasn't mocking in truth, but Rialin couldn't help but hear snark every time he spoke.

"Nothing." The last thing he wanted was advice from the Order's golden boy. He and Iaxal had never had any trouble navigating the bond. Meristofales had even called them "preternaturally gifted" on one occasion that still brought a flush of anger to Rialin's cheeks. He realized he'd clenched his fists and forced them open again.

"Hmm," Eoradon hummed. He coughed and cleared his throat, clearly unsure of what to say next.

Silence isn't so bad... Rialin thought, just as Eoradon managed to find his voice.

"How are you feeling?" It was a poor attempt, and the prince seemed to realize it immediately, glancing away as Rialin looked up. "Sorry," he said, dropping into the room's other chair. He steepled his fingers and looked at Wik, who still hadn't given any indication she was close to waking.

"She's strong," Rialin said. He wasn't sure why he'd said it, but as he spoke the words, he found they felt true. "Meristofales wouldn't have worked so much with her if she weren't."

Eoradon nodded, his eyes flicking to Rialin for a moment before returning to the girl. "You're right." He shifted, seeming uncomfortable. Rialin raised an eyebrow as he watched the prince, clearly trying to find the words to voice something. Finally, he managed to open his mouth. "Have you ever heard of Dragonmaster Horus?"

Rialin was surprised at the question, but the name didn't mean anything to him. He opened his mouth to say so, just as Wik gasped.

The sound was so sudden, breaking the room's stillness so completely, Rialin nearly jumped to his feet before his leg reminded him why that would be a bad idea.

For his part, Eoradon *was* on his feet immediately, moving toward the girl. Wik was drenched in sweat, thrashing like someone who was waking from a nightmare. Which, Rialin supposed, she probably was. He wheeled himself toward the table, but Feordan, now very much awake, jumped in front of him and went to her side. The old Rider took the girl's hand in her own, feeling her pulse. Then she placed her hands on either side of Wik's face and forced their eyes to meet.

"Wik," she said, her voice as calm and cold as steel. "Wik, look at me. It's Feordan, look at me. Do you know where you are?"

Wik's big dark eyes darted all around the room, seeming to look at everything but Feordan. Finally, though, she managed to settle, seeming to realize where she was. Her breathing slowed, and she managed a weak nod of her head.

"The monastery," she croaked, her voice rough and hoarse. "I'm in the monastery." She closed her eyes, breathing deep.

Feordan nodded. "Good girl. Yes, you are. Now, tell us: what happened?"

Wik's eyes snapped open, and Rialin saw the tears gathering on their lids. The girl wrenched her lips together, and it was clear she was holding in a sob. But if she was a dam, she was breaking. She opened her mouth to speak, but a choking wail was all that escaped, and she collapsed into Feordan's shoulder, seeming much younger of a sudden. After a moment's surprise, Bonestitcher recovered, patting her back, softly shushing.

"It's okay," she said, so quiet Rialin barely heard it. "It's okay; you're safe." Rialin thought he heard stifled tears in *her* voice, too. And his heart sank. Something had happened, and a glance at Eoradon said he knew it, too. The prince's face had gone white as bone, and his hand shook as he drew it up to his mouth.

"Oh, by the Six," he muttered, leaning against the wall. "Oh no."

"What happened?" Rialin demanded, panic rising in his chest. "What do you all know that I don't?"

The eyes in the room turned to regard him, and Feordan's red-eyed expression was far too pitiful for his liking.

A stone settled in his chest, dragging his heart down. A vast emptiness had opened beneath him of a sudden, and he couldn't stop that weight from dragging him in. "No," he said, his voice small as a child's. "No, he can't be..." And as suddenly as the void had opened, a tidal wave of rage rushed to fill it. Gone was the concern for the dragon, gone was the pain in his leg, gone was the damnable uncertainty.

"Tell me," he whispered through gritted teeth, more growling than speaking, his fingers curling into fists.

Wik sniffed, then wiped her nose. "Uanari says—"

"What?!" The entire room exclaimed at once. Rialin felt his spirits rise for a moment.

"He's alive." Wik nodded. "I don't know how, but he survived and...he's in *my* head somehow."

Silence. Rialin swore he could hear the heartbeats of the others in the room.

"No." Eoradon's voice was hard. "No, that's not possible."

A presence shoved at the boundaries of Rialin's mind. By the expressions on the faces of Feordan and Eoradon, he could tell they felt it, too. Rialin panicked, pushed back, but the presence was indomitable, marching ever onward through his mental defenses. When the voice spoke, it was the rolling of thunder, the crack of lightning, the roar of the ocean in a storm.

I remain.

The breath was stolen from Rialin's chest. This should not be possible. It was an affront. Meristofales would never have wanted—

What he wanted is immaterial, Uanari said, reminding Rialin that the privacy of his own thoughts was forfeit to the dragon. *Neither of us wanted this, but I am still alive. And so long as I live, so long as the fire of the world's making burns in my chest, I must go on. As must we all.*

The next few minutes passed in a blur as Wik relayed what had happened while she slept. Rialin found himself numb. Meristofales was dead. And Uanari had somehow been bonded to Wik? It defied sense. The thought of bonds made his mind slip back to his dragon, and he forced himself away from that train of thought.

When Wik finished her story, Uanari confirmed it was true. The great dragon seemed subdued, far away somehow. Rialin hated having him in his mind, but felt powerless to force him out. Uanari didn't seem to be connected to him beyond their ability to communicate, but it still made Rialin uncomfortable, having it forced on him.

"So," Eoradon said, speaking slowly as he worked through the new information. "You two are bonded now? Dragon and Rider?"

Wik didn't speak, instead clearly communicating with Uanari

in her mind. Rialin could no longer hear the dragon, and his overwhelming presence had seemed to retreat as Wik had finished her story. He breathed a little easier without the pressure in his head. "We think so," she finally said. "But even we're in the dark. This hasn't happened before, as far as Uanari is aware."

Feordan nodded. "You wouldn't know this, having never bonded a dragon, Wik. But the bond is supposed to be a commitment. The ultimate trust between two beings. A Rider's very life force is bound to his dragon's, and vice versa." She glanced meaningfully at Rialin. "With some obvious exceptions." He looked away, feeling his cheeks go flush as the confrontation with Ferao continued to replay in his mind.

"All that to say," Feordan looked back to the rest of those gathered, "this is a...*new* sort of bond." Wik looked down, clearly uneasy. "You two will have to discover for yourselves what it means, what its limitations are. And the rest of us will do all we can to aid you." Eoradon nodded as the room turned to face Rialin.

He shifted uncomfortably, but nodded.

Eoradon sighed, then crossed his arms over his chest, his brow furrowing. "Where is Uanari now? Can he get home?"

Wik looked up to her periphery again and Rialin suppressed a huff. She'd have to stop doing that or everyone would always know when she was communicating with Uanari.

"He's hurt," she said, her voice taking on a worrying tinge. "He doesn't think he can make it home on his own."

Eoradon nodded. "Iaxal and I will go retrieve him."

"No!" Feordan and Wik responded in unison, startling both the prince and Rialin.

"We just lost a Dragonmaster." Feordan's voice was thick

with emotion. "We cannot lose another." Rialin coughed to clear the knot in his own throat.

"She's right," he said. "Much as I don't like it, you're the one he appointed. And he did it for this very reason. The monastery needs you, Eoradon."

The heir to Ir-Anan glanced at Rialin, uncertainty crossing his face as he looked for a way out. Rialin knew the man never wanted to lead like this. That was supposed to be *his* path.

Damn leg, he cursed inwardly.

"And he's bonded to *me,*" Wik said, her voice suddenly full of fire. "If anyone is going to him, it will be me."

Eoradon sighed. "You can't just set out on foot, Wik. Not with that...thing still on the loose." His voice was full of venom, and Rialin could relate. Meristofales had been more than a leader to them; he was the closest either had to a father. Especially after what happened to Liran.

Rialin frowned at the thought. *How many fathers has he lost now?* A sudden feeling of sympathy washed over him as he looked at his rival.

"Send Ferao," Rialin said, and the entire room turned to look at him. Feeling the need to explain, he went on. "He's a competent fighter, a damn good flyer, and we don't have anyone better at caring for the dragons. If Uanari's hurt, he's the one you want to go." Wik caught his eye and he could see the fire in her eyes. It was familiar, and made Rialin smile a little as he thought of the old man. "Send her with him. She's right; if she and Uanari are bonded, she should be there." The girl smiled and she nodded to him in thanks. Her eyes didn't soften though, and Rialin wondered suddenly if that fire was hers, or if it belonged to the one who dwelled in her mind.

Careful, Wik, he thought. *Don't lose yourself in the bond.*

Eoradon sighed and suddenly looked ten years older. "Fine," he said. "I will tell Ferao to ready himself to leave by the morning." He turned his gaze to Wik. "Get whatever you need. Travel light." She nodded excitedly and turned to leave. "One more thing," Eoradon said, stopping her. "Where is Uanari now? You never said."

A pause while Wik spoke with the dragon. Then she looked back at Eoradon and said, "He's near a volcanic emergence? He said you'd know it." And then she was gone through the door, leaving behind her a room of stunned silence.

Eoradon's face had gone even whiter than before, his complexion suddenly ashen in the room's low light. For his part, Rialin didn't feel much better. His stomach had dropped through the floor at the mention of the words as memories came to him unbidden from the recesses of his mind.

Flames, screams, spurting blood, grinding stone, choking ash.

He shook himself, but the Dragonmaster looked close to passing out. Their eyes met.

"He died there." Eoradon seemed to choke on the words, his voice a rasping whisper. "Oh, Six, he died beneath the banner of my failure." Before Rialin could speak, the heir of Ir-Anan swept from the room, taking off in a sprint into the night.

Chapter Nineteen

The Wildness of Flame

20 Years Ago

Eoradon grasped the horn of his saddle in a white-knuckled grip as Iaxal bucked unexpectedly, her tail cracking like a whip. Not long ago, she'd managed to throw him from her back with a maneuver like that, and now found it to be a very entertaining way to make sure he didn't fall asleep on long flights. For his part, Eoradon *had* stopped sleeping in the saddle.

You're having too much fun, Eoradon chided her.

And you're *too serious,* she replied, sending annoyance through the bond. *How can you be so dour up among all this splendor?*

Eoradon looked out at the open sky and was forced to admit she had a point. There was a part of this that never grew old. He laughed, rubbing her absently where her jaw and neck met. *It's just what's expected of royalty.*

She shifted her weight, rolling almost halfway to the side.

The equivalent of a dragon rolling their eyes, he figured, and laughed as he turned to look out at the horizon.

They'd taken a path over rocky cliffs, jutting out into the salty waters of the Bay of Kings. To the West, the shimmering white towers of Iannivar glittered in the dimming sun like a diamond ring on the hand of a giant. Spread out before them were the seemingly endless waters of the Bay. Of course, Eoradon knew the waters weren't *actually* endless; far to the North, the waters changed from warm and welcoming to icy and treacherous as they lapped upon the frozen shores of Wulthoff.

Riders rarely ventured so far North, as the cold made flying difficult for most dragons, but of course they knew it was there. Virsk had even found his way from the frigid place to the monastery as a child, somehow. Eoradon made a mental note to ask his friend about it when he returned home.

Eoradon breathed deep, letting the salty air fill his nostrils. Beneath him, Iaxal let loose a satisfied breath. The heir to Ir-Anan leaned down close to the dragon, feeling the warmth emanating from her, and closed his eyes. Waves crashed against the rocks far below, while gullcalls filled the air above them and wind swept across his face, warming in the dying sun.

Cries pierced the moment of peace. His eyes snapped open to see a ship, barely out of port, listing and in danger of capsizing. As he watched, more flames winked to life in the recesses of Iannivar's harbor. They were ships, Eoradon realized with sudden horror. All the ships in the harbor had gone up in flames at once.

What happened? He asked.

I don't know, Iaxal responded.

Eoradon's mind raced. From the city, a low, long horn blast

sounded, carrying out over the water of the bay. Eoradon shook himself, then lowered his body closer to Iaxal's scaled form.

Let's go.

She dove, snapping her wings open and gliding across the water toward the ship. As she drew close, she flapped her wings once, slowing slightly while Eoradon launched himself away from her, landing in a roll on the deck. As he did, he felt his ankle give way under him and turn over painfully. Coming up from his roll and trying to look as confident as possible, he suppressed a grimace and grabbed a sailor who ran by with a bucket of water.

"What happened?" he asked, but the man shook his head, responding in broken Imperial.

"Pirates! Down below!" And then he tore from Eoradon's grip and was off again.

There are pirates on board, he relayed to Iaxal, who'd executed a corkscrew and was coming back around for another pass. The deck of the ship was in chaos around Eoradon. Flames were licking high on the main mast, and the vessel was still listing badly to the port side. Or was it starboard? Mentally, he cursed himself for not taking the time to learn anything about boats, and made for a door that looked like it might lead down below.

I'll go under and see what's happened to the hull, Iaxal said in his mind, and he distantly noticed her dive under the water. Dragons were known for their flying capabilities, of course, but they were also very capable swimmers. As Eoradon opened the door to start down the stairs, he was bowled over and knocked to the ground by a crewmember running up top.

The sailor landed sprawled on the ground and cursed loudly

as he dropped his armful...of stolen goods. Jewelry scattered across the deck, spilled from a box the man had been carrying. As he watched a golden ring go bounding overboard and into the water, Eoradon's mind pieced things together.

"Imperial dog," the pirate snarled as he climbed to his feet. Eoradon found his footing and spun to meet the man, who he noticed was now wielding a sword, long and wickedly curved.

I don't have my blade, Eoradon thought. *And he was down below when we flew in. He doesn't know I'm a Rider*.

Eoradon reached for his sidesword and realized he'd left it in his pack, which was currently in the saddlebag on Iaxal's back. He cursed to himself and adopted a hand-to-hand fighting stance, dropping low and putting both arms out in front of his body.

The pirate smiled, showing off a mouth missing most of its teeth. He was dressed in Meloran fashion, wearing a vest with no shirt and loose-fitting cloth pants. He moved forward, fast and clearly practiced with a blade, slashing at Eoradon's neck. The Rider slipped back, letting the blade pass inches from him, and made to step in and close the distance between them.

The pirate, for his part, saw this coming, and lurched forward at the same time, crashing into Eoradon and spinning off him. Eoradon fell to the ship's deck, while the pirate simply spun and came at him with an overhead slash. Eoradon rolled to the side, letting the blade impact the wood of the deck with a *thud,* then kicked out with his foot at the man's exposed ribs. But again, the pirate slipped backward, ripping the blade from the deck and spinning away. Eoradon climbed to his feet and readied himself again.

As the pirate made to move toward him this time, Eoradon

dropped low, rolling under the swing and coming up behind him. The pirate whirled, faster than seemed possible, but Eoradon stepped inside his grip and caught his arm at the wrist and elbow. The man's face twisted in horror as he realized, too late, what was happening. Eoradon wrenched the arm, and the sickening, wet sound of snapping bone and ripping tendon filled the air.

The man screamed, but Eoradon cut it off with an elbow to the throat. He stumbled back, mutilated arm hanging limp as a black and purple bruise was already spreading from his crushed windpipe. Eoradon took one step forward and leveraged a kick to the pirate's chest, crushing his sternum and caving in his chest cavity with a *crunch* as he flew back, disappearing over the rail and splashing into the surf below.

Eoradon stood there, panting as the sound of rushing blood filled his ears. He shouldn't be winded from that, he knew; a mortal man fighting a Rider should be no different than a baby fighting a grown man. But still, when he'd broken that man's body and given him to the sea, something had snapped inside Eoradon, and air wouldn't come. He dropped to his knees as the ship rolled hard to the side again. All around him, men screamed. Tears gathered in his eyes. He'd fought his peers countless times, run through training forms on the dummies in the training yard even more.

But there was no fear in a dummy's eyes when your sword found his neck. He did not have regrets, or wish he'd lived differently. He did not wonder how he'd come to this end. He did not die namelessly in a foreign ocean for nothing more than a few trinkets.

Eoradon knew the tears didn't make any sense. He should not cry for a pirate who'd tried to kill him, who'd tried to kill all the men on this ship. There were still people who needed his help. But there he was; sobbing into his hands on the deck of a sinking ship, all for the life of a man who'd wanted him dead.

Rodo! Iaxal's voice seemed far away, like light through a black curtain. *You need to get up! The ship is capsizing!* Cold water sprayed across Eoradon, shaking him from his stupor. Iaxal had exploded up from beneath the surface and doused him in droplets of ocean spray.

Standing on uneven legs, his balance sacrificed to the rolling ship, Eoradon tried to take in his surroundings. Sailors ran in all directions, trying to secure goods, tying off ropes in a futile attempt to save the vessel, or occasionally, simply leaping from the deck into the foaming water below. Seeing he was nearly out of time, Eoradon set about forcing the more stubborn members of the crew to evacuate.

He grabbed the muscled forearm of a man nearby, still frantically trying to tie off a rope to the main mast, for what purpose Eoradon couldn't say.

"It's time to go!" The Rider yelled to the sailor, who made no move to come with him, and instead tried to pull away. Frustrated, Eoradon tightened his grip on the man's arm, took hold of the back of his soaked-through shirt, set his feet, and threw the sailor from the ship. He cried out in surprise, then disappeared over the railing, much in the same way the pirate had only moments before.

Dive, Iaxal! Eoradon called out to the dragon through the bond. *Get them out of the water!* She didn't respond, but the glittering visage of her scales, aflame in light reflected from the sinking sun, circled broadly overhead, then dove streaking down, slamming into the water and sending spray cascading thirty feet into the air.

Eoradon continued to move across the deck, pulling sailors from whatever menial tasks they'd decided were important enough to risk their lives for, and forcing them from the deck. Iaxal was making trips to shore, carrying two to three sailors at a time, then returning for more. When the deck was finally clear, Eoradon himself leapt from the vessel and crashed into water below. The other pirates hadn't shown themselves, leaving Eoradon to wonder if they were out here, bobbing in the water, trying to blend in with the crew.

A few minutes later, he was atop Iaxal as they circled the site and looked for survivors in the water. The wind was doing a decent job drying his soaked clothes, and the sailors Iaxal had deposited on shore were now making their way back to Iannivar to find out their next steps.

Eoradon was just about to tell Iaxal it was time to head to the city and report to the Duke when he heard it: a long, low horn blast reverberated in the distance. Eoradon turned his gaze toward the sound, and at first, could see nothing in the fog that had settled on the water of the bay. After a moment, though, the bow of a ship cut through the thick fog, and Eoradon saw it was not alone. A small fleet was converging on Iannivar.

What should we do? Iaxal asked in his mind.

Eoradon's mind raced. His first instinct was to head for the monastery and let the city handle it themselves. But of course, that was not the Riders' way, and almost certainly more people would die if he ran, even though the thought of killing again made him want to lean over and empty his stomach to the sky.

He could attack them outright, he knew. He saw a few

ballistae on the ships as they drew closer, but at enough speed, dragon's fire would chew through their wooden boats before anyone could land a shot. Or so he figured, anyway; all his battle knowledge was ultimately hypothetical.

He smoothed his hair away from his face with a sweaty hand as he turned to the city, a bell now ringing from one of the white towers, fingers of a hand reaching endlessly to an almost-dark sky. The sun had nearly disappeared over the watery horizon and twinkling stars now took their place in the sky, awaiting the arrival of the twin moons and the bisecting pattern they would cut through the pinprick tapestry of the night.

Eoradon! Iaxal was screaming in his mind. *What are we doing?*

He breathed deep, reminding himself of his name, of his heritage. He was the Prince of Ir-Anan; these were his people, and he would not abandon them.

Make for the city, he said. *We need to speak with the Duke and organize a defense.*

A beat of Iaxal's great wings sent them toward the coastal city at speed. As they flew above the massive harbor, where at least a hundred ships now burned, Eoradon felt his stomach clench with realization. The pirates on board the sloop they'd intervened to help were simply the first wave. These ships could provide no resistance to a blockade by sea.

Eoradon's eyes swept out again across the incoming fleet. It wasn't large, maybe twenty ships, but with the bulk of Iannivar's own ships decimated, they could blockade this port and functionally hold the city hostage. Eoradon swallowed and tightened his grip on the saddle.

Nevermind, he said, his resolve strengthening as he realized what he must do. *We go to sea. That fleet cannot be allowed to blockade the city.*

We're outnumbered, Iaxal said, flashing anxiety through the bond. *I see ballistae, Rodo.*

We stay low and fast, don't give them a shot. We can do this, Iaxal. He wasn't sure if his own words were working on him, but he felt a knot easing in his stomach as he readied himself. *They can starve this region if they take the port.*

Iaxal was silent for a long moment. Then she banked toward the ships and flashed resolve. *Then we will ensure they do not. Hold on.* A beat of her wings increased their speed, then another, and another, and suddenly Eoradon wished he'd taken the time to put on a mask. He leaned low, hugging himself to the dragon and feeling the warmth seeping through her scales. Whether it was that warmth or the fact he was plunging into an actual battle, he could not say, but he felt a heat spreading through his chest, as well. His muscles tensed, his breaths came fast and hard through his nose, and blood thundered in his ears.

Silently, he reached out to his Rider blade and felt the sword respond. It hovered up from where it was affixed to the saddle and flew alongside them. The ships were close now, only a few hundred yards away. He sent the sword speeding ahead, so fast it would make arrows seem slow. It rocketed away, just above the surface of the water, the wind from its passing sending sprays of water into the air around the sword before it disappeared into the belly of the lead ship. Eoradon couldn't hear the wood splintering, but he saw it. The guts of the ship exploded in a cascade of shattered beams and planks, showering the ocean with its detritus. The sword passed out the stern in a similar display, then slowed as Eoradon directed it to turn around and make another run at one of the nearby ships. He couldn't keep this up for long without taxing himself too much, but it was as good an opening salvo as he could hope for.

Dive! He screamed in his mind. Iaxal obliged, dropping beneath the water without slowing. Eoradon took in a large gulp of air just before breaking the surface and entering the vast darkness of the bay. Beneath him stretched an inky black abyss with seemingly no end, while the water above him was illuminated only by the pinprick light of stars, shimmering through the shifting curtain of the sea. After a moment, that light was blotted by the shadowy forms of ships as they passed beneath the small fleet.

Up! He roared. Again, Iaxal obliged, exploding up through the water toward one of the ships at the back of the group. Eoradon clung close to her, closing his eyes and lowering his head, flattening himself as much as possible. The only sound for a heartbeat was the water rushing around him, until they collided with the underside of the ship and burst through it. The shattering and cracking and twisting of wood filled the air as they flew up through the holds of the ship, the crown of Iaxal's head forming a scaly battering ram with wings. In what seemed no time at all, they burst into the air, the wind whipping at Eoradon's soaked hair and clothes. He opened his eyes, looking down at the vivisected boat, now in the process of breaking fully in two, its midsection brutalized as it was.

Eoradon tasted metal as water ran in rivulets down his face and onto his lips. Wiping his face, his hand came back red. Below, men were leaping from the ship if they were able, but many were not. He'd known this would happen. Men were in those holds when they'd broken through. They wouldn't have even known what was happening before they came to a bloody end in the gore now dripping from him.

Eoradon shook his head and wiped his eyes. No time for that. Not right now. He forced his revulsion down and blew out a deep breath.

Light it up.

They dove again. This time, Iaxal pulled up before plummeting into the water and opened her massive jaw as she angled toward a line of ships. Eoradon heard a sharp intake of air, then a snap as she ignited it.

A gout of white-hot flame exploded from Iaxal's mouth, impacting the ship, made of wood and tar, with physical force. It caught fire instantly, as dried wood and accelerants often do. Iaxal was already moving on to the next one. As they passed the end of the line and banked out to go back for another pass, Eoradon heard popping sounds, followed by a massive explosion as one of the ships lit the bay with its final report. Wood and other debris vaulted hundreds of feet into the sky, raining down on their compatriots who had yet to meet such a violent end.

They made pass after pass, lighting the ships aflame. When they were done, they sat hovering nearby and watching the small fleet burn and sink, the sounds of popping fires filling the air when the screams subsided. There were few survivors. They'd not expected a dragon, clearly. Not one ship got a ballista shot off before they fell.

It was a massacre, Eoradon thought numbly. *They couldn't even fight back.*

It was needed, Iaxal said, sending calm through the bond.

You said yourself, they would've blockaded the city.

Right. Eoradon couldn't think about it any more. The wall he'd kept up during the fight, if it could even be called that, was coming down now that it was over. He clenched his hands into fists to stop them shaking. His Rider blade hovered back up to him from where it had been, zipping between the ships, punching holes, and generally hastening their end. It settled back into its place on the saddle.

His gaze slid over to the city of Iannivar, where a small crowd had accumulated on the docks to watch the slaughter. That seemed foolish to Eoradon, considering the pirates had set fire to many of the boats moored there, but people are drawn to spectacle.

We need to report to the Duke before we head back. Iaxal flashed agreement and they headed off toward the city.

A few minutes later, they dropped to the ground in the square of the ducal residence: a large garden, crisscrossed with dirt pathways laid on top of cut stone. The garden was verdant and in bloom, dimly lit by hanging lamps which provided a sense of romantic atmosphere to the place. Which probably explained the several young couples, walking hand in hand while gazing at the garden's bounty, who were forced to scurry away as the dragon landed hard on the circular stone platform that marked the center of the garden.

Eoradon dropped from the saddle and took in the confused and frightened faces of the lovers in the garden.

"I need to speak with the Duke," he said. No one moved, except to look from him to Iaxal and back. He sighed, fatigue seeping into his bones, and rubbed his face. Then he called down his Rider blade from the saddle and slammed it into the stone, where it stood firm, not even shaking. "I am a Rider of Mun-Alin!" He called out, raising his voice for emphasis. "I have defeated an invading force in the bay, and I need to speak with the Duke *now!*" He roared the last word, and Iaxal thrummed along with him, letting a low growl emanate from her and shake the ground ever so slightly.

The people ran from the garden in terror, and a servant in the livery of the Iannivaran Ducal House came sprinting up to him, bowing low as he did.

"Master Rider," the man said. He was thin, with a hooked nose and rapidly thinning head of hair. "My name is Brisk, a servant in the house of Duke Weston of Iannivar." He rose to his full height, a few inches shorter than Eoradon, and looked up at him from under thick blond brows gone gray with age. "Please follow me. Duke Weston will be happy to receive you in the throne room."

"I'm sure he will," Eoradon said, trying and mostly failing to keep the snark from his voice. He turned to Iaxal and spoke aloud for Brisk's sake. "Wait here. I won't be long." She thrummed in response and settled down to rest.

Brisk led him down a series of twisting hallways, lined with windows looking out on the city. The ducal residence sat high on a hill and was, like much of the city's more notable architecture, a massive tower. Thus, it gave anyone walking these halls a breathtaking view of the city stretching out below, like a carpet of light leading to the docks and the glittering bay beyond. Of course, on this night, flames still raged on the docks, and thick tendrils of smoke twisted from the wreckage further out in the waters of the bay as the invading ships made their final voyage down under the dark water. Eoradon looked pointedly away from it, focusing instead on following the servant, who still moved slightly ahead of him.

The ducal throne room was grandiose to a degree that stunned Eoradon. Maybe he'd been away from the pomp of royalty too long, but this display would've been extreme, even in the Imperial Palace of Ir-Anan. Massive white pillars, so thick Eoradon's arms would only reach halfway around them, lined the walkway to the throne, which was itself carpeted with a plush red fabric. The enormous pillars ended their vertical ascent a hundred feet above, at a ceiling covered in murals depicting moments from the Empire's—and, more specifically, Iannivar's—history.

Huge glass windows reaching halfway to the ceiling lined the room's lone exterior wall, looking out on the city below. At the base of these windows were doors that led to small balconies, where the Duke would entertain guests and show them his dominion.

Duke Weston of Iannivar leaned against the stone railing of one such balcony, a glass of deep red wine swirling lazily in a hand hanging haphazardly over the near-thousand-foot drop to the streets below.

As Brisk led him closer, Eoradon made out more details about the man. Weston was young, in his thirties, with gray just beginning to touch the hair at his temples, which was otherwise dark. He was clean shaven and dressed in a uniform that looked military in design, though to Eoradon's knowledge, he'd never spent any time soldiering. Like most royals in the Empire, Weston had come to his throne via appointment after his father retired.

My father probably appointed his father, Eoradon thought as he trailed behind Brisk and approached Weston from behind.

The servant held up a hand, halting Eoradon's approach.

"Your Grace," Brisk called. Weston turned ever so slightly toward him. "Announcing Master Rider..." he trailed off and turned to Eoradon. "Pardon, sir, what is your name?"

Eoradon nearly gave his real name, then thought better of it, being in the presence of, technically, Imperial royalty. "Kieran," he said, using the name of a member of the royal guard from his childhood.

Brisk nodded and turned back to the Duke, who looked to be growing impatient. "Announcing Master Rider, Kieran of Mun-Alin." After a beat, Weston nodded in ascent and Brisk stepped aside, taking his place nearby, should he be needed.

Eoradon approached the Duke, who didn't bother to turn and face him.

"Rider, eh?" Weston's voice was regal, with all the pomp and authority granted by a life of never being questioned.

"Yes, Your Grace." Eoradon took a breath and calmed himself. He wanted to give his report and be away, but the Duke seemed to want a conversation.

Weston beckoned him forward and extended a hand to gesture to the railing upon which he leaned. Eoradon came to a stop next to him, but chose to remain standing, rather than lean.

"I hear you saved our city," the Duke said, still not looking at the Rider. "Come to collect a reward?"

Eoradon's brow creased in confusion. "Reward? No, Your Grace, I simply—"

"Good," Weston huffed, cutting him off. "Because there won't be one. Doing your duty, that's all."

Eoradon swallowed as the memories of his duty crawled up

to meet him. "Yes, Your Grace. If you don't mind, I'd like to give you an official report—"

"Ha!" The Duke laughed and cut him off again. "Official report? Like you're a member of my guard?" Weston turned to face him now, and Eoradon saw his eyes were ringed with red and heavy with bags.

Must have started on that wine before the ships even showed up, he thought.

"You know you don't have to give me any report." Weston took a deep drink from his glass and wiped his mouth on his sleeve before continuing. "You Riders just do whatever you like. We have no say."

Eoradon cocked his head. "Your Grace—"

"Oh, stop pretending," Weston said. "Call me Weston."

Eoradon cleared his throat and forced down the contemplation of what he'd do if this man cut him off again. "Weston. I have no interest in operating with impunity. But that force was bearing down on the city and your ships were already being decimated. There was no time to allow them to form a blockade."

Weston sighed and hung his head. "Right. No time. Blockade." He waved a hand. "Consider your report given, Rider. You saved the day." He turned and resumed his gazing out at the city. "Now please, leave."

After a confused moment of hesitation, Eoradon turned and left the Duke and the strange conversation behind. As he walked away, he heard the Duke mumbling to himself.

"Such a waste. All for nothing."

Stamping down a growing feeling of unease, the heir to Ir-

Anan moved away, following Brisk back through the winding halls to where Iaxal rested in the garden. And after hardly a moment to bid the servant farewell, he leapt into the saddle and all but begged her to take to the sky.

It was two days later when they landed hard in the courtyard of the monastery. Autumn had come to the midlands of the Empire, blanketing the land in the red, yellow, and orange vibrancy of the changing season. But the monastery at Mun-Alin was mostly unchanged. Stark, gray, and stinging cold, the coruscating landscapes of the midlands were a long-forgotten memory here, replaced by the unyielding march of winter.

After landing and sending Iaxal with the stablemaster Grija, under whom Ferao had begun training, Eoradon made straight for Dragonmaster Rykas's study. It was early in the day, the sun barely risen, and a dull orange light bathed the stone of the monastery as Eoradon trudged through the halls toward the Dragonmaster's quarters.

He found Rykas bent over his desk, deep in a book. The man's long dark hair had gone mostly gray over the years, as had his goatee, which now drooped down past his chin, nearly to his chest. He looked up at Eoradon from beneath neatly trimmed brows as he entered.

"Ah, Eoradon, my boy." Rykas's voice was gone gravelly, and he'd taken on a much more grandfatherly disposition these last years. "Come in, come in."

Eoradon nodded and proceeded into the study, piled high with scrolls, books, and trinkets, the uses of which he doubted he could discern with a year of free time. He took a seat in the chair

Rykas indicated, and the old man turned to face him.

"What can I do for you?" The Dragonmaster asked. Eoradon recounted the events at Iannivar, not pausing until he reached his conversation with the Duke.

"Duke Weston," Eoradon said, "seemed...less than enthusiastic about our intervention."

Rykas pondered that. "How so?"

Eoradon shifted uncomfortably. "Well," he started, "he seemed more upset we'd stopped the attack than relieved. And as I left him, I heard him mutter under his breath about how it was 'all for nothing' and 'a waste.'"

Rykas's eyes widened and he blew air out from his aged lips. "That is certainly a strange reaction." He said. Then his eyes met Eoradon's. "What do you think?"

Eoradon shuffled uncomfortably, not wanting to voice it. Eventually, though, the weight of Rykas's gaze proved too much. "I think he might've been in on it. I don't know why, but I can't shake the feeling there's something here we're missing."

Rykas sat back in his chair in thought. After a moment, he nodded. "I agree." Eoradon sagged with relief, glad to have been believed. "You should go investigate it."

The heir to Ir-Anan snapped back to attention. "Me?" He asked, unable to keep the shock out of his voice.

Rykas chuckled. "Aye, boy. You were enough of a Rider to obliterate a fleet and free a city from a potential blockade. I think you're enough of a Rider to go ask Duke Weston why he wasn't happier about it." Seeing the hesitation written plainly on the young Rider's face, Rykas smiled and added, "I'll send Liran with you, to make it all look that much more official."

Eoradon exhaled. *Liran will be with me,* he thought, and was immediately upset he wasn't more relieved. He and his mentor had been more distant in the last couple years. Liran had spent much of his time away from the monastery, on special assignments from the Dragonmaster. And even when he was there, he was usually locked in his quarters, sleeping or studying for whatever his next job would be.

Still, he thought, maybe it would be good to spend some time with the veteran Rider. Rykas dismissed Eoradon, sending him to eat and rest, to ready himself to leave the next day. As Eoradon left the old man's quarters, he nearly bowled over Meristofales in the hall.

"Whoa there, your majesty." The First Ranger smirked wickedly and set Eoradon back on his feet where he'd nearly been knocked down. "I know you royals are above us commonfolk, but watch out underfoot."

Eoradon forced a chuckle and nodded. "Aye, Ranger. I will. My apologies." Meristofales gave him a good-natured slap on the back.

"Go on, then. I've got to see the old man." He swept past the prince and through the door into Rykas's study, leaving Eoradon to collect himself and begin gathering provisions for the next day's journey.

The next morning found Eoradon in the stable, checking and re-checking Iaxal's saddle, as well as his own weapons, armor, and riding implements. Liran arrived not long after Eoradon and set about readying himself. He said nothing to the prince, and so they went about their business in awkward silence.

Eoradon watched as Liran whipped his massive Rider cloak around his shoulders. The long end of the deep purple garment was down around his feet, so he bundled it up and draped it over his shoulder, in a style many Riders used when walking around with their cloaks on.

A short time later, Eoradon was surprised to hear an aged voice calling his name. He poked his head out to look around Iaxal's hind leg, where he'd been busy scrubbing some mess away from her scales, and saw Dragonmaster Rykas approaching, flanked by Feordan and Meristofales. Eoradon moved around Iaxal's backside to greet his superiors, and that was when he noticed what Rykas held in his hands.

A cloak; deep green, interwoven with strands of gold, folded over itself a number of times, until it made a neat square in the Dragonmaster's hands. Eoradon's words caught in his throat as he tried to speak, and the old Dragonmaster just laughed.

"I never tire of seeing their expressions." Rykas said to Feordan, who was herself smiling broadly. Turning back to the stunned prince, he said, "Eoradon, take this cloak, as well as my blessing, and go forward as a Rider of Mun-Alin." He extended his arms, offering the cloak to Eoradon, who took it in trembling hands.

"Yes, sir." He managed to croak as he ran his hands along the garment. It was beautiful, and easily the finest needlework he'd ever seen.

Did you know about this? he asked Iaxal.

No, Rodo, she said, a smile in her voice. He looked at her over his shoulder, and saw her massive eye glinting as she looked at him. *But you earned it.*

It doesn't feel real, he said.

But it is! she said. *Now put the damn thing on!*

He laughed as he swung the cloak over his shoulders and clasped it across his chest. Meristofales stepped forward, taking the hem of the cloak and wrapping it around the prince's waist, like a large cloth belt.

"Can't have you getting it dirty before you even get a chance to let it fly in the wind," he said, winking and gesturing at his own cloak, an impenetrable black curtain, wrapped around his waist in the same way.

"Thank you, First Ranger," Eoradon said. Meristofales waved away the honorific like a pesky gnat.

"I'll have none of that nonsense," he said. "Not from a fellow Rider."

Eoradon smiled and dipped his head, trying to cover the blush that flooded his cheeks. Iaxal laughed at him in his head. He exchanged more thanks to the other Riders, stifling his surprise when Feordan wrapped him in a tight hug.

"You deserve it," she said, and he felt himself go red again. He was going to make a joke and thank her, but as they separated, he noticed a profound sadness crowding her eyes, and was stunned into silence. As he glanced at the imposing First Ranger, he thought he saw something similar in his slate grey eyes, but it was gone as fast as he'd noticed it. And then they were leaving, wishing him well, and he wondered, not for the first time, what game was being played, and what he'd missed.

As he turned around, he saw Liran, arms crossed, leaning against Xialan and watching the exchange. When their eyes met, his former mentor smiled broadly, and Eoradon caught a glimpse of the man he'd known as a boy.

"There he is," Liran said, his voice free of whatever burden he seemed to always carry with him these days. "Prince of Ir-Anan *and* a Rider of Mun-Alin. You collect titles like girls collect dolls."

Eoradon laughed. "Don't let Feordan hear you say that."

Liran waved his concern away. "Oh, I'm not scared of Feo." He sighed then, settling back against Xialan, who seemed to barely notice Eoradon's presence. "This is a big step," he finally said. "Your first undertaking as a real representative of Mun-Alin." He smiled, all warmth and friendship, and clasped Eoradon on the shoulder, squeezing slightly. "I knew you'd do it." And then he turned and resumed his preparations, leaving Eoradon to return to Iaxal and do the same. As he turned, though, he couldn't help but notice Rialin in the entry to the stable, turning and stalking away, fists clenched angrily at his sides.

Eoradon had to stop himself turning around and looking at his cloak, shimmering brilliantly in the early afternoon sun. The cloak was long, extending a little past the tip of Iaxal's tail. Rider cloaks always were long like that, though. It was a symbol as synonymous with their order as the telepathic blades they used to fight. Part accessory, part life-saving implement, the cloak was a vital part of the Rider's accouterments. And now, he had one. Eoradon felt as though a piece of him he'd been missing was now returned; he was now, finally, his whole self.

The land passed beneath the Riders and their dragons in an autumnal blur, the world finally exhaling the breath it had been holding through the summer heat and humidity, staining the leaves red and yellow and brown as it readied itself for the long sleep of winter. The air had taken on a crispness Eoradon appreciated. They brought the dragons down low, to fly maybe fifty feet off the ground as they soared over the carpet of maturing leaves and frigid creeks. Eoradon noticed the villages and hamlets readying themselves for fall harvest festivals, their carts laden with all manner of foodstuffs to be traded in preparation for the coming cold.

As night descended and the twin moons rose, they camped off the main road, in a copse not far from one of the many small rivers that crisscrossed the midlands of the Empire. Smoke rose from hearthfires as the village just on the horizon and within their view settled in for the night. The ground here was hilly, but not treacherous, and fields of long grass spread in every direction for several miles, the only trees being found in copses like this one, or along the rivers' edges.

Eoradon and Liran sat by the fire, set by Xialan before she and Iaxal left them to go hunt for their own dinners, and chewed on their packed rations of dried meat and fruit. Truthfully, Eoradon could've done with some of whatever large game the dragons were sure to find, but he didn't worry over it, and instead found his eyes flitting to his cloak, which lay folded by Iaxal's saddle, which he'd removed and laid near the fire.

"You were like a child with a new toy today." Liran's voice startled the prince, and he looked over to find the Rider watching him intently from his hooded eyes. He couldn't shake the feeling of unease as he looked in those eyes, which seemed so diminished from the brightness they'd held when Eoradon had been young.

"It was an exciting day," Eoradon said to his old mentor. "I'm sure you were the same when you received your cloak."

Liran smiled, but it did not reach those eyes, ringed in bruises. "Aye, I was." And for a moment, he was lost to memory. "But it was a long time ago now, and that—" he gestured to his own cloak, tossed haphazardly over the log he sat upon "—is just a piece of cloth."

Eoradon felt a flush rise to his cheeks at that. "It is not!" he said, with more force than he'd intended. "It's an honor."

Liran chuckled. "I'm sure you think so, Prince." He took another bite of his dried meat, chewing it like cattle chew cud.

Eoradon wasn't sure what made him speak next; whether his rising hackles at being treated like a child, or Liran's disingenuous use of his royal title, but the words came on so fast and hard, he could no more stop them than he could prevent Uanari taking flight.

"What the fuck happened to you?"

The words hung in the air between them, and Eoradon swore the breeze that had been ruffling his hair just a moment before had stilled as he spoke. He regretted the words as soon as he'd spoken them, but they were out there now. And in truth, he *did* want to know what had caused the changes he'd seen in Liran. So he said nothing, and tried to stifle the flush that burned his cheeks now.

For his part, Liran hardly moved. "So, you got a cloak and a sword, and now you think you're a man?" He took another bite of his meat, ripping it away with his teeth. "You may be a prince, Eoradon, but I don't answer to you. Not when you were a boy, not now that you've draped that bedsheet around your shoulders."

Eoradon couldn't make sense of it. Just earlier that morning, this man had congratulated him on earning the cloak. Now he all but spit on it? Why? He almost asked Liran that very question, but the burning he saw in Liran's eyes, coupled with the relatively isolated surroundings, gave him pause. Instead, Eoradon chose to settle in and try to get some sleep. There were still many miles between them and Iannivar, and he wanted to be fresh for the next day.

Eoradon awoke to a world-splitting roar.

Wake up, Eoradon! Iaxal was screaming in his mind.

What's happening? he asked, trying to shake himself to full wakefulness. The sound of ringing steel forced him to look around. The fire had died, but it was replaced by a dancing, spiraling orange flame in the top of the trees under which they had camped.

Your sword! Iaxal cried. *Get your sword!*

Eoradon called for his Rider blade and felt it rocketing toward him from out of the darkness. *Strange,* he thought. *I thought it was right beside me.* As his hand wrapped around the well-worn grip, he looked around the camp and quickly realized why his things weren't where he'd expected. Their packs had been upended and dumped out, the saddles flung away, even the log Liran had been sitting on the night before was brutalized, split down the middle.

A cry went up from somewhere behind him. Eoradon spun and saw a man flying at him out of the darkness. He wore mismatched leather armor and wielded a battle axe, which was lofted over his head, ready to fall and cleave Eoradon in two.

The prince of Ir-Anan stepped forward and caught the falling axe on the massive cross guard of his sword, then twisted his grip and tore the weapon from the bandit's hands. As the man was still gawking after his stolen weapon, Eoradon reversed his stance and swung the massive sword, light as a feather in his hands, across the man's neck. His head went careening off into the chaos, while his body dropped to the ground with all the grace of a sack of grain.

Eoradon felt a vague urge to throw up, but stifled it and turned to find Liran. The veteran Rider made it easy. He was surrounded by three bandits, weaving between them like a needle through thread. Using a sidesword, he deflected and turned away their blows like it was nothing. He sidestepped a sword thrust and jabbed his blade through the man's open mouth and out the back of his head. As the man fell, he let the sword go, spun and dropped to a knee to let a sideways chop pass an inch over his head, then sprung up, driving a dagger from his boot through the bottom of the bandit's jaw. Then, in one fluid motion, he pulled the knife free, spun back toward the third man, and cut his throat. As the bodies dropped gurgling to the grass, Liran ripped his sword free of the first man's mouth and marched toward Eoradon.

"Bandits," he said when they came together. He wasn't even breathing hard.

Eoradon suppressed the urge to vomit again.

"Why would they attack us?" He asked. "There must be easier prey on the roads than two Riders and their dragons."

Liran rolled one of the dead men over with his boot and bent to examine him. Eoradon tried to look him over, too, and noticed what the older man must be looking at.

"They're emaciated," Liran said, confirming his suspicions. "Hunger and desperation can make men do all manner of stupid things."

Eoradon was about to respond when Iaxal interrupted him.

More of them! And he saw a large black shadow, silhouetted against the stars, dive from the heavens and unleash hellfire on the approaching would-be killers. Eoradon could see about ten men caught in her strafing attack, but another five managed to make it past and were sprinting toward their camp.

Eoradon gripped his sword, feeling the leather of the grip creak in his hand. As he was about to rush forward, another sound filled the air. It was a dragon's scream. He looked up and saw another shape against the stars, diving hard. Fire exploded from the dragon's mouth and the remaining men were vaporized.

Who is that? Eoradon asked Iaxal.

I have no idea, she said.

Then the dragon moved nearer the flames, and the Rider became visible. Eoradon felt the grip on the sword, which he had loosened, tighten again. Rialin hopped down as his dragon, which he had neglected to even name, landed hard in the clearing beyond the copse that had been their campsite.

As he approached, Eoradon saw Rialin was still cloakless, but as always he walked with the air of a person whose every footfall was a hangman's lever being pulled. Eoradon exhaled, trying to straighten his back. He held onto his Rider blade, rather than letting it float nearby.

"Rialin," he said matter-of-factly. "What brings you here?"

Rialin looked at him briefly, then turned to Liran. "Meristofales sent me," he said, "as backup."

Liran looked him up and down. "Pretty sure that's why *I'm* here." He inclined his head toward Eoradon. "Tell him the truth."

Rialin looked down, then glanced up at Eoradon, and those eyes filled with fire. "Fine." He spat the word. "I followed you."

Eoradon's brows creased in confusion. "Followed me? Why?"

"Because you haven't earned that!" He jabbed a finger toward Eoradon's cloak, laying on the ground in a heap a few strides away. "And I came to prove it to you. Out here, where Meristofales and Feordan can't step in and save you." His teeth were clinched, and spittle flew from his lips as he spoke. He was pure rage.

Eoradon spread his arms wide and met the commoner's gaze. "You're *that* jealous? You want the cloak? Why don't you come and take it?"

Both of them looked to Liran, who was wiping his sword on the grass to clean the blood from the blade. He sighed with disinterest and rubbed his brow.

"The time may have come," he said, sounding far away, "for you two to put an end to this."

Rialin nodded. "A duel?"

Liran shrugged. "As good an idea as any. Beat on each other for a bit, then we'll all go to Iannivar together."

Eoradon found himself nodding along. Liran was right. It *was* time to end this. His eyes slid to Rialin, who was still fuming. And despite himself, he felt his own ire rising. Years of hatred, boiling barely concealed just under the surface, was finally laid bare. Eoradon rolled his shoulders and flexed his grip around the hilt of his Rider blade.

Rodo, this is a bad idea, Iaxal said in his mind.

This is what they've chosen, he replied, surprising himself at how ready he was for this fight. *I won't hurt him, Iaxal. But he needs to know I am his better. Not just by birth, but by skill. By merit.*

Iaxal sighed, then he saw her drop from the sky and settle

nearby, just in the range of the flames' reflection, which glinted from her green scales and made her look like molten gold in the night. *I am here if you need me.*

He nodded to her. *I won't.*

"No dragons," he said to Rialin, who had retrieved his own Rider blade.

He chuckled. "If your beast interferes, I'll make sure you both regret it."

Iaxal flashed anger in Eoradon's mind.

"Fine," he forced through gritted teeth.

Liran had sheathed his sword, and was now reclining on the ground, taking in the spectacle. "Begin on my count." And he held up three fingers.

The first finger fell.

Eoradon breathed deep, blew it out through his mouth. Rialin danced from foot to foot, testing his balance. Eoradon met Liran's gaze and his old mentor gave him a reassuring nod. He felt his chest swell with unexpected emotion.

The second finger fell.

Their eyes met. Rialin's brown irises danced with reflected flames. Eoradon resolved to remind this commoner of his place.

The third finger fell. And they moved.

The Rider blades met in a shower of sparks as the blades ground together. They broke apart, and Eoradon went low. Rialin parried, twisted, and stabbed for Eoradon's gut. The prince danced to the side, surprised by the speed of the attack. Rialin never moved like that when training. He was all chops and cuts, no finesse.

What else is new, I wonder?

They came together again, and again sparks flew. This time, Eoradon leaned in and spun off the other warrior, swinging for a pommel strike to the back of the head. But Rialin dropped to one knee, whipped around and chopped for Eoradon's knees. He evaded the attack and tried to drop a knee into Rialin's face. Again, the commoner twisted away and found his footing while the royal floundered.

Eoradon shook himself, tried to refocus. They met again, blades so fast he could barely track them. But the ringing of steel and showers of sparks told him they were still matching swings.

What is this aggression? Eoradon wondered.

He's not just dueling, Rodo. Iaxal's voice was uneasy. *He looks like he's swinging to kill.*

Rialin raised his blade and stepped in, dropping a vicious downward slice, which Eoradon caught on his own crossguard. They locked together, snarling faces only inches away from each other. Eoradon's gaze slid over to Liran again. He mouthed two words.

"Do it."

Eoradon growled and pushed back, separating himself from Rialin and getting some distance. He was breathing hard, but rage still coursed through his veins.

"*Come on!*" Eoradon screamed. Rialin responded with a cry of his own as he leapt forward, blade striking out viciously fast. Eoradon barely got his own sword up to block. Sparks exploded as the blades met again and again. Eoradon feinted high, then went low, but Rialin leapt the strike and stabbed forward. A shift of the shoulders let the blade slide past, but Eoradon's own riposte was wide, and the two warriors ended up spinning away and circling one another.

Eoradon was breathing even harder now. He felt his arms begin to tire. His swings lacked the bite they had before. He was a touch too slow. Rialin landed a blow on his leg, then his arm, then nearly took him through the eye, but the blow glanced off his temple and left blood pouring into his vision.

Eoradon was a capable duelist, and against normal men and normal arms, he was as good as a god. But Rialin fought like a demon. He was faster, stronger, sharper, more brutal. And most of all, he fought with hate in every swing. And Eoradon knew the commoner would kill him, if given the chance.

That chance came. Eoradon barely dodged a vicious backhand that might have split him in two, then stabbed forward. It was a lazy strike, but he could hardly breathe now, much less fight. Rialin batted the swing away, and the sword flew from Eoradon's grasp. He tried to recall it with his mind, but he was too foggy, had lost too much blood, and it did not obey.

He dropped to a knee, trying to prop himself up, give it another go. But there was nothing left. He was spent.

Rialin loomed above him, and he might as well have been the bearer of the end of days. Wreathed in flame, carrying a sword, he looked every part a devil given form. Eoradon lifted his hand.

"I yield," he croaked. Rialin stopped short, head cocked.

Behind him, Eoradon saw Liran rise, sidesword in hand, and take a step toward them. Rialin hadn't noticed. Eoradon could see the conflict written plain across his face. Liran was closing now, and it was clear to see what the Rider was going to do.

A roar split the air for the second time that night. Eoradon looked up and saw Iaxal had leapt through the air, and was bearing down on them. Liran scuffled back to avoid being crushed, but he wasn't her concern. The dragon pounced on Rialin, who barely had time to dodge her enormous claw, which bit deep into the ground in front of Eoradon. He fell to the side, tried to crawl away, but his eyes were fixed on Rialin, standing, sword out in front of his body. He could see it happening. But it was too late.

Iaxal spun toward the Rider, sweeping her foreleg down, claws extended and looking like greatswords. She was moving with rage. And the rage of dragons was a frightening thing to witness up close.

But not for Rialin. He stepped deftly to the side of that downward-swinging claw and brought his sword down in a brutal arc, gripped in both hands.

Eoradon's vision went white as pain overwhelmed his senses. His arm burned. Iaxal screamed so loudly, he thought he'd gone deaf, his ears doing nothing more than ringing. When his vision came back, he saw Iaxal, thrashing on her side, her tail whipping this way and that, and Rialin, standing at her neck, sword in the air.

And fire burned in Eoradon. He still could not stand, but he forced his arm up, aimed at Rialin. He called on the shimmering pool of power within him.

And it answered.

Power flooded his body, and his tired mind tried to make sense of it. He thought he heard Liran screaming, but he paid no heed. He called on the wind, sharpened to a point. He was going to cut Rialin in half; he knew he would. He called that power together in his hand and exhaled.

Nothing happened. His left hand, outstretched to kill Rialin and save himself and Iaxal, did nothing.

But power coursed through his *right* hand. Currently knuckle deep in the earth, the hand exploded with a current of strength like he'd never known. It fired hard, straight down into the dirt. And it was not wind, but flame. His rage had called forth fire when he'd asked for air, and it had been poured directly into the crust of the world.

An explosion sounded, deep in the ground beneath them. Then another. And another, further in the distance. All of the Riders' eyes lifted, following the cascade of explosions toward the horizon, from which hearth smoke still curled from the small village they'd seen the night before.

There was a beat of silence as the world held its breath.

Then, a cacophony as it exhaled.

The foundations of the world, the ground itself, split wide like a horrible mouth, and Eoradon swore he saw a great hand, with fingers made of mountains reaching out of that gaping split in the world. The ground shook and raged, throwing all of them to their backs as they were tossed on a sea of dirt and rock and flame. And as they bounced along on that horrible tide, Eoradon's body finally gave out, and darkness claimed him.

His eyes fluttered open to a world deafened of sound, as a blanket of fresh snow drifted lazily down from orange heavens. He shifted from side to side, managing to free enough space to sit up and look around. The ground was covered in a foot of the thick flakes, and they fell from Eoradon's legs in large clumps as he shifted them.

His body ached. A dozen small wounds screamed for attention as he climbed first to his knees, then his feet. On top of his physical injuries, he felt as though his very spirit was drained. He looked inward, to his well of power, and found it over halfway drained. It alarmed him. He'd never used more than a pinch of his ability before. Which turned his mind back to the moments before he blacked out.

And as those memories flooded back into his mind, he fell back to his knees and retched in that snow. As he cleaned the sick from his mouth, he turned and looked to the horizon, where that great hand had reached from the earth, and nearly fell back to unconsciousness.

Where the little village had been previously, now stood four enormous towers of molten rock, the shortest still at least five-hundred feet high. They belched smoke and lava into the air, turning the clear night sky into a sooty black blob. He lifted a shaking hand to his brow and wiped away a fresh accumulation of snow. And only then did Eoradon realize it was not snow.

It was ash.

The tears came unbidden and unstoppable as the weight of his failure hit him with what felt like a physical force. It pressed down on him, bowing his once-proud royal back and forcing him to hands and knees in the ashfall.

How many lives? he thought. *What have I done?*

The ash continued to fall, twisting down from the glowing sky, but he did not care. And there, a foot deep in the floating remnants of his greatest sin, the Heir to the throne of Ir-Anan, Rider of Mun-Alin, laid down and gave up, allowing that horrible snow to cover him.

Strong hands took him firmly by the arm and hauled

Eoradon from the ashfall, which looked to now be three feet deep at least.

"Damn fool boy," said a gruff voice.

"Meristofales?" Eoradon said, struggling to force words past his cracked and dry throat and mouth. "What are you—" He was cut off as a hacking coughing fit racked his body. His chest felt like it was full of rocks.

"Aye," Meristofales grunted. Eoradon was barely aware as the First Ranger lifted his limp form up onto Uanari's saddle. "Stay here while I find the rest of your little coalition of idiots."

Eoradon hardly noticed the passage of time, drifting in and out of consciousness as he was. But he could hear the belching mountains of flame he'd called forth, spewing an apocalypse into the sky with each report.

Meristofales returned some time later, carrying Rialin, who he hefted up next to Eoradon on the saddle. A glance told Eoradon the man was unconscious. He hardly cared. The anger he thought he might have for his rival wouldn't come forth.

He started the fight, Eoradon thought. *But I ended the world.*

Eoradon gasped as a shock of relief flooded through him.

Eoradon? He nearly burst into tears when he heard Iaxal's voice. *Oh, stone and sky, Rodo!*

Iaxal! he screamed. *Iaxal, are you okay? Your foot—*

I'm fine, Eoradon. Her voice was flat and unconvincing, but Eoradon moved on.

What have I done, Iaxal? How many have I killed?

She hesitated before responding. Eventually she said, *It's bad. The village is obliterated, from what I can tell from the air. But I can't get very close. The smoke is suffocating.*

Tears filled his eyes again and he fought to sit up in the saddle. Uanari was lying in the ashfall, resting while they waited on Meristofales, and this position gave Eoradon a perfect view of what he'd wrought.

The ground was cracked wide, with a thunderous split heading straight out from where he'd been when he set off the chain reaction. Smaller cracks split off from the main vein, leading Eoradon to wonder if there might be other catastrophic reactions elsewhere.

Where the village had been, there was now only chaos. The mountains had risen from beneath the crust of the planet, splitting the ground like a hand breaking the surface of water. The fingers of that hand stood high, extending all the way into the clouds above and lighting the night a bloody orange and red.

We will find a way forward, Iaxal said. *Eoradon, believe me, please. There* is *a way forward.*

Eoradon barely heard her. He simply stared at the visage of his great failure.

He couldn't say how long it had been when Meristofales came trudging through the ever-higher ashfall.

"I can't find Liran or Xialan," he said. "And Rialin's mount is damn wild and won't come to me. Iaxal's foot needs to be treated, and Feordan needs a look at you two before anything else is done."

Eoradon nodded dumbly.

The flight back to the monastery was spent holding tight to Meristofales, the past echoing forward, refusing to be forgotten. Much like the first time Meristofales had saved Eoradon's life, he could not help but listen to the voices in his head, reminding him that he would never belong. He did not argue with them. The ashes drifting lazily to the ground beneath him as he ran from what he'd done were all the proof they needed.

Chapter Twenty

A Moment by the Water

Sinners' Pass to the south has been opened, freed from the Kerani blockade. Apparently, a warrior broke the defense almost on his own. Maybe I should've listened when they asked me to train him.

-Log of Dragonmaster Rykas, 874th Lord of Mun-Alin

Sen stretched and breathed deep the salty air. A pair of gulls wheeled above, their calls audible even above the wind coming in off the ocean that stretched endless before him. It met the horizon of a sky turning lavender as the eastern sun just barely peaked over the tops of the Crags, still dominating the view back to the east. A glance behind told him the others were still asleep, so he decided to indulge himself, slipping his feet out of the fancy boots he'd been given in Kanavar and plunging his naked toes into the cold sand.

He couldn't say how long he'd been standing there, feet

becoming ever more submerged in sand, eyes closed and feeling the breeze, when the boy padded up and joined him. Sen opened his eyes and looked down to see Erick imitating his posture, checking and rechecking to make sure he was doing it right. A smile tugged at the corners of Sen's mouth as he watched the little boy, now inextricably linked to him.

They'd ridden hard out of Kanavar, powering straight through the night and not stopping until Sen was confident they weren't being pursued. Brynne had been sure no one would come for her, saying they'd prefer to fight over the throne of Kanavar than risk her coming back alive, but he wasn't going to take any chances.

The sun had risen the next morning and found them approaching the southern reaches of the Crags, where they'd traversed the valley of Sinners' Pass, always in the shadow of the enormous mountains. When they'd emerged from the Pass, they'd been looking at the sun dipping low over the waters of the Western Ocean. So they'd camped on the beach, and now, they were here.

Erick had been all but attached to Sen the entire time. No one had told him how Sen had freed them, and he didn't seem to care. But he'd frozen when Sen had asked where he'd been while they were separated, and that was enough for the old man to ensure the slaver Jund missed a few meals.

A sour taste infiltrated his mouth as he thought of the slaver, so he spat into the waves and put his arm around the boy, pulling him close.

"Does it go on forever?" Erick asked, a touch of wonder to his voice.

Sen chuckled. "No, son. It doesn't." He thrust a finger toward the horizon. "Far away, past where you can see, lie the shores of

Vaelyn."

The boy's face screwed up in confusion. "Vaelyn? What's that?"

Sen squeezed his shoulder. "A faraway place and a story for another time." He freed his feet from the sand and picked up his boots, then turned toward camp. "Come on, let's find something to eat."

Brynne was stirring as they arrived back at camp. Sen looked her over. She'd discarded the ridiculous ballgown within a few hours on the road, opting instead for a linen shirt, buttoned up to her neck, and a pair of dark wool trousers and boots.

He should hate her, he knew. But in their time on the road, she had proven to be a capable survivor. He was sure there was more to the woman than met the eye, but he couldn't get anything from her. Not surprising, he figured, given she had met his other half.

Sen shuddered involuntarily as images of his old life rose unbidden to the surface of his mind. He'd built a name doing the dirty work of the Duke. Senran Vallos was a name still feared across the Empire. But for all he'd built, he hated that name and the weight it put on him. Senran Vallos couldn't have a family or find peace. He couldn't get away from the death and chaos he'd wrought. But Sen could. And he had, for the most part. He shook off the memories, but the weight of what he'd lost was as present as ever, lurking on the periphery of his thoughts.

Sen moved around to the rear of the wagon they'd been provisioned back in Kanavar and was assaulted by the stench wafting from the cage they'd been pulling behind them. Jund was lying on the floor of the too-small transport, shivering. Sen grimaced at the sight of him, then kicked the side of the cage. Jund startled awake.

It had only been a few short days, but he looked like he'd lost a not-insignificant amount of weight already. He was filthy, stank like old meat, and cried incessantly. Sometimes, when he stopped crying for a while, he begged and bribed and pleaded to be free. No one had said anything to him beyond whatever words were necessary to give him his meager rations or tell him to be quiet. Even Erick seemed indifferent to the man's cries.

This morning, though, Jund seemed less hysterical and more resigned to his situation. He wiped sleep from his eyes, which were significantly less puffy than the previous day, and sighed.

"It's been three days," he said to Sen, his voice still raw from all the crying.

Sen turned to him as he hefted an armful of dried meat and some fruit and vegetables to prepare a breakfast. "And?"

Jund eyed him. "Well, you said you're sending us back after three days, right?" An edge of pleading had crept into his voice.

"I said I was letting Brynne go back after three days," Sen said, his voice hard enough to crush the mountains whose shadows still stretched over them. "I said nothing about you."

Jund spluttered. "You—you can't do that! You said three days!"

Sen let a wicked smile split his face. "Slaves don't get a say in what I do. Isn't that how it works, *slaver*?" He turned on his heel and returned to the other side of camp, where Brynne and Erick had managed to get a fire going. Jund's wails ramped up quickly to their previous volume, but Sen paid them no mind.

"Nicely done!" Brynne said as he dropped the ingredients of

their breakfast down beside the fire. She patted Erick on the back and Sen could see the boy revel in her approval. It pained him, but he knew the boy longed for a mother. Not that Brynne could be that for him, but it was good to see him smile, either way.

Erick turned and looked up at Sen as he approached. "Look, Sen! I made a fire!"

"Aye, I see that. And it's a good one, too. Well done." He flashed the boy a genuine smile and ruffled his hair. "Now why don't you take your sword and go practice forms on the beach while I talk to Brynne?"

The boy nodded enthusiastically, retrieved the wooden practice sword Sen had made for him, and ran to the beach. Sen watched for a moment as the boy ran through the basic forms he'd shown him, then sat down by the fire with a groan and turned to Brynne.

"It's been three days," he said.

"I know," she said, not looking at him as she busied herself preparing breakfast. Sen couldn't help but notice a slight tremor in her hand as she placed the pan over the now-roaring flame.

"I'm not going to kill you," Sen said, lowering his voice in case Erick came close enough to hear. "I said you could leave after three days and I meant it."

She chuckled, and Sen thought he could hear tears in her voice as she spoke. "You might as well. Kanavar will be out of my grasp by now. I can't go back there." She slammed her hand into the half sand-half soil mix upon which they sat. "After all I did to build that backwater hole into a real city—"

"You mean after all *the slaves* did to build it." Sen stared at her flatly.

Brynne sighed. "Yes, the slaves. I'm sorry, I've told you time and again, I'm sorry."

Sen shook his head. "You still don't understand." He jabbed a finger toward the back of the wagon, where Jund's cries had diminished to a burbling sob. "I think he might be able to explain it to you better than I can now."

Brynne sighed again as she dropped the ingredients into the pan in a puff of steam. "The point is, I can't go back."

Sen nodded. "You're probably right. So where *will* you go?"

Her eyes met his for a moment. "I could stay," she said. It wasn't a question, or an offer, but a statement.

Sen nodded thoughtfully, though he already knew what he was going to say. "No."

She gaped. "No? What do you mean, 'no?'"

"We're going to Ir-Anan. I assume that's a place where you might have enemies."

She stammered. "Everyone has enemies. It would be fine."

"I doubt it," Sen said with a chuckle. He gestured at Erick, now doing more playing than practicing. "I can't put him in any more danger. He doesn't need to be dragged into whatever games you're going to be playing."

"So you're putting me out?" she huffed. The breakfast sizzled and popped, momentarily forgotten.

"No. I'm telling you, go find your own way. You're a smart girl; you'll be fine."

Brynne rubbed her eyes as though she was crying, but Sen knew better. She'd expected this, for all her acting. "I suppose you're right. I shouldn't be anywhere near Ir-Anan anyway." She looked to where Jund sat in his cage. "What about him?"

Sen laughed. "Oh, he'll either go with you or go his own way, but if he tries to stay with me, I'll kill him for certain."

Later, the sun blazing fully overhead, Sen watched as Erick told Brynne goodbye. He hugged her, trying to stifle tears in that way young children do, and she played with his hair and told him to be a good boy. Then he ran back to Sen, who scooped him up and held him. Brynne nodded to him, turned, climbed on her horse, loaded with the provisions Sen had given her, and slowly walked out of their camp.

Jund went after her, stumbling and still pleading to be allowed on the horse.

When they disappeared over the rise and into the valley of Sinner's Pass, Sen returned to the wagon. Their camp was already packed, so he placed Erick on the seat next to him, took the reins in hand, and bid farewell to the relative calm of the morning, fixing his eyes north.

To Ir-Anan.

Chapter Twenty-One

The King Rises

The Emergence looms over the midlands of the Empire, a testament to all the ways we've failed. Something had to be done.

-Log of Dragonmaster Meristofales, 875th Lord of Mun-Alin

Wik held fast to Ferao as they soared over the verdant plains of the Imperial Midlands. They'd passed over forests, thick with trees and burbling streams the prior day, and now looked down on fields of long swaying grass, extending as far as Wik could see in all directions.

Seeing as she'd grown up in the monastery, and never set foot off the mountain outside of her training sessions with Eoradon and Iaxal, these fields looked like a different world to her; something from a painting brought to life. In her mind, she felt her connection to Uanari growing stronger every day, even if the

monstrous black dragon fought feelings of betrayal with every step.

It feels wrong, he rumbled in her mind, as if in answer to her thoughts. *I'm not supposed to be alive if Meristofales is gone.* Wik swore she heard thunder as he spoke, but the skies were clear.

I know, she replied, trying to project empathy. *But look at it this way: you can still fight. You can avenge him.*

Uanari scoffed. *What good is vengeance to the dead? If I fight, I will do so because* I *deem it worthy.*

Wik tried not to shrink before his magnitude. In so many ways, Uanari was a force of nature, more than a thinking, feeling creature. Or at least, that's how she'd felt before getting to know him. In truth, the dragon was extremely observant and detail-oriented. To the point where she wondered to herself who'd *really* been the Dragonmaster between him and Meristofales.

If Uanari knew she thought of such things, he didn't mention it. Wik chastised herself. She wasn't used to sharing her mind yet, but she had to remember Uanari could hear everything that passed through her head.

How close are we to you? she asked him.

After a pause, during which Uanari apparently looked through her eyes, he said, *Not long. The mountains of fire should be visible to you within the hour.*

That sent a chill up Wik's spine. She'd heard the gist of the story from Ferao: Eoradon and Rialin fought; Eoradon lost control and ignited the volcanoes. Iaxal lost a foot in the fight, and their mentor disappeared, apparently killed in the explosion, before Meristofales could arrive to save them. It was an insane tale, and Wik wondered why no one had told her before.

Because it was not for you, Uanari said firmly. *It still isn't, but you needed to know what these mountains mean to the rest of the order*.

Wik said nothing, again chastising herself for not better guarding her thoughts.

Uanari wasn't wrong. In less than an hour, Wik noticed the sky darkening as the mountains appeared on the horizon. They were magnificent, in a horrific sort of way. They loomed over the landscape, dominating the view and calling attention to them, rising from the ground like fingers on the hand of a dead god. From the tips of those fingers belched smoke and fumes, glowing an evil orange and red.

"It's going to get warm!" Ferao yelled to her over his shoulder. Beneath her, Wik felt the stablemaster's dragon, Paxavan, bank to the right and begin a slow descent. "We can't stay up in the clouds!" Ferao explained. "The smoke is too thick right now. We'll come in low and find him!"

Wik nodded, but the knot in her stomach had grown even larger, and was threatening to double her over.

I am here. Uanari's booming voice sounded in her mind. She looked down to the ash-covered ground and managed to spot a small hill that seemed to be moving.

Only after a moment did she realize it was not, in fact, a hill, but the massive form of Uanari the Black. His enormous wings unfurled, exposing their thick membranes to the open air as he shook his body clean of ash. Right away, Wik saw he was pained by injuries; injuries she could also now feel. One of his forelegs and both of his hindlegs had been ravaged in the fight with the opposing dragon, his wings were ripped and torn in multiple places, and the tip of his tail had been bitten off. His face bore a deep scar across his snout where claws had raked him, and his body was adorned with similar such marks all over.

Wik was surprised at the depth of anger she felt upon seeing Uanari's injuries. It took her a moment to realize it was not her anger at all; it was his, sent to her through their bond. She shuddered and held closer to Ferao.

"We have to get down there," she said to the stablemaster.

"Aye," Ferao said. "Those injuries are more significant than I realized." Paxavan banked hard down and to the left, heading straight to Uanari's resting place. The large brown-scaled dragon slowed their descent with beats of her wings, sending ash billowing into the sky. As she settled down to the ground, Wik couldn't help but notice her feet sank deep into the accumulated ash. The ashfall's depth was confirmed when she slid off the dragon's back and sank waist-deep in the sooty stuff before her boots touched the hard earth underneath.

She plowed through it, lifting her feet higher with each step, wading through the ash like water, until she reached Uanari's side. Ducking under his massive wing, she slowed as he turned his head and regarded her with yellow eyes, large enough to consume her whole.

This close, she could feel his every inclination, every thought as though it were her own. She dipped her head down, touching her forehead to the bridge of his nose. Heat poured from his scaled body, and as they touched for the first time since she'd accidentally formed their bond, she felt tears welling in her eyes.

This was not the grief that had so overwhelmed her at the monastery. It was something different, more intimate. Uanari missed Meristofales more than she knew it was possible for one being to miss another. But he also felt a deeply-held guilt that thrummed through her body now. That, coupled with what he saw as a newfound obligation to the young Rider who'd done something they all thought impossible, created a storm of emotions within the dragon, producing something she'd never expected to find there.

Fear.

Uanari was terrified of losing her, of failing the Riders or his own kind, of dying himself. She removed the glove covering her right hand and placed it on the dragon's snout, breathing deeply with him.

I am here, she said through their bond.

Uanari breathed out, sending more ash billowing away to be caught and carried away by the wind.

I know.

Hours passed, and as the sun sank low beneath the cloud of ash hanging over their heads, Ferao finally deemed Uanari's injuries tended enough for him to move.

Wik looked into her partner's vast yellow eyes.

Are you ready? she asked.

He huffed, sending hot air flowing over her, lifting her dark hair to the wind. *Let us be away from this place.*

Wik nodded, and the dragon shifted his huge bulk, rising to his feet. He was unsteady, wobbling back and forth as he stood. Initially, Wik was afraid he might lose his balance entirely and crash back to the ground. But after a moment, he righted himself. As he rose to his full stature, Wik glimpsed the ground beneath him and her breath caught in her throat. Uanari must have sensed her shock through their bond, because he spoke almost immediately.

I could not leave him, he said, a sad tinge to his voice. Wik nodded, tears welling at the corners of her eyes, unable to speak.

"What is it?" Ferao approached from behind her. She watched as his eyes settled on the body. For a long moment, he said nothing. Wiping his eyes, he turned to regard her and breathed deep. "We bring him home." It wasn't a question.

An hour later, Meristofales's remains in tow, the group set off. Uanari was still not comfortable with the idea of Wik riding on his back, so she remained with Ferao astride Paxavan. They flew straight through the night, despite their collective fatigue. Uanari would not be stopped. Wik got barely a word from him, but could sense he was in pain. She did not know if it came from his physical wounds or his grief, but he was silent to her either way.

Finally, her bones aching from fatigue, she glimpsed the monastery, high on Mun-Alin, barely visible in the pre-dawn twilight.

Eoradon dragged himself from bed and dressed, reluctantly setting the iron circlet of the Dragonmaster on his head. Haggard, he opened the door from his private quarters and was assaulted by the cold wind, as winter was fully taking hold of the monastery now.

They're coming in now, Iaxal said through their bond. *You should be in the stable to greet them.*

Aye. It was all Eoradon had to offer her. He'd barely slept, and the weight of knowing Meristofales had died beneath the ash mounts he'd brought to the surface all those years ago had poisoned what little rest he did get. He was assaulted by images from that night and chased to waking by memories of what he'd done.

Iaxal flashed worry across the bond. *Rodo, you were barely more than a child,* she said. *Rykas never should've sent you on that errand.*

He sent Liran, too, he reminded her.

Iaxal's worry turned to fury in an instant. *That fool was no better than a child himself. He should've sent Meristofales.*

Eoradon shrugged. *It doesn't matter. He sent Liran. His reasons were his own. And it's not like we ever got the chance to ask him.* Rykas had died before Eoradon had recovered from his wounds. A sudden illness had taken him, and that was that. Meristofales succeeded him and the order of sequester was enacted, all because of Eoradon's stupid mistake. *Meristofales knew how dangerous we were. He locked us away from the realm for a reason. I showed everyone the Riders of Mun-Alin were not to be trusted.*

Eoradon wiped tears from his eyes. He'd already cried himself to sleep, but a Dragonmaster had to be strong.

Even if he wasn't.

Eoradon entered the stable just as Uanari thudded down, followed by Paxavan, carrying Ferao and Wik. He had to contain his shock at seeing the massive black dragon. Uanari had never seemed anything less than a force of nature to the Dragonmaster. Not a *who* so much as a *what*. But now, the sun rising over the eastern horizon and bathing him in red and orange light, illuminating each and every one of his wounds, he seemed very weak.

Eoradon's eyebrows knit in confusion as he saw Uanari cradling something in his enormous foreclaw. He was baring teeth at any who drew close. The accumulated crowd of Riders split as

Eoradon approached. Uanari's lips peeled back to reveal a mouth full of teeth the size of greatswords and twice as sharp. Eoradon hesitated, but proceeded slowly.

Uanari pressed into his mind, his sudden presence nearly overwhelming.

Stop. The voice was thunder and lightning, power incarnate.

Eoradon's eyes rolled to the bundle clutched in that claw.

I don't want to take him, he said, finally sure of what it was the dragon held. *I just want to see him.*

A moment passed between the two. Then, slowly, Uanari opened his claw and allowed Meristofales's remains to lie on the cold stone floor between his forelegs. Eoradon nodded, then approached hesitantly, always aware of Uanari's enormous head hanging over him.

The Dragonmaster peeled back the fabric to look on his mentor's face. He was horribly disfigured by way of what must have been the killing blow, and the time since hadn't been kind to the corpse, but it was still good to see him one last time. Eoradon set his jaw and replaced the flap of fabric.

As he stepped back, he placed a hand on Uanari's leg by way of understanding. The dragon said nothing, and his presence retreated from Eoradon's mind.

When the Dragonmaster looked back to the gathered Riders, his breath caught. Feordan was standing at the front of the group, face ashen, rings around her eyes which were red with tears both old and new. Their eyes met, and she choked out a small sob.

Eoradon caught her in an embrace, and they held each other tight. He wasn't sure who was supporting whom in that moment, but he let the tears come, appearances be damned. If these hard men and dragons thought him weak, he could live with that. He was done living by the expectations of others.

The crowd eventually dispersed when it became clear Eoradon would be making no speeches. They were probably all reeling from the site of Uanari being very much alive when Meristofales had died, but their explanations could wait. When Eoradon eventually broke away from Feordan, he found that only Rialin, still bound to his chair, Wik, Ferao, and a few of the various dragons had remained. Uanari looked exhausted and haggard, as did everyone who'd gone on the expedition to retrieve him.

"Rest now," Eoradon said as Wik and Ferao approached him. "There will be time to discuss what comes next."

Uanari's presence pressed on his mind again.

No, he said. *You must know what comes.* His voice was urgent, hurried.

Eoradon's brow knitted in confusion. *What do you mean?*

I was too weak to show Wik across such a great distance. Meristofales and I saw it before that interloper attacked us. Images flashed in Eoradon's mind. An army, Iannivar in flames, a force martialing to attack...

His blood ran cold as Uanari led him to the natural conclusion of what they'd seen.

"Ir-Anan," he said, not meaning to speak aloud. "They're marching on Ir-Anan."

An hour later, Eoradon sat in the meeting chamber where, what seemed a lifetime ago, Meristofales had announced his departure. He was accompanied around the stone table by Feordan,

Rialin, Ferao, Virsk, and Wik. Taking in the room and his fellow Riders, the Dragonmaster was taken aback by how withered they all looked.

Meristofales was your guiding light, Iaxal said. *Losing him has weakened you all.*

You're right, Eoradon admitted. *But an army marches on Ir-Anan, and we must be ready.*

Ir-Anan has not called for aid, she said.

Anger rose in Eoradon and he did his best not to direct it at Iaxal. She was right, he knew, but he'd already decided it didn't matter. Ir-Anan was his home and the Imperial capital. He would not allow it to fall.

Is Ir-Anan your home? Iaxal asked, knowing his thoughts as always. *Or is the monastery?*

I am a child of two worlds, Eoradon answered, feeling stupid even as he said it.

But you wear a crown of one.

He sighed. *The Riders serve the realm. Ir-Anan is in danger, and we must respond.*

Then, infuriatingly, she said, *I agree. But you must give thought to all avenues, if you are to lead.*

Sighing inwardly, Eoradon rose and leaned over the table, upon which was etched a map of the continent. "Uanari says the army was at Iannivar when last he saw it." He jabbed a finger at the coastal city. "If they're moving on Ir-Anan from here, it stands to reason they will go north to circumvent the Crags via Mourners' Pass." He drug the finger up to the northernmost crossing of the Crags to show his meaning.

Virsk rose and looked at the map. "We could hit them in the pass," he said. "Maybe stop them before they reach the city."

It will not work, Uanari said in all of their minds at once, a dizzying and disorientating experience. *They will have too much of a head start, and Dyraxian and his Rider will be on high alert after...what happened.* His booming voice quieted some on the last words.

Eoradon rubbed his jaw. He was frustrated by something Uanari had said, and felt the need to prod him. A silent warning from Iaxal crossed their bond, but he ignored it.

"Uanari," he spoke aloud, knowing the dragon could hear him through Wik. "How do you know this other dragon?"

Silence pervaded the mental bond they were all currently sharing, but an unmistakable rumble passed through the floor beneath their feet as Uanari thrummed down in the stable.

I do not know *Dyraxian,* Uanari said after a moment. *But I know* of *him. He is a dragon of legend, thought long dead.*

For what felt like the hundredth time in the last hour, confusion washed over Eoradon. He saw it mirrored on the faces of the others. *What do you mean?*

Dyraxian was a wild dragon and servant of the old gods, prior to the ascension of the Six.

That revelation struck the gathered Riders with a physical force.

"That's impossible!" Ferao said immediately, slamming his open palm on the table. "That dragon would be ancient beyond belief!"

"Nevermind that," said Virsk in his northern lilt. "If he

served the old gods, he should be dead with his masters."

"It's shite!" Ferao was standing now, his face going red. "It cannae be the same dragon."

The floor rumbled again. *Do not question me, stablemaster!* Uanari's voice was all lightning, pretense falling away. Ferao looked cowed, and sank back to his seat. *I do not know how he lives, but there is no other dragon alive like Dyraxian. He is immense, both in physicality and ferocity. There will be no parlay for Ir-Anan, no walls high enough to stop him.*

"What about the Rider?" Rialin spoke for the first time, his voice quiet and thoughtful. "Who is he?"

I do not know, Uanari replied, his voice full of venom. *And I do not care. They must be ended, Rider and dragon.*

Eoradon nodded. "So we will go to the aid of Ir-Anan." He leaned over the ancient table on his fists, eyes fixed on the little facsimile of the place he was born. "And we will fill the sky with dragon calls."

Chapter Twenty-Two

The Capital

I struggle to imagine what it looked like, the day the mountain was cut in half. Splithalf and Otherhalf together would have been at least twice the size of Mun-Alin.

-Log of Dragonmaster Horus, 873rd Lord of Mun-Alin

Splithalf loomed on the horizon, foggy in the quavering distance. Sen squinted and could make it out, barely. By his estimate, they should reach the mountain and, by virtue of that, the city that rested at its cleaved base, by dusk. Ir-Anan barely twinkled at the bottom of that massive black rock, a tiny diamond at this great distance.

Sen breathed deep and exhaled, expelling the nerves which had settled over him since spotting their destination, now looming suddenly very close and starkly real.

"Look," Sen said, nudging Erick and pointing at the shimmering speck on the horizon. "That's Ir-Anan."

The boy squinted, leaning forward in his seat. “It doesn’t look like much,” he finally said.

Sen chuckled. “Just wait ‘til you see it up close. It’s the gem of the Empire.”

Erick shrugged, then looked down, where his feet rested against the wooden bottom of their cart. Sen regarded him for a moment before taking a breath and asking, “What’s the matter?”

Erick shrugged again before looking up at that distant city. His small hands fiddled endlessly with the hem of his shirt. Sen could see the tears welling in the boy’s eyes, hear the hard swallow as he tried to stop himself from crying. The old man put his arm around the small boy and pulled him close. Erick buried his face in Sen’s side and the tears came. The boy cried hard, wetting Sen’s shirt as his hands curled into fists, grabbing hold of his cloak.

Sen was taken back to one of their first nights together, huddled around a fire in the forest surrounding Aneving, and a young boy woken screaming from a nightmare. It had only been weeks, he knew, but somehow the boy looked so much *older*. He patted Erick’s back and held him close.

A few minutes passed before the boy’s sobs came to a shuddering end, but he continued to lean against Sen. The old man did not fight the affection, instead gripping him tighter. The boy was so still, Sen thought he’d fallen asleep, but after a while, he finally spoke, in a voice so small and quiet, Sen barely heard the words.

“Are you going to leave me when we get there?”

“No.” The old soldier hadn’t meant to sound so firm when he spoke, but it was out there now, and nothing to be done. He wasn’t sure when he’d come to the decision, but somewhere in the cells under Kanavar, he'd realized how much he cared for the boy. "No, son, I'm not going to leave you. Not for anything or anyone."

Erick huddled even closer to Sen. "Good." Then, almost as an afterthought, as he was yawning and drifting to sleep, "I love you."

The words hit Sen square in the chest, stole his breath. He felt the tears gathering in the corners of his eyes and tried, fruitlessly, to blink them away. When he spoke, his voice was a choked rasp, an animal fighting its way through a cage. He spoke the words with the same voice that had screamed battle cries to foes, sneered curses at opponents, threatened enemies of the crown. But for all that fervor, he'd never *felt* the words so fully as he did now.

"I love you, too."

As the sun first dipped beneath the horizon and red-orange light bathed the world, Sen and Erick's cart rattled up to the Field of Hylenor, spread out for the mile surrounding the southern side of Ir-Anan. It was, much as its name implied, a massive open field. The grass was cut short, and even now, flags were situated every hundred yards from the gate, useful for showing archers the direction and strength of the wind. The Hylenor made an assault from the South nearly impossible, as approaching armies would be visible for miles as they neared, and then be forced to cross a massive open space while the city's catapults rained down on them.

It was because of all these defenses that the road cutting through the Hylenor was almost exclusively used for trade. On this day, it was packed with carts, wagons, and caravans awaiting entry to the city. Ahead of their spot in the line, Sen could see the gate guards checking wares, pulling back tarpaulins, and even frisking some people and confiscating weapons. He grunted and felt his sleeves, ensuring his throwing knives were fully-concealed. He turned to Erick, who was craning his neck up the enormous city, layers on top of layers, stacked like rings on the finger of a god. .

"Keep your head down," he whispered to the boy. Then he slipped a sheathed dagger into his hand. "And keep this hidden." The boy opened his mouth to ask a question, but Sen silenced him with a shake of the head, then turned and pulled his cloak up, hunching his shoulders. In his hand, he held tight to the writ of Aneving. Finally, after an achingly long time, the cart rolled up to the gate of Ir-Anan, and a guard there approached them.

"Wares?" The guard, who couldn't have seen more than eighteen summers, asked. His voice was high, and he was trying to force it lower. Sen stopped himself from chuckling. Boy or not, he could still see them confined to a dungeon for the night, or expelled from the city altogether. And Sen had no intention of finding himself a prisoner ever again.

"Just our supplies," Sen answered the guard. "And this." He produced the writ and extended it to the other man, who regarded it for a moment before turning to get his superior. As the officer, recognizable by the knee-length, sleeveless blue coat he wore over his light armor, approached, he took the paper from the younger man's hand and his eyes scanned it. Then those eyes slid up to Sen, over to Erick, and back to the paper as he read it a second time. Then he folded it and gently placed it in the pocket of his coat.

"Come with me." And then he turned and was off, clearing a path through the other people trying to enter the city. He directed Sen to a stable, which he quickly realized belonged to the city watch. They left the cart there, and proceeded to follow the officer on foot through the city.

"Is something wrong?" Sen asked.

The officer looked over his shoulder. "We're getting all sorts of refugees in from Iannivar," he said, worry written plainly across his brow. "But this is the first we've heard from Aneving. The Council will want to see you."

Sen's heart dropped. "Iannivar? It's..."

"It's gone." The man's voice was heavy. "So far as we can tell, anyway. The flames are still burning, from what the people at the gate have said."

They're closer than I realized, Sen thought, and his stomach dropped. If they'd already attacked Iannivar, the army would almost certainly proceed through Mourners' Pass, meaning they could be at Ir-Anan within a week, depending on their speed. He swallowed his concerns before bending down and scooping Erick into his arms.

"What's your name?" Sen asked the officer.

"Varen Skald," he said. "And yours?"

Sen hesitated, then sighed before responding in a tone barely above a whisper. "Senran Vallos."

Skald nodded, a slight gleam in his eye. "Understood." Sen mentally exhaled as the captain didn't seem awestruck by the name.

Varen Skald led them through the streets of Ir-Anan, which was bustling and busy at the calmest of times. But now, there was a tinge of fear settled over the crowds. Sen could sense it in the press, as people jostled for position in the street, in the furtive glances spared to the sky. Those people must've heard about the dragon, he decided. *Or maybe they were unlucky enough to see it attack Iannivar*. Sen could certainly go the rest of his life without ever laying eyes on the monster again. Without even meaning to, he voiced his concerns to Skald.

"Does Ir-Anan possess mounted ballistae?"

Skald gave him a quizzical look before answering. "At one time. Truth be told, I'm not sure what's left of them. I think most were dismantled."

Sen could tell the man was holding something back out of that general distrust of outsiders people gain during wartime. He hoped the city had at least some ballistae that were fully functional and stocked. The feeling in his gut told him they'd be needed, if Ir-Anan was to survive the next few days.

The trio made their way through the streets, eventually coming to the Central Line, a vertical shaft cut into the face of Splithalf, rigged with moving platforms that could take individuals of means to any level of the city they wished. From the bottom, where they currently stood, few residents held enough coin to make the trip. But with a wave of Varen Skald's credentials, they boarded an elevator and shot toward the top by way of a system of counterweights. Sen hated these elevators, and his stomach leapt as they began to ascend. Erick wriggled out of his arms and stood by the railing, watching with wide eyes as the ground rushed away from them.

When the platform came to a rest, they found themselves standing on the top level of the city, and the differences were immediately apparent. For one, this level was still under construction, as most buildings were covered in scaffolding and other signs of ongoing work. Additionally, the streets were nearly empty compared to the first level. The materials used in building were also different; the bottom levels were standard brick and mortar, but up here, builders incorporated metals, giving everything a shimmering quality Sen found disorienting.

Erick was dumbstruck, his jaw hanging open as he stared at the beautiful buildings, and the beautiful people walking between them. Sen had to all but drag him away as they trailed behind Skald. It took only a moment for the old soldier to realize where they were being led.

The Imperial Palace. Sen swallowed hard as he looked up at the immense facade which, like much of the top level, was still being constructed. The palace was actually built as an enormous pillar, running vertically through the entire city. This latest iteration was gold-plated, adorned in massive likenesses of dragons and wolves, which Sen couldn't help but find a little humorous, given their current predicament.

Varen Skald led them though the huge golden doors at the base of the opulent carvings with only a cursory glance from the guards stationed there. Sen assumed there wasn't much cause to guard a door a thousand feet off the ground, so these guards wouldn't often have cause to question the people passing by them.

The officer led them through the palace's winding halls, passing by walls devoid of plaster, half-finished ornamentation, and a whole lot of workers who barely paid them any attention. Eventually, they came to a stop in front of another enormous gold-plated door. Sen could not help but roll his eyes and seethe at the unrestrained opulence.

And all this for a palace with no king, Sen thought. *Who is this meant to impress?*

Varen Skald knocked lightly on the door three times. After a brief pause, it swung inward. The room on the other side took the rest of the palace's spectacle and raised it to even more ludicrous heights. It was a large, high-ceilinged chamber with a floor of smooth marble inlaid with gold. The walls were carved with more of the same images of lions, wolves, and dragons that Sen had seen throughout the palace. It was furnished with plush couches and chairs, beautiful deep-brown wood tables, and a desk that would put most kings to shame. The room's most striking quality, though, was the fact that its outermost wall was missing. Or, it was meant to *look* as if it were missing. In lieu of a standard stone or wood wall, an enormous pane of glass made a window as large as the room itself, looking out on the city and the verdant landscape laid out beyond it. A pool of still blue water took up the area of floor in front of the enormous window.

Sen kept his jaw from hanging open, barely. Erick lacked any such composure, and stared around the room with a look of stunned amazement. Varen Skald strolled in like he couldn't even see the grandeur. The officer walked up to the room's lone occupant, who sat with his back turned to Sen and Erick, lounging on one of the room's couches, looking out the window. A glass of wine sat on a small table next to the couch, which he downed in one gulp after listening to Skald's words.

The man rose, and Sen took a deep breath as he turned and fixed his gaze on them. He was, Sen thought, mostly unremarkable. Average height and build, looked to be in his forties, with dark shoulder-length hair and a trimmed, tightly cropped beard of the same color. He wore robes of a deep navy blue over brown trousers, tucked into shining leather boots. As he rounded the furniture and moved toward the old man and the boy, Sen could see his purposeful gait, the broad smile spreading across his face, his hand extended in greeting, and instantly judged him to be a politician. He groaned inwardly.

"Gentlemen," the man said. His voice was resonant, but not deep, and carried an authority he seemed very comfortable with. "Councilor Ciran Ylannos." He took Sen's hand in a well-practiced grip and shook it once. Turning his attention to Erick, he flashed him a brilliant, disarming smile and tousled the boy's hair, making no mention of what must have been a filthy, greasy mop from their time on the road. Sen's hand itched to go for his sword at seeing the gesture, but a deep breath kept him grounded to the moment.

Ylannos turned back to him, dark brown eyes boring into him. "Captain Skald tells me you and I need to talk." He gestured to the room's plush sofa. "Please, join me."

Sen hesitated, scanning the room for threats. But outside of Skald and Ylannos, there seemed to be no one else of note in the vicinity, and Sen felt confident he could dispatch them both if things got violent. He nodded, then followed Ylannos to the couch. The doughy sofa nearly swallowed the old soldier, who scooted up close to the edge, fumbling awkwardly with his sword.

Ylannos gestured to the blade hanging from his hip. "Captain Skald can take that, if you—"

"No." Sen spoke a little too forcefully, but he was damned if he was letting anyone take his sword again. "No, I'm fine, thank you," he corrected, with as much apology as he could muster. Skald nodded in understanding and sat lightly in one of the armchairs.

"So," Ylannos began, trying to regain his composure after Sen's outburst. "What does the Duke of Aneving need badly enough to send *the* Senran Vallos as a messenger?"

Sen swallowed. "Aneving is gone." The words felt like knives in his throat, but he forced them out. The temperature in the room seemed to drop in the wake of his declaration. Ylannos's placid mask slipped ever so slightly before he righted it.

"Gone?" he asked. "How?" Though his tone indicated he already knew.

"The dragon," Sen said. "And the army. Same as attacked Iannivar, I'm sure."

Ylannos rubbed a hand over his well-groomed jaw as he pushed himself to his feet and set to pacing. "The bastards are burning their way across the Empire." Skald was staring straight ahead, a look of glassy contemplation written across his face.

"What do they want?" Ylannos fumed.

"Nothing," Sen cut in, and again all the eyes in the room turned on him. He could feel Erick snuggled into his side, completely oblivious to the import of this conversation and was glad for the boy's presence.

"What do you mean?" Skald asked.

Sen breathed deep and blew it out. "They never made demands," he said, recalling a similar confusion gripping Aneving's ducal advisors in the days preceding the attack. He'd ignored it as boring politics then. No longer. "They just started burning and killing. It was a slaughter—not a battle."

Ylannos closed his eyes and took a deep breath, composing himself before speaking again. "We need to make preparations. Captain Skald, ready your men. I will call a meeting of the High Council and we will strategize how to meet this foe." He turned his hard eyes on Sen. "Master Vallos, I would beg you join this meeting and lend your expertise." Sen nodded in response, though he groaned inwardly. Ylannos's broad smile returned, but it did not reach his eyes. "The city of Ir-Anan will not fall this day, gentlemen. Now, to your task, Captain. Master Vallos and..." He trailed off, seeming to really look at Erick for the first time.

"Erick," Sen interjected, seeing the councilor struggling to remember the boy's name.

"Erick." Ylannos rolled the name around in his mouth as he said it, then looked back at Sen. "He's your grandson?"

Sen grunted, looking affectionately at the boy, now nearly asleep against him. "Of a sort. He's my ward."

Ylannos nodded. "Well, Masters Vallos and Erick, I will have rooms prepared for you. Please, rest and recuperate. I will send for you when the meeting is called."

And with that, they were ushered out of the councilor's apartment, down a winding hall, to a room with an enormous plush bed, table full of hors d'oeuvres, and thick curtains to block the sun. Sen placed Erick on one side of the bed, then laid down next to him. Tired as he was, sleep took him in moments, and he was swept away to the land of nightmares that inhabited his dreams.

A knock on the door wrested Sen from the embrace of sleep.

"Master Vallos? The Council meeting has been called and your presence is requested."

"Aye, I'm coming." Sen tried to keep the gruff edge from his voice, but mostly failed. Wearily, he rose and strapped on his sword. A glance at the bed told him Erick was still asleep, so he chose to let him rest. Stepping into the hall, he followed a servant back through the maze of corridors to a nondescript door. When the servant swung it open and Sen looked inside, he realized it was another elevator platform, and his stomach instinctively dropped.

"The council meets in the old throne room, down on the first level," the servant said, evidently seeing Sen's trepidation. "I promise, the lift is perfectly safe." His tone was encouraging, but Sen still had to swallow unease to get in the closet-sized opening. The lift's descent began as soon as the door shut on him, but he was relieved to realize it was neither as fast nor as rough as the lift they'd taken up initially. It descended slowly and mostly without incident, only bumping against the walls a couple of times. After what felt like an eternity in the crawling dark, Sen came to a stop. The door in front of him opened, and he was greeted by another servant, this one a young girl of no more than fifteen. She led him wordlessly through yet more hallways, eventually coming to a stop in the mouth of the old throne room of Ir-Anan.

Sen couldn't help but marvel at the space. White marble columns supported a massively tall ceiling, adorned with intricate paintings of battles and victories eons past. The floor was made of intricate multicolored tiles, now faded and worn from millions of footfalls. And in the center of the cavernous chamber stood the Imperial Throne of Ir-Anan, where the Emperor had ruled for thousands of years. Right up until some forty years ago, when the emperor and his entire family had been slain in the night. The younger prince's body had never been found, and rumors of his survival had persisted for decades. But Sen knew the world and what it could do to orphaned children on their own, so he refused to hope. That thought led his mind back to Erick, still sleeping over a thousand feet above his head, and he silently prayed to the Six for his safety.

"Master Vallos," Sen was pulled back to the moment by Ciran Ylannos's voice. He looked up to see the councilor smiling at him and gesturing to a chair next to him. "Would you please join us?" Sen obliged and took the seat next to the man. Ylannos nodded to him in greeting, then turned to the others gathered at the table. Sen counted six people; four men and two women, aside from Ylannos and himself. They were all dressed in finery, necklaces of jewels around their necks. Sen couldn't help but wonder if any of them ever came to the lower levels aside from attending these meetings. He couldn't help but notice their ages; they were all elderly, significantly older than himself. Ylannos was by far the youngest of their number, though he commanded the room.

"My fellow members of the High Council," Ylannos began, his full voice echoing off the ancient stonework around them. "I have received grave news from the province of Aneving to the east." He gestured to Sen. "Master Senran Vallos has been sent with a message from the Duke. Aneving is gone, fallen victim to the dragon and the army which left Iannivar a ruin." Murmurs went up from those gathered around the table, only to be silenced by a raised hand from Ylannos. "As we speak, that army marches here, to our doors. We must raise our own army and meet them on the field of battle."

An ancient man at the other end of the table raised a quivering hand. "We must attempt to parlay with this army before resorting to military action. We cannot waste thousands of lives on a battle that could be avoided."

Sen saw his opportunity to cut in and took it. "They do not come with demands. They burned Aneving, even though we had no army left by the time they arrived at the gates. The dragon is an indiscriminate killer. There will be no quarter given." He turned to Ylannos, who looked to be about to speak, and cut him off.

"However, meeting this foe in an open field is a good way to lose your entire force. The army isn't your concern. The dragon is. The walls should be outfitted with ballistae at all possible points. Don't let it get near, or it will level the city on its own."

Ylannos looked to consider his suggestion, though his eyes lowered at the mention of ballistae. "Ir-Anan has only one working ballista, on the highest level."

Sen had to stop his mouth falling open. "What?"

Ylannos shrugged sheepishly. "I speak the truth. Ir-Anan has one ballista."

Sen rubbed his eyes. "It won't be enough. You need to evacuate."

The murmurs of the gathered councilors turned to outraged cries at that suggestion.

"There are two million souls in this city!" came one call.

"Impossible!" said another.

"This man is no general," said the old man who'd spoken earlier. "Why should we listen to him?"

Ylannos had to shout over the din to be heard. "Councilors! Please! Senran Vallos is a veteran of a hundred battles, with more time spent holding a sword than most of us have spent holding a pen. His advice should be heeded." He turned his dark eyes on Sen. "However, my colleagues aren't wrong, Master Vallos. Evacuation on a large scale would be impossible."

A moment of silence passed as each councilor came to understand what he was leaving unsaid. "However," an old woman, sporting at least three diamond necklaces said. "An evacuation of the highest levels could be achieved."

Sen was disappointed, if not entirely surprised, by the lack of pushback on that idea. Even Ylannos seemed to consider it. Then the councilor glanced at the enormous marble throne looming over them and Sen saw his face harden in resolve.

"No." The word rang out with a strength Sen hadn't expected. "We are the Empire. We will not run and hide when challenged. This city has never fallen. It will not do so while in my keeping."

In your keeping? Sen thought. *I see no crown on your head.*

But the old soldier had to admit Ylannos was a damn fine speaker. Even the decrepit members of the High Council were bobbing their wrinkled heads.

Ylannos began issuing directives, turning to each councilor in turn. "We will ready the mounted ballista in the Mountain Tower. Construction should begin immediately on mobile artillery to be stationed on all levels throughout the city. We need scouts to head north and check Mourners' Pass. We must know how long we have. I am instituting a curfew, effective immediately. The army must be called and readied for battle. We will remain within the walls, though. They are our greatest strength, and Master Vallos is correct —we must not open ourselves up to unnecessary risk where the dragon is concerned."

There were more orders and things to ready, people to speak with, and so forth, but Sen was content to watch the High Council attempt to make itself ready. Their efforts were admirable, but he knew it would be in vain, and he had no intention of Erick getting caught in the middle of it. He managed to slip away while Ylannos was in the midst of further demands and make his way back to the lift. He took it to the top of the palace, then found his way back to the room he shared with the boy. When he slipped inside, he found

Erick sitting up, eating from the trays of food on the table, the curtains pulled back to reveal a sky quickly darkening to the black of night.

"Sen!" The boy jumped up and impacted Sen in a crushing hug, which he returned.

"Did you sleep well?" Sen asked. Erick nodded, his mouth full. He chewed diligently, then swallowed before speaking.

"That bed is great!" he exclaimed. It warmed Sen's heart to see some childlike exuberance returned to the boy's eyes, and he ached for what he was about to do.

Sen grabbed his pack and began bundling up the food and stuffing it inside.

"What are you doing?" Erick asked, his eyes betraying worry he tried to keep from his voice.

Sen stopped and looked at him. "We have to go."

"What? Why?" Fear tinged Erick's voice and it broke Sen's heart.

Sen put a hand on his tiny shoulder. "The dragon is coming." The color drained from Erick's face and the apple he was holding plummeted to the floor as his hand shook. "If we leave now, we can get away before it gets here," Sen continued. The boy's eyes locked to Sen's, feverish with fear. He nodded.

They were packed and proceeding toward the palace doors within five minutes. Sen kept a hand on Erick's shoulder as his eyes darted around them looking for any and all threats. But under the cover of night, and with Ylannos running things from the first level, the palace was mostly empty.

He pushed open the ornate doors that led onto Ir-Anan's top level and found himself standing face to face with Varen Skald.

"I didn't figure the great Senran Vallos for one to run from a fight," he said, his voice even.

Sen sighed and gently guided Erick behind him. "Not running," Sen said. "But I won't have the boy caught up in this. He's lost too much to the dragon already."

Skald nodded. "I can respect that. I've got a child of my own. Little girl. I don't want her caught up in it, either. But if we run, how many other little boys and girls don't get to grow up at all?"

Sen rolled his eyes. "My being here won't make the difference. That dragon will level this city."

"Maybe," the Captain conceded. "Maybe not. Either way, you're supposed to be the greatest fighter on the continent, right? I can't see how that wouldn't make a difference."

Sen laid a hand on the pommel of his longsword. "I understand. And I feel for you. But I'll not be putting the boy in harm's way for you or anyone else in this city."

Skald's eyes flicked down to Sen's hand on the sword and a slight smile cracked his lips. "I'm not foolish enough to fight you. Do what you will. But you should know, the rest of us will be here, sword in hand, whatever happens." He stepped aside and let Sen pass. "And that dragon took something from you, too. Don't forget that."

Sen stopped at that. Images flashed through his mind of his home, of the Duke, of all the people who'd called Aneving home. He saw the brutality of the dragon's attack, too. People exploding into nothing but smoking red ribbons, ripped in half by claws and teeth, screaming as their bodies were eviscerated. His hand tightened around his sword.

Sen's eyes slid down to Erick. How far could they even get?

This army wasn't going to stop of their own accord. They were conquerors, clearly bent on naught but destruction.

When he spoke, it was toward Skald, but his eyes never left Erick's big brown orbs. "Can you get him out?"

Skald didn't miss a beat. "Aye. My wife and daughter are packing as we speak. They'll head to her family's farm, two days' ride south from the city. He can go with them."

Erick looked to be realizing what was happening, and fear gripped the boy's features.

"No, I want to stay with you," the boy said, his voice quavering as he shook his head. "No, please, Sen. Please!"

Sen swallowed a cry, then knelt down to look Erick in the eye. "I'm sorry," he began. "I'll find you after."

"Why do you have to stay?" Tears ran down his face as he sniffed loudly.

Sen smiled sadly. "Someone has to. And I have a score to settle with the dragon." He hugged the boy close to him and kissed the top of his head. "But hear me, son: I *will* find you when this is through."

Sen felt Erick's small arms wrap around him as tightly as the boy could manage. They held each other like that for a long moment. When they finally separated, tears stained both of their faces. Erick's big brown eyes looked deep into Sen's, and the old man saw a strength there that should not be required of one so young.

"I love you, Sen." The words were spoken in the boy's small, quiet voice, but they impacted Sen like a sword to the heart. He dropped to a knee and hugged the boy again, drawing him close and whispering into his ear in a voice thick with emotion.

"I love you, too."

Chapter Twenty-Three

Made Whole

No one else sees it, but I know Feordan. That woman is stronger than the others give her credit for. What she lacks in swordsmanship, she makes up for in being able to put a body back together from scratch.

-Log of Dragonmaster Meristofales, 875th Lord of Mun-Alin

Rialin left the meeting with his heart in his throat. His hands pushed the wheels of his chair through the corridors and hallways of the monastery with fervent speed, and he caught up with Feordan not far from the meeting chamber.

"Feordan!" he called. "Bonestitcher!"

She turned and regarded him with weary eyes, and in all the years he'd known the woman, Rialin didn't think he'd ever seen her look so *old*. Her normally bright eyes were subdued, red and puffy from tears, her sockets deep-set and bruised.

"What do you need, Rialin?" Her voice quavered, sounding brittle and frail as she rubbed absently at the back of her neck.

Rialin rolled to a stop in front of her. "I need your help." He gestured at his legs, still hardly usable. "I need to be ready for this fight. Please, I need your special brand of healing."

Feordan regarded him with a stony glare for a long moment, then sighed, then wordlessly turned and walked away, beckoning him behind her.

Once they arrived back in her infirmary, Feordan had beckoned Rialin back up onto the slab of a table he'd occupied while comatose. He managed to climb up onto the table with some difficulty, then lay panting and exhausted.

"Take off your shirt," Feordan ordered. "And anything else on your upper half." Rialin soon found himself sitting up on the slab, shirtless and feeling suddenly very cold. Feordan bid him to lay back and close his eyes. He could feel her moving around, preparing whatever it was she had to prepare. Truth be told, Rialin had only seen her do this sort of thing a couple of times. Using magic to heal wounds was extraordinarily difficult, and it drained the healer's magical reserves more than any other magic usage.

A cold hand came down on Rialin's chest, just above his heart, which beat faster every minute. "This process is...imperfect," Feordan said. "I should be able to significantly speed up the healing process, but do not expect to be as you were. Your injuries were just too severe to undo entirely with magic. Natural healing is slower, but more complete." Rialin tried not to be too disappointed. But still, even if he was only half the man he'd been, that would be enough. He nodded for her to go on.

Without warning, Feordan closed her eyes and drew in a breath. Her body glowed as she pulled from her reserve. As she breathed out, Rialin felt the power course through his limbs. That power was intoxicating, and his pain was suddenly and totally forgotten. Until the power turned from an incredible fiery passion to an unbearable burning in his veins, at which point his pain returned with double or triple the force it'd had previously.

His back arched, and he let loose a scream as he felt the flames wend through his blood, coursing through his body. It moved slowly, so slowly, until it reached his ruined legs. The bones and muscles knit themselves back together with a series of ripping, tearing cracks, eliciting another scream from Rialin. Or maybe he'd never stopped screaming in the first place? He felt his muscles contracting, pulling in, hardening. His fingernails bit into the stone of the table, and then there was blood pouring from his fingers, hot and slick as it ran through the stone slab's imperfections like water into a dammed-up river.

Rialin sucked in a breath and his lungs expanded, and he thought they were going to burst from his chest. Dumbly, he remembered Wik bursting a lung in training and fear gripped him. More flames pulsed out from the place where Feordan's hand met his chest, and for a dizzying moment Rialin wondered if his sternum was about to crack, or if his heart might explode.

But they didn't. His body somehow held together long enough to get through the healing, and he was left lying in a pool of his own sweat—or, at least, he hoped it was sweat—panting for breath. Rialin's eyes opened slowly and looked at Feordan. The old woman had slumped back in a chair and looked almost unconscious.

Rialin struggled to a sitting position and, even with the fatigue he felt looming over him like a personal rain cloud, he could tell he was stronger, more complete than he had been before. He was dying to check his legs, but he needed to be sure Feordan was alright first. Leaning over, he took her bony shoulder in his hand and shook her. When her eyes fluttered open, Rialin allowed himself to exhale.

"Are you okay?" He asked.

She nodded dully. "I'll be fine." A sadness passed across her eyes. "My reserve runs low. I'm old, Rialin, and soon I'll be all used up." A tear welled at the corner of her eye and she wiped it away with a shaking hand. Then she sucked in a breath and composed herself. "How are you?"

Rialin did his best to swallow the guilt he felt prodding from his stomach and looked down at his body, which seemed much sturdier than it had a few moments ago. Hesitantly, he turned and placed his feet on the floor and, testing them, stood. It took a moment to get his balance and stop his head from spinning, but once that subsided, Rialin was surprised to find himself able to stand on his own two feet. A broad smile spread across his face, and he turned to find Feordan smiling back at him, though hers was notably more subdued.

"Go," she said, rising slowly. "I'm going to lie down. You have a battle to prepare for."

Rialin's preparations led him down to the stable. The walk there had informed him that he still bore a limp, and he assumed he probably always would. But it was still a vast improvement over where he'd been just earlier today. Part of him wondered why Feordan had waited so long to use her magic like that, and he resolved to ask her when she was feeling better. As he entered the stable, he told himself he was only going to check his saddle and gear and see if the dragon was ready to fly. But when he laid eyes on the red dragon, lying curled up in the back corner of the stable, a feeling of profound loneliness washed over him. Ferao's words came back to him unbidden.

"He saved your life!"

As if it knew his thoughts, the dragon's eye opened slowly and regarded him. Rialin met its gaze. The eye was a deep blue, contrasting sharply with the metallic sheen of red on his scales. Rialin wasn't sure what the dragon was feeling behind that gaze, but *his* insides were roiling. He stood there, finally somewhat stable on the leg this monster had shattered, but found himself feeling devastatingly alone and cold.

He strode toward the dragon, his feet moving of their own accord, and stretched out a hand. The dragon lifted his snout. Inches from each other, Rialin paused. Words were clawing at his throat, but he didn't know if he was strong enough.

"Thank you," he finally croaked, and laid his hand gently on the dragon's snout. The touch was enough to beat back the deep sorrow welling in Rialin's chest. He wouldn't allow himself to fully bond, but he felt somewhere deep in his soul that this dragon was more than just an animal.

"I'm sorry for how I've treated you," he said. At this, the dragon regarded him with those deep blue eyes again and clicked in its throat. Moving on, Rialin said, "Has Uanari told you what we're doing?"

Click click click.

Rialin assumed that was a 'yes' and pushed on. "We're going to be fighting together. So we need to be on the same page. But I just...I can't let you in my mind. Not yet." He raised his eyes to meet the dragon's gaze. "So, it's your choice. Will you fight by my side?" Then, feeling the weight of those words, added, "As a friend?"

The dragon hesitated, thrumming slightly in its chest. Then, it dipped its head and elicited a trio of *clicks*. Rialin let himself exhale and smile, then rubbed the dragon's chitinous snout again.

Wik leaned against Uanari's hide, his warmth keeping the bite of winter at bay. Her hands worked at polishing her axe, freshly retrieved from Mel's forge. The smith had been working at fashioning it into a true Rider blade, but hadn't yet been able to make it work. In the meantime, Wik settled for it being a beautiful and deadly weapon on its own, telekinetic powers or no.

You are restless, Uanari thundered in her mind, causing her to jump. She still wondered if she'd ever get used to the dragon's presence in her head, though she now found it more comforting than alarming...most of the time.

Of course I am, she said. *The Riders are going to war, and our bond is still so new.*

But I am very old, Uanari said, and Wik thought she caught a touch of amusement at the edge of his voice. *I will handle the fighting.*

You mean to keep me away from the battle? Wik asked, incredulous.

Your safety is paramount, Uanari said, sending calming emotions through their bond. *If you fall, so do I. That will be two powerful allies lost for the Riders, who are all inexperienced in real combat.*

I am not a child! Wik stood and faced her bonded partner. *How are we ever going to grow together if you don't trust me?*

The massive dragon fixed a yellow eye on her. *I do not trust you.* The words threatened to crush Wik under their weight. *You prevented me from joining Meristofales in death, as it is meant to be, forced me into a bond I never wanted, and now demand I see you as an equal.* Wik's gaze fell to the floor, but Uanari did not relent his verbal onslaught. *I will go and fight.* You *will remain out of harm's way and not slow me down. And when this is done, we will evaluate our bond, and what it means.*

Wik stumbled back from the dragon, unsure of what to do with his words. Tears stung her eyes, but she could see other Riders and dragons watching her, and she refused to give them the satisfaction of seeing her cry. Her hand over her mouth, she turned and fled the stable.

Running through the monastery's halls, her mind raced through the scenarios. She knew Uanari was unhappy to be left here while Meristofales passed into the ether, but she thought they'd made progress while returning home. Truly, their bond had felt stronger with each passing day. But now, he seemed so angry, so full of hurt. It made her question everything.

Wik looked up to find herself, somehow, standing in front of Feordan's door, with no idea why she'd come here. But if anyone knew what to do about Uanari, it would be the woman who'd loved his Rider. So Wik raised a trembling hand and knocked.

Feordan took longer to answer the door than she'd expected, and when she did, Wik couldn't help but notice the older woman's haggard features. Her eyes were sunken, her posture stooped, and even her hair seemed grayer and thinner. Like she'd aged years in only a few hours.

"Feordan?" Wik asked, her own concerns temporarily forgotten. "Are you okay?"

Feordan waved away her concern and beckoned her inside. Once inside the infirmary, Feordan seated herself and sipped from a steaming mug. From what Wik could smell of it, she knew it was an herbal remedy of some sort.

"Are you alright?" she asked again.

"I'm fine," The Bonestitcher replied. "Rialin required healing magic before this battle everyone's talking about. It takes more out of me than anything else." She shrugged. "I'll be fine in a few days."

Wik nodded, her concerns ebbing away slightly. "So, I take it you're not riding to war with everyone else?"

Feordan barked a laugh. "No, child. I think my days of warfighting are over." She sipped the tea again, her eyes growing distant. "Besides," she said, barely more than a whisper. "I feel I've lost the war already."

Wik's chest stung at the comment. So much had happened, there hadn't been time to mourn Meristofales properly yet. She reached out and grasped the older woman's hand. "We will honor him," she said. "You know Eoradon will make sure he's remembered for the leader he was."

Feordan nodded and patted Wik's hand. "I know." Her voice was thick as she fought tears. Then, showing the resolve that had brought her this far in life, she exhaled and straightened before asking, "What did you need?"

Wik shook her head and rubbed her eyes, unsure of how to

even describe her feelings. "Uanari rejects me, rejects our bond," she finally said. "He doesn't trust me, and I don't know how to convince him otherwise."

Feordan regarded her for a moment before speaking. "Uanari has suffered a loss unlike any dragon in known history," she said, speaking slowly. "It would be less like losing a partner or even a child, and more like your own soul being split in two. I'm unsure how you saved him, but it's clearly been distressing for him. And Uanari is prickly at the best of times." The old healer inclined her head for a moment without speaking. "Visyn says you should give him time, not push him too hard. He will come around."

Wik sighed. "But that doesn't help us win this battle. He says he intends to leave me away from the fighting and handle it himself."

Feordan sighed. "Wik, I'm afraid you won't convince a dragon to change his mind easily. Especially one like Uanari. But I assure you, he can handle himself. And he won't be alone. The monastery's strongest fighters ride with him."

Wik buried her face in her hands. "I should be helping."

She felt Feordan's hand come to rest on her shoulder. "I know you feel the weight of this on your shoulders. But in saving Uanari, you have already provided the strongest weapon the Riders could possibly have in this fight."

Wik nodded, but it didn't feel true.

Chapter Twenty-Four

To War

I must protect them. I only hope they'll forgive me.

-Log of Dragonmaster Meristofales, 875th Lord of Mun-Alin

Eoradon looked himself over in the mirror, and found it hard to recognize the man staring back. Clean-shaven, he wore a light metal cuirass over his leathers, tinted green with gold inlay showing the sigil of the monastery—Mun-Alin in front of a rising sun. His green cloak flowed over his shoulders to be tied at his waist. His sidesword was sheathed at his hip and his Rider blade hung light as air on his back, the black leather grip poking his shoulder. And to top it off, the brutal iron circlet of the Dragonmaster sat on his brow, above his long blonde hair, pulled into a tight bun at the back of his head.

He hated it.

You look like a warrior, Iaxal surmised. *It suits you.*

I look like a fool, Eoradon shot back. *I'll attract all sorts of attention with all this metal shining for the world to see.*

As opposed to the dragon you'll be riding into battle, which is, of course, the picture of stealth. Iaxal chuckled, and the Dragonmaster found he couldn't stop himself from smiling at the sound.

How go your preparations? he asked. As they spoke, Iaxal was in the stable, being outfitted in all the vestiges of a wartime dragon.

They go well, she said. *I am suited to this.*

Eoradon chuckled to himself, despite his dread about what loomed ahead. *That you are, my friend. That you are.*

After giving himself another once-over, Eoradon turned and walked from his study. As he passed over the threshold, he thought of how strange it felt, to call it his own. Meristofales was truly gone, and the responsibilities of Dragonmaster were his alone.

You are not alone, Iaxal said, her words a balm to his worries. *Where one of us treads, the other follows.*

Eoradon smiled to himself. The walk to the stable was a quick one, and he soon found himself staring up at Iaxal's majesty. Her saddle had been reworked, inlaid with gold and green ornamentation and emblazoned with the sigil of the monastery. Her scales had been burnished to a mirror shine, making her stand out even more than normal.

All around the cavern, Eoradon saw his fellow Riders readying themselves for battle. Virsk was climbing into his saddle, fastened to his dragon, Kranavoss, whose scales were a deep blue. Ferao was astride Paxavan already, his face a mess of emotions swirling like a hurricane. Rialin had climbed onto the poor creature he rode with his half bond, though Eoradon noticed how much calmer the red and blue dragon seemed.

And then there was their king. Uanari unfurled his body and stood, stretching in much the same way a house cat might. When he straightened back up, his head, ringed in a crown of small horns, nearly scraped the cavern's stone ceiling. His deep yellow eyes took in his kin and their Riders and a low rumble emanated from his throat. Eoradon felt the dragon's presence in his mind and stopped himself recoiling from the thunderous voice.

Dragonmaster, Uanari said, and Eoradon detected a deep ache as he said the word. *How many ride with us?*

Eoradon looked around the room and felt embarrassed as he answered. *Five.*

Uanari nodded his huge head in a startlingly human expression. *It will be enough.*

I wanted more, Eoradon said with a sigh.

A calm washed over him from Iaxal. *It will be enough, Rodo.*

Dyraxian is strong, but he is only one dragon, Uanari said. *With only one Rider*.

Eoradon nodded. *We leave at first light,* he said. A glance out the stable's massive entrance told him dawn was still an hour away.

I will be ready. And with that, Uanari the Black withdrew from his mind and resumed his position of rest on the floor. Eoradon looked around the chamber again, and thought for a moment he could *feel* the apprehension from his fellow Riders. He knew what he asked of them. None of these people had seen real combat, and beyond that, no one that he knew of had fought a dragon since the wild clans had been eradicated millennia ago.

They need their leader, Iaxal said. *They need you.*

Eoradon suppressed a chuckle. *I doubt Rialin wants an inspirational speech from me.*

The Riders need their Dragonmaster, Rodo. They are strong, as are the dragons, but still they fear what they will find in Ir-Anan. Gentler, she added, *And so do you.*

Eoradon smiled a little to himself. He could hide nothing from her. *I do not fear Dyraxian, his Rider, or even the army they lead.* His eyes returned to the opening at the other end of the cavernous stable, to the darkness, slowly turning from the black of night to the blue of pre-dawn. *I fear what happens if we win. And I fear what happens if we don't.*

Confusion came through the bond. *You fear victory?*

No, Eoradon said. *I fear what it will mean. I am the rightful leader of Ir-Anan. I am the Emperor, in truth. If I lead a force to liberate my own city, should I not sit on its throne? Should I not lead my people?*

The Dragonmaster, the Prince, the Heir, the King. His emotions were in a freefall, and he struggled to force back the bile that burned his throat. Since he was a boy, he'd wrestled with this question: where was home? And now, whether he wanted it or not, he was racing toward an answer.

You are who you choose to be, Iaxal said, her words a salve. *King or Dragonmaster; it makes no difference. Today, you are a Dragon Rider of Mun-Alin. You lead your forces to war. You will protect the people, as the members of this order have done for countless generations. And when that is done, we will decide—together—what is next, and where we belong.*

Eoradon nodded and breathed deep of the chilled early-morning air. His hand found its way, as it so often did, to her scaled jaw. *You're right.*

She chortled. *I always am.* Eoradon laughed, and felt the weight of their task retreat, if only for the moment. His eyes drifted again over the gathered Riders. *Let them hear you,* Iaxal said. He turned and met her golden eye, and nodded. He patted a hand on her snout before turning and walking to the middle of the room.

"Riders!" His voice echoed off the stone above and below, and the Riders—*his* Riders—along with the numerous dragons, turned to look at him. Suddenly, standing there with all eyes on him, Eoradon thought the chill of the morning seemed to carry much more bite. He breathed deep and pushed forward.

"An army marches on Ir-Anan. A Dragon Rider—one of our own—is at its head. The city would fall in a matter of hours on its own." He breathed, letting the silence linger. "But Ir-Anan does not stand alone. The Dragon Riders of Mun-Alin stand with them. For too long, we have cowered behind stone. But a dragon's place is in the sky. Darkness encroaches on the people of this land, and the Riders of this monastery will be there to meet it, as we have for thousands of years. We will fill the skies with dragon calls, and Ir-Anan *will not fall!*"

Silence stretched as the final words of Eoradon's speech bounced off the cavern's ceiling. Then, like a pebble tumbling down a mountainside, a *thump thump thump* emanated from behind him. Eoradon turned to find the source and nearly passed out.

Rialin was rhythmically beating his fist against his breast. After a moment, the red dragon next to him joined in, thrumming and stomping one foot. Virsk took up the rhythm next, as did his dragon. And around the stable it went. Iaxal opened her jaws and gave a mighty roar, spouting fire skyward, and the other dragons joined in, so loud they shook the cavern. Eoradon cast a nervous eye on Uanari, silently hoping the huge dragon would refrain. He inclined his head ever so slightly, and Eoradon felt the same as if he'd shouted his name from the mountaintop.

Eoradon held his hands up to stop the cheering. "At first light, we take to the skies. Go and finish your preparations. Eat. Get your mind right. And I will see you up there."

The Riders dispersed from there to whatever tasks they needed to complete before departing, leaving Eoradon alone, save the dragons.

It will be enough, Iaxal said. We *will be enough.*

Eoradon nodded and rubbed her snout again, hoping against all hope that she was right.

Feordan walked, slower than she would've liked, to the stable, cursing her bones with each uneasy step. Healing Rialin had been hard, harder than it should've been. She was old, she knew, but Meristofales's death had aged her what felt like years in only days. But still, she found herself eventually standing before the great head of Uanari. The dragon was looking like he'd aged, too, she thought.

"Uanari," she said, injecting as much confidence in her voice as she could manage. Visyn drifted closer to her from the cavern's edges, his gold and silver scales reflecting the torchlight that lined the walls.

Feo, he said through their bond. *I do not think this will work.*

I have known Uanari almost as long as I have known you, she told him. *He will listen to me.* Visyn projected doubt through the bond, but acquiesced to her judgment.

The huge black dragon had yet to acknowledge her, though, continuing to sleep. Or at least, pretending to sleep.

Can you wake him? she asked Visyn.

The dragon balked at the idea. *That would be a bad idea.*

Feordan sighed. *Fine.* She strode closer, until she was a foot away from Uanari's scaled snout. At this distance, he all but filled her vision, and the circle of spikes on his crown loomed intimidatingly large, each the length of her arm.

She kicked the dragon square in the nose.

The great beast huffed, bathing her in hot air that smelled of smoke and coal. His eyes fluttered open and fixed on her as he lifted his head to look down his nose in her direction. Instantly, she felt him pushing on her mind. She let him in, and maintained eye contact, regardless of how intimidating he wanted to seem.

Bonestitcher. His voice was the cracking of stone in her mind, unthinkably loud, and she struggled to remain on her feet when he spoke. But remain standing, she did.

Uanari, she said, trying to calm her nerves under the weight of his gaze.

What do you need of me? Uanari's voice had quieted now, allowing her to listen without being overwhelmed. He'd made his point, she guessed.

Wik, she said simply.

Uanari groaned, if that was even possible for a dragon. *She is headstrong, and thinks to demand things of me.*

She's young, Feordan said. *Of course she doesn't know how this works. She's supposed to learn it* with *the dragon she's bonded to. But you're over two hundred years her senior.*

Exactly! Uanari said, rage boiling over their connection. From the corner of her eye, Feordan spotted Visyn sidling closer. She held up a hand to signal she was okay, then returned her focus to Uanari.

She didn't mean to bond you. Feordan lowered her voice and lifted a hand, palm-out, to signify she meant no offense. *She simply reacted when she felt…what happened.* She still couldn't bring herself to say it, and even talking like this made her chest feel like it was full of stones. Though, she knew this dragon was the only person who truly knew the pain she carried. So she reached out and touched his scaled foreleg.

I miss him, too.

The rage that permeated their mental connection faded away, replaced with a well of grief so deep, Feordan felt it had no bottom.

I failed him, Uanari said as the waves of grief broke against her. *And if I couldn't keep Meristofales alive, how am I supposed to help Wik?*

Oh, Uanari. Feordan felt tears stinging her eyes, and did not fight them, letting them form rivers in the wrinkles of her face as she pressed her forehead to Uanari's leg and felt the warmth there. *It wasn't your fault.*

If I'd been stronger or faster, able to defeat Dyraxian quicker…

You cannot live your life in 'ifs.' We must live in the truth. Meristofales had a sword in his hand when he died. He was not helpless. She paused, then proceeded. *And neither is Wik.*

If something happens to her—

You will be together, she said. *There are worse things. She needs your trust, or your bond will erode.*

Uanari said nothing, but she felt him considering her words.

I will do what I can to keep us safe, he finally said. *But you make a good point. She deserves the chance to prove herself.* Feordan felt herself exhale, glad with what she'd accomplished here. *But I cannot fully trust her.*

She sighed and nodded. It would have to do for now.

Fly well, my friend. Come back to us. She ran a hand over his snout, which he lowered for her.

I will do my best to avenge him, he said.

She shook her head. *Protect the city. That's all the vengeance he'd want.*

Wik strode into the stable, hand resting on the axe hanging from her hip. A round shield was slung over her back, and she'd opted for leathers over metal armor. She'd not earned a cloak, so her dark hair fell down her back in a thick braid, sprouting from the base of a light helmet with an open face.

Her stomach was in her throat. She'd not spoken to Uanari since their argument, and she had no idea if he was even going to allow her to accompany the Riders. She shook herself and calmed her mind.

It doesn't matter, she thought. *I'll find a way. I am a Rider of Mun-Alin, and I will fight with my order.*

Steeling herself, she crossed the stable with confident strides to where Uanari was standing, stretching his massive membranous wings. Wik was relieved to see he was already saddled. Someone else must have done it, but Uanari would never wear one if no one was going to be riding on his back.

He turned his head and regarded her with those piercing yellow eyes. Now more than ever, Wik realized, they looked like the eyes of a predator, searching for prey.

Wik, he said. *Are you ready?*

She chuckled a little, feeling him soothing her through their bond. *Not even a little.*

She climbed into the saddle and surveyed the cavern. All around her, the other Riders had mounted up and were looking to the front of the stable, where Eoradon sat astride Iaxal, her brilliant green and gold scales flashing in the blazing sunrise that peaked over the mountains.

The Dragonmaster turned and closed his eyes as he let the sun bathe his face. When he looked back, his eyes were harder, his jaw set.

'To Ir-Anan!" He screamed, arm pointing out at the world. "To war!"

Part Three

The Battle of Ir-Anan

Chapter Twenty-Five

Drums of War

Ir-Anan has stood for centuries. But now, with the emperor dead and the Empire divided, I worry for the capital, should Meloran finally march west.

-Log of Dragonmaster Rykas, 874th Lord of Mun-Alin

As the wind carried thick flurries of snow across the uppermost level of Ir-Anan, Sen found himself standing at the balustrade that overlooked the many descending tiers of the city. They ran down and down and down, growing progressively poorer and less maintained, until they met the massive outer wall, which ringed the city's lowest layer. And beyond that, the Field of Hylenor spread out in every direction to the south and west until it met the Field of Igdranon to the north.

All of that might as well have been snow on the wind, though. Because all Sen could see was the massive army spread out beyond the Igdranon, slowly migrating south from the mouth of

Mourners' Pass.

"We could bombard them when they're in range," said one of the gathered crowd—a commander of some sort, Sen thought.

"Yes, that's the plan," Varen Skald said, just the hint of exasperation tinging his voice.

Sen liked the man. Ylannos had promoted him directly to General, a move the councilor had justified by pointing to the practicality of needing a true chain of command. But Sen thought it was more to tighten his grip on the city by putting the standing guard under the control of someone who owed him.

"General Skald," Ylannos began, sweeping an arm across the city. "Run us through the current state of our defenses."

Skald took a breath before continuing. "Yes, Councilor. As instructed, my men have set up mobile artillery by moving catapults and the new wheeled ballistae into positions along the outer rings of levels four, five, and six. The ballistae will be held back, hidden, not to fire until I give the command." He turned and pointed to a lone guard tower at the end of the main wall of this uppermost level. "And the ballista in the Mountain Tower is fully operational. Though..." He trailed off, seeming unsure of what to say next.

"Out with it," Ylannos snapped.

"We don't have anyone capable of manning it," the General finally said.

"We don't have anyone," Ylannos repeated, his tone incredulous, "who can manage to point and shoot?"

"It's not that simple," Skald said. "That ballista can turn in a full circle, adjust levels, and fire accurately up to six-hundred yards, but it's a far more delicate weapon than the mobile ballista we've set up throughout the city. And to be frank, Councilor, no one has been trained on it because the council never saw defense from dragons as a priority."

Councilwoman Vayne Branor, who Sen had come to learn was occupying her late husband's council seat, spoke up to say, "There hasn't been a hostile dragon in thousands of years! Of course we didn't prepare for it!"

Skald opened his mouth to reply, but Ylannos put up a hand to stop them. "It doesn't matter," he said. "We need to get someone up there to man the tower."

Sen exhaled. "I'll do it."

All eyes turned to him.

"You can operate the weapon?" Skald asked.

Sen nodded. "I trained on similar contraptions in my youth. I'm sure it'll be familiar enough."

"Master Vallos, the Empire thanks you," Ylannos said, sighing. "General Skald, please accompany him to the weapon and make sure it is fully operational." He turned to the other gathered onlookers. "The rest of you, come inside. There is still much to be done." And with that, the group of feeble rulers of Ir-Anan moved away, toward the comfort of warm hearths and reinforced walls.

Sen and Skald watched them go. Then the General turned to him and nodded.

"Let's go take a look at that weapon."

The two of them walked along the edge of the city's uppermost layer until they reached the entrance to the Mountain Tower. As they went, Sen couldn't stop himself looking out at that great black mass slowly migrating across the land. The army was enormous, larger than he remembered from Aneving. Though, he had to admit, it had been dark and raining, plus there was the dragon. He took comfort in that, oddly. Aneving had been surprised, woken from its dreams to find an army beating down its door. Ir-Anan would be fully awake when they came. He only hoped they'd done enough.

The Mountain Tower was situated all the way at the city's edge, against the flat surface of Splithalf. It started on the base level and grew in height with the city, so each level had an entrance for the tower and the inside was mostly a mass of spiraling stairs punctuated with flat open spaces where guards could watch whatever level of the city they found themselves on. Apparently, as Skald told Sen on the walk over, the top level this time had been affixed with the advanced ballista as a way of bestowing honor on its inventor.

As Sen followed Skald up the seemingly endless stairs to the tower's top, he couldn't help but hope the training from his youth would see him through this.

Maybe, he thought, *this will give me a chance to bring down the dragon.*

The weapon was, unfortunately, more complex than Sen had expected, even after hearing Skald's explanations. It consisted of a seat, situated in front of the ballista. That much was pretty familiar, at least. The foot pedals that controlled the user's angle of attack and elevation were less so. But, after allowing himself some time to gain familiarity, Sen found he was able to adjust his aim much faster than traditional ballistae, and could feasibly track moving targets. Adjusting for the bolts' flight time would be harder, but he was confident he could manage.

As they descended the steps to the tower's base, Sen finally felt secure enough to ask Skald the question he'd been holding in all day.

"Did they get out?"

Skald never slowed down. He simply maintained his pace down the steps. "Far as I know. They should be well to the south now."

Sen nodded, relieved on the one hand because Erick would be away from the battle. On the other, he hated the feeling of being separated from the boy.

"Good," he said.

The pair reached the bottom of the stairs and began making their way back to the balustrade overlooking the city and, by extension, the fields and the approaching army beyond.

"The dragon hasn't shown itself," Skald said as he stared at that creeping mass of enemy soldiers. "Even our scouts didn't see it."

Sen grunted. "It was the same at Aneving. The army attacked first, drew all our forces out so the dragon could lay waste to any opposition." He shook his head, remembering that paltry attempt at fighting back. "Not that there was much to begin with. The Duke and his advisors sent the cavalry and the bulk of the Keep's armed men to meet the force in hopes of preventing a siege. Damn fools."

Sen had tried to warn against that action. But of course, none of them could've predicted a dragon on the battlefield. And all their planning wouldn't have mattered, he knew. Aneving was doomed the moment that Rider decided he wanted them.

Skald nodded contemplatively as Sen spoke. "I'm sorry about Aneving," he said. "But I'm glad you came to us. We would've been caught with our trousers around our ankles for certain if you hadn't."

Sen nodded. "Aye. I just hope it makes a difference."

"It will," said Skald, and Sen could see the muscles on the side of his head working as he clenched and unclenched his jaw. "It has to."

Sen leaned against the railing and looked out on the city. It was quiet, which was odd for the largest city on the continent. But Sen had seen cities on the verge of battles before, and he knew well the anxiety that had settled over Ir-Anan; the people could sense the coming death, and fear had gripped them.

Sen didn't blame them. There would be much death in Ir-Anan before this was through.

Sen woke to a long, low horn blast, followed by two more straight away. He hastily strapped on his sword belt, complete with freshly-sharpened longsword, and affixed his various other knives and daggers before pulling the black cloak he'd been given by Brynne's people in Kanavar around his shoulders and making his way out into the hall.

As he pushed open the doors of the palace to the frigid night air, the horn blew three more times into a cloudless sky. Sen looked up and saw both moons were hanging huge and full in the sky, the stars behind them a tapestry upon which their cosmic beauty was painted. The wind had died down, and a thin layer of white snow tinkled like diamonds under those huge moons.

Sen made his way quickly to the balustrade where he'd stood earlier, and found he wasn't the only one here. Skald, Ylannos, and a number of important-looking people he didn't know were also looking out into the night. As he drew close, Sen saw what they were staring at.

The army was here.

Sen's breath caught as he took in its enormity. It stretched on for what seemed an eternity; a great roiling mass of black armor and torchlights, marching across the Field of Igdranon.

"Shall we begin the bombardment, sir?" Someone was asking Skald, but the general's eyes were locked onto that enormous force, massing outside his city's walls.

"Not yet," Skald said. "I want to draw the dragon out. The last thing we need is a surprise attack from the air in the middle of the battle."

The man who'd asked the question seemed to hesitate, unsure of what to say next. "So what do we do?" he finally asked.

Skald breathed deep, then expelled it in a foggy breath that dissipated into the cold air. "We let Ir-Anan do what it has done for thousands of years. We hold the line. Let them come. We will hold them at the gate." He turned to some subordinate lurking by his shoulder and barked the relevant commands, sending the man running off to organize the city's defenses.

Sen didn't hear them. His eyes were fixed on the army. It moved slowly, getting into position. From this distance, he couldn't hear the various officers barking orders, getting their men into lines, but he knew it well enough from his own memories. For a moment, he was on a different battlefield, many miles and many years from this one. He remembered vomiting on his boots as he got into formation.

But he'd come through it. Every time, he'd come out alive. And through it all, he'd forged a reputation. He'd hated the man those battlefields had turned him into, but he knew the story he'd written in blood was far from fiction. His knuckles cracked as his hand squeezed the hilt of the longsword at his hip.

A rhythmic *boom boom boom* drew Sen out of his ruminations.

The drums, he thought, remembering that pounding from Aneving. And then, all at once, the army lurched into motion, moving toward the gate. Sen could see war machines dotting the landscape beyond the wall; catapults and ballistae rolled along with the mass of the army.

The army moved slowly, step by agonizing step as the drums heralded their arrival. Around him, Skald was giving orders to runners who would carry them to the relevant captains and lieutenants. Ylannos and the other councilors were being ushered away from the battlement. What civilians were left were rushing to their homes or gawping at the assembled men outside their city. And above, the moons hung still in the blue night, ever the wardens of man's folly.

Silence. All at once, the drums ceased. The march came to a halt. The chattering around him dwindled to nothing as all eyes turned to look out at the Field of Igdranon. The city of Ir-Anan held its breath.

The first catapult launched with a *twang* as its payload was loosed. A massive boulder flew through the air, tumbling over and over as it passed through the windless night. It crested, then dropped, crashing into the city somewhere further down in a cacophony of shattering stone, followed by screams. The first blow had been struck, and Ir-Anan was bleeding.

More catapults were loosed in the aftermath, and the screams increased with each impact. Sen was reasonably sure they couldn't reach the top levels, so once again the poor would suffer while the rich took in the battle as if watching an opera from the balcony. Sen gritted his teeth, pushed those thoughts away.

Can't help them now, he thought, squeezing the grip of his sword so hard the leather wrapping creaked. *Focus on what's in front of you.*

The drums resumed, and with them came a new sound: a rhythmic pounding of the battering ram on the massive wooden gates. Then Sen saw the siege ladders going up. They'd done this at Aneving and found only castle guards and the newest recruits to fight back.

This day, they would find much more.

"Where are you going?" Skald called as Sen turned to leave.

"To the wall," Sen offered over his shoulder.

"We need you on the ballista when the dragon gets here!" Skald was shouting over the commotion.

Sen turned to face him. "I will return when the beast joins the fight. But until then, your boys need help on the low wall. We cannot lose the gates."

Skald's face was conflicted, but he eventually gave Sen a curt nod, which the old man returned. Sen was going with or without permission, but it was still nice to be on a general's good side for a change.

Van watched as the ladders rose to an apex and fell toward him. He'd been told the ladder crews were often the most crazed men the enemy could find, and looking at them now, falling with rapidity toward him, he believed it. Atop the ladder closest to him, he could see a screaming man, naked from the waist up, a serrated short sword in his hand, head shaved clean. The man looked like he'd not bathed since their march across the continent began, and the mouth of rotten teeth he put on display only confirmed Van's suspicions.

He swallowed hard and gripped the longsword in his gauntleted hand. On either side, he stood shoulder to shoulder with his brothers in arms, men he'd come through training with. On the right stood Bern, wide as a drawbridge and nearly as eloquent, his bushy beard stuck out beneath the standard-issue half-helm all members of the Ir-Anan City Watch wore.

On his left was Janek, tall and somber. He more than made up for Bern's silence, talking regularly and reminding them of all the sad books that existed for them to read. Van found himself hoping his friend had found time to read some books on warfare, instead of just sad, romantic poetry.

The enormous siege ladder crashed into the wall in front of the group, vicious metal hinges biting deep into the stone. The shirtless lunatic leapt from the ladder, his serrated blade lashing out toward Bern. The big man leaned back, and the knife passed through his beard, sending a chunk of red hair flying.

Van turned on the spot and drove his sword between the attacker's ribs, drawing a gasp as the blade punched through his lungs. Then his arm whipped out with the serrated sword again, and Van was sure it would find its way into his throat. But Bern was there, catching the man's arm and forcing it up. Then he wrenched hard and the crazed man's mouth opened in a wheeze that might have been a scream if not for the blade in his chest cavity. The blade clattered to the stones, followed shortly by the body of its owner, pouring blood from the gaping chest wound.

Van looked down at the blood on his blade and found his mind whirling. The red liquid crept down the length of the sword, crawling ever closer to his hand. He fought the urge to throw the weapon. All at once, the cacophony of the battlefield hit him with a near-physical force. The acrid smell of smoke and blood overwhelmed him. Every breath felt like he was inhaling fire. His stomach threatened to empty when his eyes slid over the still body of the man he'd killed.

Killed.

The finality of the word took root in Van's mind. He'd killed a man. He was looking at the blood again. Trying to see anything else, he cast his glance around and found nothing but more dead and dying. Over the wall, the army stretched on for what seemed eternity. The smoke from torches and flaming catapult ammunition rose to clog a cloudless night sky and hide the stars. Bern and Janek were fighting a group of three invaders and looked overmatched.

They're going to die, he realized with sudden, stark clarity. *We're all going to die.* His fingers loosened on the hilt of his sword as his feet turned, ever so slightly preparing to run, as panic gripped his heart.

Then a boulder rushed past him and barreled into the three men fighting Janek and Bern. Van blinked and the boulder coalesced into the shape of a man, taller than Janek and broader than Bern, whipping about himself with a sword. His bald pate betrayed his age, but his movements were lithe and whip-fast, his sword arm darting in and out, up and down to occupy three opponents at once while his off hand deftly directed would-be killing blows away.

In the span of three heartbeats, Van saw the warrior slide effortlessly between multiple fighting styles, using a brutal, hacking method to break one man's guard before switching to a style more befitting a soldier to quickly and efficiently run him through. Then he twisted, letting the downward chop of an axe pass an inch by his head before driving an elbow up into his would-be killer's nose. As the invader stumbled back, hand clasped over his gushing face, the old man dropped his sword, seizing the axe that nearly killed him. Taking it in two hands, he brought it up high overhead, took one step, and let it fly. It crossed the space between them in an end-over-end spiral and buried itself deep in the attacker's chest. He cried out as the impact drove him back and he stumbled over the wall.

The old man spun to face the third attacker, who had disengaged from his bout with Janek and looked to be considering his options. He didn't get the chance to run. The old warrior whipped an arm out, sending a knife Van hadn't even seen him draw to whistle through the air and embed itself in his throat.

As his third victim slumped to the ground, clutching at his opened throat, their savior turned to face the three of them. His eyes passed over each of them in turn, and Van was struck by their intensity. Nodding, he retrieved his sword and sheathed it on his hip, then turned to the siege ladder, still anchored to the wall by its massive hinges. Van saw his intention and rushed to help. Janek and Bern followed in his wake. Together, the four of them heaved until the ladder wrenched free and fell in a crash to the battlefield below.

Van turned to ask the old man his name, but he was already moving to leave.

"Wait!" Van yelled. The warrior turned to face him and again Van was struck by the weight of his gaze. "What do we do?"

The old man's eyes moved to the ground beyond the wall, where another ladder was reaching its apex. "Just knock down the damn ladders."

Sen turned from the three guardsmen, leaving them to their task. He hoped he'd done enough for them, but he could see other units being overwhelmed up ahead and needed to press on. The ladders were spread along the wall's length, but much of the fighting was clustered above the North Gate. That was his destination.

As he ran, the smell of the battlefield brought Sen back to another time in his life. How many times had he found himself here? The stink of war surrounded him and he drank it in—blood, smoke, and piss filled the air. The screams of dead and dying men were music to his ears.

Senran Vallos was home.

He ducked under an incoming axe strike, unsheathed a dagger from his boot, and slid it under the wielder's leather armor, raking it the width of his belly. Sen kept running as the man dropped the axe to grab at his intestines as they tried to flee his body.

Up ahead, a guardsman was on his back, one of the laddermen standing over him with a greatsword raised to deliver a killing blow. Sen launched the dagger and watched it sink to the hilt in the flesh of his bicep. He tottered, howling at the pain as his fingers, now limp, dropped the oversized sword.

Sen was on him in a second, freeing the dagger from his arm and ramming it through his eye. The blade stuck there and Sen was unable to free it, so he let the dead man keep it as he fell to the stones, now slick with blood reflecting the twin moons' baleful gaze. They looked down in horror, Sen knew, but he would not stop. He could not. There was no other choice. He was here now, but he knew he must return to Erick. Thinking of the boy spurred his feet to greater speed and he pounded toward the gate, every footfall carrying him closer to that knot of bodies.

When he arrived, he found a cluster of guardsmen trying—and mostly failing—to repel the siege ladders. They prodded with spears and fought to knock down the ladders, but they were so vastly outnumbered, such efforts were proving more and more futile. As Sen watched, a red-faced captain screamed a command and two guardsmen came forth with a large pot of boiling liquid.

Pitch, Sen realized, watching the men struggle to the wall's edge and tip the pot over, spilling the steaming contents onto the invaders below. The pitch oozed from the pot, viscous and terrible as it fell onto the attackers. The screams were inhuman. Pure agony, something like a dying animal, tore from their throats. They were incomprehensible—not words, not cries, simply the anguish of the dying. The smell wafted up to the battlement and Sen was unable to avoid it. The odor of burning skin and hair thickened the air. Sen saw more than one man retch at the stench. He barely suppressed his own queasiness, but a lifetime of warfighting had acquainted him with many things that could make one ill.

The rhythmic pounding of the battering ram on the massive wooden gates ceased as the invaders scrambled to recover from the pitch. But the ladders never slowed. Sen fell in, trying to help push them back, but for every ladder they knocked down, two more replaced it, all teeming with maddened warriors, thirsty for blood.

Sen fought, and stabbed, and killed over and over and over again. His mind centered, blocking out everything but the battle. He was nothing but the movements of his sword arm: in, out, up, down, thrust, slash, chop. The various aches and pains he'd picked up during the course of the fight faded until they were nothing. A cut on the leg, a growing bruise on his hand, a scratch above his eye causing blood to leak down and obscure his vision: all points along the battle's visceral timeline.

The battering ram picked up again after a little while, and the constant *boom boom boom* vibrated through the stones of the wall, causing them to tremble slightly under Sen's feet. He gritted his teeth together in a growl and shoved against the sword locked against his, pushing the snarling man back and freeing his blade. His sword arm whipped out, taking the man in the jaw and chopping deep, nearly to his nose.

Sen freed the sword, ripping a chunk of the man's cheek free as he did. He stopped, heaving breath that stank of smoke and blood, and looked around. The gate hadn't fallen yet, but it was coming. They were too outnumbered and too green. The city guards had fought well, but this army was at the end of a long campaign, and every one of them was in prime fighting shape. Sen turned and found the captain, still flush in the face, still yelling meaningless orders to "Hold, boys!" and "Bow up!"

"We need to fall back!" Sen shouted over the din, grabbing the man by the arm. "This gate is about to fall!"

The captain tried to brush him away. "No!" he cried. "The gates of Ir-Anan have never been breached!"

Sen spun the man back around as he tried to walk away. "They're about to be! You need to sound the retreat! Fall back to the city and take up defensive positions around the lift!" Sen wagged a finger in the general direction of the lift mechanism. "They must not be allowed to access the lift!"

The captain wavered, looking back toward the city. Then he turned and opened his mouth to yell something to his men.

A black-fletched arrow took him in the open mouth, landing with a *thunk* and exploding out the back of his head. Dumbly, Sen thought it must have hit his spine, because the light went out of his eyes as he dropped, dead before he hit the stones. Sen looked away from the dead man to the scores of men who would soon be dead without action. He took a deep breath and called on something from deep in the recesses of his memory; another man, from another time.

"RETREAT!" He bellowed, waving his sword in the air. "FALL BACK TO THE LIFTS! THE GATE IS LOST! DEFEND THE CITY!" At first, no one noticed. So he yelled again. Heads started turning toward him. First one, then three, then five, then fifty, then a hundred, until nearly the entirety of Ir-Anan's defenders were staring at him. And then they moved.

Like a wave of polished, blood-burnished steel, they washed across the battlements, descending the stairs and moving into the city proper. Sen was among the last to leave, sparing time for one more glance out at the thousands of men coming to ravage this city and kill them all.

Not while I can still swing a sword, he thought, his grip tightening around the haft of his sword. Then he turned and ran after the rest of the city's defenders, the sound of splintering wood chasing him from the wall.

Sen thundered down the street, buildings and homes flying past. The rest of the men were ahead of him, trying to organize into a loose line to meet the oncoming enemies.

He could hear them behind him, a growing din of yells and war cries and stamping feet. The march was over; Ir-Anan was the prize, and these men would raze it to the ground.

"SHIELD WALL!" Sen yelled as he ran, gesturing vaguely with his sword. "SPEARS BEHIND!"

By the Six, he thought. *I hope they know how to make a decent shield wall.*

They did not. The line was loose and full of holes, but Sen didn't have time to teach them. Silently, he cursed the High Council for allowing things to get this lax as he pounded between two shield holders, neither of whom seemed to have a spearman behind them. Almost as an afterthought, he grabbed a lost-looking spearman by his gambeson and thrust him toward the shield wall and continued toward the back of the force, where the lifts were.

As he walked, Sen spotted the trio of guardsmen he'd assisted on the wall and roughly grabbed the shorter one, with the tuft of blond hair sticking out under his helmet, turning the man to face him.

"Hey, what do you—" The soldier's complaint died on his lips as he met Sen's eyes. "Oh! It's you."

"Aye," Sen said impatiently. "What's your name?"

"My name? Ah—Van, sir. Vanmark of House—"

"Don't care," Sen cut him off with a raised finger, which he then thrust toward the lift. "Van, take this lift to the top level. Find General Varen Skald and tell him what happened at the gate. Tell him the lowest level is lost." Sen met the young man's eyes, fever sharp with fear and the thrill of battle. "Do you understand?"

The man nodded. Before he turned to run, he asked, "Sir! Who should I tell him is in command?"

Sen sighed, feeling every one of his years in crystal clarity as he heard the enemy's first charge crash into the makeshift shield wall.

"Senran Vallos."

Then he turned, raising his sword, to face the enemy.

Chapter Twenty-Six

Winged Death

The generals of the old gods were fearsome creatures. Uanari believes some may still lurk in the shadows of the world. Let us hope he is wrong.

-Log of Dragonmaster Meristofales, 875th Lord of Mun-Alin

General Varen Skald's hands were fixed in a white-knuckle grip around the banister of the top level of Ir-Anan. The defense of the wall was going poorly. If the gate hadn't fallen yet, it would. And once they were inside the walls, Skald knew the city was as good as lost. They could destroy the lifts to buy a little time, but eventually the enemy soldiers would flood the streets of every level.

And that didn't even factor in the dragon. Skald groaned and pinched his nose between his gloved thumb and forefinger. A sharp pain emanated from behind his eyes, like a pickaxe in his brain.

After a moment, the sensation passed and Skald shook his head to right himself.

"Commander Africh?" Skald said through gritted teeth.

"Yes, sir?" The 'Commander' was really just an old aide-de-camp he'd been forced to promote when no one else came forward, but he did his job well enough.

"Loose catapults."

"Aye, sir." And he took off to roll the words down the chain of command.

Skald leaned forward on the banister, his eyes set on the Field of Igdranon and the huge black stain roiling across it. After a few moments, he heard the *twang* of the catapults launching from all levels of the city. Ahead, chunks of rocks, boulders, bricks, and whatever other refuse they'd been able to shove into the weapons took to the air, filling the night sky with dark shapes. He couldn't hear shouting from this distance, but he knew the men down below were scrambling to get out of the way of the catapulted payloads.

They were not successful.

Even from his vantage, so high, Skald could hear the ground-shaking *thud* of the boulders and chunks of stone landing and rolling through the enemy forces, crushing men by the dozen and opening gaping wounds in the black scar on the land. Still, they were many, and the catapults had limited efficacy. Truth be told, Skald knew they were more useful for *attacking* a city than defending one, but he hoped it would at least give the attacking troops a moment of pause.

A commotion behind him drew Skald's attention away from the battlefield. He turned to find a guardsman approaching in a full sprint. He arrived, breathing hard, and snapped a salute.

"General Skald?" the soldier asked. Skald could see now he was young, with a tuft of blond hair visible around the helmet he wore.

"Yes, Soldier?" Skald eyed him up and down.

The young guardsman dropped his salute. "Sir, I've come from the first level. The gate has fallen." A murmur moved through those gathered around to hear the soldier's message. "We have fallen back to defend the lifts."

Skald gritted his teeth and squeezed the leather grip of his longsword. "Does Captain Horvath request reinforcements? We have little to send."

The soldier shook his head. "No, sir. Captain Horvath is dead." The murmur grew louder.

"Then who's in charge down below?"

The young man hesitated slightly before answering, his eyes betraying a touch of disbelief. "Senran Vallos."

Somehow, Skald found himself both relieved and dismayed. If Vallos had taken charge, they still had a chance to hold the opposing army at the lifts. But without him, they had no one to manage the ballista. Then, as Skald looked the young guardsman over, an idea occurred to him.

"Soldier, what's your name?"

"Van, sir."

Skald pointed to the Mountain Tower, where the new and improved ballista resided. "How's your aim?"

Sen fought until his legs threatened to go out from beneath him. Every movement was agony. He lifted his sword, parried an incoming stab, slid his blade across the attacker's throat, and moved on to the next enemy. He barely took notice of them anymore.

A battle axe came screaming out of the press of bodies, and Sen jerked his head back, letting it pass an inch in front of his face to bounce off the stones of the street. Sen stumbled back, tried to plant his foot, slipped in the blood and dropped hard to one knee, sending a shock through his leg, into his body, grating his teeth together. A grating sound told Sen the axe was coming back around.

Glancing up, Sen saw the blade coming at him sideways. Seeing no other option, he dropped flat to the ground and let it pass over him, scoring a line of hot pain across his back. He cried out, rolled to his back and found himself staring up at a snarling, bearded face, axe held tightly in both hands. He brought it up, aiming to swing down and split Sen in half.

The old man rolled, feeling all his years in aches and pains as he did, and the axe crashed down, striking sparks from the stones. Sen's hand found the hilt of a dagger at his belt, and he ripped it free, plunging it into the axe-wielder's knee and eliciting a howl of pain from him. He dropped the axe, his hands going to the new wound as his knee gave out and dropped to the blood-slicked ground. Sen was already on one knee. He gripped the man by the beard and pulled him in for a headbutt that broke his nose. Then he drew back his fist and thrust it into the bastard's face, one, two, three times until he heard crunching bones beneath his hand. He dropped the big fool, leaving him to scream and writhe on the ground.

Sen climbed wearily to his feet, retrieving his sword from the ground. He tried to look around, gauge his surroundings, but found the press was so cloying and choking, he could scant make out who was winning. Though, he had a sinking feeling it wasn't his side.

He was surprised to find a blazing sunrise breaking through the night sky, bathing the world in purple and orange vibrancy, illuminating the smoke and blood-filled battleground. Someone cheered behind him.

Damn fool, Sen thought with a roll of his eyes. *Cheering so we can die in the sunshine.*

And then it came. The screeching, world-shaking scream, followed by the sound of beating wings.

Sen felt fear grip his chest. In the thick of the fight, he'd had no time to think, to be afraid. But everything stopped now, as both sides looked to the sky. Sen thought he caught a look of trepidation flash across the faces of the attacking army.

The dragon came from over Splithalf, gliding over the city with its wings spread, the sunrise illuminating in full its silver scales, interspersed with red along the ridge of spikes on its back, as well as along its legs and wings. On its back, barely visible from this vantage, sat its Rider, clad in full plate armor, tattered black cloak whipping in the wind, nearly as long as the dragon itself.

Sen felt dread taking root in his chest, threatening to turn him craven. The beast was so vast, a monster from stories. As a child, dragons and their Riders had felt so far off, so separate from the world of men. But now it was here, its presence visceral, reaching to a deep, ancient part of Sen's mind. Something there, like a memory from lifetimes ago, whispered to him.

Run.

Sen fought that urge, willed his feet to remain rooted.

No, he thought. *I will not run again.* His grip tightened around the hilt of his sword.

Dragon or not, the lift still needed defending.

Skald and the rest of his cohort dropped low as the dragon screamed overhead. Hesitantly, the general peaked over the banister and looked down on Ir-Anan as the dragon glided over, its shadow passing across the city like a wave of prophesied death.

The breath caught in Skald's throat. The dragon was incomprehensibly large, the infant sunrise glinting off its silver scales nearly blinding in its intensity. Whatever he'd thought about their chances before, he knew now they had next to no chance of bringing that beast down. And that was to say nothing of the Rider astride the monster's back, torn black cloak billowing in its wake, an apocalypse given form.

"Oh, by the Six," he whispered, his voice quavering involuntarily. "We're all going to die."

The dragon banked low over the city, letting loose a roar so loud it seemed to shake the very air. It flew out over the army, turned in a wide arc, then looped back up toward the higher levels, where it came to a hovering stop, held aloft by the beating of great membranous wings. As it hovered, Skald got a clearer look at it: long and lean, like a snake the size of a building, given the wings of a huge bat, then covered in plate armor. Its head alone must have been twenty feet long and ten feet wide, its mouth bared in a venomous imitation of a smile, full of teeth the size of a man. The Rider stood on the beast's back, his balance perfect despite the bobbing of the dragon and buffeting of the wind that pulled at his cloak.

"People of Ir-Anan." His voice, amplified by some force Skald couldn't place, washed over the city and pimpled the flesh of his arms and the back of his neck. It was grinding, grating, like words being spoken from between stones being bashed together. As they waited for the Rider's next words, Skald couldn't help but notice how eerily quiet the city had become.

"I have come with a message from your gods." Skald's brows knit in confusion at this, but the Rider moved on before he had time to consider. "You have grown fat on your cowardice, from a life lived behind walls. You believe yourselves brave, but you have simply forgotten your fear." The helmeted head of the Rider fixed suddenly, and Skald could've sworn he was staring directly at him. "I have been sent to remind you. The gods are hungry."

At this, the dragon opened its maw and unfurled a burst of flame that impacted the level below Skald's cohort with a physical force, rattling the ground beneath his feet with a concussive strength. He could feel the heat radiating up as the screams found his ears. Horrible, rending screams that transcended simply being heard, and instead were felt right down to his bones. Skald gritted his teeth and gripped the hilt of his sword.

Twang.

With a sound like a huge bowstring being loosed, followed by a whistle and *thud*, the dragon's barrage ceased, leaving behind the acrid stench of smoke and the sickly-sweet odor of burnt flesh. Skald looked up in time to see the dragon recoiling, a large bolt protruding from its hindquarters, where it had impacted the meat of the beast's thigh. Skald's eyes snapped to the Mountain Tower, where Van had fired the ballista, and saw the opportunity the young man had given them.

He stood and ripped the longsword from the scabbard at his side, thrusting it toward the dragon, which was contorting its body, trying to reach the bolt in its leg. The Rider's head whipped up and met Skald's furious gaze and he noticed for the first time the twin trails of purple smoke curling from the slit in the helm. The general forced a smile, a wolf's grin, hungry, and ready for blood.

First blood to you, he thought. *But Ir-Anan bites back.*

"LOOSE BOLTS!" he bellowed, hoping beyond hope the soldiers manning the hidden ballistae throughout the upper levels heard him. The dragon must've realized what was happening, as it ceased fidgeting with the bolt lodged in its hindquarters and beat its wings in furious retreat, the Rider dropping low to hug his body to the dragon's scales.

A series of loud *twangs* erupted from the levels immediately below Skald, and a dozen bolts, each double the size of a spear, raced across the open air toward the monster. Skald had to give credit where it was due: the dragon was more agile than he'd expected, given its size. But it was too large a target, and numerous bolts found their marks. One ripped a hole in a wing, two lodged in its armored side, one glanced off its brow, and three more cut knicks on the dragon's flanks and back. With a roar, the dragon dove back to the lower levels of the city, out of range of the ballistae.

Skald breathed deep as he returned his sword to its scabbard. Behind him, someone whooped and he rounded on them, fury rising in his throat. It was one of the gathered, hastily-promoted captains.

"Quiet, fool!" Skald seethed. He thrust a gloved finger toward the still-descending dragon. “We bought time. They’ll be back, and that trick won’t work a second time. So unless you have another hidden armory I don’t know about, we are sitting ducks once that thing has licked its wounds.”

A hush fell over the group as Skald’s words sank in. They’d scored a hit on the dragon, and he knew it was significant. But he also knew the dragon would have its due. Ir-Anan would bleed more before the day was done.

Sen couldn’t see what caused the dragon to flee, but whatever had sent it back to ground outside the walls had given the opposing army pause. They looked at each other, their faces painting a clear picture for Sen. They were afraid. Unsure.

He would make them pay for it.

“Attack!” he screamed, thrusting his sword forward to the enemy ranks. After a beat, the men responded with a roar, and the defenders of Ir-Anan surged into the black-armored mass of enemies. Sen was at the front, hacking and cutting at the meager defense given by the attackers. In a handful of heartbeats, the men of Ir-Anan had cut a swath through the ranks of enemy soldiers. Sen could feel the momentum shifting with every swing of his sword. The fear in the eyes of his enemy woke something primal, deep in his bones, in a place he’d thought long buried.

Because he remembered. He remembered the stench that rose in the air as Aneving burned. He remembered the screams of those he’d trained, dead and dying all around him. He remembered the wails of the woman who’d thrust Erick into his arms. Snarling, he cut another man down. And another. And another. They were barely fighting back. Clearly, they'd expected more from the dragon.

Choke on your expectations, Sen thought as he parried a halfhearted thrust and decapitated the perpetrator. *You could never have planned for me.*

Finally, there came a break in the carnage as the enemy turned and fled to the gates, which they still held. Sen looked up and realized what had happened. The force they'd fought at the lift was a vanguard, meant only to soften their defenses enough for the larger body to sweep through, take the lift, and sack the city. Of course, they'd not been able to break through, leaving the ballistae on the upper levels undiscovered.

As he watched the enemy soldiers sprinting away, back to the gate where already he could see they were building barricades, Sen felt fatigue lay its claim to him. One of the soldiers standing by his side turned to him.

"Sir," he said. "What do we do now?"

More than anything, Sen wanted to sleep for a day or so. He wanted a hot meal. He needed to piss. But, as he watched the backs of the enemy running behind a makeshift barricade, he had an idea. It was reckless; something he would've done as a young man. He turned to regard the men—*his* men.

"Defenders of Ir-Anan," he called, taking a step away from them. "Those men have brutalized your home. Tried to kill you." His eyes drifted to the shattered windows of businesses and homes, some buildings already aflame in the dim early-morning light. "They have taken your peace." He lifted his sword and pointed it toward the enemy encampment. "General Skald has struck a blow to the dragon. These men are confused and unsure. They have forgotten the mettle of those who call Ir-Anan home. I'd like to remind them." His eyes scanned the men standing before him. He saw fear, trepidation. He also saw fury, burning hot as well as smouldering beneath the surface. He thrust his sword in the air. "Charge!" Then he turned and ran directly at the enemy.

He was halfway across the span of open cobblestone when the first soldier overtook him, broadsword in a two-handed grip. Another caught them within a moment. Then there were four, then five, then twenty, then a hundred, all roaring to hell and back, weapons raised as they charged thundering across the stones, their very footfalls shaking the earth. Ahead, the enemy soldiers still constructing their fortifications glanced at each other and broke, turning away from the charge of the men of Ir-Anan.

The front line crashed into the barricades, breaking through with little more than a pause, sweeping away the meager fortifications. The first opposition they met wasn't ready, still tired from their hasty retreat. They turned, raising weapons, but fell under the wave of steel and screaming men. Sen was in the middle of it, hacking and stabbing and howling like a beast. He gave in fully to the old bloodlust that still lurked in his veins, and the Vallos of old reared his head as he took lives like breaths, barely conscious of the bodies as they came apart around his blade.

When Sen next took inventory of his surroundings, he found himself standing in the remnants of the shattered North Gate, alone, looking out at an army that had taken a measured step back. Behind him, soldiers were coming running with fortifications to rebuild the gate. He took a step forward, but a pain in his foot nearly caused him to fall. He looked down to find the hilt of a knife sprouting from the top of his boot.

When did that happen? he thought dumbly.

Before he could fall, another soldier was under his arm. He vaguely recognized the big man. One of the companions he'd saved on the wall, what felt like a hundred years ago.

"Come on, sir." The big man boomed in his ear. "Time to take a break."

Sen shook his head, but the soldier had him tight and the pain in his foot was enough to keep him from arguing too much. As he settled, leaning against the exterior of a guard shack on the other side of the wall, he turned to the soldier to issue a final command.

"Soldier," he said. The big man turned to regard him, grime-streaked face split with that mad smile soldiers sometimes had in battle. "Your name?"

"Bern, sir."

Sen nodded. "Bern." He met the man's eyes, injecting as much authority as he could muster into his gaze. "Hold the line. Fix the gate." Then, his eyes drifting up, "Watch the sky."

Bern nodded, his face turning grave. "You should go up to General Skald, sir. He'll need to know what's happening, and you need to rest."

Sen hated the idea of leaving the men, but Bern had a point. Skald needed to know they'd reclaimed the gate. And Sen still needed to piss. So he nodded, turned, and started limping toward the lift.

Sen stepped off the lift as he shoved the new knife—just removed from his foot—into his belt. He tried not to limp as he made his way to where Skald and the others looked over the city and organized the battle plans. As he walked, he took note of the many people, citizens and soldiers alike, who stared at him. He knew he must be a mess; he'd been fighting for hours. He was covered in blood and viscera, grime, dirt, sweat, and the stench of a battlefield—which was more piss and shit than most expected.

Sen ignored the stares and tried to hurry, which only served to exacerbate his limp. He finally reached Skald and his commanders, set up right near the balustrade that looked down at the whole of Ir-Anan. As he approached, Skald turned from the man with whom he was in deep conversation—one of the councilors, Sen realized with surprise—and visibly exhaled.

"Thank the Six," Skald said, walking over and clapping him on the shoulder. "We were sure you'd fallen in defense of the lift."

Sen shook his head, taking an offered chair and sitting on the hard, wooden seat. "The lift is secure."

Skald nodded, leaning against a table stacked with various maps of the city. "That is good news."

"And," Sen continued, pouring himself a cup from a nearby carafe of water, "we've retaken the gate."

Skald nearly slipped and fell. "Retaken the gate?" He repeated, incredulous. "How?"

Sen recounted the reckless charge and use of the dragon's fleeing to bring the gate back under their control. Skald listened intently, only speaking when Sen was done and taking a long draught from his cup.

"Well. Shit." The general shook himself and looked back out at the city. The sun was higher in the sky as they neared midmorning. He leaned against the balustrade and Sen got up to join him.

"Where's Ylannos?" Sen asked, looking around at the various

people bustling from one responsibility to another, the councilor's face not among them.

Skald gestured vaguely toward the palace. "He and most of the other councilors are holed up in there. Not much for them to contribute to battle strategy."

Sen nodded. "And the dragon?"

Skald grunted and passed a long tube-shaped looking glass to Sen. "See for yourself."

Sen put the looking glass to his eye and the world instantly shrank to a single point, far in the distance but magnified to appear as if directly in front of him. He could see the dragon in stark detail as enemy soldiers worked to free the various bolts from its armored body.

"By the Six," Sen muttered. "Look at that monster." Through the looking glass, Sen could see the dragon's silver and red scales in brutal detail. It was enormous, horrifying in a beautiful way. The sun glinted off its scales, creating a nearly blinding visage. The Rider was there, too; still sitting astride the beast. Sen shuddered at the sight of him, in full plate armor, tendrils of purple smoke trailing from his visor. There was something distinctly *wrong* about the Rider, and Sen felt cold run up his spine. He set the looking glass down and turned back to Skald, who had a knowing look in his eye.

"We surprised them once. We won't get that chance again."

Sen nodded. "So, what's the plan?"

Skald sighed from somewhere deep in his bones. "I don't suppose you've bonded a dragon in the last few hours?"

Sen barked a laugh. "Sorry to disappoint."

Skald shrugged. "Ballistae operators have been told to fire as soon as it's in range. Hopefully they kill it before it kills all of us."

Sen sighed. "Let's hope so." He turned toward the palace as fatigue washed over him. "You think we've got some time?"

"I think so. Get some rest." Sen nodded and turned to go. "The city owes you, Vallos. As long as it stands."

Sen raised a hand in acknowledgement as he made his way back to the palace and, hopefully, a bed and a piss.

Sen crossed the threshold to the palace not long after, his fatigue growing with every step. As he passed an open door, through which voices could be heard, someone called his name.

"Vallos! Sir!"

Sen stopped and turned to look in the room. Councilor Ylannos sat inside on a plush sofa, surrounded by the other councilors and their families. He swirled a goblet of deep red wine in one hand, and his eyes told Sen he was thoroughly drunk.

Sen didn't have the energy left to be angry, though he felt it in his belly and the way his fists clenched involuntarily.

"Councilor," he all but growled.

Ylannos had stood and was tottering toward him, eyes moving up and down, taking in Sen's appearance.

"My word, Master Vallos. You're positively *disgusting*." He made an exaggerated gesture of holding his nose and wafting air away from his nose, then laughed to himself as he sipped from the goblet again. Thin trails of red wine ran down his cheeks to his finely-trimmed beard before he wiped them away with the purple sleeve of the fine linen shirt he wore.

"Aye," Sen said, moving his gaze away from the drunk councilor to scan the rest of the room's occupants. Most of them seemed to be at least a little intoxicated, trying to forget what he and the soldiers had been doing down on the lower levels. "Seems like you lot are having fun."

Ylannos backed away, looking stung by Sen's words. "We're just trying to survive, my dear man."

Sen sighed. "Right. I'll leave you to it, then." Ylannos was still talking as Sen turned to leave. Just before he was back through the door and into the hall, his eyes slid over a young boy and stopped him in his tracks.

The boy looked like Erick. It took him back to the decision to send the boy away. Though, now that the assault had begun in earnest, Sen was glad he'd made that decision. He imagined Erick in this boy's place, waiting out the battle, terrified of what was to come.

Then the boy turned around and Sen had to stop himself from falling over.

Erick's eyes went wide when he saw Sen. In an instant, the boy had crossed the room and caught the old man in a tight hug around the waist. Sen, still processing, knelt and scooped him into his arms. Erick was crying into Sen's filth-covered shoulder as he rounded on Ylannos.

"How?" he seethed, trying not to yell and potentially scare Erick.

The councilor shrugged. "He was found trying to leave the city and some guardsmen brought him back."

"I sent him away, you fool!" Sen grated through teeth clenched so hard, they were close to shattering. "And you brought him back to this death trap and didn't tell me?"

Ylannos held up two hands in a show of surrender. "You were out there! I couldn't have told you!"

Sen took a breath, forced his clenched fist to open, fought to regain composure. Killing a councilor wouldn't help them win this battle. And now that Erick had found his way to the middle of it, winning the battle was all that mattered. Sen leaned the boy back and looked into his face, wet with tears and streaked with dirt from Sen's shoulder.

"Have they been feeding you? Keeping you safe?"

Erick nodded.

"Good. That's good." Sen tousled his hair and the boy smiled, that full-mouthed smile children seemed to call upon with ease, but which escaped adults. "Stay here, okay? I'll come find you when it's safe."

Erick nodded, but his eyes were unsure. At Sen's questioning look, he leaned in close and whispered, "I heard it. The dragon."

Sen sighed and silently cursed that monster. "Aye. It's here." The boy's face filled with fear as if poured from a carafe. "But don't worry," Sen said hurriedly. "I'm going to take care of it." He hugged Erick tightly and set him down on the floor, and the pain of their separation dwarfed all his other aches.

"How?" Erick asked as Sen stepped toward the door. The old man looked back at him and forced a smile.

"I guess I'll have to kill it."

Sen hurried back down the hall and out the door, his need for sleep forgotten in an instant. He *did* find an opportunity to take that piss, though. He found Skald much like he'd left him, not even an hour prior.

"They didn't get out," Sen said as he approached. Skald looked up.

"What?"

"Your family. My boy. They didn't get out. Some guards brought them back, according to Ylannos." The color drained from the general's face. "I just saw Erick in there with the councilors and their families."

"Damn it!" Skald said, the flat of his hand coming down on the table he'd been poring over. "Those damn fools. I *told* the gate guards to allow them passage. How could this happen?"

"I don't know," Sen said simply. "We can find out when this is done. But we need a new plan for the dragon. Has it moved?"

Skald produced the looking glass and stepped to the balustrade. Sen followed him.

"Not yet," Skald said. "They're still working on the bolts. But there are only a few left. It won't be long." He removed the looking glass from his eye and turned to face Sen. "What are you thinking?"

Sen sighed. It was a terrible plan, and he knew it. But something had to be done, and this was the only thing he'd come up with.

"If the dragon gets airborne again, we're done for," he said. "Right now, it's on the ground. We can fight it on the ground. I'll lead the soldiers who defended and retook the gate. We'll fight our way to the dragon and kill it."

Skald laughed without any mirth.

"That's a terrible plan."

Sen nodded. "Aye."

A sigh escaped Skald's lips. "I'll come with you."

"No." Sen turned and faced the general, who was already turning to give orders to one subordinate or another. Skald turned back to him.

"No?"

"No," Sen repeated. "We need you here, keeping things together. I can handle this." And with that, he turned and strode away, back toward the lifts.

Skald watched Vallos walk away and felt a profound sense of doom settle over him. *If he fails...*

Skald's eyes slid from Vallos's departing form to the ornate entrance to the palace, and a seething rage bubbled in his guts. His mind raced as he worked through the possibilities. They were supposed to have been out of the city long before the battle began. They should've been past the walls and into the country a full day before the army arrived.

His brow knit together in frustration as the possibilities hung in the air before him, unspoken but starkly real. Skald resolved to bring his concerns directly to Ylannos when this was done.

If we live, he thought bitterly, turning back to the balustrade and gazing out over the city. His mind turned to Senran Vallos. Since he'd met the man, Skald had felt strongly that he was not the demon the legends spoke of. Generally, he'd found him to be quiet and thoughtful, considering his words before speaking them. But now, as Ir-Anan's fate, and the fate of Skald's own wife and child, rested on Vallos's wild gambit, he found himself hoping beyond hope that he was wrong.

Ir-Anan needed the Vallos of legend.

Chapter Twenty-Seven

Time to Die

Some among us believe their dragons make them invincible.

They are wrong. All things bleed.

-Log of Dragonmaster Forund, 19th Lord of Mun-Alin

Sen blew a breath out his mouth as he stared at the hastily-reconstructed portcullis, propped up in place of the previously destroyed North Gate. Even now, he knew there were likely to be groups of enemy soldiers breaking away and moving to the city's other gates, to the south and west. He hoped the soldiers there could hold.

Not that it will matter, if this fails. He checked the straps on the shield he'd procured. It was a nice, strong kite shield, large enough to cover most of his body. But it was heavy, dragging his arm down already, and would certainly slow him down. He'd chosen the shield to make up for his injured foot, but as he stood there, waiting to run out onto the battlefield, he questioned his judgment.

Sen shook himself and focused. This was no time for second-guessing. He had the shield, and he knew how to use it. Besides, it didn't matter what armaments he used. He was the weapon, and he was sharpened to a point. This was, he knew, the maddest thing he'd ever tried. But the dragon needed to die, and he was the one here to kill it.

Just another beast, he thought as the portcullis was pulled aside with a groan by the small knot of soldiers who'd been assigned the undesirable task. On the other side of the large grate, Sen could see the opposing army, thrown into chaos by the dragon's crash landing and being rebuffed from the gates. They were out of sorts, barely even paying attention to the gates. As he watched, Sen saw one of their number—a young man, no more than fifteen summers—point at the portcullis and call out. Shouting followed, as they hastily tried to get into formation.

Sen's heart thudded into his throat. It was time. Like a stallion at the starting gate, he stamped his injured foot, driving pain into his leg, gritting his teeth. Blood thundered in his ears. Beside and behind him, he could hear the rattle of weaponry being adjusted as his men readied themselves. They were a small faction, meant to achieve victory through surprise and speed, rather than overwhelming force. Still, Sen had martialed a half-thousand soldiers from the city's guard and the men who defended the walls and the lifts.

The soldiers, heaving with effort, lifted the twisted metal of the broken portcullis to the side. Sen roared, thrusting his sword toward the enemy, who was just now realizing they were coming as he took long strides out from under the gatehouse and into the cold air and bright sunshine. The men of Ir-Anan charged alongside him, and the tide of their fury washed across the snow-dotted dead grass that made up the distance between the two forces.

The opposing army was turning, still trying to get into a formation, but it was too late. The Imperials crashed into them like the tip of a spear, breaking their ragged line. Sen formed the spear's point, knocking away a sword lifted in halfhearted defense and running the wielder through.

And then, he was among them; swinging, chopping, snarling, killing. Every movement brought blood, to the point Sen scarcely knew who he was attacking. The press was hot and bloody, steaming the cold air with the sweat and screams of dying men. Beside him, Sen heard a scream and turned to find a young soldier, no older than sixteen, his stomach split open by an axe. His intestines spilled onto the dirt and he scrambled on his hands and knees, trying to force them back in. Sen noticed a brown stain leaking from his pants and realized he'd shit himself. He was screaming for his mother. Sen didn't stop the enemy soldier with the axe from bringing the blade down on the young man's neck, ending his cries with a *thunk* as the axeblade chopped into the dirt.

Sen's sword split the axe-wielder's head in half, a great spray of blood fountaining three feet over their heads to fall like steaming rain on the killing field. It sprayed across Sen's face, covering his vision with red and filling his mouth with the taste of metal. He freed his sword from the remains of the head, then wiped his eyes with the back of a gloved hand and turned back to the battle.

Heat. The sensation was sudden, visceral, and overwhelming. It happened no more than thirty feet in front of Sen. A gout of flame, so bright and hot it could've been the sun, exploded through the press of bodies, eviscerating soldiers of both sides without so much as time to scream. Sen watched as bodies exploded, men turned into blotches of red viscera on the ground, undone by the dragon's flame.

Sen's eyes followed the flames to their source, and saw the beast. The dragon's immense body was raised, like a snake about to strike. The flames dissipated, leaving smoke to billow from the monster's mouth, roiling from between its man-sized teeth to rise into the sky. From this distance, the light glinting off the dragon's scales was nearly blinding, and Sen had to squint to look at it. But he could see its red eyes, rimmed in yellow, scanning the battlefield, looking for its next target.

It didn't have to look far. The dragon's jaw opened, a great maw of teeth split by an undulating tongue, and it drew in a great breath. And with a sound like flint striking stone, more orange flames burst from the creature's mouth.

Sen moved away from the flames, fighting to get around to the dragon's flank. The army had turned into a mob, everyone fleeing for their lives as the dragon rained horror on them all, regardless of allegiance. Moving along with the great wave of human fear, Sen eventually found himself standing in open space as people surged away from the beast. He was staring at the dragon's tail, moving from side to side in a rhythmic motion, like a flag in a breeze. The torrent of flame had stopped, and the dragon looked at the people fleeing before it. As Sen watched in horror, its massive head lurched forward, jaws snapping closed around three men. Their bloodcurdling screams were cut short as the dragon lifted its head skyward, chomped once in a crunch of bone and armor, and set to swallowing its meal.

Something had changed. Sen could sense that much. The dragon had turned on the army. *Or perhaps,* he thought, *it's simply broken the leash.*

Either way, he knew this was his only opportunity. Sen sprinted across the open ground, boots thudding into the frozen dirt, turned muddy by the now-melting snow fall. He ducked as the dragon's great muscled tail passed over him in a rush of wind, and moved to the flank, where he noticed a large ballista bolt still jutting from the dragon's thigh. To his horror, it seemed the beast had been freed of the other spear-sized projectiles.

It could fly.

Sen reached the dragon's hind leg as the crunching from its mouth began to slow. As he reached up to grab hold of the massive saddle strapped to its back, something pulled him back, throwing him to the frozen ground with a *thud* and driving the air from his lungs. A cloud settled in front of the sun, bathing Sen in shade. As he looked up, though, he realized with a cold dread that it was not a cloud.

The Rider, clad in full plate armor, wisps of purple smoke trailing from the slit in his helmet, stood above him. Sen's eyes took in his silhouette, a warning sounding in his mind. The Rider cut a terrifying figure, the hilt of his massive sword poking over his shoulder from where it floated, tattered cloak whipping in a suddenly frigid wind.

The Rider's leg came up, and Sen saw the bottom of his boot, caked in mud and viscera. He rolled to the side, pain shooting across his back as the boot smashed into the dirt. Sen rose to one knee, turned in time to see the Rider's gauntleted fist coming straight for him. The kite shield came up, catching the blow but pitching Sen to his back again. He kept the guard raised and blocked another stomp.

The shield was dented, cutting into his forearm and sending a trickle of blood down to his hand. Sen rolled away again, climbed back to a knee, managed to unhook and discard the heavy shield as he made his way to his feet. His left arm was cut badly and warmth ran down to drip from his fingers. The Rider's head silently turned to look at the wound, then snapped back up to meet his gaze. Behind him, the dragon had moved into a new position, great yellow and red eyes gazing hungrily at Sen from over the Rider's shoulder. Blood still dripped from its maw.

Sen's blood ran cold as he felt his resolve weaken. What had he been thinking? This had been suicide.

By the Six, he thought. *They'll all die*. And he knew it was true. His mind flashed with images of the men he'd led out on this field, bodies ripped apart, blood scattered to the dirt and the wind. Skald, dead with his city, bodies piled high as the Empire burns. Erick, eyes lifeless, a meal for the beast.

And with that, the cold retreated, replaced by a boiling fury. Sen's hand tightened around the hilt of his sword and a growl climbed up from within his throat as Senran Vallos awoke. The Rider tilted his head to regard the man before him. Sen knew this was the moment to have words, to say something for the bards to sing about. But he had no words. Only a blind, visceral, bloody rage that burned in his veins.

The Rider took a step forward, but Sen struck before his boot hit the dirt. His sword whipped out, a metal blur with a singing edge. The Rider was caught off guard, lifted a plated arm to deflect the blow, which rebounded in a shower of sparks. Sen used the motion to whirl around and bring his blade to bear from the other side, catching his opponent on the head in yet more sparks. The Rider grunted and stumbled back two steps.

Sen did not relent. He advanced, feinting high, then striking low, scoring another hit against a knee. More sparks. Sen spun, avoiding a punch he saw coming three moves prior, came up behind the Rider and, taking his sword in two hands, smashed the blade down on the back of his head, sending him pitching forward. He braced with one hand on the dirt and Sen saw the opening.

He sidled to the right one step and brought his sword up in an arc to sever the arm at the elbow. But the Rider was recovering quickly and struck out with a kick, which Sen spun away from. The Rider was standing and, in a flash, took hold of the massive sword floating behind him. He positioned himself in a wide stance, with the sword in a two-handed grip, pointed before him. The dragon, Sen noticed, had backed off, allowing the fight to continue.

Looking at the Rider, Sen knew a duelist when he saw one. To play his game would be certain death. But he mimicked the stance anyway. And as the Rider stepped forward with a probing stab, Sen slipped to the side of the massive blade, directing its tip down into the dirt with a flick of his own sword. Then he spun, back to the huge sword's flat, drawing a dagger while his hand was obscured. As he came out of the spin, he found the Rider pitched forward, hands still on his sword as it thrust into the dirt. Sen thrust the dagger down in the gap where the plates of the Rider's armor met at the shoulder. The dagger found flesh, glanced off bone, and stuck.

The Rider grunted, taking one hand from the hilt of the huge sword and punching hard into Sen's chest. There was no avoiding the blow. Sen flew back, landing hard on his back for what felt like the hundredth time that day. His sword clattered from his grip, and he was sure the blow broke something.

But the sound of metal scraping against metal told him the Rider was advancing. He rolled to his stomach and tried to crawl away, find a weapon, anything. But there was nothing to be done. A metal boot shoved him over, forcing him to look up at the tip of a very sharp, black-bladed sword.

The Rider said nothing, just nodded at him as he lifted the blade and set the point on Sen's chest. He tried to muster the energy to fight back, but the rush of his anger and fear had dissipated. It was time to die. As the Rider lifted the sword slightly for the final blow, a roar shook the world with deafening strength. Sen saw the Rider's head snap up, first to the dragon, then out to the sky beyond Ir-Anan. Then he was gone, Sen forgotten as something else took precedent. The Rider walked with a quickened pace back toward the dragon, which was already flapping its wings and readying to take off.

Sen followed the Rider's gaze and his breath caught at the sight.

The dragon in front glimmered a brilliant green and gold, and it was followed by four more, all mounted with Riders, swords drawn as they dropped from the sky toward Ir-Anan.

Chapter Twenty-Eight

The Riders of Mun-Alin

The sight of even one Dragon Rider dropping from the sky can cause empires to quake.

-Log of Dragonmaster Grena, 805th Lord of Mun-Alin

Wik's breath caught in her chest as they dropped beneath the cover of clouds and she laid eyes on Ir-Anan for the first time. The city was enormous, made of rings, built into platforms, rising thousands of feet into the air, and all of it anchored to the slate black surface of Splithalf, which rose even higher into the cold sky.

And of course, there was the chaos taking place outside the city. A great mess of people, running all directions, but mostly just *away* from the incredible dragon that sat on that field.

Dyraxian, as Uanari had called him, was enormous, longer even than Uanari himself. His bulk was less significant, but there was no other way to put it: this was one of the most intimidating dragons she'd ever seen.

Rage flashed through her mind, so intense and sudden she had to grab the saddle to steady herself. Uanari had spotted Dyraxian, and before she even realized it was happening they had broken from the others, shooting down at a dizzying speed. Dyraxian and the Rider had gotten off the ground now, and were coming up, straight for him.

Uanari! Wik thought in a panic, her hands turning white as she gripped the saddle with everything she had. *Uanari, this is foolish!*

Quiet! Came the reply, taking her breath away with its intensity. *I will have this fool's heart!*

The wind rushed past, deafening Wik to the world. Everything was coming to a point. She could see nothing beyond Dyraxian's eyes: yellow, rimmed with red. Just as they were about to collide, Dyraxian fanned his wings out, slowing, and whirled with a speed Wik didn't think possible, bringing his huge tail around like a whip, cracking directly across Uanari's jaw and snapping his head to the side.

The noise in Wik's mind went suddenly silent as Uanari lost consciousness. The impact nearly threw her into the sky, but she managed to keep her grip and stay in the saddle. Then they were falling, tumbling through an open sky toward the ground. Wik thought about screaming, but instead gritted her teeth together and squeezed her eyes shut. The ground rushed up to meet them with a deafening crash.

The last thing Wik remembered was the saddle horn smashing into her face before darkness enveloped her.

◆◆◆

Eoradon looked over at the growing cloud of dust where Uanari and Wik had crashed down and gritted his teeth. *Dammit,* he thought. *Can you sense Uanari?*

The waters are muddied, Iaxal responded, sounding strained. *Dyraxian is clouding my senses.*

Eoradon cursed to himself and tightened his grip on his Rider blade. He turned from side to side, trying to locate the huge silver dragon. He wasn't hard to spot, making a loop and heading back toward Uanari.

Clearly they think he's the biggest threat, Eoradon said through the bond. *Let's correct them, shall we?* He felt Iaxal smile inwardly as she banked hard and took off in pursuit. Behind him, Virsk, Ferao, and Rialin, along with their dragons, were dropping low to begin dealing with the army. Vaguely, Eoradon could hear roars as they unleashed flames on the enemy.

Who are they? Iaxal asked.

The army? I have no idea, other than what Uanari said. Could be Meloran.

Iaxal let it go, but he could tell she wasn't satisfied. Indeed, he knew there would be more questions to answer when this battle was done. But first, they had to survive it, and the only way to do that was to deal with Dyraxian and his Rider.

Iaxal came in above the silver dragon as it descended to where Uanari fell. Eoradon felt the intake of breath swell her abdomen as she prepared to unleash fire on the Rider. As she breathed out and he heard the telltale *click* as the flames lit, the Rider's head snapped up, giving Eoradon his first glimpse of the creature. He pushed down disgust and clung tight to Iaxal. The Rider lifted a gauntleted hand and a torrent of flame shot from his hand, pushing them back and forcing Iaxal to abandon her plan. She quickly fell back into her pursuit as Dyraxian abandoned Uanari to take to the skies.

The chase was impossible for Eoradon to follow. The dragons writhed, spun, dipped, climbed, and dropped in an effort to gain an advantage. Iaxal stayed on Dyraxian's tail, using her smaller size to maneuver more easily around the larger dragon's movements. Occasionally, Eoradon caught glimpses of Ferao and Virsk driving the army away from the city. A wall of flames rose on the Field of Igdranon now.

Where is Rialin? He wondered. As if in answer, Rialin and his young dragon made themselves known, crashing into Dyraxian from the side, forcing him to take a moment to right his trajectory, at which point Iaxal's jaws shut tight around his tail.

Dyraxian bellowed, rolled, and whipped his tail about in an effort to throw Iaxal off, but she held tight. Eoradon could feel the strain in her jaws, the pain coursing through her teeth as she clamped down on the meat of the dragon's tail. Rialin and his dragon had righted themselves and came in again, trying to clamp down on Dyraxian's throat, but he thrashed violently, knocking them off-course with his bulk.

Eoradon's grip tightened on the saddle as he tried to stay astride Iaxal. Dyraxian was climbing now—or, trying to. Iaxal beat her wings, trying to pull him back to the ground. The silver dragon screamed as Iaxal's teeth cut into his tail. They were reaching a breaking point. The tendons in the tail were stretched to the point of ripping. And if Dyraaxian lost his tail, sustained flight would be nearly impossible.

Without warning, something hard and very heavy crashed into Eoradon, ripping him from the saddle so he skidded down Iaxal's spiked back, cutting gashes in his fancy armor, and throwing him into the open sky. His vision was spinning, chaotic. Ground, sky, ground, sky, ground—he managed to grab the hem of his cloak and wrap it tight in a fist. Muscle memory took over as he whipped the cloak about himself, grabbing it in both hands and allowing the wind to catch it and slow his fall. He was moving slower now, but still falling far too fast. The cobbled streets of a middle section of Ir-Anan rushed up to meet him. As he drew close, not knowing what else to do, Eoradon thrust his hand out and screamed, calling on that reserve of power that lurked in his blood.

The power answered, flooding through his body, then expelling through his hand in a burst of wind that was almost *too* strong. But it slowed him enough that he impacted with a merely bone-crunching force, rather than being splattered across the stones.

Rodo! Eoradon, are you okay? Iaxal was screaming in his mind as he forced his eyes open.

No, he groaned, wincing as he sat up. Gingerly, he felt his midsection, noting there were definitely some broken ribs. But all in all, the cuirass he'd been fitted with had taken the bulk of the abuse. Slowly, he unfastened the straps holding it to him and discarded it in a heap.

Dyraxian broke free from me, Iaxal explained. *He's going after Ferao and Virsk, trying to keep them away from the army. I'm coming to get you.*

Eoradon nodded and sent agreement through the bond as he

rose to his feet. Then he heard it: a crunching of stone, rattling of metal, and eventually a voice like a millstone grinding chaff.

"The prince," the voice said from behind him. "How good of you to join us."

Iaxal, scratch that. Go help them.

What are you talking about? What is it? Iaxal's voice was strained, worried. He felt the pain throbbing in her missing foot and his heart ached.

I've got a visitor. Go help them. Kill the dragon.

Iaxal hesitated, then sent agreement through the bond, accompanied by a message: *Be careful.*

Eoradon turned to see the rogue Rider standing there, regarding him curiously from those smoke-filled slits. Eoradon noted the damage to his armor, and wondered if all of it had come from the fall.

"Who are you?" Eoradon asked.

The Rider cocked his head as he seemed to think about the question. "I am no one. I am only the harbinger of my masters' will."

Eoradon glared at the metalclad monstrosity. "You killed my friend." He drew the sidesword in a ringing of steel and held it by his side. "I'll not allow you to harm the people of this city."

The harbinger, as he'd called himself, *laughed*. Eoradon felt sick from the sound, like something not meant for human ears.

"How noble of you," the Rider said. And then a sword was in his hand, an empty scabbard at his side. He raised the sidesword to point at Eoradon as an enormous black Rider blade floated down to hover just behind him.

Eoradon called his Rider blade down, letting it settle in his left hand as he gripped the hilt of his sidesword with his right. Slowly, he settled into a stance he liked, one leg in front of the other, weight balanced on his back heel, front toe barely touching the ground. His sidesword was positioned forward, side-on to his body in a defensive position, while his Rider blade was held aloft, over his head, point down toward the Rider.

The Rider cocked his head at the prince, then settled into an offensive stance, sidesword straight ahead while his Rider blade hovered behind.

So he's a duelist, Eoradon thought, evaluating his opponent. Before he could consider it further though, the Rider lashed out with his sidesword. Eoradon caught the downward swing on the flat of his own blade, then jabbed down with his Rider blade, which his opponent twisted away from. His own floating sword darted in then, forcing Eoradon to back away, knocking the massive sword aside, just for it to settle back behind its master.

As the Rider righted himself, Eoradon noticed him flexing the fingers of his left hand, glancing down at the appendage as he shook it, seemingly trying to regain feeling in it. And then the sword was on him again. The Rider blade came out of nowhere, forcing Eoradon to spin away from it and try to gain distance. It attacked again, and he parried it away, just in time to see the Rider lunging forward with his sidesword. He was too quick. Eoradon tried to duck the attack, but the tip of the sword plunged into the muscle of his left shoulder, forcing him to drop his Rider blade to the stones in a clatter.

Eoradon screamed as the blade bit deep into tissue, then gritted his teeth and smashed the Rider's helmeted face with a pommel strike, forcing him back and giving the Dragonmaster a moment's reprieve. As he turned to slash at the Rider again, a roar split the air, causing them both to look up. Dyraxian streaked overhead, hounded by Ferao, Virsk, and Iaxal.

Go! Eoradon called through his bond. Iaxal made no response, but he knew she heard him.

Then there was a sword streaking down toward him, and Eoradon's thoughts snapped back to the present as he parried the attack, spun away, and slashed sideways at the Rider. The attack met nothing but air as his opponent dropped low, underneath the attack, and stabbed up at Eoradon's chest. The prince stumbled back, a stinging sensation preceding a blooming wet warmth just above his ribs. He gritted his teeth against the pain and came in again. But the harbinger's Rider blade was coming for his head, forcing him to stop short and bat the attack away. He called on his own blade, which zipped up to engage the other floating sword. Then the Rider was on him, and they were exchanging blows at a dizzying speed.

In that screaming cyclone of raging metal, they danced, blade against blade. Eoradon found himself too slow, even with the Rider's apparent injury. He just couldn't keep up, and before long, the wounds were piling up. Cuts and scrapes along his arms and chest, a line of pain cut into his thigh, a punch to the face that was starting to swell his eye shut; they all grew together to paint a clear picture for the prince: he was outmatched. So, he did what he always did in moments of desperation.

He reached for his power.

Drawing from that pool, he clenched his fist and called on flames. After a split second of what he thought might be consideration, the warmth filled his bones, and fire engulfed his free arm. The punch landed square in the Rider's chest, denting the thick plate and exploding with force as it threw him away from Eoradon to tumble over the cobblestones and land in a heap.

Eoradon knew he should pursue, try to end the fight, but his body wouldn't allow it. Grimacing in pain, he leaned against the wall of a building and tried to catch his breath. The Rider was stirring, climbing to his feet. Eoradon could see he was injured, but he wasn't sure it would matter. He was an expert with his blades, a master duelist. Eoradon was a capable swordsman, but this was beyond him.

Of course, he thought grimly. *He killed Meristofales.*

A roar and a flash of pain drew the Dragonmaster's eyes to the sky, high above the city, where he saw the massive silver dragon Dyraxian wheeling, claws flashing across Iaxal's flank. She was in pain, but there was an undercurrent of fury in that pain. She beat her wings, gaining some distance to come in for another attack.

Dyraxian moved first. He spun, choosing to leave Iaxal as he wrapped claws around Paxavan's tail. Eoradon's heart leapt into his throat, but he was powerless, his vision fixed on the dragons, their battle painted on the canvas of Splithalf's onyx face. Seemingly in slow-motion, Dyraxian whirled, affixing himself to the side of the mountain with his lower claws as he spun, wielding Paxavan's smaller body like a club which he slammed into the flat stone face of the mountain.

Paxavan screamed. Eoradon looked for Ferao in the saddle, but was too far away, too weak to do anything as the huge silver dragon pinned Paxavan to the flat face of Splithalf, opened wide his maw, and bit down on the bronze dragon's head. Then, with a rending scream, he wrenched and tore Paxavan's head from his body in a fountain of hot blood.

Shock and grief speared through Eoradon's mind, and he wasn't sure if it came from him or Iaxal. It had happened so fast, Iaxal and Virsk had been left helpless.

Kranavoss screamed, his rage filling the sky and shaking the very ground beneath their feet as he and Virsk charged the huge dragon. Dyraxian dropped Paxavan's body to re-engage. Eoradon watched as the decapitated dragon fell to crash into the middle layers of the city in a plume of dust and broken stone.

"You have led them to their deaths." Eoradon turned to face the Rider, who was now back on his feet. "There will be more before this is finished. So many more." There was a hint of a smile in the harbinger's voice that sparked a rage within Eoradon, who felt his hand tighten around the grip of his sidesword.

The rain of blood from Paxavan's death had reached the city, and the blood steamed on the cold stones, creating a mist around their feet, covering both warriors in red. The Rider looked up and spread his hands wide, welcoming the gore.

"Blood rains on Ir-Anan," he said, so quiet Eoradon had to strain to hear him. "The way is being cleared."

Eoradon's teeth clenched so hard he thought they might shatter. Reaching to the reserve of power within him, he turned that magic inward, pushed it into his bones, willed his skin to knit together, even as he stepped forward.

What are you doing, Eoradon? Iaxal's concern echoed through his mind. *You can't maintain that kind of healing*.

I don't need to maintain it, Eoradon said, his voice flat and cold as he resigned himself. *I only need to hold it long enough to finish this.*

Don't be stupid!

He dies here, Iaxal. I will not have it any other way.

Eoradon leapt forward with a strike, and the Rider brought his blade up to meet it with a ringing of steel.

Wik groaned and lifted her head. Everything hurt. Groggily, she forced her eyes open to a blazing sun overhead. She reached out, groping about, trying to remember what was happening. She was laying in the mud at the base of a large wall.

Ir-Anan. The realization hit her like a thrown punch. She was lying in the mud, looking up at the walls of Ir-Anan. She rolled over, pain coursing through what she was certain were broken ribs, and found Uanari's massive body lying next to her, where he'd skidded up against the wall. She rose to her feet and stumbled to his side. He was breathing—obviously, she realized, since she was, too—but still unconscious. She tried to reach him through their mental bond, but received back only silence. And not his typical, brooding kind of silence, but real, lack of awareness.

She sighed and looked around. The world was chaos. The attacking army had broken all semblance of rank, and seemed to be flooding into the city through a shattered gate not far away. High above, dragons screeched and roared as they fought. From the other side of the wall, she could hear screaming, the clashing of steel, and she wondered if there was any real resistance left.

As she watched, a contingent of the attacking army had noticed her moving about and was looking at her. They were speaking to one another, though from this distance, she couldn't hear the words. She knew the faces, though. They were eyeing Uanari, lying there unconscious, and the glint of opportunity shone in their eyes. Slowly, they took a step in her direction, blades drawn. Wik felt her heart hammering the inside of her chest.

What can I do? she thought. She looked at Uanari. *He's still out. They'll kill us, what can I do?* Panic gripped her guts and twisted, the cold knife of fear stabbing through her. *He was right; I'm not ready!* Desperate, she felt about herself for anything to wake the dragon.

Her hand landed on the head of her axe, still strapped to her thigh.

Her breathing slowed. She looked back at the men advancing toward her. Her training—Meristofales's training—took over. She was alone. She was outnumbered. But she was *not* helpless.

She had an axe.

Her hands no longer shaking, Wik unstrapped the axe and hefted it in one hand. A wind cut across the battlefield and gathered up her long hair as the charging men broke into a run toward her. Briefly, she returned her gaze to Uanari. Then she set her jaw, turned, and ran toward the enemy soldiers.

Rialin lowered himself to the body of the dragon as they banked hard and came back for another pass. Flame exploded from the dragon's mouth and Rialin could see a small group of attacking soldiers vanish beneath the curtain of heat. He swallowed hard and cast his eyes back up, looking out on the streets of Ir-Anan. The army had breached the walls and were fully engrossed with sacking the city. Ahead, he spied some soldiers chasing a group of women down the street. The women were, each and every one, holding a child or leading one by the hand. Rialin gritted his teeth together and pointed.

"There!" he shouted. The dragon banked that direction and dropped hard from the sky, coming to a skidding stop, throwing a cloud of dust and debris all around. Rialin leapt from the saddle, cloak billowing behind him, sidesword flashing from its scabbard. Half of the soldiers had turned and run, but a smaller knot had drawn their weapons and approached the Rider, eyes mad with bloodlust.

Rialin caught the first sword on his blade and turned it away, then stabbed forward, taking the man in the throat. A spear flashed in and he ducked, letting it pass over his head as the dragon snapped out, jaws closing around the spearman's head and silencing his screams.

Rialin looked up in time to see another blade coming at him sidelong. He brought his sidesword up to block it, just as his Rider blade smashed down through the top of his foe's head and into the stones below his feet. The body fell away in two bisected halves, a shower of gore erupting from where the man had stood. Rialin wiped his eyes and bid the sword return to the scabbard on his saddle. Then he climbed back up and they were gone in two beats of the dragon's wings.

Chaos ruled the streets of Ir-Anan. Sen hobbled along in the direction of the lift, doing his best to avoid a fight. Every part of him hurt, from the slash across his back, to the stab wound in his foot, to whatever broke when that Rider punched him; he truly *felt* like a frail old man.

Regardless, Erick was in the middle of this, and it was time to leave. His last chance was to get to Erick and do his best to get the two of them out of here before the true killing started.

A group of enemy soldiers ran in front of Sen as he peaked out of an alley. He pressed himself to the wall, but they didn't notice him as they thundered past, looking for debauchery. Sen had seen this part before: the thrill of victory. These soldiers had been afraid when the dragon was killing indiscriminately, but now that Ir-Anan had been cracked like an egg, it was time to do what they'd marched across the country to achieve: loot and pillage.

Rounding a corner, Sen saw the enemy soldiers had already found the lift.

Damn, Sen cursed. As he watched, groups of them were loading on the lifts and riding up to the various levels of the city. He was sure the top level was high on the list to plunder, if they hadn't already gone for it.

A dragon's scream shook the world, and Sen let himself look up. The skies were as chaotic as the streets. Watching the giant creatures do battle was mesmerizing. He was fairly sure one of them had been killed and dropped into the city—he hoped the thought of that loot would distract the army.

Sen looked back to the lifts and tried to count the men guarding them. It was pointless—in his condition, he'd never be able to fight his way through them. His eyes scanned his surroundings until they landed on the edifice of the palace, rising above all the other buildings on the first level. Sen allowed himself a smile and took off at the fastest hobble he could manage.

The palace's doors had been caved in, but it seemed the looters had moved on to better prizes. There were no riches on the first level of the structure, anyway, Sen knew. Still, they had taken time to smash some of the various paintings and a couple busts of former rulers. Sen made his way through the throne room, past what looked like a puddle of piss at the foot of the giant marble throne, to the small private lift.

He gave a private thanks to the Six when he found the lift unmolested. He climbed into the closet-sized room, pulled the door shut behind himself, and activated the lift. In a few moments, he stepped out on the top floor of the palace and closed the door, hoping beyond hope it would still be working when he and Erick made their escape.

Sen moved through the halls of the palace as quietly as possible, passing ornate sitting rooms and offices—all of which were empty. A pit grew in his stomach as he took in the eerie stillness of the place. Around his feet, Sen stepped around the detritus of whatever escape the people here made; glasses, bottles, a few shoes and scraps of cloth. He didn't see blood, which he chose to take as a good sign. Still, his stomach was in his feet as he proceeded toward the palace door.

As he drew close, he could hear the sounds of shouting outside. Someone was giving orders, from the sound of it. Sen drew his sword, took a deep breath, and pushed through the ornate wooden door.

Outside, the topmost level of Ir-Anan was in chaos. The enemy soldiers ran amok, much as they did down below. More than one well-dressed body of the rich and untouchable lay unmoving on the ground. Sen scanned them, his heart hardly beating as he looked for that small body, that round, innocent face.

But Erick was not among these unfortunate souls. Sen nodded to himself and headed to the balustrade where Skald had been operating since the battle's beginning. As he came close, he could hear the always-distinct sounds of fighting: shouted orders, the rattle of shields, the clashing of steel. Up above, a dragon screamed again. From the distance, Sen could swear he heard explosions and rolling thunder.

But in front of him, a chaotic scene was playing out. Varen Skald, sword raised to glint in the sunlight, directed a small cadre of soldiers into a tight shield wall. The front row of soldiers' shields were tightly fitted together, while the second row leveled spears at the oncoming enemy ranks. For their part, the invaders were pressed tightly together, seemingly trying to decide how to attack this knot of clearly well-disciplined soldiers.

Sen's eyes drifted over the Ir-Ananian defenders. Beyond the two rows of soldiers stood Skald, shouting orders and waving his sword. Around him were his various attendants, some with swords drawn, others looking about to faint from fear. And beyond *them*...

Sen's eyes narrowed as a cold fury settled in his stomach. Ylannos and the other councilors stood huddled together by the balustrade, fear written like a book across their faces k. In Ylannos's case, Sen could also tell by his puffy red cheeks and lazily drooping eyes that he was drunk beyond all reason. And directly in front of him stood Erick, the councilor's hands gripping his small shoulders.

Sen felt his hand tighten involuntarily around the grip of his longsword. He stepped into the middle of the ongoing posturing, causing both sides to stop and look at him. He spared a glance for the enemy army, but when they didn't move to attack, he turned his back on them and strode toward the Ir-Ananians' shield wall. The soldiers moved to stop him, but a shouted order from Skald stopped them cold. With some hesitance, two soldiers parted slightly and let him into the knot of people. He shouldered his way roughly through the crowd, though many people stood to the side as he passed. His feet carried him directly to Ylannos.

"Sen," Erick cried, wrenching himself free of the councilor and running over to impact Sen with a tight hug around the waist. He reached down and patted the boy on the back, hugging him close.

"Hello, son," Sen said, his attention drifting from Ylannos to Erick as he pulled him in tight, holding the drawn longsword just out of view.

When Erick looked up, his eyes were large, fever bright and wet with fear. They were looking past Sen, to the sky, where the impacts of the dragons' attacks on each other could be heard even this far below. Sen looked up and saw the big silver one fighting off three smaller ones. Though, he knew they were still probably the size of a house.

He looked back down and took the boy by the chin, turning him so they were face to face.

"I'm here now," he said in the softest voice he could manage. "I'll keep you safe."

Erick nodded, setting his jaw. "Right. What are we going to do?"

Sen looked up, his eyes meeting Ylannos's. "The Councilor and I are going to have a chat." He gestured for Erick to go over with a little girl he assumed to be Skald's daughter. When the boy had moved away, he stepped close to the councilor, so close he could smell the whiskey on his breath.

"You," he seethed, "better start fucking talking." The longsword flashed into view from beneath his dark cloak.

Ylannos swallowed with a *gulp*, drunken eyes trying to focus on the blade. "What do you want to know?"

"I want to know why these people are outside the palace without weapons or training," Sen growled, gesturing around at the various councilors and civilians cowering behind the shield wall.

"Well—I—I—" Ylannos stammered, looking around as if for help. Sen took another threatening step toward the man, who realized he was against the railing, and was facing a several-hundred-foot drop to the next platform if he let his cowardice carry him further. He tried to straighten up and regain some of his composure, but a drunken slur still decorated his speech. "The palace has a lift," he said, as if that explained everything.

"You don't fucking say," Sen said. "It's how I got here, you worthless—"

"Then my hunch was right! The barbarians would come up and slaughter us!" Ylannos smiled, triumphant.

Sen punched him, catching him across the jaw, dropped his sword to the ground with a *clang*, caught him before he tumbled off the platform, and pulled him close.

"You brought children to a battlefield." Sen's voice was deathly quiet and he realized he'd dropped into Vallos's cadence without meaning to. "If we survive this, I'll have your head." And he dropped the sniveling worm, then bent to pick up his sword.

The boy was sitting huddled up with the little girl, but he turned to Sen as he approached. Sen dropped to one knee, eliciting a chorus of *pops* from his joints, and took Erick by the shoulders.

"I'm going to go help General Skald," he said. "You stay here, and you stay safe. If anything happens to me, or if they get through, you run, do you understand?"

Erick's head gave a little shake. "No, not without you!"

"You *run*," Sen said again, squeezing the little shoulders a bit harder. "And you don't stop running 'til you're free." He looked at the little girl, who had her father's stern face. But her quivering bottom lip gave away her fear. "The same goes for you, girl. Your da wants you safe and sound. Where's your mother?" The girl looked around, then shrugged. Sen nodded. "Stay together. Keep each other safe. I'll be back soon." Then he pulled Erick into his body. The little boy stiffened for a split second, then sank into the hug, throwing his arms around Sen's neck in a tight embrace. Sen squeezed him harder and the boy gave a little squeak. Sen chuckled, then whispered in his ear, "I love you, son."

The boy squeezed him back. "I love you, Sen."

Chapter Twenty-Nine

Last Chance

When the time comes, I must believe they will strike true.

-Log of Dragonmaster Meristofales, 875th Lord of Mun-Alin

Eoradon stumbled back, tried to plant his back foot, and felt it go out from under him. He dropped painfully to one knee, breathing hard, light leaking from a dozen scrapes and cuts that were healing slower and slower. Feordan's healing magic was strong—much stronger than his—but he thought even she would be out of it by now.

The Dragonmaster looked up at the Rider who walked slowly toward him. He'd scored several hits against the plate armor, but the Rider was barely slowed. Eoradon tried to rise, but found his legs wouldn't support him. Fatigue was creeping in. His reserve of power was nearly half drained. He pulled harder on that power, urging it to heal his body faster. It didn't respond, and he cursed to himself.

The Rider stopped a few paces in front of him. Eoradon could see his gauntleted hand flex around the grip of his Rider blade. He squatted down so they were eye to eye.

"Little princeling," the Rider grated. "The people of this city will never know how you fought for them." He reached out and took a handful of Eoradon's hair and wrenched his head back, forcing him to look up. Above, the dragons were still fighting, wheeling in a mess of claws, wings, teeth, and flame.

Iaxal, he reached out. She was strained in battle, and so did not reply, but he knew she heard him. *Iaxal, I'm sorry. I couldn't beat him.* Tears gathered at his eyes as understanding passed through their bond. *Please know—I have never regretted my life. All the things that happened. They brought me home. They brought me to you.* And he felt warmth wash over him. Love, through the bond.

The Rider spoke again, that voice like the breaking of stone. "When the sun sets, it will do so on the ruins of your birthright." He jerked Eoradon around again, forcing him to look into those horrible smoking eyes. "You are the prince of *nothing.*" He released Eoradon, throwing him to the ground as he raised his massive black-bladed sword. The Prince of Ir-Anan forced himself to his knees, determined to meet his end with his eyes open.

"I expected better from a duelist of Mun-Alin." The Rider's voice had taken on a mocking tone. He hefted the huge sword, preparing to drop it and split the Dragonmaster in half, thus all but ending their order.

Something drew Eoradon's eyes. A shadow, just over the Rider's shoulder. A smile crept across his face.

"I am no duelist," he said. "But he is."

The shadow passed over the Rider, who whirled, bringing his sword up into a defensive position, but it was too late. Rialin dropped from the sky, both feet slamming into the Rider's chest and throwing him to the ground.

The Rider turned his momentum into a backwards roll, rising back to his feet as his Rider blade flew through the air to his hand. He brought it up in a guard position, but Rialin hit him like the breaking of the tide. Both his Rider blade and his sidesword moved like lightning, the larger sword sweeping out in great arcs, while the smaller one darted in with thrusts and jabs. The Rider was on his back foot from the moment the fight began. Desperate, he caught Rialin's Rider blade on his own, tried to spin into the attack to strike out with his fist. But Rialin saw it coming, bouncing off the Rider with his shoulder, trapping the black-bladed sword in an 'X' between his two weapons, then twisted. The Rider's sword was ripped from his hand to clatter to the stones. Rialin dropped his own sword pommel first and let it rest on the black blade, held in place by his own force of will.

Eoradon watched, hope rising in his chest, as Rialin held the Rider at the point of his sidesword.

"Kill him, Rialin!" he screamed, trying to rise. Using his sword as a crutch, the prince managed to climb to his feet and lean against the outer wall of a building.

If Rialin heard him, he didn't acknowledge his words. He advanced on the Rider, who had straightened, sword leveled at his throat, his red cloak billowing out behind him like the standard of a warring host.

"It's different when we fight back, isn't it?" Rialin said, his tone flat, but betraying a rage boiling just beneath the surface.

"I told you," the harbinger said. "I was merciful."

Rialin's face twitched. "You," he seethed, "killed Meristofales. Your dragon killed F—" His voice caught, forcing him to swallow. "—Ferao. This is over."

Rialin stepped forward to strike a killing blow, but the Rider's hand snapped up as he expelled a gust of wind. Rialin was lifted off his feet and thrown backward, bouncing on the cobblestones, rolling over himself, and coming to rest in a heap, his sword several feet away.

Eoradon's heart sank as he watched the monastery's best duelist struggling to rise. As Rialin climbed to one knee, he tried to force himself to his feet, only to scream and fall back to a sitting position. Then Eoradon saw it: whatever magic had held his leg together hadn't withstood the force of the Rider's attack. He was crippled once again. And all their hopes had broken with his body.

The Rider advanced on him, flames coiling around his right arm while lightning danced along his left, crackling and sparking against his armor. With his attention on Rialin, Eoradon saw an opening.

He pulled hard on his reserve of power, willing it into his skin and bones, begging for the magic to respond. There was a beat of silence. Eoradon squeezed his eyes together, desperation pulling tears from him.

"Please," he whispered through gritted teeth, sweat pooling on his brow.

An explosion of power rocked him, forcing the breath from his lungs. Lines of fire traced through his veins as he struggled to hold onto the surge. Wisps of light coiled from his skin. His vision blurred, then coalesced into a more vibrant image than he'd ever seen. He could make out minute details, such as pits in the cobblestones and knicks on the Rider's armor.

His injuries knit themselves closed and fatigue fled from him as the immense power washed over him. With that relief came pain, though. It welled up inside of him, a burning sensation in his lungs and stomach, like flames threatening to be expelled. A memory flashed through his mind of Wik, lung blown apart, a statue melting in front of her.

Eoradon fixed his eyes on the Rider, who was nearly upon Rialin. He was shocked to see what looked like a massive dragon made of shadow clinging to the Rider's back, guiding his movements, working his limbs like a marionette. Almost without thought, he reached out and touched the shadow beast with his power, and it disappeared in a puff of smoke, caught on the wind and carried away. The fire and lightning that had ringed the Rider's arms vanished, and he pitched forward, as if suddenly unsteady.

The Rider whirled, and Eoradon saw the smoke coming from his eyes had stopped flowing. Then there came a tinny scream, captured by that helmet, as the harbinger rushed Eoradon in a full-blown rage.

"What have you done!?" He screamed, and his voice was the opening of a thousand graves. "Where has it gone?!" He lifted a fist, but Eoradon reached out, and caught it, arresting his motion completely and holding the Rider suspended by his hand.

He continued to struggle and rage, and the flame within Eoradon was burning, threatening to explode outward. He felt tears streaming down his face as he thought of Meristofales and Ferao and Paxavan. Then he opened his mouth...

...and screamed.

Light exploded from Eoradon's mouth, impacting the suspended Rider with a physical force. The Rider howled in pain, but was helpless in Eoradon's grasp. The light coalesced into a concentrated beam that struck the Rider in the chest. The armor there put up little resistance, melting under the heat. A hole was vaporized in the Rider's chest, cutting his scream short. When the light flickered out, Eoradon saw spots in front of his vision, and he felt suddenly very weak. The Rider dropped unceremoniously to the ground in a smoking, bubbling heap.

Eoradon staggered, darkness encroaching on the edges of his vision. *It's over,* he said to Iaxal. *He's dead.*

He's dead!? She sounded surprised.

What's wrong? he asked, dread filling his heart as he fought to stay upright.

The dragon lives!

"Oh no," Eoradon whispered, dropping to his knees and struggling to stay conscious.

They're not bonded, he thought. *Oh, by the Six, they're not bonded.*

He briefly registered the massive silver dragon throwing Iaxal off as she weakened from Eoradon's exertion. Kranavoss was spent. Rialin's dragon was coming back to his aid. Dyraxian dove for the field outside the city where, through Iaxal's eyes, Eoradon could see Wik fighting off waves of the enemy soldiers alone, desperately defending Uanari's unconscious body.

It's up to them now, Eoradon said as he slipped under the cool comfort of darkness. *It's up to Wik.*

◆◆◆

Wik slid to the side of a spear thrust, whirled and brought the hammer side of her axe to bear, staving in the helmet of the enemy soldier. No sooner had his body dropped to the ground, she was knocking away a sword strike, dipping under a sideways chop from an axe, rolling along the ground, and coming up to bury her own weapon in the face of an archer.

She spun and saw a knot of three men approaching, two swords and an axe raised high. Wik sprinted at them. A few paces away, she let her axe fly, tumbling end over end through the air to land with a *thunk* in a sword-wielder's chest. A high-to-low two-hand chop was coming down from the soldier with the axe. Wik shifted her shoulders to let it pass harmlessly by her, then thrust a hand into the man's chest, calling on her power. This time, she did not take only a thimble's worth, as Meristofales had coached her. She pulled from that reserve using nothing but instinct, and hit the man with a detonation of wind so strong he was shorn in half.

His top half cartwheeled into the sky, bathing everyone beneath him in blood and viscera. Wik looked at the final swordsman and smiled. A wolf's grin. A *dragon's* grin. He came at her, but his conviction had fled. She stepped into the attack, gripped him by the wrist and wrenched. Something popped and he screamed, his grip going slack. Wik caught the sword as it fell from his limp hand and, in one motion, spun it round and thrust it through the bottom of his jaw. The blade tore through the man's brain, breaking through the top of his skull with a *crunch* as his face went slack. She released the sword and he fell to the ground.

Wik breathed deep as she looked around. She was alone

among the corpses, all of them broken and brutalized in a way she hadn't thought herself capable of.

Maybe Uanari is rubbing off on me, she thought. Looking at the destruction she'd wrought, Wik didn't know if she wanted to laugh or vomit. Maybe both. The air was thick with the stench of blood, and her gorge rose with every deep breath she heaved in. After a moment, she could fight it no longer, and retched violently. As she rose to her feet and retrieved her axe from the man's chest she'd buried it in, she looked at the still-sleeping form of Uanari and begged silently for him to wake up.

The sounds of fighting still drifted over the city's walls, but it was broken by a different noise. A thunderclap, followed by a scream and a flash of brilliant light from somewhere in the city's middle levels. Wik had to shield her eyes at the explosive force of it. And further, she could *feel* something emanating from that. A great well of power, like she'd never seen.

What in the Six was that?

And as quickly as it had begun, it ceased, the light retreating and leaving everything darker for its having been there. A scream from the sky stole her attention. She looked up and saw Dyraxian thrashing about, throwing off Iaxal, who suddenly looked unable to put up a fight. Kranavoss and Virsk, now alone—where were Ferao and Rialin?—backed off, unable to keep up the fight. That left Dyraxian alone, and he spun in the air, diving.

Diving toward *her*.

Wik sprinted for the cover of the wall, pumping her arms, leaping over the various corpses. But all her effort, all her speed was for naught. Dyraxian slammed to the ground in front of her, his massive snakelike body coiling around behind her. The huge silver- and red-scaled head loomed over her, teeth bared in a grotesque imitation of a smile.

Wik tried to roll away from a descending claw, but Dryaxian was too fast, and she found herself pinned, axe discarded, unable to move. The enormous claw held her fast. The smell of old blood was overwhelming and she felt the urge to vomit again.

Dyraxian's head was directly over her, and her vision was filled with teeth.

Hello, little one, a voice purred in her mind. Smooth, like honey, she'd not even felt Dyraxian's presence intrude on her thoughts. But she could feel him now. Everywhere, all-encompassing, and so cold.

"Stop," she said aloud, frozen in fear. "Stop; get out of my head!"

Dyraxian laughed and ice crawled up Wik's spine. *So this is what has become of Trevathyn's heresy*. He tutted. *What a shame.*

Wik's brows knit together in confusion. *What are you talking about?*

Oh, poor thing. You don't even know your own history. Dyraxian drew closer to her and the stench of rotted meat on his breath nearly made her pass out. But that icy presence stilled her consciousness. *Pity you won't get to learn it*.

Wik felt the heat more than she saw it. The glow from his nostrils grew steadily, and soon she felt it stinging her face. She knew she felt tears gathering, but the heat stole them from her as they turned to steam.

This is it, she thought, fear wending its way through her brain. *Uanari!* she cried out. She reached for her reserve of power, but the fear kept her from focusing. She extended her mental awareness as far as she could, hoping to penetrate his sleep.

Uanari, please!

Something stirred at the corners of her mind.

Wik closed her eyes as the inferno in Dyraxian's mouth grew in intensity, the heat and stench of rot washing over her in waves.

And then it vanished in a rush of wind. Tentatively, Wik opened her eyes to a blue sky.

A colossal *thud* sounded next to her and the very ground beneath her rattled from the impact. Wik rolled to her feet and turned toward the sound.

Dyraxian rolled along the ground in a chaotic ball of snarling teeth and claws as an enormous cloud of dust rose into the sky. As it cleared, a silhouette became clear to Wik.

Uanari stood, crouched on all four legs, wings spread to the sky, his expansive bulk tensed, the crown of horns on his head glittering in the cold winter sun.

Dyraxian had regained his feet and crouched, facing Uanari, all else seemingly forgotten. With some distance, Wik noticed how beat up the ancient dragon was. Claw marks scored his body in multiple places, leaving flesh hanging in tatters. His scales had been raked and burned away in patches, showing the skin beneath. His breath was ragged, coming in gasps. Compared to Uanari, he looked haggard and worn. Still, his red and yellow eyes betrayed nothing but cold, calm fury, worn to a sharpened edge. When he spoke, he did so within Wik's mind, though she noticed other nearby soldiers looking around in confusion.

Uanari, Dyraxian's smooth-as-silk voice was tinged with anger that was mirrored on his snarling face.

No. Uanari's voice was vast in its response, and the soldiers who'd shown confusion before now displayed fear. *Not. One. More. You will* not *take her.*

Wik felt herself swell involuntarily as unexpected emotion reached up from her stomach and threatened to choke her.

Oh, Uanari, Dyraxian said with a chuckle, crouching lower to the ground. *I will take so much more from you before this is done. The girl. The lives of the people in this city. All are forfeit to me. I make ready the way for my masters, and this is* my *bounty.*

The meaning of the dragon's words were lost on Wik, but Uanari's response told her everything she needed to know.

Wik watched as the black dragon straightened, the crown of horns on his brow glinting in the sun, and saw something shift in him. All the regality and poise she'd always seen him project fell away, revealing a naked lethality of bared teeth and choking rage. He was the King of Dragons. But more than that, he was the King of *Dragons*: an apex predator who'd been taught to wear a mask of civility. But the mask was off now, scattered and forgotten as the monster of legend took over.

Hear me, wretch. Uanari's voice boomed in Wik's mind and, evidently, the mind of anyone else nearby. *I am Uanari the Black. I am the dread weapon of the Empire. I am the Living Storm. I am the Guardian of Mun-Alin, and these people are under* my *protection. You speak dominion over their lives, but words are the way of man.* The great dragon's lips peeled back, revealing rows of teeth sharp as any blade as a vicious growl emanated from his throat. *Come and claim them, by the Law of Teeth!*

There was no hesitation from Dyraxian. The silver dragon lurched, slithering across the ground like a snake at a speed Wik didn't think possible, and for a moment, she was sure he was too fast for Uanari. But as she watched, Wik realized with a start that she had no idea the extent of the black dragon's power.

As Dyraxian leapt up toward Uanari, fangs bared and mouth agape, the King of Dragons stood his ground. His foreclaws snapped up, taking hold of Dyraxian's jaw, one claw on the bottom and one gripping his snout. Membranous black wings unfurled, beat the air once, twice, lifting both dragons ten, then twenty feet off the ground. Dyraxian clawed at Uanari, but could do nothing while held in his grip. Then Uanari spun, whirling in the air so fast he blurred to Wik's vision. Dyraxian's long body whipped in the air as he was hauled bodily up and over as Uanari plummeted back down to the ground, slamming the silver dragon into the dirt face-first.

Another dust cloud billowed as the ground shook from their impact. Wik saw some stones slip from their place in the wall of Ir-Anan and hoped it wasn't too damaged.

As the cloud dissipated, Wik couldn't help but smile. Uanari stood, foot on Dyraxian's neck as he held fast to the beast's jaws, still pried open in his claws. Dyraxian's undulating tongue struck out as the back half of his body writhed and fought to no avail. Uanari had him, and there was no escape.

Uanari looked down into Dyraxian's mouth as he held it open and snarled.

My masters will remember this! Dyraxian screamed in Wik's mind. She cringed from the sound.

Uanari leaned even closer. Wik saw the light building in his throat and behind his bared teeth. Sparks danced along his body as he growled.

Good. Uanari opened his mouth as flames danced between

his teeth. Wik could've sworn his eyes even took on a fiery hue as his strength built. *Let them never forget the day they tested my vengeance.*

A plume of fire so bright it looked to Wik like a coalesced beam of pure light burst forth from Uanari's mouth. It shot down, directly into Dyraxian's open maw. The silver dragon writhed and screamed, but it was useless. In a moment, the smell of cooking meat filled the air. It took only seconds for the fire to burst out the back of Dyraxian's throat and impact the dirt, where a number of small fires instantly caught in the grass.

The roar of the flames was deafening, and Uanari did not relent until Dyraxian's savaged corpse hung limp from his grip. As the flames finally dissipated, Uanari stood there, heaving breath. Then he lifted his head to the sky and roared.

Ceran Ylannos was afraid. The roiling stench and chaos of the battlefield was *not* his arena. He whirled from side to side, looking for an escape, but there was none. All around, bodies pressed in closer to him as Skald and Vallos struggled to keep the enemy at bay. Somewhere nearby, a woman was crying as she clutched a baby to her chest.

The panic was setting in. And of course, he'd found his way through several bottles of wine already, so his nerves were frayed. He felt sick. His vision swam. He turned and vomited off the balustrade and felt a little better, but the death pressing in, ever advancing, could not be ignored.

And suddenly, he found himself standing just behind the boy, Erick.

"Master Erick!" He called to the boy, gripping him by the shoulder. He was suddenly reminded of the growing bruise spreading across his face where that brute Vallos had cuffed him. And all on this boy's account. Ceran wondered at that.

"Yes, Councilor?" Erick asked in that annoyingly polite and too-smart way he had. Almost as if he'd had some sort of formal training. Even the children who attended court functions in Ir-Anan were rarely this polished.

"Master Erick, tell me of your home. Tell me of Aneving." There was something here, but in his drunken state, Ceran was struggling to find which thread to pull.

Erick looked at the chaos surging around them. "Now?"

"Yes, boy, now!" Ceran snapped and immediately regretted it. He patted the boy on the shoulder and said in a softer tone, "I am afraid, Master Erick. Distract me with talk of the country."

Erick didn't look convinced, but he nodded. "Aneving was pretty," he said, a wistful look in his eyes, despite everything. "There was lots of trees. Birds, too. I saw a deer once when I went hunting with my daddy."

There it is. "Daddy? Who's your daddy?"

Erick's eyes fell. "He died. Mama, too. Least, that's what Sen says."

Ceran's eyes snapped up to Vallos to find the big thug separating a soldier's head from his body. "Who were they?"

Erick shrugged. "Mama washed clothes. Made beds. That sort of thing."

Ceran's heart was fluttering. He might vomit again. "And what about your daddy?"

Again, the boy shrugged. "I didn't see him a lot. Mama said I had to stay out of his way and never tell anyone he was my daddy. But sometimes he took me hunting. Once he even let me hold his sword."

It's true, then. The world spun as visions of the throne of Ir-Anan drifted further and further away. *He's an heir. His father, the Duke of Aneving. And he was sent here to take the throne.*

Anger boiled in Ceran's chest as he thought about it. *They would take it from me! This boy and old fool would tell* me *to abdicate! No! I'll not have it!*

And his mind formulated a plan. A bad one, to be sure. But a plan.

"Erick, my boy, I'm so sorry about your parents. Come here." He wound his arm around the boy's small shoulders and pulled him close. He turned him, so they were both looking out on the city. Somewhere down below, a dragon roared and Ceran shivered. Erick's little face was pushed up against the rail, and Ceran saw he was small enough to slip through. He smiled in his drunkenness. "Beautiful view, isn't it?"

And he shoved the boy off.

Varen Skald saw it happen. He couldn't believe his eyes, but he *saw* it. Councilor Ylannos shoved the boy from the balustrade. His mouth hung open. Something had happened, caused the enemy to break. And as he'd turned to shout a victory, he'd seen it.

Then he saw Vallos, staring at the councilor's back, sword in a white knuckle grip. He started forward with a heavy step, and Skald could see it happening again—death he couldn't stop. Because his shouts of warning fell on deaf ears with the din of battle all around them, and one of his soldiers put a hand on Vallos to stop him.

He waded into the press of bodies, his sword whipping out to find exposed throats, abdomens, arms, hands, fingers, eyes, mouths. His muscles ached, his knees cried in protest, but not from age or fatigue. No, they cried only for blood.

He was rage incarnate. He was vengeance. Every movement of his sword brought death; every step preceded screams. His very breath was murder.

There was only the killing. The city, the battle, the dragons all faded away, distant memories of another man—a man who had died when the boy went over the wall.

Sen had fallen away, and only Vallos remained.

The wave of death brought him closer to his target. To the coward. Another slash, another hack, another body at his feet. People were screaming, scattering. A sword found the flesh of his arm, another cut across his chest.

It didn't matter. Nothing slowed him. He was the tide. He was righteous death.

The man ran. He screamed and ran. Vallos turned, a knife in his hand, arm cocked to loose it when a searing pain erupted from his thigh. He glanced down and saw a soldier who'd dragged himself to his knees, hand wrapped around the hilt of a dagger protruding from Vallos's leg. He grunted and thrust down, burying the throwing knife in the soldier's eye and dropping him back to the ground.

He looked up and saw the man had made more distance

between them. He ripped the dagger from his leg, blood spurting from the wound. As he loosed it, his leg gave out and he crashed to his knees. The knife spun end over end and landed, burying itself to the hilt in the coward's shoulder. He stumbled, got up, and kept running, disappearing around a corner.

Vallos tried to stand, slipped in his own blood, and crashed down again. He screamed, tears welling in his eyes.

And then he faded, and was Sen again. And the old man screamed and screamed and cried, and folded in on himself as he tried to think of the beautiful child and instead saw only an accusing pair of eyes, staring at him as they fell to oblivion.

Chapter Thirty

The Exhale

I have led my people to war. I have fought beside my brothers. I have killed to protect my home. I only hope I have done you proud.

-Log of Dragonmaster Eoradon, 876th Lord of Mun-Alin

Rialin leaned heavily on his cane, groaning as he sat. He was in the garden at the top of Mun-Alin, looking out on the world. A blue sky hung over him, and a breeze pulled at his hair. A deep sigh escaped his lips as he thought of the last time he'd been here, talking with Meristofales.

"You old fool," Rialin whispered to himself in a voice stolen by the wind. He felt the tears gathering at the corners of his eyes and wiped them away before they could fall. He looked up and caught sight of Wik and Uanari flying a circuit around the nearby peaks. At least someone had come through the battle better off.

He rubbed his aching leg. Feordan had done what she could,

but it wasn't much. He knew it would never heal right now. His dueling days were likely behind him. He forced himself to relax and stop his fist from tightening around the cane. It had been worth it, he knew. Eoradon lived, the rogue Rider was dead, and the city was saved. Still, that choice gnawed at him. He could've gone to Ferao and Paxavan. He'd seen their fight taking a turn, but he'd chosen to go to Eoradon's aid instead.

Paxavan's dying screams, the shower of blood as the dragon's head descended to the city below—they'd left scars on his soul, moments stretched into eternities he knew he'd never outrun.

He leaned back on the bench and closed his eyes, letting the sun dapple his face in a warmth he'd been missing since long before they'd gone to Ir-Anan. Somewhere above him, his dragon circled. The sound of those beating wings brought him a comfort he hadn't known he needed. But still, there was more to be done with the dragon. He sighed. There was still an army out there, and it was more important than ever that they learn why exactly they'd come here, and who'd sent that damned dragon. The identity of that corrupted Rider was out there, too. His body had burned to ash while he and Eoradon were incapacitated, but someone, somewhere knew who he'd been.

With another groan, Rialin pushed himself to his feet and began the slow descent back to the lower levels of Mun-Alin.

Varen Skald loosed another throwing knife. It spun end-over-end and thudded deep into the wooden training dummy. He turned, shortsword in hand, and went to work on an old training form he'd learned as a recruit. The series of slashes and thrusts ended with the shortsword buried halfway to the hilt in another dummy. His frustration still not spent, he whirled and punched the final dummy in its blank wooden mask of a face. His hand exploded in pain, and he gritted his teeth to keep from screaming as he shook it out.

His chest rose with heavy breaths. He'd worked up a solid sweat, he realized. After he retrieved his cloth shirt from nearby and pulled it over his head, he made his way out of the training room, leaving the knives and swords where they were.

He emerged onto a lower-level street of Ir-Anan. The biting wind threatened to freeze the sweat on his skin, so he wrapped his cloak around his shoulders and pulled the hood up to hide his face. The last thing he wanted was to be seen down here. Every time the commonfolk saw him these days, he was accosted with praise for defending the city.

Nevermind that Senran Vallos led the frontline defense, he thought.

He wasn't the only one heaped with praise for something he didn't do. Though Councilor Ylannos had less trouble accepting the public's adoration. Skald gritted his teeth at the thought of the man. He'd watched him push that boy from the balustrade. He'd seen Vallos fly into a rage, the likes of which he'd never seen and hoped to never see again as he cut through more than twenty soldiers. And he'd seen the cowardly bastard of a councilor run and hide.

His fists had curled into balls, knuckles white with fury. He forced himself to take a deep breath and loosen his grip.

Up ahead, the palace loomed. Skald groaned inwardly. He'd been "awarded" a seat on the High Council for his bravery during the battle, but his stomach churned at the thought of attending these meetings. These people talked and talked and accomplished nothing. And he was forced to look at Ylannos and not throttle him.

I don't have enough people behind me yet. But that will come. Ceran Ylannos will never sit the throne of Ir-Anan.

Since the battle, talk of seating a new Emperor had reached a crescendo. The people had gone decades without one, and they were tired of waiting for a lost heir who was probably many years in the dirt. They wanted leadership, and they wanted safety. Ylannos had positioned himself well to stake a claim even before his "heroic defense" of the city.

Skald pulled the door open and ducked into the relative warmth of the throne room and pulled his hood back. His eyes settled on Ylannos immediately.

Never. You will never have it while I draw breath.

Van sprinted across the cobbled streets of the top level as best he could. The battle was dying down, the invaders fleeing. Something had happened; those bursts of light were clearly not natural, and he was pretty sure he'd seen the dragons killing each other. He'd stopped trying to make the ballista work some time back and chosen to join the fight down on the streets.

That had been a terrible idea, he decided. He'd barely survived to this point, having ended up in a half-dozen skirmishes on his way to the palace. As he drew closer, though, he found the opposition thinning. And now, he was virtually alone. Something had caused everyone to flee the area not long prior.

Van choked out a shocked sob as he came upon the place

where people had been huddled, against the balustrade, near where General Skald had been directing the defense of the city.

Bodies. Everywhere. The street was stained red with blood. Arms, legs, hands, heads: all lay discarded on the stones, the broken toys of the gods. Van swallowed the urge to retch and began checking the bodies, looking for survivors.

There were none.

Eventually, at the end of a trail of broken Ir-Ananian soldiers' bodies, Van yelped in surprise as he came across the still body of the man who'd saved him down on the wall, what felt like a lifetime ago. Van crouched by the body and looked closer, but Senran Vallos was still as all the others.

Legends really do die. Van sighed and placed a hand on the corpse.

Then he leapt back with a scream as the old warrior sucked in a ragged breath.

Eoradon's eyes flickered open to a dimly lit stone chamber. He was immediately aware of the pounding in his head. It radiated from somewhere at the core of his being, up his back, through his neck, into his brain. He tried to sit up, but a spell of dizziness overtook him and forced him back down onto a moderately comfortable mattress, with a feather-stuffed pillow.

He groaned and squeezed his eyes shut. His memory came back in flashes. He was in Ir-Anan. He'd killed the rogue Rider. Something strange had happened to his magic. It had been amplified somehow, like sunlight through a glass pane. It had worked, but when it fled, he had been drained. Curious, he reached for his reserve of power.

The pool, normally full of light, wisps of smoke curling from its surface, was empty. Only a trickle of his power remained, the only vestige of the vast reserve granted to him by his royal blood. A cold weight settled in his chest. Fear gnawed at his mind as he perceived the emptiness of that reserve. Though he knew it would eventually replenish itself—again, a function of his heritage—he felt naked, exposed without it.

Shuddering, he forced himself to try to rise again. He made it to his feet this time, and found he was dressed in a soft robe, undergarments, and nothing else. He pulled the robe around his aching body and took wobbling steps toward the door, under which he could see a ribbon of light.

He pushed the door open and shielded his eyes against the light of torches. He was cold, and the stones underfoot hurt his feet. As his eyes adjusted to the light, he could see he was in a hall. It was familiar.

Shock overcame him as he realized where he was. He was standing in the hall outside Feordan's infirmary.

He was in the monastery.

He was *home.*

Eoradon stumbled back against the cold stone of the wall and slid down into a sitting position. Tears gathered in his eyes and he let them fall. As clarity returned to his mind, he realized with a start that Iaxal hadn't spoken to him.

Iaxal! He called through the bond. *Iaxal, where are you?*

There was a beat of silence before she responded.

Rodo? Joy flowed through their bond. *Eoradon! Thank all the stars, you're awake!*

Awake, Eoradon confirmed. *And cold.* He looked around at the empty hall, noting the absence of any voices. *Where is everyone?*

The joy he'd felt through the bond retreated, replaced by a somber tone.

They're getting ready.

Eoradon's brows knit in confusion. *Getting ready for what?*

The funerals.

Memory came back to Eoradon like a burst of lightning through the brain. He saw Paxavan's head ripped from his neck, felt the shower of hot blood that covered Ir-Anan. And of course, there was the *other* body...

I need to find some clothes, he said.

As he hobbled to his chambers, he cringed as a distinct feeling of unease washed over him. He realized the Dragonmaster's chambers were now *his*. And not just temporarily. Meristofales would not be returning. This was now his role, fully and completely.

He shuddered a little at the thought. Of course, there was the other consideration. Ir-Anan was his home, in reality. He'd fought for it, shed blood for it, lost friends for it.

The weight of responsibility settled like a millstone around his neck.

But you already made your choice, Iaxal said. *You made it before we left for Ir-Anan.*

I know, Eoradon responded. *To be fair, I thought we might die, and then I wouldn't have had to face it.*

She laughed. *Oh, Rodo. Always running from who you are. It's time to stop running. It's time to be the man I've always seen in you.*

He nodded to himself, but said no more as he moved slowly through the corridors he'd lived all his life in.

By the time he was dressed in a shirt, cloth trousers, and boots, Eoradon was feeling more himself. He gave the little room a once-over, and his eyes fell once again on the group of books chained closed. He supposed he wouldn't get to ask Meristofales about those, after all. With a sad smile, he closed the door.

He found the courtyard full of his fellow Riders, gathered in a circle. All around them and in the air were the various dragons of Mun-Alin. The dying sunset caught their scales and illuminated the night in a brilliant rainbow of dazzling greens, blues, reds, golds, and of course, black. Uanari lingered high above the rest like a demon of shadow.

Wik was the first to notice him. She turned, shock written across her face.

"Dragonmaster!" Her voice betrayed her surprise. Eoradon waved off the honorific.

"Just Eoradon tonight. The real Dragonmaster is over there." He gestured with his chin to the pyre, where Meristofales's body lay, covered by his black cloak, now tattered and burned from his fight with the harbinger.

Wik nodded, then turned back to face the two pyres. One for Meristofales, and another, much larger, holding the corpses of Ferao and Paxavan. Seeing the body of his friend and his partnered dragon lying there, dead and unmoving next to his mentor and the closest thing he'd had to a father caused Eoradon's chest to feel tight. He tried to breathe and found the air caught in his throat. He choked, then coughed, spluttering as he tried to regain his composure. Then there was a hand on his back. He looked, and saw Feordan, dressed all in black, the hood of her cloak pulled up over her silver hair.

"They're gone," was all he could say as he leaned against the healer.

"I know," she said, her voice soft as she held him up, despite her smaller stature. "But the city is saved. They would've made the trade, had they been given a choice."

Her words helped. Eoradon nodded, squeezed her lightly, and straightened. Around the circle, he could see hard faces, lined with emotion, some with tears openly flowing. It had been a long time since a Rider fell in combat, and now there were two of them.

"They might want to hear from you." The voice appeared at Eoradon's shoulder. He turned to see Rialin, limping and leaning heavily on a cane.

"I don't know what to say," Eoradon sighed.

"It was your call." The words weren't accusatory—just a statement. "You should speak."

Eoradon nodded, then took a couple steps forward into the circle. The sunset set the courtyard ablaze in streams of golden, red, and purple light. High above, the dragons wheeled.

"When we went to the aid of Ir-Anan," Eoradon began, "I asked for volunteers. Ferao was the first to join in. He wanted to help, to make the world safer for the dragons he loved so much. Paxavan, his eternal friend, fought valiantly against Dyraxian. But he was overcome by one of his own kind, turned against him. But their bravery and sacrifice was not in vain. We triumphed, and their names will be remembered by all Riders, now and forever." He turned to Meristofales's body, and found words failed him. So he spoke from the heart, and hoped it was enough.

"Meristofales was my friend. He saved my life more than once. Made sure I didn't turn into someone I didn't want to be. Every day, I try to be a little more like him." He swallowed hard, choking back a sob. "I lost my father too young. But it was okay. Because I had the First Ranger."

And with that, Uanari dropped from the sky. Eoradon rejoined the circle as the black dragon beat his enormous wings and hovered above the pyres. There was a sharp intake of breath, the sound of flint on stone, and fire burst from his mouth, engulfing all three bodies. The fire took immediately, smoke winding into the sky to be caught on the breeze and swept away.

"So," Rialin said after a moment. "What's next?"

Eoradon sighed. "I think you already know."

The other Rider nodded. "It's where you belong."

Eoradon chucked. "Once, I would've taken that as an insult."

Rialin smiled slightly. "Once, I would've meant it as one."

Eoradon turned to face his rival. Rialin returned the gesture. Then, the Rider extended his hand.

"I'm sorry," Rialin said. "For all of it."

A flash of anger shot through Eoradon's mind from Iaxal, followed by a sense of resignation as she recalled Rialin saving his life.

"Me, too." They grasped forearms, and Eoradon felt for the first time like he really belonged somewhere.

But it wasn't here.

He turned to face the rising flames and followed their trail into the night's sky as stars emerged from their hiding places, and the cool breeze played with the tendrils of smoke. As the world reclaimed its dead, Uanari let loose a baleful cry, and the mountains echoed the rebounding call of the dragon's anguish as a rumble of thunder joined his cadence. In the distant sky, a storm was gathering.

Epilogue

Ceran Ylannos yawned. The council meeting had dragged on for nearly three hours, and he wasn't sure how much more could be discussed about "rebuilding infrastructure" or "housing the poor." They'd barely had the resources to fix the damaged shops on the top level, so he wasn't sure how this gathering of fools thought to fix anything down on the lower levels.

He drummed his fingers on the tabletop, thinking of how dull his life has become since the battle. The days after had been preoccupied with cleanup and counting the dead, not to mention dealing with the newly-reemerged Dragon Riders. Now, the dead were buried, the city was being rebuilt, and the attacking army had retreated. Of course, there weren't enough soldiers left to pursue them and finish the job, but with the dragon and its Rider dead, Ceran didn't worry about another attempt on the city.

He continued to tune out the droning of his fellow councilors, his attention turning instead to the massive throne looming over them. Every day, in every meeting, at every opportunity, it taunted him.

A young boy, shoved from a great height.

Ceran shook himself, fought down his rising gorge, and looked away from the throne. His time would come. He was a hero to the people of this city. Or, at least the important ones.

His eyes drifted over Veran Skald, who'd managed to get himself a seat at this table following the city's defense. Skald's cold stare stuck fast, boring into him. Ceran blushed under his gaze and turned away.

He knows, he thought. *He knows about the boy*. Panic rose in Ceran's chest, and he fought it down. *He might know, but he can't prove it. And he can't move against me yet. But soon, he might win the people. If he becomes Emperor, he'll have me killed, and he won't even need Council approval.* He swallowed hard. *Skald cannot sit the throne. It cannot be allowed to happen.*

A commotion sounded outside. People screamed before the sound of beating wings. Inside, there was a cacophonous scraping as people stood from their seats, ready to run. Skald's sword was already free of its scabbard, a ringing sound echoing through the cavernous room. But no dragonfire came.

Instead, the doors to the palace pushed open, and a man entered. Outside, Ceran could see a dragon, sun shining off its scales, resplendent in green and gold and his chest exploded with panic yet again. *They've come to take me,* he thought, his mind wheeling through images of cells in the sky, or being fed to the beasts.

The man who entered was tall, broad through the shoulders, but not bulky. His hair, golden as the sun, reached down past his shoulders and flowed free. He wore a white linen shirt and dark trousers and leather boots that made a *click-clack* noise as he walked across the marble floor. As he drew closer, Ceran saw his face: all regality, sharp features and a strong jaw, with captivating green eyes. He was clean-shaven, but a light stubble was starting to grow on his cheeks.

He approached the throne, his eyes locked to it, seemingly oblivious to the council. Ceran had had enough of the insolence and called out to him.

"Hey!" he said. "Who are you? What are you doing here?"

The man turned from the throne and slowly fixed his penetrating gaze on Ceran. When he spoke, his voice rang from the walls of the chamber like the echo of the ages.

"I am the son of a murdered father," he began, taking slow steps toward Ceran, who backed away instinctively. "I am the lost child of Ir-Anan. I am a Dragon Rider of Mun-Alin. I am a defender of this city. I am the heir to that throne." He thrust a hand out, gesturing to the massive stone seat. A small smile spread across his lips as Ceran's mind whirled.

"I am Eoradon of House Vyrentil. And I have come home."

The End of Book One of *The Law of Teeth*

Afterword

It's funny, I can write 116,000 words to tell this story, but when it comes time to write the afterword, I'm at a loss. Ultimately, I want to say I hope you enjoyed your time in this story. In so many ways, fantasy is my literary home. It's what I started reading as a child that got me into reading for pleasure (shoutout *Eragon*) and it's what I've always wanted to write. And while I'm immensely proud of the story I told in *What Blood Remembers,* this is the book I've wanted to write my entire life.

I love dragons. I've always loved them. But if we're being honest, many dragon stories in fantasy follow one of a couple formulas. And those stories are awesome! But I wanted to try and do my own thing within in that structure. I hope I succeeded.

In terms of the writing, this is one of the first times I truly sat down and tried to outline something. I am a pantser at heart, but I knew I would struggle to stay on task with fantasy. So I wrote out a page or two of notes, the general bones of the story.

Then I changed a lot of it while writing, but those bones are still there. Sen, for instance, was completely added in at the last second and fully pantsed. But man, I think that old guy might be the emotional core of this narrative.

Speaking of Sen and his story, let me just go ahead and apologize for Erick. I know, it hurts. It hurt me, too. I very nearly completely reworked the story in order to not do it. But ultimately, there was just no avoiding it. I know you hate me. I hate me, too, don't worry.

Additionally, I know there are a lot of unanswered questions here. I get it, but I only ask that you trust me. There will be a payoff when you get the answers for the questions asked in this book.

I am outlining and drafting book two now and it is looking *great*. I think it will more than satisfy the lore nerds among you.

(I am also a lore nerd, don't worry.)

Until next time, fair winds!

-Will

Acknowledgments

The list of people I need to thank is surely as long as this book, but I'll do my best.

First off, I need to thank my wife, Tana. Her unending patience for hearing about the nonsense I'm writing is key to getting it done.

My children, for giving me the heart that's necessary for any good story.

My parents, for their unfailing belief, and willingness to remind me that I need to write a bestseller and make sure they can retire comfortably.

My writing group, Maya and Trevor for their in-progress notes that helped shape this book into what it is.

My beta readers, Britt, Reid, Fair, Yahtzee, and Jonathan, for their incredible feedback.

My editor (and sister-in-law) Jenna, for her extremely in-depth notes that made this manuscript so much stronger.

My cover artist, Jason Dement, for his unbelievable work bringing Eoradon and Iaxal to life.

My cover designer, Joshua Adams for his awesome typography and layout work.

All of my friends who have helped promote this story and get it in the hands of as many readers as possible. To name a few: Noah Brisk, Maurice Africh, Z.B. Steele, Miles Lyon, A.C. Hobbs, Max (i_like_fantasy_books) and many, many others. I can never list you all, but know I have seen your posts and shares, and they mean the world to me.

About the Author

C. William Phillips was born and raised in the hills of Kentucky, and has been telling stories as long as he can remember.

He resides in Louisville, with his wife, Tana, and their brood of children.

Scan QR code to follow C. William Phillips on Instagram and stay up-to-date on book news!

www.ingramcontent.com/pod-product-compliance
Lightning Source LLC
LaVergne TN
LVHW040214110826
845146LV00005B/1277

* 9 7 9 8 9 9 9 3 5 5 9 4 2 *